Praise for *Links*

"It is a looking-glass world that the Somalian nov~~~~ ~~~~ rah takes us through in his novel. . . . ~~~~ ~~~~ ex-ile exploring his country's disin~~~~ ~~~~. . . . Only the setting is miasmic, poo~~~~ ~~~~ls and drift-high in seeming monst~~~~ ~~~~ -tirely, as Farah is artist enough to ~~~~ ~~~~nstrosity and freakishness."
—*New York Times Book Review*

"It's easy to see why Nuruddin Farah's name keeps coming up as a likely recipient of a Nobel Prize in Literature. . . . [Farah's] strange and compelling books don't just keep you awake. They haunt you. . . . Like Joseph Conrad and Graham Greene, writers to whom he can be favor-ably compared, Farah poses questions that, once asked, never go away." —*Newsweek*

"A terrifying window into a lawless country . . . a political thriller for a nation with no politics but anarchy."
—*San Francisco Chronicle*

"A nuanced tale of lives wrenched apart both by civil war and by for-eign meddling." —*Entertainment Weekly*

"Farah . . . has said he hopes to reclaim Somalia through his writing. With *Links*, he accomplishes that mission with blinding intensity."
—*TimeOut New York*

"Intelligent and complex. . . . [Farah is] *the* literary voice of his coun-try on the world stage." —*Star Tribune* (Minneapolis)

"Unsparing in its portrait of a land overwhelmed by poverty, war and corruption." —*The Baltimore Sun*

"This is the slightly abstract, slightly surreal territory where several Nobel laureates hang out, writers like Singer, Márquez, and Saramago, and it's no coincidence that Farah has been held up in their company. . . . [*Links*] is a haunting exploration of the desire to help and the atten-dant costs of doing so." —*The Christian Science Monitor*

PENGUIN BOOKS

LINKS

Nuruddin Farah is the author of eight novels, most recently the Blood in the Sun trilogy: *Maps, Gifts,* and *Secrets.* His novels have been translated into seventeen languages and have won numerous awards. Farah was named the 1998 laureate of the Neustadt International Prize for Literature, "widely regarded as the most prestigious international literary award after the Nobel" (*The New York Times*). Born in Baidoa, Somalia, he now lives in Cape Town, South Africa.

LINKS

NURUDDIN FARAH

PENGUIN BOOKS

PENGUIN BOOKS

Published by the Penguin Group
Penguin Group (USA) Inc., 375 Hudson Street, New York, New York 10014, U.S.A.
Penguin Group (Canada), 10 Alcorn Avenue, Toronto, Ontario, Canada M4V 3B2
    (a division of Pearson Penguin Canada Inc.)
Penguin Books Ltd, 80 Strand, London WC2R 0RL, England
Penguin Ireland, 25 St Stephen's Green, Dublin 2, Ireland (a division of Penguin Books Ltd)
Penguin Group (Australia), 250 Camberwell Road, Camberwell, Victoria 3124, Australia
    (a division of Pearson Australia Group Pty Ltd)
Penguin Books India Pvt Ltd, 11 Community Centre, Panchsheel Park, New Delhi - 110 017, India
Penguin Group (NZ), cnr Airborne and Rosedale Roads, Albany, Auckland 1310, New Zealand
    (a division of Pearson New Zealand Ltd)
Penguin Books (South Africa) (Pty) Ltd, 24 Sturdee Avenue, Rosebank,
    Johannesburg 2196, South Africa

Penguin Books Ltd, Registered Offices:
80 Strand, London WC2R 0RL, England

First published in the United States of American by Riverhead Books,
a member of Penguin Group (USA) Inc. 2003
Published in Penguin Books 2005

10 9 8 7 6 5 4 3 2 1

Originally published by Kwela Books, South Africa, in a significantly different form.

THE LIBRARY OF CONGRESS HAS CATALOGED THE HARDCOVER EDITION AS FOLLOWS:
Farah, Nuruddin, date.
Links / Nuruddin, Farah.
p. cm.
ISBN 1-57322-265-8 (hc.)
ISBN 0 14 30.3484 7 (pbk.)
1. Mogadishu (Somalia)—Fiction.   2. Americans—Somali—Fiction.
3. Political refugees—Fiction.   4. Somali-Americans—Fiction.   5. Mothers—Death—Fiction.
6. Abduction—Fiction. I. Title.
PR9396.9.F3L56   2004   2003065969
823'.914—dc22

Printed in the United States of America
Designed by Stephanie Huntwork

The image on the title page is an aerial photograph of the Somalian Coast.

FOR ABYAN, KAAHIYE, AND MINA,
WITH ALL MY LOVE

If you don't want to be a monster, you've got to be like your fellow creatures, in conformity with the species, the image of your relations. Or else have progeny that make you the first link in the chain of a new species. For monsters do not reproduce.

MICHEL TOURNIER

The individual leads in actual fact a double life, one in which he is an end to himself and another in which he is a link in a chain which he serves against his will or at least independently of his will.

SIGMUND FREUD

A dog starved at his master's gate
Predicts the ruin of the state!

WILLIAM BLAKE

LINKS

PART 1

THROUGH ME THE WAY INTO THE SUFFERING CITY,
THROUGH ME THE WAY TO THE ETERNAL PAIN,
THROUGH ME THE WAY THAT RUNS AMONG THE LOST.
. . .
"For we have reached the place . . .
where you will see the miserable people,
those who have lost the good of the intellect."

(CANTO III)

"Your accent makes it clear that you belong
among the natives of the noble city." . . .
My guide—his hands encouraging and quick—
thrust me between the sepulchers toward him,
saying . . . "Who were your ancestors?"

(CANTO X)

"They said he was a liar and father of lies."

(CANTO XXIII)

DANTE, *Inferno*

1.

"GUNS LACK THE BODY OF HUMAN TRUTHS!"

Barely had his feet touched the ground in Mogadiscio, soon after landing at a sandy airstrip to the north of the city in a twin-engine plane from Nairobi, when Jeebleh heard a man make this curious statement. He felt rather flat-footed in the way he moved away from the man, who followed him. Jeebleh watched the passengers pushing one another to retrieve their baggage lined up on the dusty floor under the wings of the aircraft. Such was the chaos that fierce arguments erupted between passengers and several of the men offering their services as porters, men whom Jeebleh would not trust. Who were these loiterers? He knew that Somalis were of the habit of throwing *despedida* parties to bid their departing dear ones farewell, and of joyously and noisily welcoming them in droves at airports and bus depots when they returned from a trip. However, the loiterers gathered here looked as though they were unemployed, and were out to get what they could, through fair or foul means. He wouldn't put it past those who were armed to stage a stickup, or to shoot in order to get what they were after. He was in great discomfort that the Antonov had landed not at the city's main airport—retaken by a warlord after the hasty departure of the U.S. Marines—but at a desolate airstrip, recently reclaimed from the surrounding no-man's-land between the sand dunes and low desert shrubs, and the sea.

Jeebleh observed that after retrieving their baggage, the passengers congregated around the entrance to a lean-to shed, pushing, shoving, and engaged in acrimonious dispute. A minute later, he worked out that the shack was "Immigration," when he saw some of the passengers handing over their passports, and the men inside receiving the documents and disappearing. If the lean-to was the place to have his passport stamped, who, then, were the men inside, since they had no uniforms? What authority did they represent, given that Somalia had had no central government for several years now, after the collapse of the military regime that had run the country to total ruin?

Turning—because the man spoke again, repeating his remark about guns—Jeebleh saw the stranger's late-afternoon shadow, and decided that he and the man had never met before. If they had, he would have remembered, because this man boasted a mouth that wasn't much of a mouth, with a pair of lips that appeared tucked away, virtually invisible. He was very tall and unnaturally thin. Jeebleh couldn't help wondering to himself whether the man hadn't been looking after himself in the style to which he had once been accustomed, or whether he had always been thin. But seeing his dignified posture and the way he carried himself, Jeebleh couldn't imagine how anyone could survive and prosper in the conditions of Mogadiscio, described to Jeebleh by Somalis in the know as cloak-and-dagger, man-eat-man politics. The man was probably educated, and perhaps had held a high position during the former brutal dictatorial regime, whose popular overthrow had led to the ongoing strife. Or he may have been a well-regarded academic at the National University, now to all intents and purposes defunct.

"What do guns lack?"

The man repeated, "They lack the body of human truths!"

Jeebleh thought: There you are! For it was no accident that the first sentence spoken to him by a stranger began with the word "guns." This was emblematic of the civil war vocabulary, and times being what they were, he was sure he would have many opportunities to listen to everyone's take on guns and related terms.

He looked away, and his gaze fell on two youths with missing limbs, asking passengers and onlookers alike to take them to an outlying shack where they might make telephone calls, or escort them to a depot not far away where they could get transport to the city. He quickly averted his eyes, turning his full attention back to the man. Jeebleh felt weak, and sensed vaguely that something wasn't right.

"Everyone calls me Af-Laawe," the man said.

Jeebleh was embarrassed for his lack of manners in not shaking the man's extended hand, and for his own failure to reciprocate and introduce himself.

Af-Laawe continued, "You need not bother yourself, because your reputation precedes you. So let me welcome you home, Jeebleh!"

The sun moved in a dazzle. And as though in a daze, Jeebleh looked about, certain that at a conscious level he was not sufficiently prepared for the shocks in store for him during this visit, his first to Mogadiscio in more than two decades. He would have to adapt to the new situation. He reminded himself that he had felt a strange impulse to come, after an alarming brush with death. He had nearly been run over by a Somali, new to New York and driving a taxi illegally. He hoped that by coming to Mogadiscio, the city of death, he might disorient death. Meanwhile, he had looked forward to linking up with Bile and, he hoped, meeting his very dear friend's niece Raasta, who had lately been abducted.

"How do you know who I am?"

"I'm a friend of Bile's," the man responded.

"How is Bile doing?"

"It depends on who you talk to."

"What do you mean?"

"Bile has many detractors, people who associate his name with terrible deeds!"

"Are you one of his detractors?"

The question seemed to throw Af-Laawe off balance, and he fell silent. In the meantime, Jeebleh made sure he had his carry-on and his shoulder bag, in which he kept his documents, firmly between his feet. Distrustful of the thin man's motives, he tried a different tack to come to grips with his discomfort about everything since his arrival. "Did Bile know I was on this flight?" he asked.

"Maybe Nairobi rang to alert me."

"You speak as though 'Nairobi' were someone's name," he said, and waited for Af-Laawe, who was proving hard to pin down.

Af-Laawe was clearly happy to steer the conversation away from Bile. "Some of us think of the cities we know very well and where we've lived as intimate friends."

Jeebleh knew what he meant, knew that in moments of great anxiety, one may mistake the self for the world. But he explicitly checked his precautionary measures, pulling his shoulder bag and carry-on onto his body. He had his few clothes in his shoulder bag. On advice from friends in Kenya, where he had spent a couple of days, he had left a bigger suitcase in Nairobi, depositing it at the left luggage of his hotel. He had brought more books than clothes with him to Mogadiscio, assuming that reading material would be more difficult to come by in a city ruled to ruin by gunrunners.

Now he massaged his right shoulder, which was giving him cause for worry, because one of the bags contained many hardcover books—gifts for Bile, who would appreciate them, he was sure. Jeebleh had stashed away much of his cash, a few thousand U.S. dollars in large denominations, in his wallet. He had to bring his money in cash, as there were no functioning banks here. "Tell me more about Bile's detractors."

"He still runs The Refuge."

"What is to criticize about running a refuge?"

"Our country is full of detractors, out to defame the name of anyone ready to do good things," Af-Laawe responded. "Bile has his fair share of detractors because he is successful at what he's doing. As a people, we have the penchant for envying achievers, whom we try to bring down to where we are, at the bottom."

"But tell me more about Bile. Why so much detraction?"

"People question the source of the money with which he set up The Refuge."

"How did he get the money?"

"His detractors speak of murder and robbery."

"Bile murdering and robbing?"

"Civil wars have a way of making people behave contrary to their own nature," Af-Laawe said. "You'd be surprised to know what goes on, or what people get up to. At times, it's difficult to tell the good from the bad."

"Not Bile!"

"You have heard about his niece?" Af-Laawe said. "That she's been abducted, rumor has it, by men related to the people Bile has allegedly murdered and robbed? Supposedly, the kidnappers have said they won't set his niece and her companion free until he has given back the money he stole, or confesses to having committed the murders." Af-Laawe watched silently as Jeebleh stared at him with so much distrust spreading over his features.

"A lot of what you've told me is news to me," Jeebleh said, and after a brief pause added, "From what I know, the abductions have a political motive. In fact, I recall reading somewhere that StrongmanSouth, the warlord, is implicated."

"Where have you read that?"

"In the American press."

"What do Americans know about things here?"

The man had a valid point, and Jeebleh chose not to challenge him until he knew more. He was silent for a long while, pondering how to continue this conversation. Finally he asked, "Were Raasta and her companion abducted together or separately?"

"Raasta and her playmate, Makka, who has Down's syndrome, shared a room," Af-Laawe replied. "They were inseparable. You saw one, you saw the other, you thought of one, you thought of the other too."

"How's Bile taking it?"

"He's devastated."

Jeebleh shook his head in sorrow, as he remembered reading an article about the abduction in *The New York Times*. The article had described Raasta as a symbol of peace in war-torn Somalia, the stuff of myth, seen by the city's residents as a conduit to a harmonious coexistence. Jeebleh could remember parts of the story word for word: "People believe that they will not come to harm if they are in her vicinity; they feel safe from arbitrary murder, from stray bullets or from the pointless death of a mugging. This is why ordinary people seek shelter at The Refuge, where she resides."

"If Bile just returns the money, will they be set free?"

"There's no guarantee," Af-Laawe said.

"Does anyone know who the abductors are?"

But when Jeebleh turned to hear his response, Af-Laawe was gone, and he was face to face with three armed youths. Terror-stricken, he wondered if he had conjured the man, with a little help from a friendly jinni, out of desperate need for a guide to help him navigate the anarchic city.

WHAT BEASTLY MOTIVE DID THESE ARMED YOUTHS HAVE FOR TAKING UP POSITION so close to where he was standing? Nonplussed by their devil-may-care postures and ragged outfits, Jeebleh supposed they were not acting with the authority of the police, who would have had uniforms and badges. He was certain that even if they had been in uniform, they would hardly have looked the part. And in any case, Somalis would not defer to someone simply because of his uniform: he would still be an armed thug trying to maintain authority.

Jeebleh remembered seeing a German play when he was a student in Italy, a play set in Prussia at the end of World War I, in which an ex-convict, with no papers, dons an officer's uniform. Saluted and deferred to wherever he goes, his every word deemed to contain the voice of authority, he is welcomed everywhere; unlimited credit facilities are extended to him. Somalis never defer to the authority of a uniform in the way the Germans do, Jeebleh thought. We will defer only to the brute force of guns. Maybe the answer lies in the nation's history since the days of colonialism, and later in those of the Dictator, and more recently during the presence of U.S. troops: these treacherous times have disabused us of our faith in uniformed authorities—which have proven to be redundant, corrupt, clannish, insensitive, and unjust.

Then he heard the word "Passport," and turning, found himself before a man, neither in uniform nor bearing a gun, who seemed to arrogate authority to himself. Jeebleh looked him slowly up and down, questioning the wisdom of surrendering his passport on the say-so of a total stranger. Yet he dared not ask that the man show him proof of his authority to make such a request. Suddenly Af-Laawe was back, and no sooner had Jeebleh opened his mouth to speak than Af-Laawe broke in, his voice low and firm, advising: "Do as the man says. Give him your passport and twenty U.S. dollars cash. He'll stamp the passport and return it to you, together with a receipt."

Was he being set up? And if so, what should he do? Af-Laawe seemed to wield certain power hereabouts, but could he be trusted? And who were the gunmen? Being from New York, the Metropolis of Mistrust, Jeebleh decided not to part with his American passport. He reached into his shoulder bag and pulled out the Somali document, recently issued by the embassy in Rome, and a crisp twenty-dollar bill. He left his American passport where it was, together with the cash, in his wallet. The man leafed through the pages and demanded, "Why do you give me a Somali passport, not at all used, and with no visas in it?"

Jeebleh turned to Af-Laawe, and with a touch of sarcasm addressed both men: "When has it become necessary for a Somali to require a visa to enter Mogadiscio?"

"Is he taking us for fools?" the man protested.

"Please take the twenty dollars," Af-Laawe told him, "accept his Somali passport, and return it stamped, with a receipt. *Pronto!*"

For a moment, the man paused, and it seemed he might not be willing to oblige. Af-Laawe pulled him aside and out of Jeebleh's earshot.

Jeebleh's thoughts drifted back more than twenty years, to the last time he had used a Somali passport. It had been at the Mogadiscio international airport, about forty kilometers south of here, and he recalled how a man—not in uniform, and without a gun—had taken his passport and disappeared for an eternity. Jeebleh was on his way to Europe, and he worried that he might be prevented from leaving the country, then under the tyrannical rule of the Dictator. Bile and several others, who had apprenticed themselves to Jeebleh politically, had been picked up by the National Security the night before. There was every possibility that, as their mentor, he too would be arrested. And he was.

He had been driven straight from the airport to prison. He was brought before a kangaroo court and sentenced to death. Several years later, he was mysteriously taken from the prison in a National Security vehicle and driven to the VIP lounge of the same airport, where he changed from his prison rags into a suit. He was handed a passport with a one-year Kenyan visa and put on a plane to Nairobi, all expenses paid. Someone whose name he could no longer remember suggested that he present himself at the U.S. embassy. There he was issued a multiple-entry visa for the United States. He still wondered who had done all this for him, and why.

Now, as he waited for Af-Laawe to return, he held the two contradictory images in his mind. In one, he was dressed in a suit, being roughly handcuffed and taken in a security vehicle, sirens blaring, straight to prison; in the other, he was in rags, being driven back to the airport, to be flown to Nairobi. In one, the officers escorting him to prison were crass; in the other, the officers were the epitome of courtesy. That's dictatorship for you. This is civil war for you!

With every cell in his body responding to his restless caution, he wished he knew where danger lurked, who was a friend and who a foe. He had once been used to the arbitrariness of a dictatorial regime, where one might be thrown into detention on the basis of a rumor. That had been exchanged here for a cruder arbitrariness—a civil anarchy in which one might die at the hands of an armed youth because one belonged to a different clan family from his, if there was even that much reason.

Af-Laawe was back, telling him that his passport would be returned shortly, duly stamped. There was much charm to his lisp, as he commended Jeebleh for having surrendered the Somali document rather than the American one. Jeebleh couldn't decide whether his self-appointed guide was a godsend or not. Nor could he decide whether the man had hidden motives.

"Any chance of a lift or a taxi?" Jeebleh asked.

"I've arranged that already."

"I see no taxis anywhere."

"Not to worry, you'll get a lift," Af-Laawe assured him.

"Tell me something about yourself in the meantime."

"There's very little to tell."

"Then tell me what little there is."

"I'm a friend of Bile's," Af-Laawe said.

"So it was he who sent you to meet my flight?"

"The pleasure of coming was entirely mine."

Impressed with the man's smooth talk, yet frightened by it too, Jeebleh wanted to know how Af-Laawe had managed to survive in this violated city, with his wit and his dignity—or at least his composure—intact. For all that, however, something didn't add up. Af-Laawe reminded Jeebleh of an actor in a hand-me-down role for which he was ill suited.

"If you won't tell me anything about yourself," Jeebleh said, "maybe you can tell me more about Bile, whom I haven't set eyes on for more than two decades."

"Everything in due course, please," the man responded.

Jeebleh wondered whether he should put Af-Laawe's evasiveness down to discretion, or to the fact that he knew of the bad blood between Bile and Jeebleh, both personal and political, from long before. The bad blood had to do in large part with Bile's being kept in prison, while Jeebleh had been released and mysteriously put on that plane. It was no surprise people believed that Jeebleh had betrayed the love and trust of his friend.

"Where does Bile live?" Jeebleh asked.

"In the south of the city."

That Bile chose to base himself in the south of the divided metropolis did not surprise Jeebleh at all. His friend was of the same bloodline as Strongman-South, the warlord who ran the territory, supported by clan-based militiamen. Jeebleh was of StrongmanNorth's clan, but he felt no clan-based loyalty himself—in fact, the whole idea revolted and angered him.

Jeebleh returned to the basics: "Will you help me find a hotel?"

Af-Laawe appeared discomfited. He looked around nervously, seemingly out of his depth, as put-upon as a babysitter asked to take on the responsibility of an absentee parent. Guessing that Af-Laawe knew more than he was prepared to let on, Jeebleh had the bizarre feeling that whoever had sent him had asked that he arrange a lift, but not book him into a hotel. Had Af-Laawe come under someone's instructions, and if so, whose?

Now Af-Laawe was again conveniently wearing the confident look of a veteran guide, able to steer his charge through to safety. "We will have you taken to a hotel in the north, where we think you will feel safer! You see, in these troubled times, many people stay in the territories to which their clan families have ancestral claims, where they feel comfortable and can move about unhindered, unafraid. However, if you wish, we'll have you moved eventually to the south, closer to Bile. Possibly Bile himself will invite you to share his apartment, who knows."

Jeebleh took note of Af-Laawe's use of "we," but was unable to determine whether it was a gesture of amicability or whether someone else was involved in the arrangements being made for him. Was this "we" inclusive, in the sense that Af-Laawe was hinting that the two of them belonged to the same clan? Or did Af-Laawe's "we" take other people into account, others known to be from the same blood community as Jeebleh? "What about Calooshii-Cune?" he asked.

Although Calooshii-Cune—Caloosha for short—was Bile's elder half brother, he and Jeebleh were of the same clan. Curious how the clan system worked: that two half brothers sharing a mother, like Caloosha and Bile, were considered not to be of the same clan family, because they had different fathers, and that Jeebleh, Bile's closest friend, was deemed to be related, in blood terms, more to Caloosha, because the two were descended from the same mythic ancestor. For much of the former Dictator's reign, Caloosha had served as deputy director of the National Security Service. Many people believed that he had been responsible for Bile's and Jeebleh's imprisonment, for the death sentence passed on Jeebleh, and also for his eventual, mysterious release. Bile had remained in prison until the state collapsed, when the prison gates were finally flung open.

"Caloosha lives in the northern part of the city," Af-Laawe said, "near the hotel you'll be staying in. Say the word, and we'll be only too pleased to take you to him, any day, anytime."

Jeebleh was disturbed to learn about Af-Laawe's intimacy with Caloosha, but wanted to wait until he knew more. "He is all right, Caloosha, is he?"

"He's a stalwart politician in the north," Af-Laawe answered, "and on the side acts as a security consultant to StrongmanNorth."

Rumor mills are busiest, Jeebleh thought, when it comes to politicians with shady pasts. He had gathered, from talking to people and interesting himself in the affairs of the country, that many politicians with dubious connections to the Dictator had found safe havens in the territories where their clansmen formed the majority. The way things stood, Jeebleh should've expected that Caloosha would be chummy with StrongmanNorth, who would guarantee him immunity from prosecution for his political crimes. Of course, Jeebleh had no intention of looking Caloosha up, and he did mind staying in a hotel in the north of the city, close to this awful man's residence. Yet who was he to raise objections about these things now?

"But staying in a hotel in the northern section of the city won't prevent me from moving about freely, will it?" he asked.

"Crossing the green lines poses no danger to ordinary folks," Af-Laawe replied. "Unarmed civilians and noncombatants seldom come to harm when crossing the green line. However, the warlords and their associates do not cross the line unless they are escorted by their armed guards."

"Where do you live?"

"I live in the south."

"In your own property?"

"No, I'm house-sitting!"

"House-sitting?" Jeebleh had read and heard about questionable dealings when it came to the practice of house-sitting.

"I've entered into an arrangement with a family who own a villa and who've relocated to Canada since the collapse," Af-Laawe explained. "An empty villa in civil war Mogadiscio is a liability as well as a temptation. I live in the villa for free and look after it."

In the local jargon, "house-sitting" meant the taking possession of houses belonging to the members of clan families who had fled, by members of families who had stayed on. Not all house-sitters were squatters, pure and proper. Some lived rent free. Others were paid to look after the properties of people living abroad, who hoped they would find them in good condition to do what they pleased with them once peace had been restored and a central government put in place. Of late, though, there had been a number of cases in which men claiming to be the owners of the properties they were looking after had sold them.

As Jeebleh was about to ask what kind of house-sitter Af-Laawe was, he was gone again, only to reappear with the immigration man in tow. Af-Laawe turned to the man and took the document from him. Then, sounding satisfied, he said, "Let's see."

The man bearing his passport wore the pitiful look of a son cut out of a wealthy parent's will. Maybe he had hoped to receive some baksheesh and was unhappy when he saw he would not. Or maybe there was another reason, indecipherable to Jeebleh. Af-Laawe scrutinized the passport on Jeebleh's behalf, then handed it to Jeebleh, who put it in his pocket without bothering to open it.

"What about the lift?" Jeebleh asked.

"Give me a few minutes," said Af-Laawe.

WHILE WAITING, JEEBLEH LOOKED AT THE DISTANT CITY, AND SAW A FINE SEA of sand billowing behind a minaret. He remembered his youth, and how much he had enjoyed living close to the ocean, where he would often go for a swim. Time was, when the city was so peaceful he could take a stroll at any hour of the day or night without being mugged, or harassed in any way. As a youth, before going off to Padua for university—Somalia had none of its own—he and Bile would go to the Gezira nightclub and then walk home at three in the morning, no hassle at all. In those long-gone days, the people of this country were at peace with themselves, comfortable in themselves, happy with who they were.

As one of the most ancient cities in Africa south of the Sahara, Mogadiscio had known centuries of attrition: one army leaving death and destruction in its wake, to be replaced by another and another and yet another, all

equally destructive: the Arabs arrived and got some purchase on the peninsula, and after they pushed their commerce and along with it the Islamic
faith, they were replaced by the Italians, then the Russians, and more recently the Americans, nervous, trigger-happy, shooting before they were shot
at. The city became awash with guns, and the presence of the gun-crazy
Americans escalated the conflict to greater heights. Would Mogadiscio ever
know peace? Would the city's inhabitants enjoy this commodity ever again?

From where he stood, the trees were so stunted they looked retarded, and
the cacti raised their calluses and thorns in self-surrender, while the shrubs
cast only scant shadows. The clouds of dust stirred up by successive armies
of destruction eventually settled back to earth, finer than when they went up.

Jeebleh did not look forward to seeing the desolation that he had read and
heard about. He was heavy of heart to be visiting his beloved city at a time
when sorrow gazed on it as never before. Mogadiscio spread before him, as
though within reach of his tremulous hand, a home to people dwelling in terrible misery. A poet might have described Somalia as a ship caught in a great
storm without the guiding hand of a wise captain. Another might have por-
trayed the land as laid to waste, abandoned, the women widowed, the children orphaned, and the sick untended. A third might have depicted it as a
tragic country ransacked by madmen driven by insatiable hunger for more
wealth and limitless power. So many lives pointlessly cut short, so much futile violence.

"What's it been like, living in the city?" Jeebleh asked.

Af-Laawe replied with what seemed to Jeebleh a non sequitur. "Danger
has a certain odor to it, only there's very little you can do to avert it between
the moment you smell it and the instant death visits."

"What are you talking about?"

"I'm smelling danger, that's what," Af-Laawe said.

"I don't understand. Can you smell danger now?" Jeebleh asked.

He didn't wait for an answer. Instead, he followed Af-Laawe's gaze, and
saw the three armed youths who had stood guard over him earlier, now in a
huddle, mischievously whispering among themselves. And they were also
glancing at the stairs of an aircraft being boarded.

"What are they up to?" Jeebleh said.

"I overheard their conversation as I went past them. They were taking bets."

"What were they betting on?"

"Our city's armed youths are in the habit of picking a random target at which one of them takes a potshot, then the others aim and shoot, one at a time. It's a sport to them, a game to play when they are bored. The one who hits the target is the winner."

"And that's what they are doing now?"

"I suspect so."

"Can't we intervene?"

"I doubt it."

"What if I talk to them?"

"Why take unnecessary risks?"

"Because somebody has to."

"If I were you, I wouldn't!"

Before Jeebleh could move, a shot rang out. They heard a woman scream, and then pandemonium. From where Jeebleh stood, it would have been difficult to piece the story together in the correct sequence. Yet it wasn't long before somebody explained what had happened: the pilot of the Antonov, a Texan, had offered to help the woman, a passenger, carry her plastic containers into the aircraft, and she followed him up the stairs. Perhaps the gunman had aimed at the pilot, who, fortunately for him, stepped out of harm's way a second before the shot was fired. Or perhaps the woman and her children were going up the steps too slowly and so had become the targets. Whatever the case, the first bullet struck the woman's elder son. The crowd at the foot of the stairs exploded into panic. Two of the youths trained their guns on anyone who might dare to approach or dare to disarm them. The people cowered, silent, frightened.

The three youths were overjoyed, giving one another high fives, two of them extending congratulations to the marksman. Meanwhile, the woman and her surviving child were screaming so loudly that the heavens might fall. The youths moved slowly, and facing the crowd as if afraid of being shot in the back, clambered into a van, which sped away in a trail of dust. The people moved, as one body, toward the bottom of the stairs where the corpse of the ten-year-old victim lay in a gathering pool of blood.

Was it true, as they said, that in this hellhole of a city, no one did anything for you when you were alive, but when you were dead, everyone would rush to bury you, fast? It was evident from the conversation Jeebleh now overheard that everyone was relieved that the American pilot had not been hit. Jeebleh was shocked that no one in the crowd of people still milling about had been willing to confront the gunmen, to try to stop them from playing their deadly games. And where was Af-Laawe? He had disappeared again. Yes, there he was, climbing the stairs of the aircraft, presumably to help. The woman and her child kept wailing, and Af-Laawe bent over them in an effort to comfort them.

Maybe there was more to Af-Laawe than met the eye. He was shrewd enough, all right, and was resourceful, and courageous too. But was he trustworthy? Was he his own man, or a vassal to one or the other of the Strongmen? It would be atypical, Jeebleh thought, to find in Mogadiscio a man not solely devoted to serving his blood community, but working in pursuit of his own ideals.

An instant later, Jeebleh looked up and saw the first carrion-eaters—strong-headed, keen-eyed, with deadly claws capable of tearing into two disparate halves the surrounding cosmos.

"NO BODY BAGS, PLEASE!"

Those had been the parting words of Jeebleh's elder daughter as she implored him to take good care of himself. His wife's advice was simply that he should trust no one. In different circumstances, Jeebleh and Af-Laawe might have struck up an immediate friendship, exchanging telephone numbers, promising to look each other up. Here, however, things were far more complicated. And now this: A ten-year-old boy killed just for fun!

Jeebleh knew it would be unwise to talk about any of this to his wife and daughters, who would ask him to return home immediately. And if he tried to discuss his shock at the crowd's inaction, his wife would reflexively refer to "the Somalis' lack of moral courage," even though, in her heart of hearts, she wouldn't want him to take a risky moral stand. His elder daughter, a senior at NYU, would tell him that it would be unbecoming of him—a man of such a venerable past, whose life was full of countless instances of moral courage— to die in vain. His younger daughter had speculated that if he was killed, it was unlikely he would be sent back to New York at all. "You'll just be buried within five minutes of dying. We would never even get to see your corpse. One of us would have to fly to that god-awful country to bring your body back so we could give you a decent burial." They had opposed his visiting Mogadiscio.

He had heard it all before, the arguments for and against getting involved in any political or moral activity that might lead to death. He remembered his mother fondly, especially because even though he was her only son, she had never once suggested that he shouldn't risk his life by engaging in dangerous political work, when many parents in the days of the dictatorship discouraged their children from taking a stand. His mother was an exception. "You live only once, and I'd like you to live your life with integrity," she would say. But he doubted that even she would have wanted him to risk his life unnecessarily in this instance—if, as Af-Laawe said, there wasn't much he could do.

The arrival of more crows, marabous, and other carrion birds set him loose from his memories. Had these birds learned to show up as soon as they heard shots, knowing that there would be corpses? They perched restlessly on the telegraph wires, waiting. People stood by, looking helpless. Af-Laawe led several men, who carried the dead boy's corpse to a vehicle with the words "*Noolaadaa dhinta!*" on the side, and below that the English translation: "Who lives, dies!" When at last Af-Laawe joined him, Jeebleh asked if the van in which the corpse now lay was his.

"It belongs to a charitable organization that gives decent Islamic burials to the unclaimed corpses littering the streets of the city whenever there is fighting," he said. "I set it up in the early stages of the civil war, when there were bodies everywhere, at roundabouts, by the side of the road, in buildings. A large percentage of the dead had no relatives to bury them. They had belonged to clan families who had been chased out of the city."

He fell silent, and looked in the direction of a four-wheel-drive vehicle that was arriving, bearing a VIP, perhaps a clan leader or a warlord on his way to Nairobi. Several youths with guns alighted from the roof of the vehicle and others stepped out of it, before an elderly man, whom Jeebleh recognized, emerged limping. A hush descended; even the bereaved woman, now in Af-Laawe's van, stopped her wailing. Jeebleh, a changed man, was far more frightened than when he had landed. He wished he could pluck up the courage to speak to the venerable politician as he walked toward the plane.

"Now here's how things are," Af-Laawe was saying. "I had intended to take you in my van. You can still come with me, only I must warn you that I now have other passengers, including a corpse, a bereaved mother, constantly wailing, and several gravediggers. I am driving straight to the cemetery. Or I can organize a lift for you in that fancy car."

"What are the chances of that?"

"I'll talk to the driver. I know him well."

"And he'll know where to take me?"

"I'll tell him."

Everything was done in haste, because Af-Laawe wanted to get the boy's body buried before night fell. Before leaving, he gave Jeebleh his business card, which on one side had the words "Funeral with a difference!" and on the other *"Noolaadaa dhinta!"* Jeebleh found himself thinking that maybe someone with a dark sense of humor was having a bit of fun by sending a funeral van to meet him on his arrival. Only Caloosha would be likely to send him such a veiled message, with a death threat threaded into its cloth. Alas, Jeebleh couldn't tell whether he should take it lightheartedly, or with the heedfulness of a man being forewarned.

"Good luck," Af-Laawe said, and he was gone.

2.

JEEBLEH WAS UNCOMFORTABLY SQUEEZED IN THE FRONT OF THE VEHICLE, pressed between the driver and a man responding to the title of Major. In the seat immediately behind them were three youths with assault rifles. Perched on the roof were several others with grenade launchers and belt-fed machine guns. That he was uncomfortable sitting so close to so many guns in the hands of teenagers was obvious; he remained alert, and watched for the tell-tale signs of imminent danger.

As they moved, and once he was accustomed to his discomfort, his eyes fell on a young man lying in the rear. The handsome youth had the whole seat to himself, his right leg, which was in a cast, extended in the dignified attitude of someone showing off a prize possession.

Perhaps mundanely, perhaps revealing more about how much more American he had become than he would care to admit, Jeebleh wished that the driver, the Major, and the youths in the back would all refrain from turning the vehicle into a smokehouse. He kept quiet about his preoccupations, doubtful that they would oblige, and feeling silly that he would expend more energy on their cigarette smoking than on the fact that they were so heavily armed. Instead, he asked the Major where he had been when the state collapsed and the city exploded into anarchy.

The Major replied: "Here and there and everywhere."

"But you were in the National Army, were you not?"

"How did you decide that?"

"I assumed, because of your title, Major."

Saying nothing, the Major blew out rings of smoke straight into Jeebleh's eyes, irritating him no end. The driver sensed the tension building up and stepped in. He addressed his words to Jeebleh. "We're all shell-shocked on account of what we've been through—those of us who stayed on in the country. I hope people like you will forgive us our failings, and we pray to God that He'll forgive us our trespasses too."

The Major cursed. "What fainthearted nonsense!"

Minutes passed with only the sound of the engine. The youths engaged in agitated whispers in a hard-to-follow dialect commonly spoken in a southern region of the country where militiamen came from.

"Where do you know Marabou from?" the Major asked.

Jeebleh looked from the Major to the driver and back, as he had no idea what this meant. His lower lip caught in his teeth; biting it, he mumbled, "Marabou?"

The driver helped him out. "'Marabou' is the nickname by which the guy who runs Funeral with a Difference is known in some circles of our city."

"He introduced himself as Af-Laawe," Jeebleh said.

"And you met him for the first time today?"

When Jeebleh nodded and the driver vouched for him, this angered the Major. He turned on the driver, saying, "Why do you keep speaking for him?"

"Because I'm the one who offered him a lift, that's why," the driver said.

And when the Major continued to stare furiously first at him, and then for a considerably longer time at Jeebleh, whipping himself into a giant fury, the driver was compelled to add, "I know this gentleman's reputation, and of the high respect his name is held in, in many quarters. What's more, I know this to be their first encounter, because Marabou told me so."

There was silence.

A few minutes later, the driver said, "I am reminded of a story in which Voltaire, who is on his deathbed, receives a visit from Satan. Eager to recruit the French philosopher for his own ends, Satan offers him limitless pleasures that would make his afterlife more comfortable in every possible way. But Voltaire turns down the offer, and speaks a stern rebuke to Satan, saying that this isn't the time to make enemies, thank you!"

In a fit of pique, maybe because he had no idea what to make of the parable or why the driver had recounted it, the Major barked a command. "Stop the car!" he shouted.

No sooner had the vehicle come to an abrupt halt than the armed youths leapt from the roof, fanning out, their guns at the ready. But the youths inside did not move at all. On edge, the Major got out.

"Why this unplanned stop?" the driver asked.

Miffed, the Major said, "I'll return shortly!" He went around to the driver's side, and told him, "You're a volunteer, and I'm in charge of this outfit, and you take orders from me. Keep in mind that we're at war, and I'll have you come before the disciplinary commission of the movement if you disobey my orders." Then he swayed off down a dusty road, along with two youths detailed to escort him, their weapons poised menacingly.

"What's eating him?" asked one of the youths in the vehicle.

The handsome youth with his leg in a cast speculated that the Major was due to go on a dangerous mission, and was living on his nerves.

Everyone retreated into the disarray of an imposed silence, embarrassed. Jeebleh sat unmoving, like a candle just blown out, smoking its last moments darkly.

OUTSIDE, THERE WAS A FAINT WHIRLING OF SAND. AND THERE WAS LIFE AS Jeebleh might have imagined it in its continuous rebirth, earth to dust, dust to earth, wherein death was avenged.

With the vehicle parked by the side of the road and the Major and his young militiamen off on some mysterious mission, Jeebleh felt increasingly like a sitting target. His heart beating faster from fear, it occurred to him that they could all be dead at the pull of a trigger. The dead would be mourned and buried—Marabou would see to that—but the militia would regret the loss of the vehicle more. In the mid-eighties, before the collapse, corruption having reached unprecedented levels, poems had circulated on cassette about the ill-gotten money that had brought many Land Cruisers into the country. Jeebleh wished he could remember the words. Nowadays, many of these four-wheel-drive vehicles had ended up in the hands of the fighting militiamen, who mounted their weapons on them, turning them into the battlewagons that became a staple of the civil war footage shown on CNN and the BBC. He kept a wary eye on what was happening outside, in the dusty alleys. Two of the armed youths who had climbed down from the roof of the vehicle stood with their backs to each other, in imitation of what they must have seen in American movies. They nursed immense bulges in their cheeks, great wads of chewed-up *qaat*, a moderately mild stimulant. They might have been cattle ruminating.

The driver spoke: "Once again, I feel I must apologize for the behavior of our countrymen, who do not know what is good for them, or how to say thank you to those who mean them well. Our moods swing from one extreme to another, but we haven't the courage to admit that we've strayed from the course of moral behavior. I suppose that is why the civil war goes on and on, because of this lack in us, our inability to appreciate what the international community has tried to do for us: feed the starving and bring about peace in our homeland."

Jeebleh wanted to know more about Af-Laawe. "What is Marabou's story?" he asked.

Thunderclouds of worry gathered on the driver's forehead; readying to speak, he made throaty noises similar in intensity to the rumble before a lightning bolt splits the heavens. "Marabou, for a start," he finally said, "has many aliases, and he changes them as often as we change our shirts."

Jeebleh wondered to himself whether Af-Laawe—meaning "the one with no mouth"—was also an assumed name, which, to a Dante scholar, might allude to the *Inferno*. He asked, "How well do you know him?"

The driver answered in a burst of impassioned speech, "How does one know anyone in a land where people are constantly reinventing themselves? How well can anyone know an Af-Laawe who does his damnedest not to be known?"

"My impression is that you've known him a long time."

"True, I've known him for long, since his student days, when he was doing his doctorate in Rome. Then, I was the head of the chancellery at the Somali embassy there. I remember him coming to see me, when he learned that
the National Security had put his name on a blacklist and issued a directive
instructing us to discontinue his government-sponsored scholarship. Knowing I couldn't help him, I asked a junior officer to deal with him. He left the
chancellery, angry and abusive. A few days later he visited me at home. This
time, he pleaded that I extend his passport. I told him that there was no point
in extending his passport if he no longer had a scholarship allowing him to
live in Italy, but my son assured me that Af-Laawe, who was his friend, had
received another grant to help him continue his studies and all he needed
was a valid passport, with a valid residence. I renewed the passport, at some
risk to myself, I must add, and heard no more about him until I met him several years later in France, with an Italian woman, his fiancée. By then he had
set himself up somewhere in Alsace, in a town called Colmar, and he eventually married the woman."

"And when did he get here?"

"Soon after the U.S. troops flew into Mogadiscio. I'm told he carries
French papers now, and speaks several languages. It's said that he was hired
by the European Union at a very high salary, with the vague job description
'facilitator for all things European.' He was sent out on some sort of trouble-
shooting mission, and had a driver, a cook, a bodyguard. He lived in a huge
three-story house by himself, testimony to his high-rolling lifestyle."

"What happened?"

"It's rumored that together with two other Europeans, a Frenchman and a
Norwegian, he effected the disappearance of some four million U.S. dollars
from the United Nations coffers. Nobody knows how it was done."

"Four million dollars?"

"Didn't you read about it in the American press?"

"I don't recall anything about this!"

"Rumor has it too," the driver went on, "that he lost his job with the EU
because they suspect him but can't prove anything. And he doesn't dare return to Colmar, where his two teenage children and wife live, because the

Frenchman and the Norwegian will ask him to hand over their share of the heist. Those in the know think that he was the brain behind it all, and many Mogadiscians assume that the money is buried somewhere in Somalia, and he is the only person who knows where."

"If the money is here, how come the two Strongmen, or their minions, haven't forced him to show them where he buried the cash? It seems so incredibly far-fetched, no?"

"Maybe the two Strongmen know things we don't."

"What do you mean?" asked Jeebleh.

"Maybe they know the money is already in Europe, deposited in a Swiss bank, and waiting to be signed for, on submission of a coded number," the driver speculated. "Or maybe they're waiting until our man joins the Frenchman and the Norwegian who helped him spirit away the UN funds, and then Marabou will collect his cut, and share it out. Maybe an associate of one of the Strongmen is Marabou's principal protector."

"Like who?"

"Do you know of Caloosha? His name is often mentioned," the driver said. "I hear too that Af-Laawe is quite friendly with a brother-in-law of his, who is StrongmanSouth's deputy. Ours is an incestuous community, and the man has protectors all over the place."

"What are his links to Caloosha?"

"I wouldn't know, to be honest."

The youths inside the vehicle were becoming fidgety, and looked out anxiously in the direction from which they expected the Major to appear. The one with the cast pointed out that as a highly placed officer often entrusted with dangerous missions, the Major ought to know that it wasn't safe for them to remain stationary in one place for such a long time.

"We'll give him another minute," the driver said.

"And then we'll go," the youth insisted.

No sooner had the driver turned the key in the ignition than they saw the Major with his escort, carrying something in a plastic bag. Cursing under his breath, he appeared still very edgy as he entered the vehicle. The engine started and the vehicle moved.

3.

"WHAT TOOK YOU SO LONG?" THE DRIVER PUFFED HUNGRILY ON THE cigarette he had lit in a moody silence.

"We had to break the safe," the Major explained, "because the woman couldn't find her key. Apparently her old man had taken it with him."

"The movement is broke and we need to raise funds from the usual sources, our clansmen in the U.S., am I right?"

The Major was on the point of accusing the driver of divulging a secret to a nonclansman, but then his face took on the expression of a man deciding to put aside his differences with another for the sake of peace. Surprisingly, he lapsed into a friendlier mood, even smiling, if a little uneasily. Maybe he had retold himself Voltaire's admonition while breaking the safe, and had come around to the view that it wasn't wise to make unnecessary enemies. He turned to face Jeebleh, and asked, "Have you ever met StrongmanSouth?"

"No."

The Major said, with an odd mix of fear and pride. "I know Strongman-South very well."

"What's he like?" Jeebleh asked.

"The man is raving mad."

Jeebleh remained silent and sullen. He had no idea what to expect or where their conversation might lead.

"And you know what?" the Major went on.

'What?"

"For his breakfast, he eats cakes of soap."

Jeebleh wanted to remain silent, but couldn't help himself. "Why in God's name would he do that?"

"To prove that he's tough!"

Jeebleh caught a glimpse of the Major's rage rising and felt he might explode any minute; he looked at the driver, hoping he would step in to calm things. And it appeared as if he might do just that, but then he seemed to change his mind, and he too remained quiet.

The Major was now raving. "I've known StrongmanSouth for what he is for years—a lunatic with a madcap notion of what he can achieve. I served under him in the Ogaden War. I know him to be a pushover, and that's why I am not afraid of him. In fact, he's no trouble at all. Never mind the myth that's been built around his name by his clansmen and supporters." He threw his cigarette butt out of the window, and turned to Jeebleh as if expecting him to applaud. "He invaded our territory, conquered it. His ragtag militiamen rape our women, his clansmen have helped themselves to our farms. He's turned our ancestral land into an extension of his power game, and we're part of his bargaining strategy when the different interest groups come to the national reconciliation tables to set up an all-inclusive government. I keep telling my men that no one is able to rule over a people if they're prepared to fight. We're ready to kill, we're ready to die until our ancestral territories are back in our hands."

When the Major fell silent, the relief was not just Jeebleh's. They felt it all round, and took it in with a fine dose of the dust coming in through the window, cracked open because of the heat.

"To someone like you," the Major started up again, "we're all nuts, we're ranting mad. You probably think we're all fighting over nothing of great importance. You'll say, 'Look, your country is in ruins, and you keep fighting over nothing.' Those of us who've stayed on and participated in warring against the invaders of our territories feel maligned. We feel belittled when those of you who left, who have comfortable jobs, and houses with running water and electricity, somewhere else, where there is peace, speak like that. Has it ever occurred to you that some of us carry our guns, as the good everywhere must bear arms, to fight and die for justice?"

"But what makes you think that I believe you're fighting over nothing of great importance? I've said no such thing."

"I've met and heard many like you!"

Jeebleh chose not to answer and looked away.

The Major continued: "We're fighting for a worthy cause, the recovery of our territory. We're fighting against our oppressors, who're morally evil, reprehensibly blameworthy, every one of them. I see StrongmanSouth as evil for wanting to impose his wicked will on our people."

Jeebleh knew a lot more than he was prepared to let on, knew that the Major's armed movement was engaged in acts equally reprehensible as those of StrongmanSouth's militia, knew too that, as part of its policy to gain total control of the region, it had "cleansed" its ancestral territory of those hailing from other regions. From what Jeebleh had read, the leaders of the movement to which the Major and the driver belonged condoned the killing of innocent people who belonged to other clan families with ancestral memories different from theirs. Jeebleh considered the acts of all these armed movements immoral. Even so, he doubted there was any point engaging the so-called leaders in debate.

"Why are you here, anyway?" the Major demanded.

"Just visiting," Jeebleh replied.

"Who're you visiting?"

Jeebleh took his time before responding, because he didn't like the Major's aggressive tone. To calm himself, he studied the early hints of darkness coming at them in waves, and enjoyed this intimation of his first night in Somalia descending. His silence made the Major more impatient; he insisted on his question. "Are you visiting anyone in particular?"

"I'm visiting my mother's grave," Jeebleh said quickly.

But he felt ridiculous even to himself as soon as the words had left his lips. Granted, there was no gainsaying the fact that he had intended to call at his mother's grave, but he had planned to achieve other things during his visit, including a good air-clearing session with Bile about their unfinished business. He saw the Major and the driver exchange knowing glances; both looked at Jeebleh and then back at each other.

"Did your mother die recently?" the driver asked.

"Close to nine years ago."

"She died without you having seen her for years?"

Jeebleh nodded.

"Any idea where she's buried?"

"None whatsoever."

"During the last few years," the driver said, "a lot of terrible things have been done both to the memory of the living and to the spirit of the dead. I'm glad you've come on a visit to ennoble her memory, and honor it. Even though, if I permit myself to be cynical for a moment, your mother was fortunate to die when she did. This way she was spared many of the horrors of the civil war."

"How will you find her grave?" asked the Major.

"I am pinning my hopes on my mother's housekeeper and caretaker, who will most probably know where she is buried," Jeebleh said. But, he revealed, he had no idea how to find the housekeeper, who was actually in his employ, in that he paid her salary in the form of monthly remittances from America, directly into her account in Mogadiscio. Jeebleh was sure the housekeeper held the key to many secrets, and he was eager to talk with her.

"Don't you have any blood relations in the city who might know?" the Major asked.

Although he was tempted, Jeebleh chose not to talk about his motive to visit, or admit that he was hoping he might be able to locate his mother's story in the context of the bigger national narrative. So he kept it simple: "There are no surviving relations that I know of, or that I'm in touch with. But I have a couple of friends I plan to look up, and I'm pretty sure they'll help in leading me to where my mother is buried."

"How odd!" The Major sounded shocked.

"What?"

"I cannot believe that you have friends in the city, but no surviving blood relations." He repeated the word "friends," pronouncing it with a mocking distaste. "This is what America does to you."

"What's America done to me?"

"It's made you forget who you are."

"No, it hasn't."

"You'll see for yourself when you've been here for a couple of days that there are no longer 'friends' you can trust, anywhere in this country," the Major asserted. "Here we don't think of 'friends' anymore. We rely on our clansmen, on those sharing our ancestral blood."

"I find it hard to believe that you don't have friends," Jeebleh said.

"Only a fool not in touch with the realities of this country and our current history would insist on placing 'friends' above the station occupied by blood relations."

The driver shook his head. "I don't agree with you, my dear cousin," he said. "You and I know that even in the worst times of the civil war, many of us have been saved, given shelter, and then helped to safety by our friends."

"This is no longer the case, and you know it!" the Major replied. "Let's not kid ourselves with these and other lies. Nor is it that this fellow doesn't have any surviving blood relations here—he has plenty of them. Only he chooses to have nothing to do with them, believing they'll relieve him of his American money, which he doesn't wish to share with them. He thinks our reliance on blood kinship is backward and primitive. He is saying that he has money, that his family is safe and in America, that he belongs to the twenty-first century, while we belong to the thirteenth. Can't you see what he's saying?"

The driver said, "No, I can't."

"He's saying that we're backward fools, because we think of our kinsmen. Listen to him. He's here not to visit the country or some relations, but to call at *his mother's grave.* And on his way to her tomb, he'll make the time to look up a couple of his old friends. He's a modern man. We're primitive, we have our heads in the sand."

The militiaman with the cast said, "I think he should go to the south of the city, where they're all crazy, to look for his mother's grave. I agree with the Major, there's something wrong with this man!"

The driver winced like a parent in whose presence a child has been rude to a guest.

The Major now launched into a new tirade on how people like Jeebleh were on show-off visits "as false as their teeth." He devoted a few enraged remarks to their mannerisms, their clothes, their shoulder bags, the Samsonites-on-wheels in which they carried steam irons with which to press their stonewashed jeans. "The man is here to be gawked at," he said. "You can bet he left America after paying a visit to his dentist, who scoured his mouth for possible repairs, and after calling on his physician, who prescribed his tablets against malaria. A tangle of pretenses, that's what he is!"

He paused for a moment, but he wasn't done with Jeebleh. He turned to the driver and said, "Ask him who his friends are, since he has no blood relations in the land. Ask him."

Jeebleh was silent, but the driver answered the Major: "I suggest you lay off!"

Midway through the last rant, Jeebleh had decided not to rise to the Major's provocation, because he felt apprehensive. It worried him that he thought of the Major as someone behaving like a damaged person who placed his own inherent failures at the center of his self-censure, and who laid all blame at someone else's door. But he knew this notion wasn't right, and he didn't like the fact he was thinking it. Instead, Jeebleh eavesdropped on the conversation coming from behind him and was shocked to hear so much hate pouring forth from the militiamen, directed at StrongmanSouth and his tattered army that had laid their region to waste. Jeebleh looked for a long time at the wounded youth, with as much pained empathy as he could muster.

The driver jumped into the opportunity the silence had afforded him to change the subject, telling Jeebleh, "Our young warrior in the back stepped on an antipersonnel mine buried by StrongmanSouth's militiamen in a corridor of the territory we control. In the opinion of the surgeon in Nairobi, he was lucky to get away with injuries only to his leg—he could've been blown sky high."

It grieved Jeebleh to note that many of the militiamen laying down their lives in the service of the madness raging all around were mere children. It pained him too that those in the vehicle with him were so full of adult-inspired venom, their every third word alluding to vengeance, to death, and to shedding more enemy blood. They had lost their way between the stations of childhood and manhood. To judge from their conversation, many of them preferred dying in the full glory and companionship of their kin to being alive, lonely and miserable. Jeebleh remembered what Oscar Wilde said: that simply because someone is willing to die for a cause doesn't make the cause just.

The Major said, "What do you, in America, think of us?"

It dawned on Jeebleh that there was something doglike about the Major: his tongue in a mouth forever ajar, throbbing with deadly menace. But after studying it for a few moments, he decided that the tongue hung out not like a dog's, but like laundry left on the line to dry.

"It's very hard to judge from there. I've come here to learn and to listen," Jeebleh said.

"Then there's hope for us yet!"

"In some ways, I admit things were a lot clearer when I was last here, in the days of the dictatorship. But despite everything, and despite the prevailing obfuscation, I've come to assess the extent of my culpability as a Somali."

And he imagined seeing corpses buried in haste by his kinsmen, the palms of the victims waving as though in supplication. Similar images had come to him, several times, in the comfort of his home, in New York, and on one occasion, in Central Park, he had been so disturbed that he had mistaken the stump of a tree for a man buried alive, half his body in, the other half out. This was soon after he had watched on television the corpse of an American Ranger being dragged through the dusty streets of Mogadiscio. Those images had given him cold fevers for months. Now he felt the strange sensation of a many-pronged invasion, as if his nightmares were calling on him afresh. His throat smarted, as with an attack of flu coming on.

Abruptly the Major again gave the order for the car to stop. As before, the young gunmen dismounted from the vehicle's roof and took up positions facing the shanties at the roadside and spreading out fast, covering every possible angle. The Major got out and beckoned to several of them, and gave them instructions in a self-important way. He bid Jeebleh farewell, saying, "I hope you find your mother's grave!"

He vanished into the village, one armed youth ahead of him, another behind, and two others on either side—a VIP with his own security detail, presumably on his way to the money changer's.

"SO, YOU AND THE MAJOR DIDN'T EXACTLY HIT IT OFF," THE DRIVER SAID.

There were half a dozen people left in the vehicle, including the wounded youth in the back. The driver did not move off right away, but waited for the Major's escorts to return. The engine kept running; everyone was now more relaxed.

"Is he on a dangerous mission?"

Jeebleh took it that the driver knew the Major better than he was prepared to let on, and gathered from the man's body language that he was comfortable in Jeebleh's presence. But would he take him into his confidence, tell him things?

The driver spoke, his voice almost a whisper. "When he was in the National Army, he was trained in intelligence gathering and sabotage. Now he's been assigned to sneak into the area controlled by StrongmanSouth, where he'll do a couple of jobs. I've no idea what these are, because I have no clearance."

Jeebleh remembered reading about the region that the driver, the Major, and these youths came from: their ancestral territory had been turned into a battleground between bloodthirsty warlords. Many of the people had fled their towns and villages, fearful of being caught up in the fighting or of being massacred by drug-crazed militiamen on instructions to do as much damage as possible. The area had become known as the Death Triangle.

When the youths returned from having done their escort duty, the driver announced that he was ready to move. But no sooner had he done so than an argument erupted among the militiamen, those who had been on the roof insisting that they exchange places with those inside: Voices were raised; triggers were touched; death threats were made. Jeebleh prayed, Oh God, please, no shooting! He feared, for the second time since his arrival, that he might die in a mad shoot-out involving hapless youths.

Against the driver's advice, he stepped out of the vehicle, injudiciously volunteering to sit on the roof with the youths on guard duty. To his relief, his ploy worked, because those on the roof consented to remain there—as one of them put it, "for the time being, in honor of our guest."

Jeebleh had barely pulled the door shut when he heard one of the youths on the roof lashing out at those inside for being favored by the Major, to whom as cousins they were closer than the youth was. Admitted into the intricacies of kinship, Jeebleh learned that the Major was in fact showing preference to his cousins, whom he kept close to himself, inside the vehicle and farther from danger, whereas he assigned roof duty to those more removed. For Jeebleh, this proved clearly that the family thread woven from a mythical ancestor's tales seldom knitted society into a seamless whole. He assumed that the driver and the wounded warrior had stayed out of the dispute because their subclan was loyal to an altogether different set of bloodlines.

Once peace had been at least temporarily restored between the youths, the vehicle was on the move again, but not for long. The driver, as courteous as ever, apologized for the time it was taking to arrive at Jeebleh's hotel. "It won't be long now," he added.

"Where are we?" Jeebleh asked.

"We are in the north of the city, where our clanspeople have relocated to, having fled because of StrongmanSouth's scorched-earth policy," the driver said.

The vehicle had scarcely come to a halt when Jeebleh noticed a change in the behavior of the militiamen. They showed a united front to the hordes of men, women, and children who came from the shanties all around. There was a lot of mingling, a lot of primordial rejoicing. As he watched the shambling efforts at camaraderie, Jeebleh thought nervously about the ingrained mistrust between the youths, who belonged to different subclans, and about the unreleased violence that stalked the people of the land: friends and cousins one instant, sworn foes the next.

From inside, Jeebleh looked on as a woman in some kind of nurse's uniform instructed a group of teenagers how to lift the wounded fighter out of the vehicle. The teenagers were rough-hewn in speech and manner, and struck Jeebleh as being careless, picking the wounded youth up like a sack of millet, despite the nurse's warnings—"Careful, careful!" Jeebleh was reminded of inexperienced furniture movers taking an eight-legged table out of a small room into a bigger one through a tiny door.

The driver, waiting, kept the engine running.

JEEBLEH WAS SAD THAT THE NIGHT HAD FALLEN SO RAPIDLY, AS TROPICAL nights do. He was sad that he took no account of it, when he had wanted to remain alert, from the instant he first remarked that it was coming at them in a series of waves. He wished he were able to tell the meaning of the stirrings in the darkness outside, a darkness that was imbued with what he assumed to be Mogadiscio's temperamental silence. Jeebleh heard a donkey braying, heard an eerie laughter coming to them from the mournful shanty homes. He had looked forward to the twilight hour, had been prepared to welcome it, hug it to himself, but when it did come he hadn't been aware of it.

As they moved, Jeebleh, with nothing better to do, pulled at his crotch to help lift the weight off his balls. From the little he had seen so far, the place struck him as ugly in an unreal way—nightmarish, if he dignified what he had seen of it so far with an apt description. Most of the buildings they drove past—he had known the area well; Bile's mother had had a house hereabouts once—appeared gutted; the windows were bashed in, like a boxer who had suffered a severe knockout; the glass panes seemed to have been removed, and likewise the roofs. In short, a city vandalized, taken over by rogues who were out to rob whatever they could lay their hands on, and who left destruction in their wake. Jeebleh's Mogadiscio was orderly, clean, peaceable, a city with integrity and a life of its own, a lovely metropolis with beaches, cafés, restaurants, late-night movies. It may have been poor, but at least there was dignity to that poverty, and no one was in any hurry to plunder or destroy what they couldn't have. He doubted if there was enough space in people's minds for the pleasures he had enjoyed when living in Mogadiscio.

"I feel embarrassed that my colleague was rude to you in my presence," the driver said. "I cannot apologize enough. Kindly forgive us!"

"I suppose I should've said to the Major that I had returned to reemphasize my Somaliness—give a needed boost to my identity," Jeebleh said tentatively. "Do you think that would've made any sense to him?"

"I doubt that it would have."

"To tell you the truth, I was fed up being asked by Americans whether I belonged to this or that clan," Jeebleh continued, "many assuming that I was a just-arrived refugee, fresh from the so-called clan fighting going on in our country. It's irritating to be asked by people at the supermarket which clan I belong to. Even the colleagues I've known for years have been lousy at second-guessing how I felt about clan identity and my loyalty to it. You see, we Somalis who live in America, we keep asking one another where we stand on the matter of our acquired new American identity. I've come because I want to know the answers. I also wanted to visit these heat-flattened, sunburned landscapes, and see these shantytowns, witness what's become of our city."

When he had finished speaking, Jeebleh relished the quiet drive, the silence of the hour, the fact that there was no fighting, no guns firing, no traffic in the roads. He could hear voices, but they weren't threatening or frightening. The night they were plunging into extended a hand of welcome. Would that he could challenge his demons of despair, if these got in touch. On this trip, his life felt like it was on a mezzanine suspended between a floor marked "Ennui" and another marked "Hope." While he knew that anything could happen, he was determined to do his utmost not to end up in a body bag, or in an overpriced coffin addressed to his wife and daughters, care of a funeral agency with a zip code in Queens, New York.

The driver said, "I'll give you my telephone number so you can call me when you need to. And please don't hesitate to get in touch if there's anything I can do to help."

"It's very kind of you."

The vehicle stopped in front of a hotel gate. The driver applied the handbrake, turned to Jeebleh, and announced, "Here we are!"

4.

JEEBLEH TOOK NOTE THAT THE GROUNDS OF THE HOTEL WERE MARKED off from the street by a large sign, handwritten in Somali, Arabic, English, and Italian, warning that no one bearing firearms would be allowed onto the premises.

At the sound of the horn, the gate opened slowly, and his gaze settled on two men, neither, evidently, with a gun. One of the men appeared to have only one arm, while the other was distinguished by an enormous pair of buckteeth, bright white against an otherwise obscure face.

Above the gate, up in the heavens, the sky was soaked in the blood of sacrifice: it reminded Jeebleh of the Somali myth in which the sun is fed daily, at dusk, on a slaughtered beast. He remembered being told, as a child, that the routine of feeding the sun daily at the same hour made her return for food the following day. Now that he had gained his adulthood and come back to this fragmented land, he lamented the tragic absence of a hero worthy of elevation to solar eminence. He might have been at the gate of prehistory, because the quickening darkness of the hour dyed the visible world with the dim color of yet other uncertainties. Would he be safe at this hotel? Did it have running water? How intermittent was its electricity?

Of the two men at the gate, OneArm advanced with the wariness of a chameleon, once all the militiamen had gotten down from the roof of the vehicle.

He was so dark he might have been woven out of the night. He moved around the vehicle in the stylized goose-step of a sentry on duty. "No guns, please," he told the driver, who assured him that neither he nor Jeebleh was armed.

Bucktooth stayed behind, focused with reptilian attentiveness on every possible movement, his right hand in his pocket—maybe because a firearm was hidden there. The gate firmly in his grip, he kept half of his body out of immediate danger in the event of a shoot-out.

His hands on his lap, Jeebleh was a study in concentration. He was totally taken with Bucktooth, who seemed intent on outstaring him and the driver—until they conceded defeat, and showed their hands, palms forward. In fact, Jeebleh probably would have felt bothered and offended if he had been treated differently from anyone else.

As the gates opened fully to let the vehicle through, Jeebleh was touched by an instant of remorse as the minute hands of his destiny gathered the hours of his emotion. He looked forward eagerly to calling his wife and daughters in New York, to assure them that all was well with him so far; he felt a surge of anticipatory elation.

The driver parked under the glow of a fluorescent tube with a crowd of moths around it. Jeebleh got out, and took two steps before tottering to an unsteady stop: his toes had curled up in an awful cramp. While he was stretching his legs and retraining his feet to walk, two youths, presumably bellboys, not in uniforms but in sarongs, grabbed hold of his bags, and went ahead inside.

He bid the driver farewell and, even though he didn't think he would ever get around to calling him, wrote down his telephone number and thanked him profusely. Then he followed the youths, into an enclosed area where there were tables and chairs. He could not be absolutely certain, but it was possible that he took leave of his senses for a few exhausted seconds, during which he may not have known who he was, where he was, or what on earth he was doing there.

COMING TO, HE CAST ABOUT FOR A SOLID ANCHOR AND SOON SPOTTED A rather rotund man, with a cuddly look about him, struggling to heave himself out of a threadbare chair. He was tempted to offer the man a hand, but thought better of it when he saw him extricating himself from the deep chair and straightening up, then coming forward, his right hand outstretched. He was not the handsomest of men: his mouth protruded, boasting teeth that might have been molded out of soapstone, and his lower lip curved in the unlikely shape of a kilt of clouds covering the southern half of a full moon. The man introduced himself as the manager. Jeebleh was comforted when he shook the man's fleshy palm. "Welcome," the manager said. "I hope everything has been smooth and comfortable since your arrival."

The accumulated horrors of the scene at the airport, the stress of meeting so many strangers in a city virtually alien, and now the necessity of staying in a hotel—these were taking their toll on Jeebleh, unnerving him, and making him lose his general equilibrium. Lest he should speak impulsively and say whatever came into his mind, he remained silent.

"Welcome home, our bitter home!" said the man, reading into Jeebleh's silence. He stuffed his hands into the pockets of his baggy trousers, in which you could hear the jingle of colliding coins. (Jeebleh wondered what manner of coins these might be, and assumed they were not Somali, considering the high rate of inflation: a dollar was exchanging nowadays for thousands of shillings; when he had left for the United States, it had been worth six.) "I am Ali!"

Ali offered a belated smile, as if now remembering that he had been trained to please his customers. "In an earlier life, in long-ago peacetime Somalia, I used to be the favorite of gossip columnists and the envy of other hotel managers," he told Jeebleh. "I was appreciably more adept than any other hotel manager at getting the best of jobs. In my day, I played host to several kings of the petrodollar variety, not to mention a handful of African presidents on visits to Mogadiscio, and the secretaries-general of the UN, the Organization of African Unity and the Arab League too. And even though I am suitably qualified to run hotels anywhere in the world, having taken a degree in hotel management in England, I've chosen to stay. We are the sons of the land, to which we belong, you and I. I feel no regrets, though, none whatsoever."

Jeebleh suspected he knew what Ali meant when he said, "We are the

sons of the land." He understood the manager's "we" to be inclusive: Jeebleh, Ali, and many other known but unnamed clansmen of theirs, united in
blood. But was he right to interpret it this way?

"Why have you chosen to stay?" he asked.

"I have a bedridden mother to look after."

And here he was, Jeebleh, come to pacify his mother's troubled spirits.
Yet he couldn't and wouldn't be able to say, No regrets, none whatsoever.

"Anyway," the manager continued, "we've been alerted to your coming,
and we are at your service, to offer you our best."

"Who alerted you to my coming?"

"A good friend of yours."

"A good friend of mine?"

"Af-Laawe."

Jeebleh let this pass unchallenged. Moreover, he purposefully radiated a
false sense of confidence, if only to prove to the manager that he was on top
of things. He thrust his chin forward and asked, "Where are my bags?"

For a moment, because he had no idea where the bags had ended up, the
manager cut an undignified posture; but he was quick in setting things right.
He summoned the tallest of the bellboys and inquired what had become of
the gentleman's bags. Another bellboy in a sarong informed them that he had
taken the gentleman's bags to "the suite."

"Now for the formalities, if you don't mind." The personification of courtesy, Ali placed a pen on top of some forms and pushed them toward Jeebleh.

"Would you like to see my passport?" Jeebleh asked.

"There's no need."

Jeebleh completed the forms in haste. The words for date and place of
birth, sex, marital status, and permanent address were in Italian, and spelled
incorrectly; the paper was so dry it felt to Jeebleh as if it would break if he
tried to fold it; and some of the spaces he was supposed to fill in already bore
pencil markings. When he had finished, and was preparing to go up to his
suite, he heard Ali say, "Please do not judge us too harshly!"

"But of course not," Jeebleh replied.

"Times were"—Ali gestured out toward the gates, toward OneArm and Bucktooth—"when you knew who was bad and who was good. Such distinctions are now blurred. We are at best good badmen, or bad badmen."

Because he wanted to create a small measure of trust, Jeebleh blundered forward. "Do you know Bile?" he said.

"He's a good man."

"What's the latest about Raasta?"

"Nothing, so far that I've heard."

As Jeebleh took his leave politely, half nodding, the manager asked, "Would you like to get in touch with Bile?"

"There's time for everything," Jeebleh answered.

A bellboy escorted him to his suite.

"SUITE" WAS A MISNOMER, GIVEN THE ROOM'S SIZE AND ITS AMENITIES. AND now that Jeebleh was alone, the demons were back. His agitation was due, in part, to a lack of clarity in his mind—how to define himself here. His difficulty lay elsewhere, in his ability to choose whom he would associate himself with. He was somehow sure that Ali knew that Bile was his childhood friend, but not a fellow clansman. Jeebleh revisited his earlier exchanges with the Major, a barking dog penned in a kennel with many others like him, helplessly damned. It had been one thing talking to the Major, who thought of him as an outsider; it was altogether another to be in the company of the manager, with his inclusive "we"! What was he to do? Spurn Ali, who wished to relate to him, or welcome the inclusion, and yet keep a discreet distance, for his life might in the end depend on it?

He thought of how it was characteristic of civil wars to produce a multiplicity of pronominal affiliations, of first-person singulars tucked away in the plural, of third-person plurals meant to separate one group from another. The confusion pointed to the weakness of the exclusive claims made by first-person plurals, as understood implicitly in the singled-out singular. He remembered a saying, "Never trust a self-definer, because an 'I' spoken by a self-definer is less trustworthy than a she-goat in the habit of sucking her own teats," and it made good sense when he thought about how Somalis drove him crazy with their abuse of pronouns, now inclusive, now exclusive.

Pronouns aside, he felt alienated from himself, as though he had become another person, when he witnessed the brutal murder of the ten-year-old boy earlier. Thank God, that sense of alienation lasted a mere moment or two, making him wonder whether he was not the he who had left Nairobi earlier that day. Why were the demons making him engage in a discourse of the mad, a discourse marked by pronominal detours?

He was ill at ease with the kind of discourse drawn from the obsession with pronouns. Take that inclusive "we." Assume, he told himself, that Ali, presumably a clansman of his, kills someone. Wouldn't the family whose son had been murdered take vengeance and murder, for instance, Jeebleh? Was he, as a member of a clan family, responsible for the murders committed in the name of a shared "we"? And what of the claim that violence is cathartic, capable of making people get to know one another in a deeper way, just as a person comes closer to knowing others in times of disaster?

He was sure that he did not love Somalia the way he used to love it many years before, because it had changed. Maybe love did not enter into one's relationship with one's country? Maybe nostalgic patriotism demanded its own brand of flag-waving? Was he back in the country to refurbish his emotions about Somalia with fresher affections? Can one continue to love a land one does not recognize anymore? He had never asked himself whether he loved America. He loved his wife and daughters, and through them, he was engaged with America.

He took an intent look around the room in search of a secret place where he might hide his valuables, certain—although he hadn't asked—that the hotel had no working safe. The room contained the minimum essentials: a single bed, evidently hastily made; a bedspread covering it, color discreet indigo; a bedside table with a lamp; a washstand with a jug below. Also, a threadbare facecloth, a bidet to the right of the stand, and near it, a plastic kettle. The kettle reminded him that he was back in an Islamic country, where one performed the rite of ablution several times a day.

He thought ahead, imagining that a hotel employee had stolen his valuables. Caught and found guilty, the thief would lose his hands. Jeebleh was distressed, because he didn't want to confront the hard realities of today's Somalia—where the limbs of the small fry are amputated, while the warlords are treated with deference. He pulled out the wallet holding his cash, and felt the freshness of the dollar bills between his fingers. His whole body shook at the thought of receiving an amputated hand as compensation. He replaced the cash in his wallet, and pulled out his toiletry bag.

Because he hadn't expected to find a safe in a Mogadiscio hotel, he had resorted to making his own, in the safety of his hotel in Nairobi. He was a needle-and-thread man, and seldom traveled anywhere without a sewing kit. He had picked up the habit of darning during his years in jail. In fact, his study at home in New York was replete with all kinds of threads—cotton, silk, nylon and other synthetics, and a sewing machine, an ancient Singer, received as a Christmas present from his mother-in-law. With a reel of nylon thread, a pair of scissors, and a needle, he had made a false bottom for his toiletry bag, covering the visible part with waterproof material. He now had a space big enough to hide things in once he arrived in Mogadiscio.

He unloaded his toiletries onto the bed, and made sure the inner flap of the bag had been strengthened sufficiently. He was pleased with what he had done in Nairobi. Now he peeled off enough cash for his immediate needs, and put the remainder and his U.S. passport in the envelope into the false bottom of the bag. Then he replaced the toiletries in it, and left it conspicuously unzipped and in full view on the washstand, in the hope that no thief would suspect the bag to contain anything of value. As part of his strategy of deception, he triple-locked the closets, which contained nothing but his few clothes; he hoped to mislead any intruder.

He took a bucket shower quickly and methodically. Then he went out, in search of something to eat.

SEVERAL YOUTHS IN SARONGS WERE STANDING AROUND THE LOBBY. BEHIND the counter at the reception desk was an older man, more formally dressed;

he appeared to be in charge of the desk. Jeebleh didn't think the man was familiar with the etiquette of hotel business. He was crude, picking his nose and speaking rather loudly to the young men. When he made no move to ask whether he might be of some assistance, Jeebleh assumed that he was a relation of the hotel owner, newly arrived from the rural areas. Eventually a youth who described himself as a runner came forward and offered his help, saying, "We run errands for the guests. Is there anything I can do for you?"

"I would like to eat," Jeebleh said.

"What do you want?" the youth replied. "There's a restaurant close by."

"What's available?"

"Steak, other types of meat, spaghetti."

"Spaghetti and salad?" Jeebleh doubted very much that he would eat more than a mouthful or two: he was worried that his stomach might act up, something it was prone to do. Not wanting to trust the runner with a large U.S. banknote, he lied, saying, "But I don't have cash."

"Don't worry. You can pay later." And without waiting for further instructions or Jeebleh's confirmation, the youth ran off.

Alone in the courtyard, Jeebleh was struck by the night's beauty, and gave himself time to admire its starry quality. His gaze fell on a tree in the distance, silhouetted by moonlight, and he was startled to notice a human figure wrapped in a subdued gray, sitting under the tree. The shape seemed detached from both time and space, reminding him of a well-trodden floor and a tableau vivant. He assumed he was looking at a woman, age indeterminate. Somehow, the woman's figure evoked in him a funereal sorrow. Moving closer, he realized that there were in fact two women, sitting so close to each other that their veils merged and became one. They were so still for such a long time, neither speaking, that he thought of two cows sharing a scratching post. He had never examined these veils closely. They were less elaborate than the ones commonly worn by Yemeni women when he had lived in Mogadiscio.

Then he heard a man's voice. When he turned around, the manager was standing in front of him. "A breathtaking sight, isn't it?" Ali said. "Just look at how beautiful the night can be in a place that's otherwise dreadful!"

And Jeebleh looked back up at the sky, which lay solemn in the placidity of its own composure, the stars a-scatter like maize kernels thrown into greedy disarray by two hens quarreling. He agreed: "The sky is divine!"

"I wouldn't put it past StrongmanSouth to get it into his head that it's time he owned the skies too," the manager said. "Then we'll all be in deeper trouble."

In the pause that followed, Jeebleh was unable to say much, still shaken by the image of two women merging into one. He and Ali walked back to a table surrounded by chairs. Jeebleh asked, "What manner of veils do Somali women wear these days?"

"A lot has changed since you were last here."

"I don't remember these."

The manager explained that the influence came from the heartland of Islamic fundamentalism, from societies such as Pakistan and Afghanistan, where knowledge about the faith was essentialist, or Saudi Arabia, where the people were traditionalist. He described how the "robes" were made from two widths of black material sewn together into a kind of a sack, with sleeves that were equal in width to the length of the gown. They had a face veil, consisting of a long strip of poplinette that concealed the whole face except for the eyes. The robe covered the woman from the tip of her forehead to her ankles.

"Well, I never!" Jeebleh said.

"How long have you been away?" the manager asked.

"Far too many years."

The manager looked away, stared down at his hands, and said nothing.

Peace was a luxury expressed in an evening's beauty, Jeebleh thought, in the calm into which a cricket chirps, into which the owl hoots.

"Has there been much fighting lately?" he asked.

"Every now and then," Ali said. "When there is fighting, our evenings become very ugly and we hear nothing, not even the heart of our fear."

"And the point to the fighting?"

"I don't see any point to much of it."

"But the entire nation is held for ransom," Jeebleh said, mostly to himself and the quiet night.

Then he heard a scuttle coming from behind them: two geckos bickering over supremacy or rats, he couldn't tell. He looked at the wall behind him, at the space ahead of him. Alas, he couldn't make out who or what had made the sound, no matter how hard he tried. To a frightened man, he thought, everything appears strange, and every noise poses some threat.

The youth arrived, carrying two aluminum plates, one on top of the other, together containing a runny meal. Jeebleh had no idea why the youth had brought him a steak, or why it was drowned in the sauce it had been cooked in. He hoped it was freshly cooked, not warmed up several times over. The fried potatoes were soggy and inedible, and the steak tougher than the hoof of the cow slaughtered to produce it. The manager sat forward, and made as though he might launch into a lengthy explanation. Jeebleh waited, his fork raised, mouth in a grimace. He took a bite of a sodden potato, then a tougher-than-thou bite of steak. It was possible that his grim countenance dampened the manager's intentions.

"Do you know the driver with whom I came from the airport?" Jeebleh asked.

"He was no driver in the ordinary sense of the term," said the manager.

"What're you saying?"

"Don't be fooled."

Jeebleh was thoroughly confused. He took a mouthful of potatoes and helped himself to a generous cut of rubbery steak, which he eventually swallowed.

"What is he, then, if he's not a driver?"

"He was once a top civilian aide to the Dictator," the manager said. "Now he is second man to an armed militia that enjoys the backing of Ethiopia. You want my advice: Don't be deceived!"

Jeebleh wasn't sure how to react to the information. He stared at Ali in the hope that he might continue with this line of advice. No one likes to be taken for an easy ride. Was he being fed falsehoods? A driver who was not a driver! Once a diplomat in the Somali chancellery in Rome; then a top aide to the Dictator; now a driver. Where was the truth in all this? Then there was Af-Laawe, otherwise known as Marabou, who presented himself as a friend of Bile's but at the same time badmouthed him. Someone had sent him to the airport to meet his flight, but Jeebleh was damned if he knew who.

"How did you come to meet your 'driver'?" Ali asked.

"Af-Laawe arranged a lift for me with him."

"A night has two faces," the manager commented.

"What does that mean?"

"Simply that a night has a face that's visible in the light," the manager said, "and a face that's ensconced in the mystery of the unexplored."

Jeebleh could see that the manager was enjoying himself, probably repeating something he had rehearsed previously in front of other clients like him. In repose, the manager's taut face put him in mind of a tree cut before its time. Although he couldn't wipe the agitation off his own face, Jeebleh remained silent; he would have to find out if there was a profitable purpose to the lies.

The manager sat in an unkempt huddle, his arms folded across his heaving chest. "Don't be deceived!" he repeated.

Jeebleh pushed away the inedible food, wiped his mouth with his handkerchief, and asked if there was a way to make a telephone call to America. The manager informed him, to his surprise, that this was possible. And when Jeebleh asserted that he hadn't seen a phone in his room, the manager said, "There's a one-man telephone company I can send for."

"A what?"

"A one-man telephone company!"

Jeebleh remembered that until the late eighties it had been impossible to call Somalia from anywhere because the country boasted the worst telephone network on the entire continent. You just couldn't get through to anyone living here. So how it was possible in civil war Mogadiscio for a one-man telephone company to allow him speak to his wife?

"It will cost you four dollars a minute. Shall I send for him?" the manager asked.

"Yes, please!"

HALF AN HOUR LATER, A MAN CAME TO JEEBLEH'S ROOM WITH A BRIEFCASE full of gadgets, including a telephone linked to a satellite long-distance service. Jeebleh called his wife at work, and gave her a sanitized version of what had happened so far. Lest she beg him to return at once, he omitted any mention of death or tensions. As far as he could remember, this was the first time that he had deliberately kept things from his wife.

And he realized, when he was once again alone in his room, that he wouldn't hesitate to lie if he believed that by doing so he might serve a higher purpose: that of justice.

5.

BILE SAT UP, STARTLED, CALLING OUT JEEBLEH'S NAME, HIS VOICE HOARSE and his thinking addled. He was shaking all over, shivering fitfully one instant, perspiring heavily the next.

In a dream, a young woman in search of a physician had come for him, to tell him about a neighbor's horse that had broken loose and, in the process of bolting blindly, trampled her elderly husband underfoot, wounding him badly. Hysterical, the woman had appealed to Bile to help her. And she kept repeating her plea, "Save me from becoming a widow. Have pity on me and my unborn child. You must save him from becoming an orphan." She repeated the same sentences again and again, until the words merged one into another and he couldn't separate them.

Bile sat up in the darkness of his nightmare, disturbed that he was unsure whether he had ever met the young woman, or known of her. In his discomfiture, he couldn't resolve whether the dream had called on him for a reason as yet unclear, whether it had any bearing on his life or the lives of those who mattered to him.

THE NIGHT SOFTENED INTO DAWN, AND STILL RESTLESS, BILE GOT UP TO MAKE a pot of coffee the way he liked it: black, strong, no sugar. In his pajamas and dressing gown, and still a little shaken, he moved around in the apartment in which he had lived alone for a week now, half listening for the kettle to call when the water had boiled. He felt a chill of fluster in his bones, and a deep fear surged in him. Jeebleh, his friend, who was in Mogadiscio now, and Seamus, a close Irish friend, who was away in Europe, were of the view that he was in the habit of going into silent depressions, avoiding confrontations, or putting things off. He had never grieved enough, or been able to work through his rage at Caloosha for all the damage his half brother had done to him. Bile would retort that if he hadn't acted on the deep-felt hurt, it was because he was a man of peace.

He returned to the kitchen in jitters, his hands trembling as he picked up the singing kettle. He poured the boiled water into the pot and, missing his target by a few inches, emptied much of the water on the flames, thus extinguishing the fire. He became even more agitated thinking about what Jeebleh might ask when he saw him. He was likely to ask whether Bile had done anything about Caloosha, and if so, precisely what. If Bile's reply was in the negative, his friend was bound to say, "But what's wrong with you?"

Wrapped in a fever of shivers, Bile took the coffee tray with him into his study and sat in a swivel chair by the window, whose curtains were open. He placed the tray precariously on the side of the crowded desk, because there were far too many books on the coffee table. There were books everywhere, on the desk, on the floor by his favorite rocking chair, on the windowsill, many of them open, some with bookmarks, others lying facedown. One book was splayed on its side, as though it had been knocked over recently. Bile knew the man who had written it, a fellow doctor famous more for his silly infatuation with the politics of his clansman StrongmanSouth than for his professionalism. Bile stared at a spot in the distant heavens, in the manner of someone abruptly stripped of memories, and balked at his own reaction to Jeebleh's unexpected arrival.

When he heard the muezzin calling all Muslims to their dawn prayer, he pushed his enraged emotions aside and got up, intending to find a prayer rug for the first time in many years. He had no idea why, but a few minutes later he was standing before the blackboard on the wall, a piece of chalk in his hand, adding "Clean towels, sheets for Jeebleh's bed, etc." to the day's to-do list. No sooner had he replaced the chalk and dusted his hands clean than he was appalled that he hadn't said his prayers—and on top of this he was dismayed at reading what he had just written, for he had assigned Raasta's room to Jeebleh without giving the matter any serious thought. He leaned against the wall, worried that he might sink into a delirium. With the sun's early rays falling on his face, he might have been a rabbit caught in a mighty floodlight, its warren of possible escapes blocked off. When he went into the bathroom, he felt as closed in as a rabbit seeing its frightened expression in a mirror. Studying his reflection, he felt that he was staring at someone else's face, remembering and reliving someone else's history, listening to the thought processes of someone alien to him.

Bile was fifty-eight, tall, with a back straight as a ramrod. There wasn't a single ounce of extra fat on his body. His mud-brown eyes were restless, and his lips were forever astir, in the active manner of a mystic endlessly reciting his devotions. His hair was cut short, in the style of a get-up-and-go man who hasn't the time to comb it. He typically wore either jeans or trousers that didn't need to be ironed.

Shaving, he cut his chin, and his forefinger came into contact with a trickle of blood. He dabbed the cut with toilet paper, and grew steadily calmer, until he remembered who and where he was. He dabbed the cut again, to see how much blood he was losing.

In these unsettling times, everyone's fate, actions, dreams, hates, and aspirations were seen, understood, and interpreted in stark political contexts; distrust was the order of the day, and everyone was suspicious of everybody else. If Jeebleh were to express dissatisfaction with Bile's way of doing things, Bile would contrast it to his friend's *lex talionis,* affirming that he, Bile, did not feel indentured to an Old Testament law of retaliation. There was no doubt in his mind that the dark side of wrong would not be allowed to triumph. Now this: Raasta kidnapped; her father, Faahiye, missing. Rumor had it that Faahiye had last been seen heading for a refugee camp in Mombasa.

Bile's fears and sense of despair came close to depression, as he thought of a western he had seen once in which the good characters were caught in deadly quarrels among themselves, while the bad, who posed a greater threat to the fabric of society, were all dealt winning hands in the first part of the film. He knew from personal experience how often people, like Faahiye and his wife, Shanta, eager to change the unreconstructed ways of Somali society, fought fiercely among themselves until they had no energy left to take on the reactionaries who ran the real show. In a civil war, there were no progressives and no reactionaries; everyone was a victim, seldom a culprit.

His knees and hip joints stiffening, he recalled how, with the prison gates left open after the Tyrant fled the city, he had taken his first step into what he assumed was freedom. For almost an hour, he had watched with detached amusement as other prisoners ran from their cells as fast as their feet could carry them. A few of his fellow political detainees, whom he hadn't seen for years because he was kept isolated, came by his cell on their way out. He remembered saying to one of them, "What's the hurry?" But why, why didn't he flee?

The truth was shockingly mundane. He was merely having difficulty getting to his feet, suffering, as he was, from locomotor ataxia, in which the lower limbs are numbed. Try as he might, he would rise and then fall, again and again, his feet and legs failing him, his heels hurting, his eyes in pain when he opened or closed them, his head dizzy. As a political detainee, in isolation for seventeen years, Bile had been denied his right to take fresh air, to walk about in the prison yard, or to come into even indirect contact with the world outside. He had received no letters and no books.

Kept in a tiny cubicle, where it was impossible for a tall man like him to stand to his full height, he did what he could to remain fit, exercising within the limited space. But things were made even less tolerable, physically and mentally, when a month before the collapse of the state, more draconian security measures designed to confound the prisoners were introduced. He was kept in a dark room, allowed no contact with anyone, including the wardens. Then he was taken out of isolation and made to share a cubicle with petty thieves and other riffraff. Bile couldn't say whether he preferred total isolation in a dark cubicle to confinement in the same cramped space with low-minded thugs, who wouldn't let him be.

He remembered how at long last he had risen later that afternoon of liberation, only to find that his knees had stiffened, and his hip joints were as tight as rigor mortis. Nonetheless, he took a healthy long step with the stronger leg, swung the rest of his unwilling body around, and carried himself out of prison. It was that first, willing step that eventually brought him to Raasta, his niece.

And what a girl!

Now showered, shaved, and restless, Bile went to Raasta's room, where he found himself reliving a most pleasant memory: the day she was born. The image that stood out was one of a wet thing in his embrace, curled up, fists tight, as if she held the entire cosmos in her clasp. Asleep, she might have been a kitten delighting in the sound of its own purr. She was exceptionally beautiful, eyes the shape of almonds, mulberry-colored lips forever parted.

When she was born, there were four of them in the room: Shanta, her mother, half dead from exhaustion; Faahiye, her father; the midwife; and him. Faahiye, who was prone to going off in a dark rage, reminded Bile of a bird with its wings stuck in the mud it had wallowed in, clumsily trying to fly.

The girl was a few days old when it was discovered that she drew people to herself. They came by the hundreds whenever there was fighting, which was most of the time. People fleeing turned up at the house with the big compound, where they all stayed for the first few months of the civil war. They felt safe in her vicinity. Word went around that she was "protected," and so were those who found themselves near her. As a result, more escapees in search of safety from the fighting arrived to camp in the compound. At the time, there was no telling whether Faahiye was exaggerating when he claimed that "peace of mind will descend, halo-like, on whoever holds the girl in his or her embrace." Bile bore witness to the fact that Raasta, whose birth name was Rajo, meaning "hope," was always calm. She was rarely given to crying, even when she wet herself, as other babies of her age did. Nor did she cry when she was hungry. She was a miracle child, gaining everyone's trust, serving as a conduit for peace, enabling any two people at odds with each other to talk and make up. Nothing troubled her more than words of disregard hurled by people at each other in front of her. In her presence, her parents, to their credit, tolerated each other, in contrast to their mighty quarrels when she wasn't around.

She was equally popular with children and adults, and had a way of attracting virtual strangers, who willingly fed from the open palm of her charm. Occasionally she displayed a sense of discomfort in the company of immediate members of her family, who knew no self-restraint and were in the habit of losing their tempers.

Raasta shared a spiritual closeness with Bile, whom she treated like a surrogate parent.

She was never bored; she seldom seemed lonely, even when alone. She jabbered, improvising stories with which she entertained herself. It was clear that other people were in need of her, not she of them. And she always had an entourage of children in tow. Some came from poor backgrounds and were in rags, the younger ones with wet noses and eyes crawling with famished flies; still others brought along kwashiorkor bellies, drop foot, rickets, and other complaints. At the age of three, Raasta had gone about The Refuge with pocketfuls of vitamins that she distributed to the other children, earning herself the nickname Dr. Dreadlock, bestowed on her by the Africa director of UNICEF, who was on a fact-finding mission after the U.S. withdrawal. Even earlier, her intelligence knew no bounds. Bile remembered how she learned languages as soon as she heard the first fricative consonant of the new tongue, or was asked to repeat the guttural in place of the vowel sound of a monosyllabic derivative. By the time she was three, she could speak, read, and write three languages. At five and a half, her mastery of a few more tongues was exemplary.

Bile had thought he could get used to anything, because he had survived years of detention and many more of humiliation at the cruel hands of his half brother. Getting accustomed to Raasta's absence, though, was proving impossible. She had been the only constant in his life since he regained his freedom. He might have achieved as much as he had without her help, or done whatever he had done without her input. But he most certainly would not have cherished life as the sweet thing it had become if it had not been for her. She had taught him what it meant to be happy.

At times, he believed that his most dear darling had gone simply because she was fed up with the way her parents quarreled; at other times, he believed she had been kidnapped.

TEARS OF SORROW WET BILE'S FACE AS HE RELIVED THE LAST EVENING HE had spent with his niece. It had been early evening, when, tucked in bed, comfortable, and ready to sleep, he had told a folktale to Raasta and her playmate Makka. As had been his custom, he had lain between them, each girl with her head on his shoulder, to listen attentively to a tale about two giants.

Once there were two giants. One of them was a cruel tyrant, the other a wise king. The two giants did not know of each other's existence, they had never met—even though their kingdoms were next to each other. The cruel giant was called Uurku-Baalle, "the one who has wings in his belly," a name that meant that he knew everything about people just by looking at them; he knew when they were lying, and when they were telling the truth. The good giant was Shimbiriile, and he lived in a cave. His nickname was Dirir, the bad giant's Xabbad.

The cruel king Xabbad enjoyed making people cry; he liked to see terror on the faces of his victims, and he was happy when they were sad. He delighted in satisfying every desire of his, and never hesitated to take things that didn't belong to him. He was a hoarder, and claimed that all things belonged to him. Almost every house, every farm, and all money were in his name, in that of his immediate family, or in the names of those who were most loyal to his evil doings. He knew the details and movements of his people. To appease him, his subjects paid him large tributes. The more he was given, the greedier he became. Many of his subjects fled because they were fed up. They moved out of his kingdom to others, where they felt safer and were allowed to keep the things that belonged to them.

One day a distant relative of the kind king Dirir's by marriage played host to a family seeking refuge from Xabbad's kingdom, and

Dirir came to hear of the terrible things that had been done to them. He heard more stories, as more people fleeing the bad giant's territory came to live in his peaceful realm. The more horrific their tales, the keener he became to help the weak and the innocent. He gathered his advisors and a select few of the newcomers, and they talked and talked the whole day. Then the good king said, "We must help these people, we must put an end to these cruelties."

His people gave their full support, the able-bodied men volunteering to fight, and the rich offering to help feed the army when it was at war. Dirir prepared for war. He put on his custom-made steel bangles, which served as ornaments but could be used as powerful weapons. The bangles were heavy, and so strong they could shatter even the toughest iron shield. When word reached Xabbad that Dirir and his men were ready to attack, many more of his subjects changed sides and fled his territory. They liked what Dirir was doing.

At long last, Dirir and Xabbad came face to face. And Dirir threw a *daandaansi* gauntlet in the wicked ruler's direction, insisting that he remove the boulders that he and his men had put in the way of nomads who wanted to water their beasts from the wells.

"And if I refuse, what will you do?" came the bad giant's fierce challenge.

"Then you leave me no choice but to destroy you," responded the good giant. "I cannot stand by and hear about you looting the camels belonging to others, killing many innocent people."

BILE WAS DRESSED, BUT NOT READY TO FACE THE DAY. HE SAT AT HIS DESK, which was pushed into a corner. Close to his right hand were three telephones, each linked to one of the city's networks. There was a fax machine, and two mobile phones.

He thought back to a conversation he had had years before with Seamus and Jeebleh. For some three years, they had lived together in an apartment in Padua, in Italy. He couldn't remember which of them had described their friendship as "a country—spacious, giving, and generous." They held no secrets from one another, and lived out of one another's pockets, sharing all.

At the time, Jeebleh was doing his dissertation on Dante's *Inferno*, casting the epic into a poetic idiom comprehensible to a Somali; Bile was studying medicine; and Seamus was working on a postgraduate degree in Italian. Who would've thought that the three of them had discussed even then what Somalia would be like if the country plunged into anarchy? Reflecting on the *Inferno* made Bile shift to the recent past, and a conversation from a week before, when he had taken Seamus to the airport. They were, perhaps unsurprisingly, discussing hell.

Seamus was arguing that hell was a state of mind, not a place with its own territoriality, where the perpetrators of evil were condemned to serve an afterlife of punishments. Bile had reminded his Irish friend that in the Koran, the word for "hell" was specifically derived from "fire." And he had quoted the Prophet, who, when asked to qualify the relationship between "hell" and "fire," explained that the former was "more than the fires of the world by sixty-nine parts, every part of which is equal to all the fires of the world!" A sinner experiencing hell would feel as though he were wearing shoes or thongs made of fire, as though the brain in his head were melting. "It's like being thrown into a boiling copper furnace!" Bile said. Not quite sure of his facts, Seamus wondered whether the Arabic word for "hell" was not based on the Jewish concept Gehenna. To which Bile responded that, according to the Koran, Gehenna "is the purgatorial hell through whose gates all Muslims pass."

Seamus countered with an Irish fable. A blacksmith deep in debt sells his soul to Satan in exchange for wealth. There is one proviso, however: he'll lose everything and die if he doesn't repay the loan in seven years. When the allotted time is up, Satan presents himself before the blacksmith to remind him of their contract. The blacksmith pleads for an extension, which is granted. At the end of this period, he pleads for more time, and again his request is granted. But when he asks for a third extension, Satan will not oblige. He takes possession of the man's soul. And the blacksmith dies.

The dead blacksmith comes to the gates of heaven, where he meets Saint Peter, who reminds him that because he has sold his soul to the devil in exchange for wealth, he is not welcome. With no other choice, the blacksmith goes to the gates of hell. There, the devil gleefully informs the unhappy fellow that he is not welcome in hell either. When he learns that no amount of pleading will help, he asks Satan, "But where am I to go, then? Where can someone like me go, a man with no soul, no wealth, no power, and no friends to intercede on his behalf?"

"Make your own hell!" Satan tells him.

And so, Seamus concluded, "hell is a warlord who's ransomed his soul to Satan, in exchange for elusive power." Then he got on a plane bound for Dublin, leaving Bile alone in Mogadiscio.

THREE OF THE TELEPHONES ON BILE'S DESK STARTED RINGING SIMULTANE-ously, though not in any coordinated manner, because the phone companies were owned by subsidiaries of companies based in the United States, Norway, and Malaysia, and the tones they used were different. He didn't like to answer telephones at random. Then all three phones stopped ringing, only for one to resume after a brief pause. Bile picked it up, because he knew from the code that Dajaal, his man Friday, would be at the other end of the line.

Dajaal asked, "Is there any errand you would like me to run before I see you in half an hour?"

"Yes," said Bile. "I'd like you to pick up my friend Jeebleh from his hotel, and to bring him here. In fact, I'd appreciate it if you came here first, so I can give you a note for him, just in case you don't find him there. I want him to know that I'd like to see him right away."

Dajaal asked, "Do I go armed or unarmed?"

Bile did not answer immediately, because one of the phones had resumed ringing. Then he reminded himself that this was the first time Dajaal had put such a question to him, though he had offered to serve as Bile's hit man, when word circulated that men allied to an illicit group with links to Mogadiscio's underworld had kidnapped Raasta. Dajaal knew what was what, but Bile was a man of peace; he would not countenance such a heinous thought. Carrying a firearm was contrary to everything Bile held dear, anathema to his professional ethics as a doctor. "I would prefer for you to go unarmed. And in any case, I would like you to bring my friend Jeebleh here unharmed!"

He hung up, and let the other phone ring and ring and ring. He enjoyed an inner calm, as he thought about meeting Jeebleh, hugging and welcoming him warmly.

6.

JEEBLEH SLEPT A TROUBLED SLEEP.

He dreamt of taking part in fierce clan fighting. He was serving as an auxiliary to Caloosha, who, as commander, saw to the deadly operation. Caloosha was at the wheel of the battlewagon. Trained as an attack animal, Jeebleh took pure delight in the killing spree: happy to be on such a savage mission, in which no prisoners were taken, and in which women were first disemboweled and emptied of their babies, then raped.

A rocket from a bazooka flew over their heads, hitting no one; then heavy machine guns went wild. A missile struck the battlewagon, severing it into two uneven halves. Caloosha and Jeebleh remained in the front of the battlewagon and drove off, separated from the fighters.

The two were in a jubilant mood, singing praises in honor of their common ancestor. Jeebleh wore a belt of bullets, and held a recently fired assault rifle close to his chest, hugging it as one might hug a baby. His fingers came into contact with the bloodied bayonet, as though testing its sharpness. It felt as dull as a dead tooth.

UPON WAKING, JEEBLEH WAS CONSCIOUS OF SHUFFLING MOVEMENTS, SOURCE unknown. He was bothered that he couldn't tell whether he was still in the

Faustian country of his nightmare, a recruit fighting savagely to prove his worth to the clan family, or whether he was awake and hearing living sounds, of which he would eventually make sense.

It took him a long time to identify the source of the noise: a chameleon that was making its way along the floor of his room. What business did a chameleon have with him, up in his room on the second floor? Chameleons had terrified him as a child. Had someone who knew that brought it and deposited it on his balcony, while he was sleeping? Jeebleh doubted that the reptile could have covered such a distance by itself. So who was playing a prank on him, and for what purpose?

In an instant of utter insanity bodied forth by an odd mix of fear and superstition, he got down on the floor and, supporting himself on his elbow, eyeballed his saurian visitor. He watched the reptile's effete efforts as it headed for him, its one-step-forward, half-a-step-back movement holding Jeebleh under its spell. He sensed an inner tremor as he recalled the atavistic fears Africans had for chameleons, which were believed to have carried the message of death from the heavens. A number of African myths centered death on two oral messages, the one given to a hare and guaranteeing uninterrupted life, the other to a chameleon and presaging mortality. In the myths, the chameleon delivered the message, in obedience to an ancient dark fear. The hare, however, was distracted by its playfulness and failed to pass on the message of life.

Jeebleh took the measure of his own phobia as the reptile moved its eyes in constant gyration—first clockwise, then counterclockwise. It was probably making its presence felt, like an elephant employing theatrics to instill fear in its opponents. The eyes did not seem an ordinary part of its body, because they hung in front of its face, like two monocles, and rolled like dice dipped in Benetton colors. Its tail now curled up, its tongue out, it appeared, to Jeebleh, longer, its body grossly distended and intimidating.

But once he ceased to perspire so profusely, Jeebleh started to draw courage from the supposition that death is a direction rather than the end in the process of a life, and that the reptile is a mythical representation of an abstraction. After all, while the hare kept changing direction, the chameleon did not.

Now, for some reason, it was the reptile that was changing its course and moving toward the balcony, with the pained motion of an amputee on wobbly crutches making a U-turn. Leaving, the chameleon became a mere reptile, having no magical properties whatsoever.

And then there was a knock on the door.

A YOUTH WITH A MUDDY EXPRESSION, LIKE A FROG WITH DRIED CLAY STICKING to its forehead, was on the doorstep. Loath to allow him in, lest he should see the chameleon departing, Jeebleh held the door in a tight grip. "Yes?"

"What would you like for breakfast?"

Jeebleh couldn't imagine eating a breakfast that had been handled by such a youth. "Nothing for me, only coffee," he said. "Please."

"No cooked breakfast?"

"Only coffee."

"What kind?"

"What's available?"

"Coffee in Yemeni style, or instant."

With his skin prickling, and fearful that he might break into a sweat of itches at the thought of spending more time with the youth, he said, "Yemeni style, please."

"No eggs, no bread, nothing else?" the youth urged.

"None."

But the boy didn't seem ready to leave. He stood there, ogling Jeebleh, who couldn't bring himself to shut the door in his face. The soft morning sunlight separated him where he stood, with his hair on end, from the youth. He studied the teenager from close quarters, and decided that his face was much older than the rest of his body, what with the desert cracks in his dry, neglected skin. He couldn't help thinking of the degraded state of the soil of the Sahel, with its proximity to the Sahara. The youth's eyes were the size of black ants, his teeth appeared more rotten now that the gentle sun fell on them, and they had the hue of ginger taken from a curry pot. Hunger had gnawed at his cheeks too. Years of dictatorship, the habit of chewing *qaat*, and the civil war together had brought the boy's potential and his overall health to a sad, retarded state.

"And you'll like your coffee before you go?"

It was news to Jeebleh that he was going anywhere. At least, he couldn't remember arranging to go anywhere, unless he had clean forgotten. "Where am I supposed to be going?"

"I was told you were going somewhere."

"Who told you that?"

"I don't know."

Jeebleh's breath caught in his throat. He dreaded things coming to this: appointments being arranged for him when he had no idea where or with whom. Did he have any choice but to honor the request for him to go somewhere, on someone's whim? Had he no choice in what he did, where he went and when? He was about to goad the youth into giving him the source of his information, when another youth arrived bearing two pails, presumably containing hot water and cold. The two boys greeted each other amiably, and the breakfast boy went down a couple of steps to help carry one of the pails. When they came to within half a meter of him, Jeebleh noticed something quite odd about the bath boy's features. He was missing a nostril. Maybe an untended bullet wound had turned gangrenous, damaging his face. Jeebleh indicated that they should give him the pails and he would take them in. They did as they were told, and left, holding hands and laughing luridly.

Showered and dressed casually, Jeebleh picked up the two pails, which he meant to leave in the corridor, and was ready to pull the door open and bounce youthfully downstairs, when he heard another knock on the door. This time it was one of the bellboys to say that he had a visitor.

JEEBLEH DESCENDED THE STAIRS SLOWLY, OVERWHELMED WITH FOREBODING. In his distracted state, he almost collided with a young woman going up with a pail and a mop. He regained his balance just in time, and continued down the steps, past the reception area, where several youths lounged, and out to the courtyard, awash with bright sunlight.

Af-Laawe was there to surprise him, greeting him as one Arab greets another, with the left hand on the heart, head slightly bowed, right hand touching lips moving and emitting a salvo of blessings. Af-Laawe ended his theatrics with a sweeping gesture of his right hand, half prostrating himself. Then he spoke in an ellipsis: "A nightmare of loyalties!"

Jeebleh refused to be taken in by anyone's antics, least of all Af-Laawe's. With a straight face, he replied, "Would you like to join me for coffee?"

"Yes, I would."

They sat outdoors at a plastic table with three chairs around it. The break-fast boy brought Jeebleh his Yemeni coffee in an aluminum pot, which proved difficult to hold or pour; but he managed it, then pushed the sugar bowl toward Af-Laawe, who helped himself generously.

"How was your first night back?" Af-Laawe asked.

"Thank you for arranging the lift and the hotel."

"I hope the manager is treating you well."

"He is, considering the circumstances."

"The room is all right?"

"I can't ask for more," Jeebleh said.

And then all that the driver had said about Af-Laawe returned to Jeebleh in a flash. His lips were touched with a knowing grin, in anticipation of learn-ing more about Af-Laawe's link to Caloosha's world of deceits, conspiracies, and killings. Jeebleh replaced the features of the driver with an identikit that might have been a cross between Af-Laawe and Caloosha; he superimposed this on the face of a hardened criminal wanted for a series of robberies worth millions of dollars.

"I'm glad you're having a good time," Af-Laawe said.

All around the courtyard, Jeebleh noticed vultures gathering. They ar-rived soundlessly, working to a precise timetable, one every half-minute, like airplanes landing. There were no fewer than a dozen, the largest the size of a Fiat Cinquecento, heads down, wings folded, beaks held dramatically in mid-motion. One particular bird disappeared every now and again, only to reappear a few minutes later as several more birds joined the gathering. Jeebleh found it strange to see vultures alighting in the courtyard of a four-star hotel. Where was the carrion to be had?

He fell under the spell of the spectacle. He couldn't take his eyes off the vultures, now dividing themselves into two groups, on what basis he couldn't tell. The huge vulture went back and forth between the groups, then took off quietly, and was gone for a good while. He returned with a companion of similar size and comparable build, but with a beak of a different color. The two birds went back and forth between the two groups as if ferrying urgent messages.

"Vultures, crows, and marabous have been our constant companions these past few years," Af-Laawe said. "There've been so many corpses abandoned, unburied. You will see that crows are no longer afraid if you try to shoo them away. At the height of the four-month war between the militiamen of StrongmanSouth and StrongmanNorth, the crows and the vultures were so used to being on the ground foraging, they were like tourist pigeons in a Florentine piazza. These scavengers have been well served by the civil war."

"Why the nickname 'Marabou'?" Jeebleh asked.

"Somebody has been telling you things."

"And why 'Funeral with a Difference'?"

Af-Laawe said, "I started the funeral service when sorrow felt like something emitting a bad odor that was forever there, as though it had been smeared on the inside of my nostrils. After the mosques were raided and the women seeking refuge in God's house taken out and raped, I set up an NGO to take care of the dead."

"Where did you get the funds to set it up?"

"I raised them myself," he said.

Was Af-Laawe, as he told it, a lone do-gooder in the style of the folk heroes one read about as a child? Jeebleh wondered what good a single person could do in a place where the bad outnumbered the virtuous. Maybe one must do what one can, the best one can.

Af-Laawe continued, "At least I am in the privileged position of choosing what I want to do and how I go about it. Not everyone is in this position."

Who was he, really—a troubleshooter on a fat salary from the EU; a big-time swindler, with a heist stashed away in a Swiss bank; a do-gooder with an NGO to bury the unclaimed dead; a house-sitter looking after the property of a family who had fled?

"Speaking of choices," Jeebleh said, after a long silence, "did the members of the clan families who fled the city *choose* to flee, or were they forced to abandon their properties in a city they adored?"

"These are abnormal times!"

"I can see that," Jeebleh said, and looked at the vultures holding a conference a few meters from where they were seated.

The traces of a wicked grin formed around Af-Laawe's drawn-in lips. He noticed Jeebleh's gaze. "A cynic I know says that thanks to the vultures, the marabous, and the hawks, we have no fear of diseases spreading," he said. "They clean things up, don't they? My cynical friend suggests that when the country is reconstituted as a functioning state, we should have a vulture as our national symbol."

"You wouldn't be that cynic yourself?" Jeebleh asked.

Af-Laawe stonewalled again: "These are abnormal times."

"I would agree it's abnormal to see scavengers of carrion at a four-star hotel, looking as though they are well placed to choose what they eat and where they go. They look better fed than humans."

It puzzled Jeebleh to see that Af-Laawe was upset. Had he said something to offend him? Now his drawn-in lips moved, like a baby fish feeding.

"There were far more vultures and marabous in the aftermath of the October-third debacle, when over a thousand supporters of StrongmanSouth were massacred, and eighteen U.S. soldiers lost their lives. I bore witness to the arrival of these scavengers, gathered around the battle zone, and perched on the lookout points in the neighborhood."

The words were spoken like an attack. Did Af-Laawe think that Jeebleh, as an American, would be upset if he mentioned the U.S. dead in Mogadiscio in the same breath as sighting scavengers gathering at the battle zone? Because Jeebleh assumed that Af-Laawe's badness was emerging, he prepared for an attack, and waited. He was getting to know Af-Laawe a little better at least.

Af-Laawe went on, still in attack mode. "On the fourth of October, there were as many carrion-eaters as there were human beings come to witness the massacre. But the birds had no chance to get at the corpses of the Somali dead, since these were taken away and buried by their families. A discerning person, like my cynical friend, would've seen two marabou storks, weighing no less than twenty kilograms each, discreetly following the progress of the riotous mob dragging the corpse of an American Ranger down the dusty alleyways of the city. The marabous followed the mob, and my friend tells me that their bare heads and bare necks were in clear view. Maybe they expected the crowd to abandon the corpse of the American at some point, so they might pounce on it. The hawks hung back, remaining at a distance. They didn't want to get into direct conflict with the marabous."

Jeebleh, listening to Af-Laawe, realized that he himself was infested with more venom toward Caloosha and anyone associated with him than he had thought possible, despite his years of exile.

"Do you wish to know the name of the cynic I was with?" Af-Laawe said. When Jeebleh nodded, he asked, "Have you ever met Faahiye?"

"I know Raasta's father," Jeebleh said.

"He's the cynic I was with on the fourth of October."

Jeebleh was relieved that they had changed the subject when they did, even though he doubted very much that Faahiye had said any of the terrible things ascribed to him. "Where is Faahiye?" he asked.

"A cynic, who's angry at the world," Af-Laawe said.

"No stonewalling. Where is he?"

"Faahiye hates being an appendage."

"An appendage of whom?"

"Faahiye looks forward to the day when he is his own man, not an appendage," Af-Laawe explained, "not to be referred to as Raasta's father, or as Bile's brother-in-law."

"Where is he?"

"He was headed for a refugee camp on the outskirts of Mombasa when I last heard about him," Af-Laawe said. "They say he was thin, as we all are, and the worse for wear, as we all are." After a pause he added, "He was troubled like a rutting he-dog, not knowing what to do, where to turn, because he is terribly excited." Pleased with his private joke, Af-Laawe graced his lips with a grin. Jeebleh waited, expecting Af-Laawe's exculpatory defense of his own behavior, after he had been accused of such insensitivity, but Af-Laawe did no such thing.

Now, why did the story about the marabou storks following the progress of the American Ranger disturb Jeebleh so? Before he had time to answer, a bellboy called him to the telephone. He asked who it was who wanted him on the phone, expecting it to be Bile. The boy said, "The name sounds like Baaja—I don't know."

Af-Laawe stepped in helpfully. "He means Dajaal."

"Who's Dajaal?"

"Bile's man Friday."

Jeebleh got to his feet, hurting and clumsy, and nearly toppled the plastic table. "Sorry!" he said, with guilt on his face, and he rushed off, passing the gathering of the carrion birds, their presence of no apparent concern to him.

On the phone, Dajaal said he would come shortly to take him to Bile.

7.

THE ROADS MOVED: NOW FAST, NOW SLOW.

From where he sat in the back of the car, Jeebleh saw vultures everywhere he turned: in the sky and among the clouds, in the trees, of which there were many, and on top of buildings. There were a host of other carrion-feeders too, marabous, and a handful of crows. Death was on his mind, subtly and perilously courting his interest, tempting him.

He remembered with renewed shock how he and Af-Laawe had come to their falling-out earlier. Perhaps he wasn't as exempt as he had believed from the contagion that was of a piece with civil wars as he had believed; perhaps he was beginning to catch the madness from the food he had eaten, the water he had drunk, the company he had kept. He doubted that he would knowingly take an active part in the commission of a crime, even if he were open to being convinced that society would benefit from ridding itself of vermin. He knew he was capable of pulling the trigger if it came to that. His hand went to his shirt pocket, where he had his cash and his U.S. passport. He meant to leave these in Bile's apartment, where they would be safer than in his toiletry bag.

Dajaal was in front beside the driver, and Jeebleh had the back to himself. The ride was bumpy, because of the deep ruts in the road. In fact there wasn't much of a road to speak of, and the car slowed every now and then, at times stopping altogether, as the driver avoided dropping into potholes as deep as trenches.

Looking at Bile's man Friday, Jeebleh thought that Dajaal must once have been a high-ranking officer in the National Army. He deduced this from his military posture, from the care with which he spoke, and from his general demeanor. He suspected that Dajaal was armed: one of his hands was out of sight, hidden, and the other stayed close to the glove compartment, as though meaning to spring it open in the event of need. Getting into the vehicle, Jeebleh had seen a machine gun lying casually on the floor, looking as innocuous as a child's toy gun. The butt of the gun rested on Dajaal's bare right foot— maybe to make it easier to kick up into the air, catch with his hands, aim, and shoot. You're dead, militiaman!

What Jeebleh had seen of the city so far marked it as a place of sorrow. Many houses had no roofs, and bullets scarred nearly every wall. In contrast to the rundown ghetto of an American city, where the windows might be boarded up, here the window frames were simply empty. The streets were eerily, ominously quiet. They saw no pedestrians on the roads, and met no other vehicles. Jeebleh felt a tremor, imagining that the residents had been slaughtered "in one another's blood," as Virgil had it. He would like to know whether, in this civil war, both those violated and the violators suffered from a huge deficiency—the inability to remain in touch with their inner selves or to remember who they were before the slaughter began. Could this be the case in Rwanda or Liberia? Not that one could make sense of this war on an intellectual level—only on an emotional level. Here, self-preservation helped one to understand.

"Why is ours the only car on the road?" Jeebleh asked.

"We're headed south, maybe that's why," Dajaal replied.

"The roads were crowded on your way north?"

"We're taking a different route from the one we took coming."

"Why?"

"It's the thing most drivers do." Dajaal waited for the driver to confirm what he had said with a nod. Then he continued, "They believe that taking a different route from the one they used earlier will minimize the chance of driving into an ambush."

"This is a much longer route, isn't it?"

"It is."

The driver, in a whispered aside, commented to Dajaal that he thought Jeebleh had arrived in the country only a day earlier.

Jeebleh's eyes fell on a bullet-scarred, mortar-struck, machine-gun-showered three-story building leaning every which way, as if in homage to the towering idea of a Pisa. He was surprised that it didn't cave in as they drove past—and relieved, for there were people moving about in the upper story, minding their business.

He asked Dajaal, "Have you participated in any of the fighting?"

"I've never been a member of a clan-based militia."

"So what fighting did you take part in?"

"Let's say that I got dragged into one when the American in charge of the United Nations operation ordered his forces to attack a house where I was attending a meeting."

"The American-in-charge." Jeebleh strung the words together, at first hyphenating them in his mind, to capture Dajaal's enunciation, then abbreviating them: AIC. Jeebleh had heard that that was how he was known in certain circles.

"This was the first American attack on StrongmanSouth, in July 1993," Dajaal went on. "I was at a gathering of my clan family's intellectuals, military leaders, traditional elders, and other opinion makers. It was our aim to find a peaceful way out of the impasse between the American in charge of the UN Blue Helmets, and StrongmanSouth and *his* militiamen. The July gathering has since become famous, because it led eventually to the October-third slaughter. It was the viciousness of what occurred in July, when helicopters attacked our gathering, that decided me to dig up my weapons from where I had buried them after the Dictator fled the city."

"I presume you know StrongmanSouth?"

"I served under him," Dajaal replied. "He was my immediate commander, during the Ogaden War. We didn't get on well for much of the time, which was why I declined to be his deputy when he set up the clan militia. I knew him well enough *not* to want to be near him if I could help it. The man is determined to become president, and he'll use foul means or fair to get what he wants."

The driver made a left turn, and as far as Jeebleh could tell, headed back the way they had come. He slowed down, as if to allow Dajaal time in which to gather his harried thoughts.

"I remember that Cobra and Black Hawk helicopters attacked us in the house where we were having our meeting," Dajaal continued. "Once the attack began, it was so fierce I felt hell was paying us a visit. The skies fell on us, the earth shook down to its separate grains of sand."

Jeebleh listened intently and remained still.

Dajaal went on: "I felt each explosion of the missiles, followed by an inferno of smoke so black I thought a total eclipse had descended on my mind. And the shrapnel, the spurting blood I saw, the men lying so still between one living moment and a dead instant, the moaning—I was unprepared for the shock. I remember thinking, 'Here's an apocalypse of the new order.' It's very worrying to see a man you're talking to blown away to dust by laser-guided death, deceptive in its stealth. We all lost our sense of direction, like ants fleeing head-on into tongues of flame, and not knowing what killed them."

Jeebleh dared not speak.

Dajaal's voice had in it a good mix of rawness and rage. "Coming out the door of the house, I tripped on a pile of shoes. But I walked on, barefoot, shaking with fury, until I found myself in another compound, my eyes still smarting from the black smoke. You could say I came to only after the helicopters left. I knew then that I was still alive. But I couldn't make sense of what had happened, even as the crowds gathered in front of the target villa. I learned that many of my friends had died, and that a number had been taken prisoner, in handcuffs, and treated as common criminals.

"It was a hell of a day." Dajaal was close to tears, reliving the scene, and angry too. But Jeebleh couldn't tell at whom. Dajaal resumed: "The cattle, terrorized, ran off mad, the donkeys brayed and brayed, and the hens didn't lay eggs for several weeks. Our women noted a change in their monthly cycles, and their psyches were irreparably damaged. No time to mourn, our dead were buried the same day."

"Provoked in July," Jeebleh said. "So you dug up your gun and were ready for the October confrontation, determined to take vengeance?"

Dajaal's expression, or what Jeebleh could see of it, was a touch sadder, as he nodded. Sorrow pervaded his voice. Jeebleh understood from what he had heard that badness had names and faces: those of StrongmanSouth, and of the AIC. And of course Caloosha and the Dictator too.

"Were you opposed to the Americans' coming in the first place?"

"We welcomed their coming, we did," Dajaal said.

"What happened then?"

"They were just crass, that is what happened."

"Tell me more."

Dajaal said, "My grandson Qasiir was among half a dozen unarmed boys at the international airport, then closed, doing what youths of his age do. They were fooling around, some smoking, others lounging or sleeping in abandoned vehicles. Then the Marines landed at the beach. And what was the first thing they did? They handcuffed my grandson and several others with belts, electrical cords, whatever else was handy. They humiliated them for no reason, intimidated them, and arrested them. The boys were doing no harm to anyone. Then July happened, and I was in it, as close to death as I've ever known, many of my clansmen killed or wounded, or carted off to some prison island off the coast. Then in October, my granddaughter, my son's youngest, was blown away in a helicopter's uprush of air and confusion."

Jeebleh spoke in a whisper and with the caution of someone avoiding a mine. "You were never in support of StrongmanSouth yourself?"

"Hell no, I wasn't."

Again Jeebleh spoke tentatively: "Someone must have been, for there were always crowds everywhere he went, women screaming supportively, and used as shields?"

"I can name a large number of my clansmen who wanted peace," Dajaal said, "which, in fact, was why we were holding the meeting. We didn't like where the American-in-Charge and StrongmanSouth were taking us, and we didn't approve of their confrontational styles. We thought they were so alike, the two of them, and wished they'd fight their own fight, in a duel—bang, bang, one of them dead!"

"How's your granddaughter doing, the one who was caught up in the helicopter's wake?" Jeebleh asked.

"She hasn't spoken since that day."

"How old is she?"

"She started to vegetate so early in her infancy," Dajaal said, "that we don't think about her age anymore. She startles easily, and the slightest noise causes her to burst into tears, and nothing will calm her. There's nothing wrong with her motor mechanism. Dr. Bile has been of tremendous help, thank God, but I doubt if she'll ever grow to be normal."

"What about the mother?"

"What harm did the mother do to *them*?" Dajaal raged.

In his mind, Jeebleh saw a knight on horseback, sword in hand, ready to take vengeance and die in the service of justice. "What about the mother?" he repeated.

"To calm her down, they handcuffed her. Why?"

Bile was very lucky to have Dajaal as his man Friday, Jeebleh thought. The man struck him as upright, straightforward, and honorably courageous. Yet he couldn't decide how far Dajaal's loyalty would extend to him. He watched the road ahead in silent intensity, worried, like an insect focusing all it had in the way of wiliness to avoid being hurt.

The car suddenly stopped, and the driver and Dajaal exchanged a nod. Fear can make a man sit slightly off balance, as though he were hard of hearing, listening for an ominous sound, shoulders hunched, ears pricked. Jeebleh's whole body went stiff, as he stared at the solitary Coke bottle that stood majestically in the center of the road. He didn't know what to make of it. In a coordinated manner, the driver moved in the direction of the glove compartment at the same time that Dajaal lifted the machine gun off the floor with his feet, flinging it up and catching it just as Jeebleh had imagined earlier. He had agile feet, Dajaal did, and he deployed them more adeptly than some use their hands. A minute passed. Nothing happened. Then Dajaal and the driver spoke in low whispers. Jeebleh broke the grief: "Are we at the green line?"

Both Dajaal and the driver shook their heads and then, still not speaking, allowed themselves the rare luxury of smiling, in the loaded way two adults might exchange a smile when a child asks an inappropriate question. Their watchful eyes no longer on the Coke bottle, the driver and Dajaal communicated in gestures, after which the driver pressed the horn three times, once gently, twice decisively, then paused and waited.

An old man and two boys, all with guns, emerged from behind an abandoned building, the man leprous, one boy with his right foot clumsy with elephantiasis, the other boy afflicted with wrist-drop agony. The boys lowered their weapons, their lips traced with smiles of relief. The old man, whom Jeebleh presumed to be the father and the leader of the band, aimed his gun at the vehicle. As though on a dare, the car crept up to the Coke bottle, which fell on its side. Jeebleh watched this with mixed pity and amusement. Dajaal wound down his window and threw a wad of money tied with a rubber band at the feet of the old man.

The smaller of the boys bent down and retrieved the wad. It was only when the vehicle came level with them—near enough to smell their unwashed bodies—that Jeebleh realized that all three had imitation guns, poor-quality mahogany painted black.

"What are they?" he asked.

Maybe Dajaal picked up on his unease or maybe he didn't, but Jeebleh was instantly regretful, wishing he had said "who" instead of "what."

The driver spoke for the first time, his accent clearly from Mudugh. "Down in the south," he said, "we call them 'idiots of the north.'"

"Because they are a harmless lot?"

Dajaal had had enough. "Let's get going!"

And as the vehicle moved, Dajaal explained that the "three-man militia" had their checkpoint in a no-man's-territory, in the belief that they could continue profiting from their stickups. "Myself, I'm impressed with their cunning, because they expose a major weakness in the idea of the clan. After all, they too claim to represent the interests of a clan family—even if it's the smallest unit within the larger clan to which the two principal contestants, StrongmanSouth and StrongmanNorth, also belong. It's clever of them to poach in the no-man's-territory, claiming their share in what is to be got."

The car slowed, the driver changing gears, looking this way and that. He signaled left but took a right and then—how very odd—reversed, managing to avoid a mound of dirt. They were at a crossroads. A cluster of children appeared. They stood by, watching.

"We're now entering the no-man's-territory, where the so-called green line is," the driver said, pointing at a spot in the road to his right.

This was comparable to pointing at a spot in a river and saying that one's parents had drowned there several years before. To Jeebleh, Mogadiscio's green line and the no-man's-land both expressed not so much inadequate demarcations of territories, but rather the absence of compromise between the realities and the political zeal of the warlords. Such a line, and that no-man's-land, would continue to exist as long as these incompetent men refused to reach a compromise.

The roads had no names. No flags flew anywhere near where the car was now parked, and there were no sheds, however ramshackle, to mark the spot. For the first time on this drive, there were a lot of people, busy as shoppers; buses disgorging more people; lean-to shacks, where you could have tea; stalls where women ran their haberdasheries.

"Can I step out?" Jeebleh asked.

"And do what?" said the driver.

"I'd like to have a feel of the place, if I may."

"We would advise you not to," the driver told him.

Jeebleh nonetheless got out of the vehicle, leaving the door ajar, and crouched in the bent-knee posture of a supplicant before a deity. Passersby, men and women hurrying to catch the bus that would take them somewhere, gawked at him, some looking amused, others uncomprehending. What was he doing? Humbling himself before the god of peace, or Mother Earth herself? The driver shouted to him to get back in the car.

A quarter of a kilometer later, they stopped so unexpectedly that the car slid forward when the driver braked. Several armed youths in military fatigues, who had materialized out of nowhere as far as Jeebleh could tell, flagged them down. The oldest would have been in his twenties, and none of them had proper shoes to give their uniforms respectability. They seemed thuggish to Jeebleh, all boasting the armed youth's standard chipmunk cheeks, their jaws busy chewing *qaat*. Their eyes were bloodshot and sore with exhaustion.

One of the youths recognized Dajaal, and said, "What if I hadn't recognized you? We could've shot you. Be careful next time. Now get going, and fast!"

Once the car had driven off, Jeebleh asked, "What do they do to people they don't know?"

"They make a nuisance of themselves," Dajaal said, "they open the trunk of your car, pretending to check for weapons to confiscate, or for contraband goods on which StrongmanSouth's income revenue police levy a hefty duty. Often, they take the goods themselves as their share, since they are members of StrongmanSouth's militia. I would say every major and minor warlord runs the territory under his nominal control profitably."

"Does StrongmanSouth provide them with the uniforms?"

"No."

"Who, then?"

"Gadhafi has sent a planeload of these army fatigues," the driver said, "and the AK-47s are available in the open market and cost only six dollars apiece. StrongmanSouth allows them a free run of the place every now and then, and supplies them with their daily ration of *qaat*, or at least enough cash with which to buy it."

Another kilometer and three more checkpoints, and the vehicle came to a halt. Informed that they had arrived, Jeebleh gave a sigh of relief. Here, it was all peaceful. They were before a huge building, which he remembered serving as the State Secretariat. In the sixties, soon after independence, the prime minister and other important ministers had had their offices here. Now the building was rundown, the pillars about to collapse, and thatch and mud huts occupied what used to be parking lots. Jeebleh relaxed when he saw people behaving normally, children playing, women busy at braziers, cooking or washing.

"Is this The Refuge?" he asked.

Dajaal shook his head.

"What is it, then?"

Dajaal called out the name of a man, who then came running out of a side door. He was introduced as the day watchman, and Jeebleh learned that he would take him to the apartment where Bile awaited him.

8.

JEEBLEH WALKED A COUPLE OF PACES BEHIND THE DAY WATCHMAN escorting him to Bile's apartment, serene at the sight of sunlight on the old man's bald patch. He walked in step with the man, and tried to remain attentive to all his movements, as he expected he'd be returning without a guide.

They were now in a narrow corridor, with a closed door to their left, and one slightly ajar on the right. The watchman led him past a metal gate, then down a ravaged staircase. They walked past a huge void, which may once have housed an elevator; who knows, Jeebleh thought with a chill, dead bodies may have once been thrown down the shaft. He wondered where they were, in a basement of some sort, close to a building that had been an annex to a government ministry. He was disheartened by the water he saw leaking everywhere. Scarcely had he decided that the building was not at all inhabited when he heard the distant voices of children and smelled onions being fried. Somewhat relieved, he followed the watchman down another half a dozen devastated steps before they were out of the building. Then up a stairway a-scatter with geckos, past a half-demolished wall crawling with cockroaches, past a bricked-up door, past a window with half a glass pane, and then through cavernous rooms with no doors. Jeebleh was depressed to bear witness to so much destruction, and to the fact that what the plunderers didn't have the will to destroy simply fell into destruction on its own.

Soon they exited again, and walked through an arch and into a large courtyard with a communal kitchen where women were cooking, and where toilets, their doors hanging on broken hinges, emitted a foul odor. The place swarmed with well-fed children at play, like puppies after feeding time. Jeebleh's furtive look fell on the watchman, who comported himself in the reverential way of a commoner approaching royalty: deferentially, knees slightly bent, as in a curtsy, and with a smile of sterling quality. From this, Jeebleh deduced they were on Bile's floor.

The open courtyard, kept spotlessly clean, boasted a freshly painted wall, and windows apparently recently repaired—there were X's on the panes, evidence the glass was new. They walked to a metal door, and the watchman pressed a bell. As they waited for an answer, Jeebleh read the verse scrawled in an upright Celtic hand on a plaque attached to the door lintel: "Deliver me from blood-guiltiness, O God!" He was pondering its meaning, whether it was from the Bible or some other scripture, and wondering who might have put it there, when the door opened.

BILE WAS STANDING IN THE DOORWAY, CLAD IN A SMILE OF WELCOME, HIS ARMS open and raised, in anticipation of taking Jeebleh into his embrace. The two friends hugged very warmly.

At about six feet, Bile was a head taller than Jeebleh, but Jeebleh was a lot heavier. With the tears of joy suppressed, the emotion of their reunion seemed momentarily under some restraint, as each remembered how he had visited the other in many dreams. In Jeebleh's dreams, Bile's arrival would often be heralded by the buzzing of a bee quietly, busily, and positively constructing a cosmos of harmony, a bee knowing not a moment of idleness—generous, loving, and kind to all. Jeebleh's arrival, in Bile's dreams, would be announced by the neighing of a young horse breaking loose; and when Jeebleh came to take his leave, the horse would be replaced by an eagle flying into the outer reaches of the heavens.

"How wonderful to see you," Jeebleh said.

Bile was blessed with young-looking skin of a reddish hue that reminded his friend of a light wood treated to assume the darker tint of mahogany. He wore jeans, a T-shirt, and Indian thongs, and was much thinner than Jeebleh had remembered; he had a slight stoop, the result, perhaps, of aging in a prison cell. Otherwise, he appeared to be in good physical shape, his gaze bright, with the gentlest of smiles. When they hugged again, even more warmly, the crown of Jeebleh's baldness came into raspy contact with Bile's day-old stubble.

Even though visibly happy to be reunited with his friend, Bile had the expression of a man who had just emerged from a very long night of sorrow; now frowning, now grinning, he might have been suffering from an upset stomach. His thoughts provided their own subtext, prompting a shudder in Jeebleh as Bile broke the calm by reciting the verse above the door in a booming voice: "Deliver me from blood-guiltiness, O God!"

They became conscious of the watchman, still standing at the open door, looking rather sheepish, waiting, perhaps, for baksheesh and a thank you before being dismissed. Bile brought out a wad of cash and gave it to the man. Once he was gone, Bile slammed the door shut and turned his back on Jeebleh, ready to bring his idleness to a profitable end. "Would you like some coffee?" he asked.

"Yes, please!"

JEEBLEH STOOD TO THE SIDE OF A WINDOW WITH THE CURTAINS HALF DRAWN, and Bile stood away from the window in the cautious attitude of someone spying on what was happening outside without being seen. They were so full of joy that every now and then one or the other spoke of the pleasure of being together again. Now it was the nth time for Bile to say, "It's so good to see you!"

As Jeebleh studied the scene outside the window, the devastation and the ugly shacks, he remembered his and Bile's childhood: how each was strong where the other was weak. Jeebleh tended to be obsessive in pursuit of his goals. Bile was quicker and brighter, adept at anything to which he put his mind. He was an excellent athlete, who won medals in science and art too. He was, however, weak in the department of decision making. Nor did he have the guts to speak his mind, forever postponing the day when he might stand up to the daily battering meted out to him by Caloosha. Although Bile and Jeebleh were not related by blood or marriage, they were raised in the same household, and had laid the foundation of their closeness in what they called "a land all our own." In Jeebleh's scheme of things, there was no place for tormentors. In Bile's scheme of things, life had its ugly surprises for those who were ugly of heart and cruel of mind. Desperate to move him into action, Jeebleh would have liked Bile to defend himself in word and deed. Time and again, not only would Bile balk at the suggestion that he fight back at his half brother, but he would discourage his friend from confronting Caloosha, even if they had privately decided to avenge themselves with violence. Thus there was never the choice of a truce, and many predicted that their conflict with Caloosha was set to continue until death.

Out the window, Jeebleh noticed a pile of rock-strewn earth, with stones placed on the summit. "What's that down below?" he asked.

"A child's tomb."

"A tomb in the middle of the city?"

"At times, people are so scared to go to the cemeteries that they resort to burying their young ones close by, in tombs they improvise in their own neighborhoods."

"Who are the people sheltering in the building?"

"They're some of the displaced," Bile said, "who've come here because of the fighting in their regions of the country. We get an influx whenever there are confrontations between the armed militias."

"Is this The Refuge, then?"

"No," he said. "The Refuge is close by, a few minutes' walk from here. It has its own compound and permanent staff. The displaced who live here are an extension of The Refuge, in the sense that we provide them with food, run a school for them, and see to their health needs whenever we have to. But we refer to them as 'the tourists,' because their visits are often brief. When the conflict subsides, most of them return to where they came from, to their homes and properties."

As they sat down, Jeebleh wondered to himself whether he could get used to the schizoid life that had become Bile's: living in relative physical comfort, but dealing constantly with abject poverty, disheartening sorrow. He wouldn't be at peace with his own conscience if he lived comfortably, yet so close to such miseries on a daily basis.

Jeebleh's restless gaze landed on a bit of scriptural wisdom framed and hung on the wall, a runic inscription that read: "The sun shall be turned into darkness, and the moon into blood!"

"Whose apartment is this, then?"

"Everything here is Seamus's handiwork," Bile replied. "It was Seamus who hammered in every nail, and who copied the inscription over the entrance, and the verse on the wall too."

"I had no idea that he was here," Jeebleh cried happily. "Where is he?"

"He's away, but he'll be back in a few days."

"So I'll get to see him?"

"I hope so."

"That's wonderful!" Jeebleh now looked around the apartment with a more critical eye. "Seamus built all this? I didn't know he was such an accomplished artist."

"We decided, Seamus and I, to create an oasis of comfort here. Technically, the apartment is his, but I share it on and off, and Raasta and Makka have a room where they play, and stay in when they sleep over."

At the mention of the girls' names, Jeebleh saw a cloud of sorrow covering Bile's features. And he spoke of them in the present tense too.

"Is he with an Irish NGO or something?"

"He's here to help me."

"That's very dedicated of him."

"Running The Refuge and the clinic is my principal occupation," Bile said, "and Seamus sees to the smooth functioning of both. He is very punctilious, able to tell us how much we've spent on this, how much on that, how much money we have in the kitty, and how much more we need to raise. He goes back and forth a great deal between Mogadiscio and Dublin, where his mother is ailing and bedridden. But when he's here, which is a lot of the time, he handles the daily chores and The Refuge's demanding correspondence.

I'm in charge of the core ideas, but he's the nuts-and-bolts man, who makes them work. He's our carpenter, when we need one, our interior decorator, our masseur, our male nurse, and our general advisor on matters mysterious. He's his helpful self, you'll remember that from our days in Padua. When something mechanical breaks down, he fixes it. I am not technical at all, in fact can't change a fuse. He's the man we call on when a door hinge falls off, or the roof of the clinic springs a leak. He is there at all hours, never complaining. In short, he's a godsend! On his way back here this time, he'll buy spare parts for the clinic generator, which has broken down. The young man on night duty switched it on without checking if there was sufficient oil in it."

As Bile was talking, Jeebleh noticed how awful his teeth were. Since his arrival, Jeebleh had become obsessed with teeth. He caught himself thinking about them quite often, and about what bad teeth the youths he had met had. The sight of Bile's teeth broke his heart, especially because the man seemed fit and healthy otherwise.

When Jeebleh realized that Bile had fallen silent, he felt embarrassed and guilty. But then he spoke: "I hope Seamus will be back before I leave."

"You've only just got here," Bile said. "Don't tell me you're already thinking of leaving?" Teasing, he added: "What's the matter with people from Europe and North America? Always on the go, and on speeded-up time too!"

"I may have to depart in a hurry," Jeebleh said.

"And why would you do that?"

Jeebleh didn't mean to be secretive, but he didn't want to talk about what he wanted to do. He needed time to find out more about Raasta and consider what help he might offer to recover her, and what to do about Caloosha and whom to recruit to do him in, if that was what he and Bile agreed to. He could understand Bile's looking offended, shut out, or puzzled. He explained, "We'll have the opportunity talk about things at length."

Bile stole a glance at his watch. Jeebleh felt so uneasy that he swallowed some dry air, almost choking on it.

Bile wondered whether the years separating them and the bad blood that could make each distance himself from the other had given them an alternative memory, so that they might have difficulty remaining as good friends as they once were. Maybe it was wise not to talk about the past, or about what they had each been up to since then. They did not have time for this, and especially not today, for Bile had the clinic to attend to.

"How has your visit been so far?" he asked now.

Jeebleh became as restless as a colt. He turned away from the window, and his hand came casually into contact with his shirt pocket, where he carried his passport and cash. He appeared eager to get off his chest something that had been bothering him for decades, ever since he had left the country. Instead of answering Bile's question, he sprang a surprise on his friend: "How have you dealt with Caloosha? Do you meet him often? Tell me about your relationship with him."

Bile said nothing. Maybe, in his own way, he was making a point: that they viewed Caloosha differently, which explained why, up to now, he had not done anything about him.

Jeebleh insisted, "Do you see him at all?"

"This is a divided city, and you'll discover when you've been here for a few days that you seldom run into people," Bile replied. "We remain confined within the part of the city where we live, and try as much as we can to avoid contact with others."

"What's his occupation?"

"He is a consultant to StrongmanNorth on security matters."

"Does he have his own detail of bodyguards?"

"He does."

Bile saw that Jeebleh was apparently intent on dealing with Caloosha, whatever this was supposed to mean. But Bile was not prepared to jump into uncharted waters. Now he understood why Jeebleh had spoken earlier of possibly having to leave in a hurry—maybe after accomplishing his mission?

"We'll have to talk more about all this," Bile said, and again looked at his watch, ostensibly to let Jeebleh know that they didn't have the time to do so now. And then he repeated his own question. "How has your visit been so far? I'm curious."

"No one has a kind word to say about anyone else."

"Civil wars bring out the worst in us," Bile said. "There's terrible bitterness that comes at you from every direction, everyone busy badmouthing everyone else, everyone reciting a litany of grievances. You'll hear this one is a robber, that one is a murderer, that one a plunderer. Sadly, no one bothers to provide you with even flimsy circumstantial evidence to support the charges."

The talk of robbery and plunder reminded Jeebleh of his passport and all the cash he was carrying. "Do you have a safe?" he asked.

"We do, somewhere here. Why?"

"I need to deposit my valuables."

Bile pointed vaguely to a rug on the floor and explained that underneath was the safe—custom-built by Seamus of reinforced steel, with a digital lock.

Jeebleh brought out the wallet with the passport and money. Bile was immediately up on his feet, and the two of them shifted chairs, rolled up the rug, and lifted a section of the pine flooring. "Our Seamus at his most genial," Jeebleh said excitedly.

When he had stored his things, he said, "Much of my life, when I look back at it, strikes me as a half-remembered dream. But I remember certain episodes with clarity. I remember our mothers, Caloosha and what he did to us, and of course I remember Seamus and the three of us in Italy." Jeebleh's grin was as gentle as the water's surface in the wake of a duckling. "How much of your Plotinus do you still remember?" He recited quietly: "Never did eye see the sun unless it had first become sunlike."

"In other words," Bile interpreted the philsopher's wisdom aloud, as though for his own edification, "an artist representing an image cannot presume to be an artist unless he is able to be the very figure being represented. Likewise, a man with a radical image who's spent years in detention for political reasons must act forthrightly and without fear of the consequences."

Jeebleh's gaze launched itself into the shadowed darkness of an owl, bearing in its hoot a message of doom. Was it because Bile had quietly spun Jeebleh's Italian nostalgia back to Mogadiscio? "What's the latest about Raasta?" he asked.

Bile sat up so fast that he knocked his cup over, spilling some of the coffee sediments. Now both were on their feet, clumsily cleaning, Jeebleh dabbing at the low table and then the floor with a cloth.

"Not much more than what's been in the papers," Bile said, and paused judiciously. "We're following a few leads."

"So far no harm has been done to either girl?"

"We have no way of knowing."

"How's Shanta taking it?"

"It's always hardest on a mother," Bile said. "Shanta is in the habit of going off on excursions into the land of the insane." He paused again. "It's been very hard on her."

"No word about Faahiye's whereabouts?"

"I hear he's left for Mombasa."

"I'd like to see Shanta."

His voice very faint, Bile said, "You will."

It was as though a healing heart had been broken open. Lips closed, Bile ceased his breathing as he smothered his tearful emotions.

A phone rang, and he went to answer it in the study.

WAITING IN THE APARTMENT FOR BILE TO RETURN, JEEBLEH ENTERTAINED himself with memories dating back to before he and his friend were separated. Bile in those days had thought of himself as a kindred spirit of Plotinus, the ancient philosopher, born in today's Asyut around A.D. 205. A hardworking, principled man, austere in his style of living and in the way he ran his personal affairs. He was said to be always in touch with both his spirituality and the material side of life. A man of peace, he arbitrated in the disputes of communities at war and managed to bring them closer without alienating either side. He also ran a charitable house, one section of it alive with the noise of young orphans, another part filled with destitute widows. Jeebleh recalled that after a book, *The Life of Plotinus*, had been smuggled into Bile's prison cell and he had been caught reading it, he was severely punished. Bile returned from the study. He looked fine after the phone call, but Jeebleh sensed that the world in which they found themselves was ailing.

"How well do you know Af-Laawe?" Jeebleh asked.

"What can I say?"

"What's his story?"

"You know the proverb—'Tell me the names of your friends, and I'll tell you who you are.' Caloosha is his closest associate." Bile clenched his hand tensely in a fist, his thumb inserted between forefinger and middle finger, in the vulgar Italian gesture of a fig.

"Is he a fraud?" Jeebleh asked.

"People speak of money missing from the UN coffers."

"And why his nickname, 'Marabou'? Just because of his funeral business?"

"You wouldn't think you arrived only yesterday." Bile smiled like a man who knew no sadness. After a pause, he went on: "He's described by many as a cool customer and a con artist. So watch out, my friend!"

"Any idea what's become of the stolen money?"

"I wouldn't know."

"And his NGO Funerals with a Difference?"

"He claims to bury the unclaimed corpses gratis, with free prayers for the soul of the dead thrown in for good measure," Bile said. "But there's a much darker side to his dealings. Shanta can tell you more than I."

Again the phone rang, but this time Bile chose not to answer it.

STILL IGNORING THE PHONE—THE PERSON CALLING HADN'T USED THE CODE— Bile poured more coffee. The memory of sorrow flooded his vocal cords as he spoke. "Please accept my belated condolence over your mother's death. She was like a mother to me too, and I miss her!"

"Maybe death was kind to her, coming when it did."

"Unfortunately she depended entirely on Caloosha and her housekeeper," Bile said, "and they were awful to her, I've heard. Caloosha had misled her, making her believe his version of events."

"My letters to her were returned unopened."

"I wouldn't put anything past Caloosha."

"Would you know how to reach my mother's housekeeper?"

"We'll ask around," Bile said. "Shanta might."

"And might she know where her grave is?"

"I doubt it, but we'll ask," Bile said. "Shanta has been in no state to think about anyone or anything else since Raasta's disappearance. But I'm sure that with her help and Dajaal's, we can locate your mother's housekeeper, and then her grave."

"I would appreciate it."

Jeebleh noticed some potted plants, where a mantis, comfortable in its camouflage, was preparing to ambush another insect—swaying back and forth, head raised, fragile-looking forelegs extended, delicate body elegantly poised. Despite its devout posturing, the mantis was a predator, always on the attack. Jeebleh watched it in silent fascination, remembering the chameleon's visit to his hotel room. The mantis bided its preying time, as slow as a sadist in its intention to torment its victim. Jeebleh couldn't help comparing the antics of a mantis lying in wait, readying itself to pounce, to the modus operandi of a man who was a foe in the likeness of a concerned friend. He would act like the mantis and wait, lying low, until he was able to rid this society of vermin like Caloosha, a canker in the soul of his years of imprisonment and exile.

A housefly landed on Bile's forehead: when chased away, it moved to Jeebleh, hesitating above his eyes and nose for a few seconds before finally and decisively alighting on his cheek. Not liking the housefly's noise, the mantis slunk away quietly into hiding.

Now three phones rang all at once, and kept ringing. But Bile wasn't prepared to answer them, not immediately. "I'd like you to move in with us," he said. "There's room for you. I've already prepared it, Raasta's room."

"Raasta's?"

Bile looked so pale you would think he was hearing heavy treads on his own tomb. His sad expression caught the sun in its sweep, and Jeebleh stared at the specks of dust, recently stirred up by the restless housefly.

Bile went to answer the one phone that had not stopped ringing, and when he returned, he was in some distress. He spoke to Dajaal on his mobile, suggesting that he come to take Jeebleh back to the hotel.

"We have an emergency!" he told Jeebleh.

"Can I be of help?"

"I must be on my way to the clinic. Please arrange with Dajaal when you wish to be picked up," Bile said. "Either later today, or tomorrow, or at the latest the day after."

In less than ten minutes, Dajaal was at the door of the apartment, ready to escort Jeebleh to the hotel. Both Jeebleh and Bile knew that they had a lot more to say to each other, and knew too that they had time on their side.

They embraced for a long time before parting.

9.

IN A DREAM OF THE NIGHT BEFORE, JEEBLEH KNEW WHERE THE CAPTORS were keeping Raasta and her companion—in a mud hut overlooking the no-man's-land between the two StrongMen. He was at a disadvantage, though, in that he had no transport of his own, and no one to bring him back to where he was staying, a beach cabin by the ocean. Nor did he have bodyguards to protect him in case he was attacked. Moving about was proving very difficult.

He was in an anteroom of the beach cabin, where a woman, name unknown and face unseen, lay on a mat, screaming her head off, occasionally mumbling to herself the name of the man to whom she addressed her pleas. To Jeebleh, the name sounded very much like "Caloosha." Another woman, in a nurse's uniform, was restraining the wailing woman and speaking to her in the patronizing tone that medical staff often use when chastising obstreperous patients. It wasn't clear, in the dream, whether the screaming woman had attempted suicide. When he tried to find out the woman's story and why her wrists were bandaged, an armed man in rags sealed his mouth with an asphyxiating gag. Later, after ridding himself of the gag, he tried to push his way past a bouncer with enormous sharp teeth. He was kicked in the groin for attempting to escape, and collapsed backward, in a hapless heap, groaning. He was in so much pain that he couldn't get to his feet, and he wet himself.

· · ·

AWAKE, JEEBLEH SAW THAT EVEN WITH ITS DISJOINTEDNESS AND LACK OF clarity, the dream had some highly detailed moments. He remembered the woman pleading to "Caloosha," even though he had seen no sign of the man in the dream. He decided, on the basis of the dream, that he should seek out and solicit Caloosha's help. Perhaps he would intercede with the hostage-takers.

But a few things in the dream raised warning signs, which worried and frightened him. A man had appeared, assigned to be his guide. He had eyes from which billows of smoke issued, and he held several lit cigarettes be-tween his fingers. The man, a dwarf, needed to work out his daytime contra-dictions, and was now on stilts. He was a praise singer, and claimed that he had been commissioned to compose a panegyric for the boss of Mogadiscio's underworld, "the fire of whose genius was unlike any other, and had no equal anywhere." Sadly, Jeebleh couldn't remember any of the lines, because the man whose voice reminded him of Af-Laawe had the wrong accent, his syn-tax was muddled, his diction lacked finesse, and his metaphors were mixed.

There were also marksmen in the dream, who took delight in demonstrat-ing the skill of their shooting; they hit their targets lethally without breaking a bead of sweat. One of them had a mouth with baby lips that blew bubbles. At the center of the tableau was a small girl having her hair braided by her companion.

Despite his misgivings, the dream left Jeebleh with a sense of optimism, and he rose from his bed convinced that Caloosha held the key to the girls' disappearance, and that he or one of his associates, namely Af-Laawe, knew where Raasta and Makka were being held. Quite possibly, Caloosha had helped the captors in a big way. In a moment of elation, Jeebleh believed that he would succeed in recovering the two girls from the clutches of their cap-tors. But first he had to seek an audience with Caloosha. He would show hu-mility, he would openly acknowledge Caloosha's power over them all. To steel himself, Jeebleh recited two lines from a poem in Somali in which a weak man, plotting to kill a much stronger man, humbles himself before his intended victim, pretending he is a friend and no threat at all. But when the opportunity to hit presents itself, he strikes! Jeebleh would do as the poet suggested, and wait in ambush until after the girls' release.

Shaved and showered, he took the piece of ruled paper on which Dajaal had drawn a map with directions to Caloosha's villa. Smoothing the crumpled sheet, he followed the route with his forefinger, memorizing the sequence of turns in the road. He was sure he would find it easily, no trouble at all. He went downstairs and past the reception desk, which was unusually quiet today, to have his coffee. He moved as slowly as a chameleon going uphill.

WHILE JEEBLEH WAITED FOR HIS COFFEE, THE DAY SEEMED AS DULL-EYED AS a young elephant mourning the death of its family. The sun shone competently, its rays trudging through a thick film of dust. He sat facing the open area where, only the day before, the vultures had gathered. Today there wasn't a single one. There was an Alsatian, though, pregnant by the look of it, and close to her, a crow, lonely-looking, brooding and quiet for much of the time.

Seeking out his tormentor was the last thing Jeebleh wanted to do. The decision to call on Caloosha was not an act of courage—it went against everything Jeebleh stood for and believed in. But the dream had strengthened his trust in the correctness of the decision. He would do all he could to help gain freedom for Raasta and Makka, even at the cost of feeling humiliated by a fool. Then he would figure out how to take vengeance on Caloosha, perhaps with help from Dajaal, to whom he intended to speak.

An only son, Jeebleh had been raised by a strong woman with iron determination. His father was a lowlife; he had sold the house the family lived in and the plot of land he had inherited from his own family to pay off gambling debts. After the divorce, Jeebleh's mother made it her mission in life to ensure that Jeebleh grew up to be very different from his father. She impressed into his memory his uniqueness, repeatedly telling him that he could do anything he put his mind to.

She possessed no more than a brick-and-mud single-room hut, a barn with two cows and a calf tied to poles buried in the earth, an outdoor latrine, and an undying hope in her son's future success. And even though she loved him to excess, she was firm with him. Within half a year of being divorced, she borrowed a few hundred shillings from a woman friend and started a neighborhood stall, selling tomatoes, onions, and matches spread on a cardboard box. Day in and day out, she sat on the very mat where she and her son slept at night.

One morning, two years after she had set up her *warato* stall, she became acquainted with a midwife living in the same neighborhood. The two women got talking, and they entered into a contract from which both would benefit. The midwife kept the oddest of hours, because of her vocation, and was away from home several days and nights at a stretch. Then she would be off work for a few days at a time. Jeebleh's mother agreed to look after the midwife's two sons, Caloosha and Bile, for a monthly fee. The elder of these sons was away at school until early afternoon, while the younger one, more or less Jeebleh's age, had not started school yet.

A bright-eyed, active child, Bile was as adorable as Caloosha, his elder brother, was detestable—Caloosha, who had been born in breech position, almost killing his mother in the process. The two younger boys got along extremely well, and the midwife was pleased that her son had an ally in Jeebleh, who helped deter Caloosha from bullying his younger brother. Jeebleh trained so he could defend himself, and he tried to teach Bile, but with little success.

The midwife paid for the food and the household expenses, and Jeebleh's mother kept Caloosha out of mischief as well as she could, at the same time protecting her son and Bile from his bullying. Raised as brothers in the household efficiently run by Jeebleh's mother, and paid for by Bile's, the two boys became very close.

The world in which Jeebleh and Caloosha would be meeting today, if they met at all, differed greatly from the one in which they had met as children, and from the one in which Jeebleh had been a political prisoner and Caloosha his jailer.

The youth who came with the pot of coffee Jeebleh had ordered also delivered a message: Apparently a few clansmen of Jeebleh's were at the front gate of the hotel, waiting to be let in. The men on sentry duty, the youth explained, wanted to know whether or not Jeebleh was prepared to receive them. When Jeebleh inquired how many there were, he learned that there were half a dozen, eager to speak to him about "family matters."

Jeebleh told the youth that he wanted to drink his coffee in peace. He had other things on his mind, actually, and was in no mood to entertain a group of elder men who were likely only to bring further clan-related complications into his life. He finished his coffee and left by the back gate.

THE ROUGHLY DRAWN MAP TO CALOOSHA'S PLACE IN HIS HAND, JEEBLEH walked fast, with the light-footed gait of someone who knew where he was headed. He might have been a thief avoiding an angry mob sent to apprehend him. He wanted to get away from his clansmen, that was all.

He recalled how his mother had done everything possible to make sure that she and her only son would have nothing to do with this clan business. As a young woman, she had been given in marriage to a gambler with no self-honor, because he paid a dozen cows and a donkey as a dowry to her family. She hoped to raise her son in an enlightened way, educate him and make him believe in his own worth as a man. Soon after entering into her contract with the midwife, she bought herself a Singer sewing machine and, for starters, tailored the family's clothes: her own and her son's, and the two other boys' and their mother's as well. Her son was given the nickname "Jeebleh"—"the one with the pockets"—because his shirts, shorts, and trousers had huge pockets.

It was on a day such as this, when his so-called clansmen came around to be received as his blood, that he appreciated what the two inveterate loners had created.

No doubt the clansmen were there to remind him of his responsibility toward his blood community. He remembered how often his mother had warned him against such opportunists, who would turn up at his door with their begging bowls when he was doing well—the very same men and women who would disappear when he was the one in need. She had also warned him against Caloosha, whose cruel behavior was a threat to the continued existence of the family she and the midwife had so carefully held together. "Be your own man," she would say, "not anyone else's. And beware of your clansmen. They'll prove to be your worst enemies, and they are more likely than not to stab you in broad daylight if you choose to have nothing to do with them."

He walked purposefully, his heartbeat quickening with each step. There was no authority to dreams if the happenings during one's waking hours did not tally with their thrust, he decided. He prayed himself sick, wishing for success in whatever he was trying to achieve.

A moment's distraction helped him notice a richly woven spiderweb hanging down between the open-ended spaciousness of the morning sun and a mango tree, laden with its seasonal yield. While admiring the bewitching spectacle, he saw an old man in colorful rags hungrily demolishing a mango with the self-abandon of a child. The old man's fingers must have been as sweet as a beehive, and a swarm of eager wasps descended on them, taking off and landing again, following every movement of his hands. A closer look at the man revealed a more disturbing sight: his highly unfocused gaze. The man washed his hands with water from a pitcher, then dried them, and started to speak as the mad do, wisely.

The old man was fascinating to listen to and wonderful to watch, his every gesture theatrical, and his voice a memorable baritone. Soon enough a crowd formed near him, and the space around the tree filled with curious spectators, including Jeebleh. The man spoke on and on, in speech so disjointed that not everything he said made sense to Jeebleh. But he could not tear himself away, and he stood there fascinated. The man behaved as hypnotists do, self-confident, as if aware of where his strengths lay. He seemed to be saying that the trouble with self-isolated communities was that they were "as unhealthy as a child's toenail growing inward." The crowd around the mango tree listened attentively. At one point, the man fell silent, then looked steadily at Jeebleh, outstaring him. A woman standing near Jeebleh raised her naked son so he might see what she described as "the spectacle."

The old man was now proposing that a beggar given to spurious changes of mood was a dangerous one. "So beware, my brothers and sisters, of such beggars. Beware too of our politicians who think and behave like beggars—

one day, they act normally and ask for donations from the international community, and the next day, they kill the foreigners who've come to help."

He then asked the crowd, "Are you mad?" When no one responded, he asked, "Am I mad, then?" No one spoke. "Are you mad or are you sane? I want you to separate yourselves into two groups, those who are mad, and those who are sane."

But nobody moved. The man repeated his instructions, and again nobody moved. People appeared disturbed by his indiscretion, and yet no one was ready to challenge him or oblige. Murmurs of disapproval were heard, the din growing louder as people talked among themselves. Even so, no one stood apart, or walked away, and no one declared himself to be mad or sane; everyone found comfort in staying with the crowd.

The old man changed his tack: "What if I asked you to separate yourselves into those who've murdered and those who haven't? Will all those who've murdered please gather here to my left, and all those who've not murdered or harmed anyone, who've raped no woman, looted no property, will they please stand here to my right?"

Nobody obliged, but Jeebleh's curious gaze fell on a military type, who broke into a heavy sweat. Now the old man danced a jig, and as he did so he had a smirk on his face, and his hands moved as though in imitation of a trained dancer performing the classical Indian dance-drama Kathakali—or so thought Jeebleh. The man cut a most impressive figure, with his stylized gestures now in vigorous motion, now gentle, his whole body moving in obligatory pursuit of a ritual, his index finger close to his nose, his hard stare focused on it, his squint disarming. The crowd grew, as more people came. The last group to arrive included a drummer, who beat in rhythm to the man's chants.

Having seen and heard enough, Jeebleh left the area. A man followed him. When Jeebleh slowed, he noted that the man was keeping pace with him. He turned to confront the man shadowing him, looked at him fixedly, and said with a wry smile, "Are you mad or are you sane? Are you a murderer? Are you innocent of all crimes?"

"Ask me a serious question, and I'll give an answer," replied the man, his stare iron-tough.

"Don't you think these are serious questions nowadays?"

There was something fierce about this man with rough edges, the type you see in films. The hard-stare guy introduced himself: "My name is Kaahin." And he extended his hand to Jeebleh, who remembered his encounter with Af-Laawe at the airport and decided not to shake it.

"What do you want?" Jeebleh asked.

"I want to know which group you'd join."

"I've never killed or harmed anyone," Jeebleh said.

"So you say!"

"What about you? Which would you join?"

"The murderers, of course," Kaahin said, and guffawed.

Jeebleh saw now that the man's eyes wandered away, toward two men who were standing apart, smoking. Like him, they were military types, but too old to be part of a fighting force. If they were no longer in active service, Jeebleh guessed, they would be acting as consultants to security firms, or as deputies to a warlord, or as well-paid bodyguards to a VIP or to foreign dignitaries visiting the country. To a man, their postures gave them away.

The man calling himself Kaahin said, "Where are you when it comes to brothers and blood?"

"Have you ever heard of Hesiod?" Jeebleh replied.

"Who's he?"

"A poet who lived in the eighth century B.C." Jeebleh didn't like the amused look on Kaahin's face, but he continued, trying to appear unbothered: "Hesiod advises that you take along a witness when you're in a dispute with your brother or one of your intimates over matters of great importance."

"Well, perhaps I could be of some use to you, then."

"In what way?"

"In leading you to someone you want to see."

"I'm not with you."

"I'm offering to be in your service," Kaahin said.

"What will you do for me?"

"I'll come along as your witness."

"Pray, who will I be meeting, and why do I need a witness?" Jeebleh started to walk away, pretending he had no idea what the man was talking about.

"I'll take you to Caloosha," Kaahin said.

One of the military men led the way, the other walked behind. Jeebleh was sure that several others were shadowing them from a distance, even if they were invisible to him. They moved forward, in the direction of what he hoped was Caloosha's house.

10.

JEEBLEH ENTERED A LIVING ROOM OVERCROWDED WITH FURNITURE AND immediately sensed the dark movements of a few figures, and then heard the sound of curtains being closed or opened. Likewise he could not determine whether the footsteps he heard on the staircase were gingerly going up or coming down.

In a corner of the room, a cat was trailing a spool wound with thread, which it pushed around so coquettishly that Jeebleh was quite taken with the acrobatic performance. This was when Caloosha made his staged entry. By the time Jeebleh became aware of his presence, Caloosha was already seated in the singularly placed high chair. Reduced to a sideshow, the cat pawed at the spool for a few more seconds, and then lost interest. Eventually, it walked out of the room altogether. Kaahin and his men spread out, one of them approaching Jeebleh where he stood.

"So here you are at last, my long-lost junior brother!" Caloosha said.

Jeebleh fought shy of applauding sarcastically, aware that Caloosha had worked very hard on his rehearsed delivery; he enunciated the phrase "long-lost junior brother" to give a sharp, cutting quality. He might as well have said, "Now, what have you got to say for yourself?" That Caloosha was upset was also obvious, but not why.

Jeebleh took his time, comparing his memory of Caloosha when he had seen him last with the specimen in the high chair. He was looking at a man with a more prominent nose than he remembered, a much fatter man, with so distended a paunch it spilled over his belt and lay flat in his lap. His face was puffy, the hair was thin on his skull, patchy, and peppered with gray at the sides. He could easily have done a send-up of a Buddha, only he had no wisdom to impart. Alas, the years had not humbled the fool in the least.

"It's been naughty of you to come to *my* city and to stay in a hotel," Caloosha said, his double chin trembling, his breathing uncomfortable. "You could've stayed here. I'll tell it to your face, it's been very naughty of you, very, very naughty. Yes, that's how I feel, that's how I feel, and I'll speak about it."

Ever since childhood they had been at loggerheads, and the memory of how Caloosha had again and again hurt him returned with a vengeance, causing Jeebleh to display his rage right away, and violently. The question now uppermost in his mind was how to keep from losing his cool.

"Is this a way to welcome a long-lost junior brother?" he said.

"Admit it, you've been naughty!"

"Maybe you could be nice to me for a change."

"How do I do that?"

"Humor me, but don't shout at me."

"Cut the crap," Caloosha said, "and explain how you ask to be taken to a hotel in *my* part of the city. I have this big villa all to myself."

"Af-Laawe suggested that I put up there."

"Because you asked him to!"

"Let's talk about something else."

"I've heard all about you and what you've been up to since your arrival," Caloosha said, wagging a finger in mock threat.

This gave Jeebleh a tremor of unredeemed guilt. Might Caloosha have any idea what murderous thoughts were actually brewing in his mind? "I don't like it that we're fighting on our first meeting after so many years," he said. "Can we allow peace to reign, at least for the time being? You can see that I've come to pay my respects to you, I've come to make amends, not to quarrel."

They stared at each other with the fierceness of unresolved conflict. After a long silence, Jeebleh stammered, "Unfortunately, I had no way of reaching you."

"You're a liar!"

Jeebleh was at a loss for words, and he looked about the room as if he might find there the expressions that were eluding him. He saw Kaahin and his two sidekicks, and thought that even though he didn't like what was being done to him, he wasn't a fool and wouldn't be misled into believing that he could gain anything by reacting violently. In the two days he had spent here, he had seen nothing but destruction, because none of the men at each other's throats was prepared to compromise, and none showed humility. Where would arrogance lead him? It would create further rifts, cause more deaths, and spill more bad blood! He considered the possibility too that Caloosha was playing to the gallery, showing off for his buddies. Now he said, "I'm not a liar, and you know it."

"Lying at your age. Shame on you!"

Jeebleh took a step to the right, and from the corner of his eye, he could see that Kaahin was moving watchfully closer to him. This was a badly acted piece of theater all around, and so he said, "This isn't getting us anywhere."

Then he made to leave. He didn't want to go—well aware that his departure would not bring him any nearer to learning how much Caloosha knew about where Raasta and her playmate were being held hostage, or who their captors were—and he suspected that Caloosha wouldn't let him walk out like this.

"Af-Laawe has been to see me," Caloosha blurted, "and he told me about your message to Bile, that you wanted to meet up with him. Why didn't you send word to me too, unless you're fibbing?"

"Maybe he forgot to deliver it?"

"He wouldn't dare! It was I who alerted him to your arrival and sent him to greet you at the airport."

"Truth-telling" sits awkwardly on evil men, Jeebleh thought. Caloosha's distended belly was filled with sentiments of war and wickedness, which was why he looked so ugly, and so unhealthy. Attrition retarded his brain, evil dulled his imagination, did not sharpen it.

"How did you know what flight I was coming on?" Jeebleh asked.

"Because I know everything that happens hereabouts."

Reminding himself of the purpose of his visit, Jeebleh smiled and chose not to be provoked. They might get somewhere if he didn't deflate Caloosha's inflated ego in the presence of his buddies.

"I've had you followed," Caloosha asserted, "and I know where you've been, to whom you've spoken, what comments you've made, from the moment your plane landed until you walked in here. Tell me, are you or aren't you a liar?"

Jeebleh felt like a mischievous pupil called to the headmaster's office to explain why he had behaved badly. He didn't know whether apologizing would help or play into the stronger hands of a brute, adept at exploiting a weakness in his character. He dodged and asked, "Where's the family?"

"What family?"

"Your wife and children."

A primal joy descended on Caloosha's features, and his double chin trembled. It was touching to behold the sudden change in the man, whose expression was so infectious that Kaahin and his men grinned from cheek to cheek too. Jeebleh looked like a baby with a sweet tooth made to taste salt.

Caloosha intimated with a flick of his right hand that Kaahin and his companions should leave. Then he rose, heaving himself up and out of the high chair, and waddled toward Jeebleh, with every distended part of his body waggling. Jeebleh allowed himself to be hugged for the sake of peace. Caloosha smothered him in a fleshy, all-encompassing embrace. Jeebleh thought of women submitting themselves to men they loathed, for the love and safety of their children. Part of him didn't wish to know what his life would be like after this embrace.

Jeebleh's hand was entirely lost in Caloosha's acquisitive grip. Even so, he thought it best not to withdraw, lest his action provoke a hostile reaction from his host. Now that they were standing close to each other, he saw how ugly the man was, short, fat, and always short of breath. "How are they, anyway, the family?"

"They're all well." Caloosha paced in circles as he spoke. "Do you know how many wives and how many children I have? Unlike you, I have twenty-two children, the perfect number for two soccer teams, with me as referee. I was married five times, and am currently married to three wives. I've been a grandfather seven times, all of them boys."

"You're married to three women?"

"That's right."

"Where are they, your families?"

"Almost all the children by my first five wives are in Holland, Sweden, and Denmark as asylum seekers, or in Canada and the U.S. as naturalized citizens. One of my wives is in Canada with her five children, another in the U.S. with seven, and so on and so on. In Canada and the U.S. my children changed their names to those of their mothers, fearing being linked to me, because of my earlier job. What a bore! But they're all doing well, earning enough and living comfortably. In fact, the two oldest girls send me monthly remittances, but the boys think more often about themselves, their latest fads and the cars they drive, and seldom about their old man. But we thank God for His great mercies!"

Jeebleh said, "You must be relieved that they are all out of the country and out of harm's way, what with the fierce fighting and all."

"One of my current wives is here," he said, and nearing Jeebleh, spoke in a whisper. "She's somewhere in this villa, the latest acquisition of an old man ready to retire." Crassly, his left hand went to his crotch, and made a show of caressing it.

"How did you *acquire* her?" Jeebleh asked.

"We blundered into each other," he replied.

"Blundered into each other?"

"That's one way of putting it. She and I blundered into each other out of fear, out of the loneliness of old age on my part, and out of the aloneness of youth on hers."

There were no more mysteries to the brute, and Jeebleh could have killed him for that. If he did not act upon his visceral loathing, it was because the extent of Caloosha's ugliness was so overbearing and revolting at the same time, and of course, he hadn't the wherewithal to follow it through. Nor had the fool any sense of shame. The latest acquisition of an old man, indeed!

"Where did you find her?" Jeebleh asked.

"I found her alone after looters had emptied her family home and killed her parents. She was fifteen years old at the time, and was hiding in the attic, frightened out of her wits."

"She could've been your granddaughter!"

"She's very pretty, of Xamari descent," Caloosha said with a grin and a wink. "And as I said before, we thank God for all His mercies, great and small. She's been a blessing to me in my old age, my young thing."

Jeebleh wondered what Caloosha had been doing in the girl's family house after the looters had killed her parents and emptied the house of all that was useful. But because he doubted he would receive a true answer, he thought better of asking. Besides, such a question might take them away from where his own interest lay. Now he dwelled on Caloosha's face, and concentrated on his eyes hooded with fat and hair, suspecting that he might read the man's motives from his expression. As a ploy to humble himself, Jeebleh sat on a low three-legged stood diagonal to where Caloosha was standing. His gaze wandered leisurely across the settees, ottomans, and armchairs scattered about in spectacular disarray. Caloosha stopped moving in circles and took tortoise steps to a lounge chair, where he sat down. Not much of the furniture in the living room matched. Had he acquired the pieces through his various marriages, or from his looting sorties into the vacated homes of families who had fled the city, which was up for grabs during the initial stages of the civil war? Jeebleh was so upset he felt like the commander of a militia unable to hold a bridgehead seized in enemy territory.

"Whose house is this?" he asked.

"Mine," came the answer.

Jeebleh believed that Caloosha was lying, that the house wasn't his. There was something visibly aseptic about the place. It might be a minor warlord's home, where he stashed away all his plunder. It looked too clean, like that of a small-time thief who regularly brought stolen goods into his private living space. Or could it be that the heavy furniture came with the young wife?

"Where is she?"

"My wife?"

"The young thing for your old age."

"Have pity on a man of my advanced years, Jeebleh." Caloosha displayed a kind of humor Jeebleh hadn't thought him capable of.

Maybe the light footsteps on the staircase when he came in had been hers, Jeebleh thought. Was it also possible that the soap opera dialogue in Arabic that he could hear was coming from her satellite TV? He was tense, his tongue as heavy as a wet hammock. Married serially five times, currently the husband of three, with twenty-two children, seven grandchildren, all of them boys: maybe the man had a right to all the furniture that was on disorderly exhibition in the living room. Who would've thought that the phoenix of Caloosha's day would rise from the ashes of his evil deeds after the collapse of the regime he so wickedly served? But there you were, he was alive and well and lording it now in the city of his clan family.

"How about your family?" Caloosha asked Jeebleh.

"I've spoken to them twice since coming here."

"Your daughters are both of college age?"

Jeebleh nodded.

"The younger one is left-handed, yes?"

"No, it's the older one who is."

As though no longer certain of his facts, Caloosha hesitated, then asked, "One of them had a Burmese cat, the other a dog, yes?"

Jeebleh was unprepared for this, because he knew he hadn't given these details to anyone in Mogadiscio, except maybe to his mother, in his chatty letters to her. Had the housekeeper been sharing secrets with Caloosha?

"If you're asking yourself how it is that I know a lot about your wife and daughters," Caloosha said, "it's because I make it my business to know how things are with the people I feel close to."

Angry words not to be freed now clung shapelessly to Jeebleh's tongue. He was relieved that he didn't let go of them, and that he changed the direction of their talk. "Can you do me a favor?" he said.

"If it's in my power to."

"Can you help me reach my mother's housekeeper?"

"I'll see what I can do."

"I'd be most grateful," he said, meaning it.

Caloosha stretched out his right hand and pressed a bell, which rang on the upper floor. A young woman, evidently the maid, came down the stairs and walked over to a table partially hidden from Jeebleh's view. When he craned his neck, he saw her standing in front of two flasks, and as she prepared the coffee, water first and then an undrinkable instant, Caloosha explained that his younger brother from America took his coffee black, no sugar. The young woman went about her job with more professionalism than the youths at the hotel had done. From having seen the maid, who was from the Rivers People, he assumed that Caloosha's wife would most likely be veiled, in which case she might not be permitted to meet him. Maybe the truth about her not coming down was even simpler. Caloosha spent much of his time downstairs with the military types, and his young wife and the maid spent all theirs upstairs, watching soaps on satellite TV, as bored housewives did the world over.

HE HATED THE TASTE OF HIS INSTANT COFFEE, AND ALMOST ASKED FOR SUGAR and milk. But then he didn't like the thought of the bell's ringing and the maid's coming all the way down to serve them. He was formulating the question "Where were you when the state collapsed?" but lest it sound tacky, didn't ask it. Instead, he said, "Where were you when the Dictator fled the city?"

"I was here."

The blueprint of a lie stared Jeebleh in the eye. But he chose not to allow the lie to blind him to his ultimate purpose. "Which side were you on, then?" he said. "With your employer, the Dictator, and against the militiamen fighting to overthrow him, or against him and with the militia recruited from the rank and file of the clan?"

Caloosha's features resembled a boarded-up house that hadn't enjoyed fresh air or sunshine for some time: a lifeless house, without light.

After a long pause, he said: "I did what I had to when I was battered by a blind storm: I organized myself, and discovered that I could only work on a short-term plan to survive. I thought hard when everyone helped themselves to the properties left empty by the 'chased-out' families!"

"What did your short-term plan produce?"

"When you work on a short-term plan, you think about yourself, not about the past, where the problem began, nor about the future, where there'll be other problems waiting in ambush. I prepared myself for peace."

Before he knew it, Jeebleh was shouting: "Was peace uppermost in your mind when you locked us up?"

"You know the answer to your question."

"I'd like to hear it from you all the same."

Caloosha was in the shade, the sunlight in the room having moved on, as though shunning him. He seized up, his eyes narrowing, his sight dimming, and broke into a cold sweat, his forehead ringed with beads of perspiration. "I trained in the Soviet Union, where obedience was drilled into me, obedience to my superiors first and last," he said. "That was what the manual taught us. I was trained to act as though I was stationary while in motion. One of my Soviet instructors liked to compare his students who were training to be in the national security business in their countries, to hunters moving with the stealth of one who is prepared to kill and be killed. I am not an intellectual, you and Bile are. I am a military man. I obey the instructions given to me by my superiors."

"Why was I released?" Jeebleh could feel that the intensity of the conversation was pushing to the brink of something disastrous, but he couldn't stop himself.

"Those were my instructions."

"Why was Bile kept in prison?"

"You're putting your questions to the wrong man, and you're making me unnecessarily nervous. I'm not the man you should ask." Caloosha paused, perspiring liberally. "You don't need me to tell you that a dictator makes his decisions without advice from his subalterns. I don't need to tell you that a tyrant's fickle decision is law. Why are you putting these questions to me?"

Jeebleh was on his feet, shaking. He heard a bell ringing faintly somewhere, then saw suspicious movements outside, among the trees. Was he imagining things? Could there be snipers at the ready waiting for him, men like Kaahin, lying flat on their chests, preparing to shoot? This talk about Soviet instructors drilling obedience into their students' heads reminded him of his English teacher Miss Bradley, who was fond of repeating, "Memory is a bugger!" Now he watched the garden, imagining that it was crawling with armed men of dubious loyalties, military types working on commissions, on the completion of deadly assignments. He could get killed, and no one would know, for he hadn't told anyone he was coming here.

Caloosha asked, "What's brought you here?"

"Deaths, lies!"

"I haven't killed anyone," Caloosha said.

Jeebleh remembered his earlier encounter with the Kathakali dancer, who asked the murderers in the crowd to separate themselves from the innocent. "Have I accused you of being a murderer?" he said.

"You can't pin anyone's death on me!"

Yet Caloosha had been accused of murder, when he was young, hadn't he? His own mother had suspected him of murdering her husband, his stepfather. But she didn't have the evidence. Moreover, there were other murders that could be pinned on him, once the International Criminal Court charged Somalia's warlords and their associates with crimes against humanity.

Caloosha had risen out of his chair. Now he was threatening: "Watch out!"

"Your loyalties are despicable."

"I'm warning you!"

Jeebleh forced himself to concentrate on the pale moons of his own fingernails, to focus on the evenness of the lunar shapes. Was he showing signs of malnutrition? Peace and compromise both had gone out the window, and the two of them were on a warpath. So be it. "What were you doing in the family home of the girl who's now your kept woman?" he asked.

"I've never robbed corpses, like someone else I know!"

"What are you talking about?"

"I bet Bile hasn't told you!"

"Af-Laawe spoke of the alleged crime, all right."

"And did Bile own up to this crime when you met him?"

"We didn't get around to talking about alleged crimes, Bile and I."

"Ask him why he blacked out for a good three days." Caloosha had regained some of his composure. Both of them sat down again. "Ask him if he killed and then slept it all off, woke up, and then robbed. Or whether the robbing came first, and the killing later. We have three unaccounted-for days, three whole days. We know when he ran out, a free man, and we know when Dajaal picked him up, lost to the world. My junior half brother killed, robbed, and then slept it off!"

"Bile wouldn't lower himself to such a base level."

Caloosha applauded with an informed sarcasm, only he didn't clap with his palms, but instead knocked his fingernails together, in jest.

"Do you continue to drink the blood of your foes?" Jeebleh asked.

Caloosha had a gory sense of humor. "Maybe that's why I've been sick lately," he said, "suffering, as I do, from severe inflammation of my joints and from an abundance of uric acid in my own blood." Then he added, "You make me sick."

Jeebleh didn't know what to make of Caloosha's behavior, and he got to his feet, unsure where to go or what to say. He paced back and forth, then placed his foot on a stool. They had both gone too far, and it was his turn to compromise, if necessary, to make amends. He put on his professional act: "In the pressure cooker of a civil war, in which the sides at war have been intimates, everyone exaggerates. Okay? And when a society has lost its general sense of direction and, along with it, its self-respect, then every individual is on his or her own, miserably alone. Like ants with no hierarchy or order. Okay? I suggest we forget whatever either of us has said in anger. Okay?"

"I get your point!" Caloosha replied.

They were silent for a long while, and a semblance of calmness returned. Caloosha was where Jeebleh wanted him to be, in an amiable mood. "I am here to make peace," Jeebleh said. "Okay? The past is not here, the present is war, so we must think about the future and marry it to peace. You get me?"

"I get you."

Jeebleh hoped that it wasn't too late in the day for him to introduce the subject that had brought him to Caloosha in the first place. He thought cautiously and elaborated the question in his head. Then he straightened his back, massaged it, and yawned. "Have you seen Faahiye lately?" he said.

Jeebleh talked about Faahiye when he actually wanted to talk about Raasta, and her disappearance. Because the girl's father was as safe a topic as he could come up with at short notice.

"He came to see me the other day, to say hi."

"Alone?"

"Af-Laawe brought him along."

"When was this?" Jeebleh asked.

"I can't recall."

"What about my mother's housekeeper?"

"What about her?"

"Could you tell me how I can reach her? I'll do so without imposing on you."

"It is possible," Caloosha said, "that like Faahiye, your mother's housekeeper went to a refugee camp in Mombasa. I'll see what I can do, and get back to you when I have news of them."

How convenient: a refugee camp in Mombasa!

"What about Raasta and Makka?"

Caloosha gave the question serious thought before responding. "Faahiye assured me, when I asked him, that he knew nothing about his daughter's whereabouts. You know that the girl's parents had separated before her disappearance?"

"I would like to see Faahiye."

"If he is in the country, you will," Caloosha vowed.

"And my late mother's housekeeper?"

"If she hasn't left for Mombasa, you will."

They exchanged a few pleasantries, and Jeebleh helped himself to another cup of coffee, and then asked if Kaahin could take him back to his hotel, on foot. And of course, he would think about the offer to move in with Caloosha, thank you most kindly.

11.

BACK IN HIS HOTEL, JEEBLEH ARRANGED TO PHONE BILE. WHEN THEY
spoke, they agreed to meet, and Bile promised to send Dajaal to fetch him.
Jeebleh was eager to talk, because Af-Laawe's and Caloosha's innuendos
were beginning to bother him.

As he waited for Dajaal, Jeebleh replayed in his mind the two encounters—
with Af-Laawe his first day, and Caloosha today—and his expression clouded
over as he sadly contemplated how difficult it might be to discredit the accu-
sations. Even though he did not think there was any truth to their insinuations,
he did not want to dismiss them out of hand. It was possible that they were
trying to trick him away from the direction in which he ought to be moving.
And what better way to achieve their devious ends than to introduce such
hard-to-challenge charges against Bile's integrity? Jeebleh didn't wish to rely
only on his gut feeling: he wanted to hear his friend's side of the story too.

There was much ground to be covered. But before getting to what interested him, or asking Bile to refute the allegations or own up to them, Jeebleh
decided that he would inform him about his own activities so far. He would
tell him about being shadowed and then approached by the military types
who had escorted him to Caloosha's villa, and how the place had crawled with
suspicious movements, how he felt the armed men were out to intimidate him
and make him stop asking questions about Raasta.

Once Jeebleh and Bile were together, they were anxious to get talking before Bile was called away on some emergency or another. They spoke fast, their words now merging and working well together, now jarring and making no sense at all.

It fell to Jeebleh to make coffee for himself and tea for Bile, and to serve them both. It fell to him too to ask the appropriate questions so that his friend might build a bridge between his elusive past and the murky present in which they found themselves now.

"What was your first day of freedom like?"

"I had a harrowing experience of it," Bile responded readily, prepared for this question, "because fighting framed my life then in ways I'll never be able to communicate well to others not familiar with the circumstances." The stress on his face was evident. "My first day as a free man proved to be the most frightening day in my entire life."

"Why?"

"As prisoners, we were entirely cut off. We had no idea what was happening outside our cells. We had no idea that the Tyrant had fled the city. Someone, Lord knows who, opened the prison gates, someone else the gates of the city's madhouses, someone else the gates of the zoo. So you had humans, some mad and some not, you had animals of every shape, size, and description, all of them on the run. And running alongside them, or in the opposite direction away from them, you had the looters, and the frightened families fleeing. You had thousands of political detainees, and hardened criminals in the tens of thousands. The lions, the zebras, the hyenas, the zoo camel with its two humps—every single creature on the run. You couldn't tell who was fleeing from whom and who was chasing whom. Left to myself, I would've stayed on in my prison quarters, where I might have felt safer."

"How did you know the gates were open?"

"Several hours after they were opened, a handful of vigilantes burst into our wing of the jail," Bile replied, "and went from cell to cell, vowing to kill all the prominent politicians from the opposite clan family. The vigilantes had a dust-laden accent—they must have been recruited from the nomadic hamlets north of Balcad town. I was threatened with death because I tried to intervene, using the nationalist rhetoric of the sixties and seventies. They told me to leave, but I couldn't, because I had a problem getting up. But they didn't hack me to pieces with a machete. In the end, I left my cell, my home for so many of my prison years, when it was safer to do so."

Jeebleh poured more tea into Bile's cup. And looking outside, he saw the sky wearing the clearest of blue and the sun a very bright smile.

Bile continued: "The streets were filled to bursting with the mad, the political detainees just released, the criminals with all kinds of murderous records, and the animals from the zoo. The hard-hearted military types were busy looting the banks and city coffers. The clan militias recruited from the nomadic encampments were looking for city women to rape, and for properties to plunder and cart away in the trucks they had appropriated. The city, the whole country, was pure chaos. The advancing morning melted into high noon before I knew it. I was told of hungry hyenas scavenging in the city center, of lions on the prowl in school dormitories, and of elephants running amok in supermarkets! An unannounced eclipse at dawn: that was what it felt like, the first morning of my freedom."

A heart-wrenching noise erupted outside. They both looked up. Bile explained that vultures were making this ungodly din on the roof of a nearby building, fighting over a carcass.

Neither spoke for a good while.

"What bothered me most was that I couldn't tell the bad guys from the good guys," Bile went on. "After all—not that I had any trust in them—those in uniform, whether they were on the payrolls of the National Army or the police, were all busy looting too. I felt that before long the army and the police would fragment into splinter groups along clan lines. So I moved about in a state of utter confusion.

"I was hungry, frightened, and I didn't know where I was headed. I didn't want to go to Caloosha. I couldn't care less if he was dead or alive. But I wanted to get in touch with Shanta. I had no idea where she was, if she was in danger, or if she had fled the city. It was a nightmare from which, given the choice, I might not have wanted to awaken.

"On one occasion, while moving around, I remember coming up to a madman who took one look at me and kept out of my way—maybe he thought that I was madder than he. Of course, I wasn't mad in my own mind, because I was overwhelmed with embarrassment at the figure I must have cut—something the mad seldom feel. You see, I wasn't in a prisoner's uniform. I was in rags, so dirty not even a beggar would put them on. Part of me wanted to be touched, seen and helped, the other part wanted to hide my eyes, ostrichlike, in the sand of my imagining. In short, I felt suicidal."

"So what did you do?"

"If twenty years in jail had taught me anything," he said, "it was never to trust in luck. In any case, I ran into trouble, right where Lazaretto Road meets Stadium Road, when I was accosted by a group of men, common criminals by the look and sound of them. They chased me. I ran faster than they, and had just turned a corner when I saw a group of thugs roaming the area farther on. Luckily I was at a quiet cul de sac, where a gate opened. A boy in his early teens, dressed in sneakers, khaki shorts, and a safari hat, as if ready for a picnic, came out and looked this way and that. He retreated into the house in terrific haste. I waited. Then a big four-wheel-drive with maybe a dozen passengers of all ages, from grandparents to grandchildren, came out, the boy holding the gate open. When the vehicle had reversed out, he pulled the gate shut and got in, and the vehicle sped away. I forced the gate open— it needed only a decisive push—and went in, closing it behind me securely.

"No sooner had I taken my second step than I saw a very fierce dog waiting for me. It was medium-sized, with a short black coat, most likely a Doberman. It was growling and barking. I acted as though I was a friend. But when I moved, the dog bared its teeth and continued barking at me more fiercely than before. I snapped my fingers, tried what I could to make the dog into a friend, but it still barked whenever I moved. It didn't attack me, though, and eventually I got to a door, and into the kitchen. I bolted myself inside."

"Then what did you do?"

"I marked time."

"Doing what?"

"I made myself coffee," Bile said. "I walked around in the house, marked out my territory, after I had made sure no one else was there. I ventured up to where the bedrooms were, and disconnected the alarm. Being able to achieve this most difficult of feats helped me conquer my fear. I showered, found a wardrobe. The choices were so many. I felt like a child dressing for a birthday party. In the end, I chose a pair of jeans and a pressed shirt. By this time, I had ceased to think of myself as an intruder, and felt like the owner of the house—at least I moved about like I was. It was the kind of house I might have owned or lived in, given the chance."

"And then?"

"I thought of winning the dog's trust. I opened the front door and it came at me, growling. But it wasn't as fierce as before, maybe because I had on its master's clothes. The dog and I stood there uneasily, sizing each other up. Then I played with it, making it go fetch a ball. An hour and a half of this, and the dog and I became friends of a kind. And it began to follow me everywhere I went, and jumped into the Volkswagen Beetle in the carport when I inspected it, trying to see if it would start.

"I went into the house once I was exhausted from playing with the dog. And when the silence got to me, I switched on the radio to listen to the BBC news and, as I did so, ate some Parmesan cheese of stupendous pedigree. I had coffee and more coffee, and then more Parmesan. Heaven was coffee with Parmesan. I tasted the joy of life in the coffee I drank, and in the Parmesan I ate."

Bile had a ball of a time, living it up. He hadn't a care in the world, like someone living on borrowed time, and enjoying every instant of it. He ate cheese or what fruit there was, because he couldn't bring himself to cook a meal. And because there was not a single book in the entire house, except for school texts in Italian and Somali, he listened to the radio and exercised his leg, which was still giving him a bit of trouble. With plenty of time on his hands, he decided to use it profitably: he taught himself to read and write Somali, which was given an official orthography only in 1972, while he was in prison. And when he tired of learning to read and write, or of listening to the radio or playing with the dog, he went to the telephone and pressed the redial button in hope of speaking to a human voice. The line was either busy or the phone was not functioning, he couldn't tell.

He wished then that he were one in a crowd, where he could touch and be touched. "That was what I wanted," he said. "I had lived in total isolation for years, and hadn't touched or been touched. I envied the mad, naively thinking that they never feel lonely, as their heads are full of talk and of other people's memories. I envied the madman who could think of himself as a crowd, and behave any way he liked!"

"And then?"

"I felt depressed, miserable, and lonely. I slept for who knows how long, and woke up a new man. My memory, which I thought had gone dead on me, had been stirred into action, selectively remembering some of the things I had seen and done. I couldn't remember what I had done between when I saw the fierce dog and made myself several cups of espresso and walked about the house alone, marking out the territory as though it was mine, and when I decided to think of myself as a free man. Then I realized I didn't have to hide in one of the city's shadowy corners, or reinvent myself by changing the history of my loyalties. It was then that I finally decided to celebrate my freedom!"

"How did you do that?"

"I was going to go out."

If Jeebleh didn't ask pointed questions to get Bile to devote a few minutes to answering Af-Laawe's and Caloosha's allegations about murdering and stealing, it was because he didn't wish to interrupt the flow of the narrative. He was sure they would have the opportunity to talk about this and many other subjects too. "And?"

"It was when I was looking for some clothes to carry away for my immediate use that I stumbled on a duffel bag full of money, in large denominations, in cash and ready to go! The amount was staggeringly high, close to a million U.S. dollars. It was there all along, only I hadn't seen it."

Jeebleh stared at the scar on Bile's forehead. An inch long, and pale, no bigger than a caterpillar that would mutate into a butterfly. He stared at it, because he sensed it moving. Now he said, "What did you do?"

"I went to sleep," Bile said.

"But what on earth for?"

"Not being a thief, and not wanting to tempt fate," Bile explained, "I decided I no longer had any reason to hurry. I was determined to take my time and decide what to do with the money, whether to appropriate it, or just leave it where I found it.

"But I became afraid of the looters, whom I knew to be stronger than I, and who I knew would come. If I was clear in my mind about one thing, it was that I should ultimately hand the money over to the government. I hadn't thought about what I might do in the absence of a reconstituted national government."

He paused, helped himself to more tea, and then went on: "I'm not a religious person, but for the first time in years I thought about God and His purpose in me. I also thought about a couple of small things I might use the money for. Then Plotinus came to me. And I thought about peace, about the misery and poverty of our people, and how, if the money were mine and I used it judiciously, even a small sum could help a lot of people."

"You didn't think the owners might return?"

"I stayed on in the house with the money," he said. "I was in no hurry—remember, I wasn't a thief. And when I slept—and I slept for a very, very long time, almost three days I should think—I dreamt at one point that I was setting very, very many small things right. Then I came to, because I heard a god-awful noise!"

"What?"

"The dog was barking and barking."

"When would this have been?" Jeebleh asked.

"At dawn, I cannot be certain which day it was, my first intimation of danger was at more or less the same time as the muezzin's call. The barking, interspersed with the eerie quiet of the hour, struck fear into my heart. I thought of running away, and there was a great deal of sense in that. But I decided to sit it out. I waited and waited. No one came, and the dog stopped barking. I resolved to take the money, and use it for other people!"

"And you left?"

"In search of Shanta."

"Had you any inkling where she might be?"

"No."

"Had things calmed down by then?"

"Not much," Bile said. "But it made sense to take the car in the carport, despite the moral question—although this irked me. Would I be stealing if I took a million dollars stashed in a duffel bag ready to go, from the house of people who had looted the coffers of the state before its final collapse? Would it be a good thing or a bad thing if I used the embezzled funds to set up a charitable refuge? We could argue about these moral issues at length. In the end, thief or no thief, I said to hell with it, took the car, and quit the house."

"And the dog?"

"Where would I take the dog?"

"Fair enough. You drove off," Jeebleh said, "alone."

"In Somalia the civil war then was *language*," Bile said, "only I didn't speak the new language. At one point, a couple of armed men flagged me down, and one of them asked, '*Yaad tahay?*' I hadn't realized that the old way of answering the question 'Who are you?' was no longer valid. Now the answer universally given to 'Who are you?' referred to the identity of your clan family, your blood identity! I found the correct responses in the flourish of the tongue, found them in the fresh idiom, the new argot. I was all right. I was a good mimic, able to speak in the correct Somali accent, nodding when my questioner mentioned the right acronym. The men who flagged me down had in their gaze the shine of well-fed guard dogs. What's more, their four-wheel-drive vehicle was loaded, because they had just robbed the Central Bank."

"So they let you proceed?"

"With a warning, after I spoke the acronym of the period," Bile said, head down, as if embarrassed to have done so.

"What was the acronym of the period?"

"The initial letters of the clan-based militia movement that ran the Tyrant out of the city."

"They just let you go?"

"They suggested that I take care. I gathered from this that it would be unwise to ask if they knew where I might find Caloosha. I didn't think it likely that they would lead me to Shanta."

Bile's hands were beginning to resemble those of a baby, clutched tightly into fists. Maybe he was wishing he had done something cavalier by challenging the looters.

Bile continued, "I had barely gone a kilometer when a pack of knife-wielding urchins flagged me down. I was trying to appease them, when my prayer was answered: a man in uniform, armed but not looting, came driving by. He asked if there was a problem. The youths fled. I introduced myself to the gentleman, who told me his name: Dajaal. Taken aback, at first I assumed it was an alias, some sort of nom de guerre. When it became obvious that I could trust him, I told him that I wanted to get in touch with a sister of mine, and gave him some spiel, the gist of which was that I had no idea how to reach her. It was my good fortune that he knew my name, knew Shanta, and knew where she lived. He and I belonged to the same family—he said so right away, as if to assure me that I could trust him. That didn't matter to me as much as it mattered to him. What mattered to me was to find Shanta, and I said so. He told me to follow him, but for obvious reasons this didn't appeal to me. I wanted to get rid of the Volkswagen, I wanted to have no associations with the house I had gotten it from, or the family it had belonged to. So I got into his car and felt safe in his hands.

"Ours was the only car on the road in that part of the city, but there were pedestrians everywhere—at crossroads, ahead of us, behind us. Many were entering houses empty-handed and emerging with their loot. At one point, Dajaal nearly ran over a man carrying what appeared to be a very heavy load. I got out of the car and helped the man gather his scattered loot. I had half expected to find the roads blocked with checkpoints, and curiously, they weren't. I was relieved also that Dajaal hadn't inquired about the contents of my duffel bag!"

Bile learned from Dajaal that Shanta had married Faahiye, who was nearly twenty-five years her senior, and that she was heavily pregnant at forty-three.

"I had thought that she was past childbearing age, and reasoned aloud that if this was her first, I would have to prepare, for such a pregnancy might bring along its fair share of problems. 'A miracle baby, then?' Dajaal said."

As it turned out, by the time Bile was led to her, Shanta was in labor and in great pain. There were no doctors around, and no possibility of getting her to a hospital. Bile had to break the traditional medical code of conduct and help his younger sister in her hour of labor.

"Never mind the medical or traditional code, which I disregarded," Bile said, "it gave me great joy to deliver a lovely dreadlocked miracle baby into the world!"

"And then?"

The phone rang, and Jeebleh and Bile looked at each other. "I'm afraid that installment will have to wait," Bile said, and went to answer.

12.

JEEBLEH DREAMT THAT HE WAS A CRAB. HE HAD GONE PAST THE LARVAL
phase of transparency but gotten stuck in the stage of growing legs. His cara-
pace was not broad enough, and his legs were deformed. He couldn't scuttle
around as crabs do, he could only move slowly and laboriously. A distant
cousin of the spider crab, he looked forward to waiting in thorny flowers for
prey to pounce on. A pity that no victim came within the reach of his claws.

When he woke, he felt the urge to take a dip in the ocean. He missed the
delicate touch of its saltiness, and remembered how much he enjoyed swimming and then going for long walks, the sandy beach stretching ahead of him
and to his back, the air clean, the water as blue as the sky, and as clear. He and
Bile would spend much of their slack time on a café terrace facing the ocean.

He decided to go for a swim before breakfast, and found himself walking
sideways. At first, he was a little amused, but when he saw some youths staring at him in shock, he stopped walking altogether. He paused for a long
while, closing his eyes and taking deep breaths, concentrating his mind on
what he would do next. Eventually he moved, but only after he felt he could
walk straight.

He was wearing a sarong that he had brought from New York—a present
from his wife—a Yankees T-shirt, and under the sarong, a pair of swimming

trunks. Around his shoulders was a towel. For shoes he had a cheap pair of Chinese-made flip-flops, the only item he had purchased in Mogadiscio since his arrival, from a vendor at the hotel. When he had inquired at the reception desk about going to the ocean for a swim, the man at the reception desk seemed amused, maybe because of Jeebleh's attire. The man told him that the beach was no more than a five minutes' walk away. He was to go east, and he would soon come to it.

The water stretched endlessly before him. He stared at its immensity, and had a moment of recollection. He was in his early teens, with Bile, and the two were escaping from Caloosha. In his memory, the ocean was a place of refuge, because Caloosha had never learned to swim, despite his having been in Mogadiscio for much of his life. When the memory faded, Jeebleh looked this way and that, and noted that the beach was deserted. He took off his sarong, T-shirt, and towel, and placed them under a stone, to make sure he would find them later.

After he had been in the shallow water only a few minutes, it occurred to him that it might not be worth risking his life for a dip in the ocean. Not that he was afraid of the surf or of sharks. He saw three men on the beach looking in his direction. He suspected that one of them was armed; he seemed to have a shiny revolverlike weapon in his grip. He guessed the man could easily have taken a potshot at him.

Who were they? He reckoned they were not from one or the other clan-based militia, for they seemed to be better disciplined than those armed thugs who killed for a bit of sport. For all he knew, they were there on in-structions from Caloosha, to shadow and report on his movements. But would they harm him or protect him? It bothered him that he had no way of know-ing. He doubted that Dajaal had the wherewithal to arrange such a security detail at Bile's behest. Besides, Dajaal's authority did not stretch to the north of the city, where Jeebleh was having his swim.

He swam farther and farther out and floated. He didn't want to expose himself to sharks. He wasn't sure what to do next—stay where he was, go out farther, or get out.

· · ·

HE WAS AN EXCELLENT SWIMMER. HIS TECHNIQUE IMPROVED THE INSTANT HE exiled all worries of death from his mind. His breaststroke was as good as a competitive swimmer's, his butterfly superbly rhythmic, and his crawl extraordinarily fast. When the water proved rough, he resorted to breaststroke. When it was calm, he rested, floating. He lay on his back, contemplating the blue sky, thinking.

He recalled sitting in an apartment in Queens with his wife and daughters, and watching the main event on television: Marines in combat gear, and cameras flashing as photographers took pictures of the Americans alighting from their amphibious craft. In a moment, several of the Marines, appearing proud, would be interviewed by one of the most famous anchormen in America. Jeebleh's wife turned to him to ask whether the Marines knew what doing "God's work" meant in a country like Somalia.

It was from the ocean that all the major invasions of the Somali peninsula had come. The Arabs, and after them the Persians, and after the Persians the Portuguese, and after the Portuguese the French, the British, and the Italians, and later the Russians, and most recently the Americans—here, Jeebleh remembered how the U.S. intervention to feed the starving Somalis became an invasion of a kind, hence the term "intravasion," frequently used at the time. In any case, all these foreigners, well-meaning or not, came from the ocean. The invaders might be pilgrims bearing gifts, or boys dispatched to do "God's work"; the American in charge of the U.S. "intravasion" would be described in the reputable *Encyclopaedia Britannica* of 1994 as the putative "Head of the State of Somalia."

Jeebleh stayed in the water for an hour. He lay afloat, the sky unfailingly above him, the warm water below. These were his only points of reference. And in the farthest reaches of the sky, he saw an eagle, majestically alone and riding the heavens' sail, and around it the clouds paying homage. He sensed, even from such a distance, the determination in every feather—a bird in regal flight. What elegance!

Doing the breaststroke now, to view ahead of himself, he saw no sign of the three men. Were they gone? Did they have nothing to do with him? Was he being paranoid? Or were they hiding behind the bushes, ready to pounce? He came out of the water cautiously and walked, edging along the sea wall, faster and faster, because he was now truly afraid. Then all of a sudden he spotted one of the gunmen, who looked away, embarrassed. It was Kaahin.

The men kept their discreet distance, but still following him, until he was safely within view of the hotel gate. And when he turned, just before going in, he saw that they were no longer there.

HE SENSED SOMETHING WRONG THE MOMENT HE GOT TO THE GATE, HIS shadow as short as a set of manacles fitted around his ankles. He stamped his feet on the paved driveway to rid them of the fine sand that clung to them, and while doing so, greeted the sentries at the gate. One of them kept making signs. Not adept at sign language, Jeebleh had difficulty following the meaning. The man kept doing funny things with his tongue. What on earth was he trying to communicate? Jeebleh noticed a group of elderly men crouched in a dusty huddle, whispering to one another. These must be his clansmen. The pedestrian door, carved out of the bigger gate, was opened for him, and he walked through.

At the reception desk, he was given a thick parcel. He broke the seal and unwrapped the package, and inside found a mobile phone with a manual in Arabic—presumably it had been imported from Abu Dhabi, where most Mogadiscians got their high-tech stuff. An attached note advised him, in Italian, of the numbers that had been fed into the phone's memory. A P.S., in Bile's hand, told him not to worry about the bills.

Then the same receptionist gave him an envelope. This was thin and contained a one-page message in Somali, written on lined paper torn out of a child's exercise book. At first he thought that a child had penned it—an obviously shaky hand, some of the letters small, others large. At the bottom of the message were six thumbprint signatures and three printed names, difficult to decipher. His hand trembled as he held it, and he thought of it as a souvenir that would benefit from being framed—ideally on the walls of an adult literacy class. The message informed him that his clan elders wanted to discuss with him matters of family importance.

He took his time showering, then tried to make the mobile phone work. Being inexperienced, he pressed buttons at random and inaccurately, and got cut off or reached busy signals or wrong numbers. Just when he thought he had succeeded, Bile's number was off his screen.

He felt it was time for his Yemeni coffee. Downstairs, he asked a runner to get him a pot of coffee and to prepare several pots of tea, milk, lots and lots of biscuits, and half a kilo of sugar, and to bring these to his table. When the runner returned, he told a bellboy to show the clan elders in.

THE MEN FORMED A LINE AND GREETED JEEBLEH ONE AT A TIME, EACH OF them respectfully taking his hand in both of theirs. Then they sat down at a table, three to the right of him, six to his left, he at the head. Before anyone uttered a word beyond the greetings, Jeebleh pointed to the nine teapots, one for each of them, the biscuits still wrapped, and the bowls filled to the brim with sugar. He suggested they help themselves.

They got down to the business of pouring out their tea with the clumsiness of four-year-olds. And even though their cups were full, they poured milk, then added several spoonfuls of sugar, so that the tea spilled over the sides. They did this with such devotion you might have thought they would depart as soon as each had attended to his sweet tooth. The table was soon as messy as a toddler's birthday party would have made it. The crackling of biscuit wrappings mixed with the loud chorus of tea slurping. A host of flies arrived to feast on the sugary surfaces of cups and saucers.

The first elder to speak had biscuit crumbs on his chin and a bit of sugar on his cheek. He was of small build and looked healthy for his age. He explained that he and several other elders had come previously to greet and welcome Jeebleh, but they were informed that he had gone out. "Now we're very pleased to return with a different lot of elders who've shown interest in meeting our son, and to welcome him back into the bosom of his immediate clan." The old man requested that each of the other elders speak, but confine their remarks to a few words, because, he said, "your son is a very busy man and doesn't have a lot of time to waste." After they had done so, he invited each of them to recite from the Koran, in praise of Allah, who had brought their son back from "his worldly wanderings." Their lips astir and their voices low, each man mouthed a few verses.

Jeebleh bowed to each of them in turn, greeting them with a ritual nod, but said nothing. Then he poured himself more coffee and sipped at it leisurely. One of the men passed him the sugar bowl. He nodded his thanks as he took the proffered bowl, and watched the consternation on the men's faces as he put it aside without helping himself. Why was he drinking his coffee bitter, with so much sweetness available?

The spokesman of the elders now discussed Jeebleh's importance and the positive, commendable role he could play in the politics of the clan. Jeebleh lapsed into a private mood, a man in his own space. He did his utmost not to display unease at the thought of privileging blood over ideology. The idea of nine self-appointed clansmen making a claim on him was anathema. Of course, he meant not to anger them unnecessarily. But he changed his mind when the spokesman alluded to his mother without mentioning his father. "As it happens, we're from your mother's side of the *bah*!"

By invoking his mother's name, not his father's, the men from his mother's subclan were explicitly distancing themselves from his father, the gambler. The elders failed to mention that they had blamed his mother for her husband's wild ways, accusing her of driving him first to gambling and then to the bottle, when this wasn't the case, according to his mother's version. Some of these very men may have been present when family members had resolved to deny her a hearing—one of them was for sure, the especially ancient-looking sort with the thick glasses, whom Jeebleh thought of as FourEyes. So where was the clan when Jeebleh's mother sang her sorrow, a single mother raising him, and later a widow isolated from the subclan? Where were these men then? The first time a member of his subclan ever visited him was when he returned from Italy, with a university degree. When he incurred the Dictator's wrath and for his pains was thrown into prison and sentenced to death, they had all deserted him, hadn't they? He knew that clan elders were self-serving men, high on selective memory and devoid of dignity.

"I am insulted by the way you've formulated my identity," Jeebleh said. "Why do I feel I am being insulted? Why do you continue referring to me as the son of my mother without ever bothering to mention my father by name? Don't I have a father? Am I illegitimate? We know what he was like and what kind of man he was, but still, he was my father and I bear his name, not my mother's! How dare you address me in a way that questions my being the legitimate son of my own father?"

The gathering was thrown into a state of noisy confusion, as all the elders tried to assure him that they did not mean to insult him, or to offend his parents' memories. He was elated that their cynical ploy had worked to his advantage, remembering how, earlier, he had restrained himself from losing his temper with Caloosha. The elders were now too shocked to speak. He had them where he wanted them.

"Why have you come, then?" he asked the bespectacled man to his right, and not the spokesman, farther to his left, who, rendered speechless, covered his mouth with his hand. The men's evasive looks now converged on the face of the spokesman. He removed his hand from his mouth and shook his head regretfully: he was not going to speak, either on his own behalf or on anyone else's.

There was vigor in his voice when FourEyes now spoke. He came to the point: "Unlike other *bah*s of the clan, ours hasn't been able to raise a strong fighting militia. We do not have sufficient funds to take our rightful place among the subclans equal in number to or even smaller than ours. We've come to appeal to you for money so we may repair our only two battlewagons."

Jeebleh addressed himself to the gathering: "I'm busy with other concerns, and as you can imagine, I've not brought along with me more cash than I need for my daily expenses. So I suggest you wait until I return home and consult my wife and daughters, and I'll come back to you with my response."

There was absolute silence as the meaning of Jeebleh's words registered with the elders. Then, as if on cue, the mobile phone on Jeebleh's lap squealed. He answered it and told the gathering, "This is an important call, and I must take it in private. Please forgive me." And he walked away.

"Are we to wait for you?" FourEyes called after him.

"You needn't," Jeebleh answered. "I'll be in touch!"

The men argued among themselves, some suggesting that they should wait, others insisting that the earlier command to wait had been addressed to the caller. When he walked farther away, and they heard him ask one of the runners to show them out, they said in a chorus, "This is an insult!"

Jeebleh waved to them from the reception area, and shouted: "Go well!" And before they had a chance to say anything, he himself was gone.

AN HOUR AND A HALF LATER, JEEBLEH SAT IN THE HOTEL COURTYARD AND took note, with alarm, of three gunmen walking past the sentry at the gate without being stopped. The hotel runners entertained the three with friendly banter. Even so, Jeebleh was very conscious of the mood palpably changing. And when he called to one of the runners, asking what the gunmen were doing on the grounds of the hotel, the youth just made "Search me" gestures. The sun was burning hot, the sand seemed agitated, and the air unhealthy.

Jeebleh's wandering gaze fell on a boy in a fancy cowboy hat and jeans, ruthlessly hitting an Alsatian with a stick. He turned to the young man at the next table and asked why the gun-carrying militiamen had been allowed in, and why no one was stopping the boy from abusing the dog. "Maybe the gunmen are the boy's bodyguards?" the young man mused.

"Who does the Alsatian belong to?"

"I don't know."

The pregnant dog was writhing in agony, and actively giving birth. There was something odd about the clothes of the boy, and something odder still about a pure-bred Alsatian in today's Mogadiscio. From another table, Jeebleh overheard a likely explanation: that the dog had once belonged to an Englishman, formerly of the BBC African Service, who had been seconded to the city by UNOSOM. But why had he abandoned his pampered pet to fend for herself, knowing she might fall prey to packs of bush dogs more feral than even the fiercest Alsatian? Or be beaten to death by Somalis not given to being friendly when it came to dogs? What madness could have compelled him to leave her behind?

Jeebleh remembered how, when he was small, he had tried to stop Caloosha and his friends from molesting a dog. He had been beaten harshly himself for his impudence. (Many years later, he learned that one of the boys had met the fate he deserved: he died from rabies.)

Jeebleh took courage, and found his tongue. He shouted, warning the boy to stop abusing the dog or he would deal with him. At the sound of the raised voice, the guns of the militiamen were trained on him.

He stood up and stormed over to the boy and took him by the scruff of his pampered neck. The boy was so shaken that he choked on his scream, issuing none audibly. "If this spoiled brat disturbs this dog again," Jeebleh shouted, so everybody could hear, "I'll become violent and punish him." The dog looked terribly frightened, and Jeebleh, for his part, felt overwhelmed. But when he snatched the stick from the boy, the dog began to relax. Jeebleh said, "When you hurt the dog, I hurt."

Now the Alsatian came closer to Jeebleh, and finding her tongue, favored his extended hand with a lick. Jeebleh crouched by the dog, touching her coarse coat, stroking her gently. This provoked a ripple of disapproval across the crowd that had now gathered to watch. Whatever they might think, Jeebleh and the dog looked at each other for a long while, and he discovered her intelligence in the steady confidence in her eyes. Then the dog, racked with birth pangs, went even closer to Jeebleh, who encouraged her to keep pushing. Someone in the crowd commented favorably on his kind gesture: showing mercy to a dog in labor. Someone else said that what he had done was un-Islamic; as a Muslim, he was supposed to avoid coming into physical contact with dogs.

When Jeebleh next looked around, the armed youths were no longer aiming their guns at him. As a matter of fact, they weren't even there. Perhaps they had sensed that their threatening posture was not acceptable anymore and had slunk away.

He was now in an upbeat mood, and remained close by until the dog, having given birth, bit off the umbilical cords. He admired the compact beauty of the litter: puppies full of stir, half Alsatian, half bush dog, of exquisite grace. He wished someone with a home thereabouts would keep them and look after them. He found a quiet corner for the family, and took off his jacket and covered the puppies with it.

Walking away, he felt good, proud of what he had done, despite the shock on people's faces. As he moved toward them, a path opened before him, many shunning him because they did not wish to make any physical contact with a man who had touched and been licked by a dog. Customarily, Somalis who came into contact with dogs would cleanse themselves ritually, in obedience to the Islamic code of self-purification. He did not care a sick dog's snuffle if anyone now shunned bodily contact with him.

As he walked past one knot of bystanders, he heard a whisper: "What manner of man chases away the elders of his clan, and in the same afternoon risks his life to save a bitch?"

The fact that many people had missed out on love because of the continued strife, Jeebleh thought, did not mean that one should stand by and do nothing or allow further cruelty to be meted out to animals or humans.

13.

THE SUN SHONE BRIGHTLY, THE NOON HIGH ON ITS DIAL.

His expression sullen, Jeebleh squinted up at Af-Laawe, who towered above him where he sat. Because Af-Laawe was a friend and an associate of Caloosha's, Jeebleh didn't feel he could go to him for help, or share with him his concerns. But now that he was friendless and felt ostracized by the hotel staff—not so much for his kindness to the Alsatian as for his rude sendoff of the clan elders—he was wondering whether to seek out Af-Laawe, obviously a man with a murky history. Maybe things would work out well in the end. As he rose to take Af-Laawe's hand, Jeebleh proposed a walk in the neighborhood.

"A walk and a talk will do you good," Af-Laawe agreed.

Conscious of the hostility directed at him from all around, Jeebleh noted that even Bucktooth, the friendliest of the sentries, who had welcomed him with enthusiasm earlier, averted his visibly disturbed gaze. To make a point, though, he greeted Af-Laawe by name. There were rough edges to things, and Jeebleh was more aware of them because of the dirty politics of the place, and this was weighing down on his mind.

He who alienates his clan family is dead, he thought, as he followed Af-Laawe out of his hotel grounds into the derelict streets lined with vandalized buildings. Parting with his clansmen, leaving the hotel—these were as easily done as throwing out a rotten banana when you were well fed. Besides, it was just as well that it had happened the way it did. A confrontation between him and the clan elders over his political loyalties was bound to happen sooner or later, and he was relieved that it had occurred when it had—a few days into his visit. He would move out of the hotel at the first opportunity, and take up Bile's offer to share the apartment with him for a few days. He had a lot to do: locate his mother's housekeeper, and make sure that his mother had found peace, that her soul was laid to rest; give a hand in recovering Raasta and her companion from their captors; and recruit Dajaal to exact vengeance on Caloosha.

AF-LAAWE LED JEEBLEH IN THE DIRECTION OF VILLAGGIO ARABO, NAMED FOR the Yemeni community who had formed the majority in the district during his youth. He remembered it as a lively quarter, very cosmopolitan, its alleyways infused with spicy fragrances—the Yemeni kitchen was one of Jeebleh's favorites. He didn't need to ask what had become of the community: virtually all, he knew, had fled the city in the earlier weeks of the civil war, when the dust-laden pastoralists recruited into StrongmanNorth's armed militia turned on them, raping their women and plundering their wealth.

In the streets where Jeebleh and Af-Laawe now walked, minibuses ferrying passengers negotiated their way and almost knocked down pedestrians as they avoided potholes. There were also plenty of Angora goats that may once have belonged to the Yemeni residents, and these were forced to feed on pebbles; there were no shrubs, and the grass and the cacti were dry. The cows Jeebleh saw chewed away at discarded shoes, for which the goats had no stomach. The dogs looked rabid and were so skinny you could see their protruding ribs; they ran off at the slightest hint of threat. There were waste dumps every few hundred meters or so, where vultures, marabous, and the odd crow were having a go at the pickings. Jeebleh felt he had arrived in an area just devastated by wildfire, which had reduced it to spectral ruins, with only the charred sticks of houses remaining.

He tried to express his sense of disbelief to Af-Laawe. "This city is a disaster. I haven't met anyone who openly approves of what's happening, and yet the fighting goes on and the clan elders continue soliciting funds for repairing deadly weapons. What's going on?"

"It's like a fashion," Af-Laawe replied. "Every clan family feels that it has to form its own armed militia, because the others have them. The elders, almost all of them illiterate and out of touch with your and my sense of modernity, spend their time trying to raise funds from within the members of the blood community. In truth, it's all a pose, though, and everybody knows that the elders are doing this to make sure they remain relevant." Af-Laawe paused, surveyed the devastated street. "Incidentally, I agree with what you did, your refusal to pay for the repair of a battlewagon."

Jeebleh looked away, at a crow that was being denied access to its fair share of carrion, the smallest of the vultures chasing it away every time it approached. This is a place of grief, he thought, in which even crows starve; in which goats feed on pebbles or clumps of earth, and cows on discarded shoes. What in God's name was he doing here? He turned to Af-Laawe, silent.

Af-Laawe was ill at ease in the silence, and finally broke it. "I happened to be at Caloosha's when the clan elders reported to him that not only did you send them away empty-handed, but you were rude to them too."

"What was his reaction?" Jeebleh asked.

"He did his best to placate them."

"Why would he do that?"

"He sounded as though he had your best interest at heart. He wants to be in their good books, and wants to make it up to you too in his own way."

"I can't believe what I am hearing."

After a pause, Af-Laawe said, "The manager of the hotel phoned Caloosha, agitated."

"And what's with him?" Jeebleh asked.

"Something about the dog wore him to a frazzle."

"The hell with it," Jeebleh fumed.

His eyes focused and compact like a fruit stone, Af-Laawe recounted that the manager had called twice to lament that his hotel would now be remembered as the place where two terrible things happened, back to back, within half an hour.

It was incredible, Jeebleh thought, how speedily peoples' moods changed, friendly one moment, hostile the next. Was this what his beloved country had been reduced to, a land where the elders were unaware of being out of touch with the times, and where the young were armed and not right in the head, killing without remorse?

"You know what I think?" Af-Laawe said.

"Tell me."

"I think that because people who have lived under such stressful conditions assume they can set fire to vultures," Af-Laawe said, "they believe they will rid the country of its problems by doing so."

"But this is raving lunacy!"

Af-Laawe said nothing. He was busy responding to greetings from passersby. He nodded without bothering to pause or engage in conversation. He returned the greetings with the casualness of a superior officer acknowledging a minion.

They were joined by a mob of beggars, who addressed themselves only to Jeebleh, touching their bellies, then their mouths, asking for alms. Maybe they sensed that Jeebleh might have a softer center than his companion, who they knew was not in the habit of offering alms. Jeebleh could tell from their accent that they were from the bay region that was the center of savage wars launched by StrongmanSouth. The Major and the driver whom he had met in the previous days had hailed from the same Death Triangle.

"Does anyone help the city's displaced?" Jeebleh asked.

"These live in the buildings around here, but no one looks out for them, or care what happens to them. Many of them beg and squat in the ruined properties of those who've fled or in the buildings that belonged to the state."

"Any idea about how many there are?"

"They are about a million and a half, and they're on the increase, every time there's fighting."

You're seldom alone in the areas of a city where the poor are attracted in hope of finding help or a job, Jeebleh thought. There are beggars, shoeshine boys offering their services, urchins promising to look after your vehicle for a small fee, hangers-on, pimps, prostitutes, touts waiting to sponge on you.

One of the beggars stuck to Jeebleh, and kept saying, "God is generous!" But unlike the others, who rubbed their bellies and then touched the tips of their fingers to their lips, he asked for nothing. This made Jeebleh uncomfortable. Af-Laawe explained that the man had belonged to Mogadiscio's middle class and had held a high position in the government. A longer look at the beggar revealed the telltale evidence. The man eyed Jeebleh as if he hoped he would recognize him, a man like himself, who had fallen on hard times. And even though he appeared no different from his fellow beggars, remarkably he communicated that he knew what dignity was. As a cloud of dust stirred and swirled around him, Jeebleh sensed that sorrow skulked in every grain of sand. He asked Af-Laawe, "Who is this man?"

"In his heyday, he was known as Xaar-Cune."

So this is what's become of EatShit, Jeebleh thought. A torturer with no equal, he had taken sadistic pleasure in forcing political detainees on hunger strike to do as his name suggested. He had served under Caloosha. "How was he reduced to this state?" Jeebleh asked.

"When the state collapsed, he stayed in the city, confident that no harm would come to him. But he made a mistake while foraging for political gain: he swore total loyalty to StrongmanSouth, who for a time put him to good use as a torturer. Because his mother, like mine, is from the north of the city, StrongmanSouth assigned to EatShit the job of ferrying messages between the two Strongmen. Then came the time when StrongmanSouth suspected Eat-Shit of betraying him in an off-the-record remark to one of the local rags. He was summoned and humiliated in the presence of the in-group, and made to partake of a feast of feces."

"And he was put out to grass here?"

"He was dumped here, painted with all sorts of shit and dung," Af-Laawe said, "and everyone came out to mock him. His poor mother died soon after, heartbroken. His mind got twisted out of shape, and he fell into a state of utter malfunction."

Sad, like an owl flying into the sun, Jeebleh prayed that someone, it didn't matter who, might mete out similar or worse punishment to Caloosha. But when he considered that it might fall to him to do it, he felt like a man invited to a wake at which the dead got up to say their say, then departed, promising to return to torment those who had made their lives a misery.

"Would you like to have lunch?" asked Af-Laawe.

For a moment, Jeebleh didn't want to think about food. But he was hungry. "Is there a restaurant nearby?"

"Right here," Af-Laawe said.

Jeebleh saw a hole in a wall and a curtain billowing out. But there was no sign, no name.

Af-Laawe said, "Follow me," and Jeebleh did so.

Inside, it was dim, and candles were burning; the atmosphere was more jazz club than lunch spot. A waitress in overalls led them to a table, and Af-Laawe ordered their first course with exaggerated élan.

"DESPITE IT ALL, WE'RE ALL INTIMATES, YOU KNOW."

"We? Who do you mean?" Jeebleh asked. With his back to the wall, he watched the candles nodding this way and that. Figures sat close together at other tables as though in whispery conspiracy; he couldn't see their faces.

"Do you know why," Af-Laawe said, "when a wife is found dead under suspicious circumstances, her husband is brought in and questioned in depth?"

"Because he is an intimate?"

"Precisely."

Jeebleh was unsure what to say; he waited.

"In a civil war, death is an intimate," Af-Laawe said. "You're killed by a person with whom you've shared intimacies, and who will kill you, believing that he will benefit from your death. And when you think seriously about an entire country going up in civil war flames, then you'll agree that 'intimacy' is more complicated."

"I hadn't thought of intimacy in that sense," Jeebleh admitted.

"Do you know the Somali term for 'civil war'?"

"*Dagaalka sokeeye.*"

"Precisely," Af-Laawe asserted.

In his mind, Jeebleh couldn't decide how to render the Somali expression in English, in the end preferring the notion "killing an intimate" to "warring against an intimate." Maybe the latter described better what was happening in Somalia. He was uncertain what to say next, and waited.

Af-Laawe went on, lapsing now and then into Italian: "The phrase, as you know, is of recent coinage, and it explains quite aptly something about the intimate nature of the civil war. Questioned in depth and under the investigative powers of the police, many a husband whose wife has died under suspicious circumstances will fidget, even if he is innocent. 'Where were you on Thursday evening between nine and eleven?' Every private thing is made public, and the husband must prove his innocence."

The waitress who served their spaghetti all'amatriciana, was not the one who had taken the order, and apparently she knew Af-Laawe. "Would you like me to bring your usual with your meal?" she said.

Af-Laawe shook his head no, then asked Jeebleh what he might like to drink. Jeebleh ordered lemonade, and Af-Laawe told the waitress to make it two.

"If I remember correctly, the driver who gave me a lift from the airport, thanks to your kindness, told me that you lived in Alsace. When did you come home from Alsace?" Jeebleh asked.

"I bought myself a ticket as soon as I heard that the Dictator had been chased out," Af-Laawe said. "When I arrived, there was still a palpable joy in the city because he had fled. The mood was short-lived, however. Soon it became a matter of us and them, clan families versus clan families. Instead of celebrating victory, it was the start of the war of the intimates! I couldn't stand the thought of being part of this kind of schism, so I returned to Alsace."

"Were you here during the four-month war between the two Strongmen, when the city was severed in two?" Jeebleh asked.

"I wasn't here, but we are still living with the consequences of that war."

"How so?"

"Those four months of war made it clear that the idea of the clan is a sham, as some of us believed all along," Af-Laawe said. "More recently, those of us who think of ourselves as progressive argue not only that the clan is a sham, but that you cannot organize civil society around it."

"When did you come back to Mogadiscio?"

"I returned a few months after UNOSOM got here."

When they had finished the first course, Af-Laawe asked for his usual, which Jeebleh suspected had in it a tot of something forbidden in an Islamic country. Eventually another waitress brought baked fish in garlic sauce for Af-Laawe and pepper steak, well done, for Jeebleh, and a salad for each. Jeebleh listened, as Af-Laawe continued talking.

"Some of us are of a 'we' generation, others a 'me' generation. You mix the two modes of being, and things become awkward, unmanageable. I belong to the me generation, whereas my clan elders belong to the we generation. A man with a me mindset and a family of four—a wife and two children— celebrates the idea of 'me.' It is not so when it comes to our clansmen who visit from the hinterland, and who celebrate a 'we.' They believe in the clan, and they know no better—many of them have never been to school or out of the country. I am included in their self-serving 'we.' This leads to chaos."

Pausing, he glanced at Jeebleh, who obviously wasn't enjoying this monologue. Af-Laawe resumed: "You and I belong to the me generation. We're professionals with qualifications, and we can survive on our own anywhere. You're a university professor, and I am a highly paid consultant. So far so good?"

It wasn't, but what the hell. Jeebleh nodded.

"But while our European counterparts belong wholeheartedly to the me idea, you and I belong at one and the same time to the me and the we. After all, we have extended families to clothe and to feed, by fair means or foul. You and I, indeed many of us first-generation schoolgoers, are made up of competing ways of doing things."

Jeebleh didn't agree with the spin that Af-Laawe put on things, his belief that educated Somalis didn't believe in the clan; he, Jeebleh, knew many who did. But he chose not to challenge.

"If you peel away the political rhetoric," Af-Laawe went on, "what you have is a me grievance dressed in we clothing! And with such overriding loyalties, driven by personal ambitions, the invented memories of a me are cast in an imagined we. This way 'me' is reinvented as 'we.'"

To Jeebleh, Af-Laawe's nonsensical double-talk made mockery of his own earlier pronoun fixation, and he was relieved when the waitress came to clear their plates. Af-Laawe ordered a cappuccino, and Jeebleh a double espresso.

As the waitress walked away, Jeebleh said, "Do you have any sympathy whatsoever for the warlords?"

"How can I raise a heart of sympathies for killers?"

AS THEY WALKED BACK TO THE HOTEL, THE STARES OF THE PEOPLE THEY encountered overwhelmed Jeebleh with foreboding. He had no idea why the feeling had come over him. He wanted to be alone, that was his instantaneous reaction. In times of sorrow, he tended to enjoy being by himself. Alas, this was not possible here on unfamiliar ground. He didn't know how to get back, or where the dangers lurked.

As if to reinforce the point, as soon as they walked into the hotel grounds, he saw that the vultures were back in force. And a horde of buzzing flies hovered over a spot as red as fresh slaughter. Ali, the manager, met them in the courtyard, disheveled and distraught; you could see he was the bearer of sad news. Curiously, he spoke only to Af-Laawe, as if Jeebleh, a foreigner, did not understand Somali, or were not there at all.

Shaken by the story he had to tell, Ali spoke confusedly, starting where he should have ended. "There were two of them, both young," he said.

"Two? Who?" Af-Laawe instructed Ali to calm down, not once but several times.

His shirt hanging out, his fly open—something he didn't notice till later—the manager tried two or three times to begin from the beginning. Still, Jeebleh and Af-Laawe failed to understand. Finally he came out with: "One of them was killed."

"But who do you mean?"

"And the other, he was wounded, and has since been captured by our guards, and taken to a nearby hospital, where he is recovering."

The story became clearer in the fourth retelling. Two young men with firearms had sneaked into the hotel, and—with help from a staff member, who had since been fired—got into Jeebleh's suite and hid there. A cleaning woman noticed a suspicious presence and reported it to the reception desk. Hotel security was alerted, there was a scuffle, shots were fired, and one of the intruders died inside. ("You can see his blood on the balcony, although his corpse has been removed," the manager elaborated.) The wounded one was apprehended and interrogated. When he was frisked by hotel security, "incriminating evidence" was found in his pocket.

"What kind of evidence?" Jeebleh asked.

Ali spoke directly to Jeebleh for the first time since their return to the hotel. "He had your name and suite number written on a piece of paper. We've interrogated him, as I've already explained, and even though he hasn't volunteered a lot, we're satisfied with what we've gotten out of him."

"But this is madness!" Af-Laawe said.

The manager sobered up, perhaps at the word "madness." He continued to address Jeebleh, "There's no reason to panic. We'll change your room, give you my suite. It's much more comfortable, and a lot more secure. We'll beef up the security around you. No reason to panic. We'll take care of you, despite what's happened, or what you've done here on my hotel grounds. I guarantee that you're safe with us, safe!"

"Where's the corpse?" Af-Laawe asked.

"In your van."

"And my bags?" Jeebleh asked.

"In my suite, safe."

Jeebleh was relieved that he had had the foresight to leave his valuables with Bile. He decided to call him and ask him to send Dajaal, with a driver, to fetch him. He needed a quiet moment, to contemplate all this madness.

He stood apart, and used the mobile phone. "I need your immediate help, Bile," he said. "It's urgent."

"Where are you, what's happening?"

"I need you to get me away from this place."

"What's happened?"

"A young man found hiding in my room has been shot dead, another has been wounded." Jeebleh's voice was low, charged with a mix of anger and terror; his whole body was shaking. "I've no idea what's happening. I want to leave this place as fast as I possibly can. Please send Dajaal."

"I will."

"Thanks."

"Do be watchful," Bile advised, "and stay calm."

"I will," Jeebleh said, and disconnected. He turned and felt a nervous change in his surroundings. He heard the hotel gate open. A huge man waddled in: Caloosha, making a dramatic entrance.

At once everybody tried to be useful to him, the men at the gate opening it wider, others standing to attention. A handful of bodyguards, among them Kaahin and men he had seen earlier, walked beside him and behind, their guns at the ready. Ali arrived pronto, half running. He stopped a few meters before the visiting VIP, then bowed as if to royalty. Caloosha dismissed everyone, including his bodyguards and the manager, and moved to a café table nearby. He sat down with the slowness of a hippo that had eaten its fill, and summoned Jeebleh and Af-Laawe. As he approached, Jeebleh could tell that Caloosha was in a rage, glowering at Af-Laawe. "Where did you go?"

"To eat," Af-Laawe said sheepishly.

Now Caloosha said to Jeebleh, "Did he drink?"

Jeebleh couldn't control himself. "What does it matter if Af-Laawe has taken a drink? My concern here is about death. Did you have a hand in it? Was I supposed to be here when the youths sneaked into my room? Is this why you're asking Af-Laawe where we went?"

"There's been a lapse in your security," Caloosha said.

He couldn't believe his ears: "A lapse in my security?"

"And Af-Laawe is responsible for it."

"What does 'a lapse in security' mean?"

"Someone who was supposed to be here wasn't."

"And Af-Laawe is to blame?" Jeebleh asked.

Night had descended early in Af-Laawe's eyes, and he hung his head in despair—his ear, in Jeebleh's disturbed thinking, assumed the shape of a full-grown bat.

Jeebleh turned to Af-Laawe. "If there is something you haven't told me, please speak up."

"We were supposed to go to Caloosha's house," Af-Laawe replied, "where you were to meet the clan elders and apologize. But I took you to my favorite restaurant instead. Caloosha thinks that the incident with the dog is my fault too, because I was supposed to keep you company and out of mischief."

"Am I a child, whose every activity must be supervised, lest it be seen as mischievous?" Jeebleh said. "Am I to be told when to apologize to self-serving elders?"

"That's no way to react," Caloosha said.

Jeebleh spoke at the top of his voice, clearly impervious to the reaction of those in his vicinity. "Am I not a venerable elder myself, not of a clan, God forbid, but just a venerable elder? To earn everyone's respect, do I need to put on two robes dipped in mud and then dried before I wear them?"

Caloosha kept silent.

"Who is the dead boy?"

"The son of one of the clan elders, whom you insulted earlier today and sent off empty-handed," Caloosha replied.

"Will there be other deaths because of his?"

"That can't be helped!"

"I don't want any more deaths, not on my account," Jeebleh said. "I forbid you to let your mad dogs loose on the family of the dead boy. There have been enough mindless killings already. I forbid you to kill on my account, my conscience won't allow it."

Caloosha met Jeebleh's earnestness with sarcasm. "Sadly, I don't have a conscience."

"It's high time you reactivated one."

"I'm afraid I cannot," he said, mimicking Jeebleh's serious tone, "as I sold my conscience to the devil to pay for a mortgage on the house of my self-promotion. To date I've survived on the proceeds, and I doubt I want to buy it back, thank you!"

"Hell was invented for your kind."

"I am sure it was!" Caloosha bellowed.

Before either managed to raise the stakes any further, Dajaal was standing there between them, unarmed. Caloosha's bodyguards closed in on him and waited for instructions.

Caloosha held his rage in check, his eyes fixed on Jeebleh, then on Dajaal. "Why are you here?"

"Don't ask me," Dajaal said calmly. "Ask Jeebleh."

Af-Laawe got up and walked to a spot he seemed to calculate as beyond the range of a stray bullet. Caloosha, meanwhile, gestured to his bodyguards to relax.

"I'm going to spend a couple of nights at Bile's," Jeebleh said, "and then decide what to do."

"Why not move in with me?" asked Caloosha.

"Let's talk in a couple of days, and maybe I will." And to the manager, Jeebleh called, "My bags, please!"

"We'll beef up security," Ali promised.

Jeebleh assured him that he had wanted to spend a couple of days with Bile anyway. When he was paying his bill, he saw Caloosha eyeing the manager and shaking his head, indicating that he shouldn't accept the money.

"Take an overnight bag," Caloosha suggested, "and then return in two days. Look how well I compromise!"

"I promise I will visit you, Caloosha!" Jeebleh said. He asked Dajaal to take his bags to the car. He hoped he wasn't making more unnecessary enemies out of Caloosha, the manger, or Af-Laawe. He was determined to buy himself time: to think, to figure out whom to trust, to plot. "I want to see you both," he told Caloosha and Af-Laawe, "when I come to the north. Now, before I go, do you have any news about Faahiye, Raasta, or my mother's housekeeper?"

"We're working on the assignments," Caloosha said, his mockery gentler, even friendly, now.

"Patience!" Af-Laawe added.

Jeebleh waited in silence until everybody seemed relaxed, in particular Caloosha's bodyguards. He stole a glance at Dajaal and by chance intercepted a communication between him and Kaahin. He didn't know what to make of it; didn't know whether he should view it as harmful to his own prospects for survival. Death is your most intimate neighbor when you are in Mogadiscio, Jeebleh thought, as he went out of the hotel gate, speaking to no one but also showing no sign of fear.

PART 2

O vengeance of the Lord . . .
I saw so many flocks of naked souls,
all weeping miserably. . . .
Some lay upon the ground, flat on their backs;
some huddled in a crouch, and there they sat
. . . supine in punishment.

(CANTO XIV)

. . . With all of Ethiopia
or all the land that borders the Red Sea—
so many, such malignant, pestilences.
Among this cruel and depressing swarm,
ran people who were naked, terrified,
with no hope of a refuge or a curse.

(CANTO XXIV)

DANTE, *Inferno*

14.

JEEBLEH WAS IN SUCH DISTRESS THAT HE FELT HE COULD LIVE ONLY ONE minute at a time. He was unable to remember things in any detail; concepts like "an hour ago," "yesterday," "tomorrow," "last week," "next week" were meaningless with all that had taken place.

He was certain that staying on in Mogadiscio would not be the same— even if he had no way of knowing whether his own actions had factored into the killing of the youth in the hotel. He reviewed the events, and everything became suspect. Was the young man running away, out of the room, when the bullet struck him dead? Did he mean to kill Jeebleh, and if so, why? Was it because he had insulted the clan elders, or because he had been kind to the Alsatian in labor?

Disoriented by the urgency of his existence, and stymied by the demands on his time, Jeebleh had acquired other priorities, besides and beyond finding his mother's grave and paying her his respects. He had lost his way in the labyrinthine politics of the place, and the labyrinth seemed to have Caloosha at its center. The man had had a wicked hand in his and Bile's detention; another in encouraging the elders of the clan to call on him to extract the funds they needed; and yet another in having him shadowed from the instant he landed. If he had the wherewithal to have Jeebleh tailed to wherever he went, to "provide him with protection," as he put it, it followed that he also had the means to have him killed if he so chose.

Jeebleh hoped that he wasn't losing his marbles, becoming paranoid and joining Mogadiscio's multitudes of borderline schizophrenics. He remembered Ali's pleading with him, when they first met, not to judge "them" too harshly. Jeebleh was quitting the north of the city, where his clansmen formed the majority, and taking up residence in the south, where Bile's folks reigned. He found it ironic that he felt safer outside his clansmen's territory.

In the car, he broke the silence, saying to Dajaal, "Tell me a little about Kaahin."

Dajaal did not answer immediately. Waiting for an answer, Jeebleh was haunted by two images: in one, Kaahin and Dajaal communicated secretly, in a way that suggested conspiracy; in the other, Caloosha and Dajaal exchanged burning looks. The silence lengthening, Jeebleh noticed that the same driver was taking the same route as before to Bile's. Then a third image came to him: a vulture, the size of a Cinquecento, flying off into high heaven with a baby goat in its claws!

"Kaahin and I were very close at one time," Dajaal said. "We were both army officers, we'd see each other at the mess frequently. And we were tennis partners. But we fell out just before the collapse of the state. Over a family matter."

"You aren't related, are you?" Jeebleh said.

"We could've been, but we aren't."

He fell silent, knowing that this wouldn't make much sense. Embarrassed, he looked away, averting his gaze from the driver too. He rubbed his face, like a monkey reflecting. There was an eerie quiet in the vehicle now, as though all three men had taken temporary residence outside of time, and were dwelling in a nightmare of family disloyalties and dissonance. The driver nodded at Dajaal, as if encouraging him to say what was on his mind.

"We came to fierce blows, Kaahin and I, when I learned that my youngest sister's child was his, and yet he wouldn't own up to it. Lately, since he admitted that he is the biological father of the boy, who is now eleven and living in Canada, we've been meeting to try to work things out."

"Do you meet in secret or openly?" Jeebleh asked.

"In secret, of course," Dajaal said.

"Because it would upset Caloosha?"

"It would, yes," replied Dajaal. "Anyhow, I doubt that Kaahin would talk of this to anyone, least of all Caloosha, who would use it against him. It's not in my favor or his for such things to come to light."

A whirlwind gathered and blocked the sun from Jeebleh's vision. He wondered whether Caloosha's discovery of these secret encounters of Dajaal and Kaahin might start another battle between the warring factions. He imagined fingers on triggers, imagined the joy on the faces of drug-crazed youths shooting and watching, as their victims collapsed in a heap of death.

"Here we are!" the driver said.

WHEN HE AND BILE MET IN THESE CHANGED CIRCUMSTANCES, THE ONE A host, the other a guest, Jeebleh was unable to recall things in as much detail as he would have liked. But he managed to tell Bile what had happened and in little time, fearing that he might not carry the telling through to the end. Bile listened without comment or interruption. When he was finished, Jeebleh felt restless, so he stood and opened the windows, wandered about, and then opened his shoulder bag, out of which he took the books he had brought as gifts. He presented them to Bile without ceremony, and then sat down, again without ceremony.

"Do you feel betrayed?" Bile asked.

"I hurt!"

Still restless, Jeebleh rose again and paced back and forth, agitated one moment, depressed the next, up and moving purposelessly one instant, down and wincing the next. At some point, he was surprised to find himself facing Bile, who had gotten to his feet too.

"Let's go!"

Jeebleh didn't ask where.

HE FOLLOWED BILE DOWN A FLIGHT OF STAIRS AT A RUN; THEN DOWN ANOTHER set of steps, which he approached with caution; past a knot of women, some washing their babies, others busy cooking at braziers; past a group of men sitting uncomfortably on a mat, playing cards.

Jeebleh was becoming two people, one leading a familiar life, the other a life that was unfamiliar; one looking in from the outside, the other looking out from inside. Alive to his surroundings, he was able, with his active side, to spot the security detail shadowing them. He could see Dajaal and two young men tailing them. His more contemplative side wondered whether the civil conflict was being driven as much as greed—the quick gains and limitless profits available for the warlords—as by bloodlust, shedding the blood of others to settle centuries-old scores. He questioned Bile as they walked.

"Money runs the civil war's engine, all right," Bile agreed. "There are the corrupt commissions paid to the warlords for a start, the money they make from hiring out militiamen to foreign delegations on visits. There's the money paid to the warlords in the form of tributes by foreign firms operating in the country. And Mogadiscians also pay other tributes to the warlords, who levy road tax and duties on everything imported through the entry points of the city, which they control."

Jeebleh remembered being stopped in the car, and StrongmanSouth's armed youths in fatigues readying to extort money when they recognized Dajaal. "Why do most vehicles on the roads have plates from the Arabian Gulf, and why do they all look just-bought?" he asked.

"Bringing vehicles in from the Arabian Gulf is a racket, all right!"

Jeebleh waited for an explanation.

"When a vehicle is in an accident and is written off somewhere in Europe or the USA," Bile said, "a mechanic puts it back together and has it repainted, makes it look as good as new. An import dealer brings the reconditioned vehicles into the Gulf, usually into the Emirates, which specializes in import/export. The cars are quickly re-exported to Mogadiscio or Nairobi.

Many vehicles stolen in Europe end up in the Gulf in the same way, and they're sent on to other countries with little or no customs control."

Jeebleh was amazed. "There's a racket everywhere you turn, isn't there? And I bet the rackets are run by the same people who run the guns!"

Bile explained that vehicle owners hired gunmen for protection, and the more expensive the car, the more gunmen needed. But in the earlier days of the civil war, cars had their fuel tanks rebuilt in a way that reduced the fuel intake. In those days it was common to see two-liter plastic containers on the floor of a vehicle, by means of which the engine was fed, through a hose. You couldn't travel great distances, because you ran out of fuel frequently, and had to refuel more often. But your car was safe from potential carjackers.

"An American journalist described Somalia as an ideal model for the rest of the continent," Jeebleh said. "In his view, Africans could do away with governments by studying what's happening in Mogadiscio, where telephones work better now than they did when there was a state. The same journalist pointed out that whereas there used to be only one daily newspaper—the government's mouthpiece—now there are no fewer than thirteen dailies, with opposing views. What do you think?"

"What do I think? Where's this journalist on education?" Bile challenged. "Where is he on providing hospitals, or security and other social services to the ordinary person with no gun? Every Somali not in the pay of a warlord would agree with me that even an inefficient and corrupt government will offer better services than those provided so far by the warlords, who are in the business not of building institutions but of demolishing them. The services may be faulty and faltering in other countries, but any central government, however weak it is, will do better than these murderous warlords and their cartels. Just look at this city! You know what it used to be like."

"Are the warlords subservient to business cartels?"

"As long as they are from the same blood community. Fact: The warlords and the business community stand to profit from every skirmish, every confrontation. Fact: Most fighting takes place outside business hours, in the late afternoon, when the markets have closed for the day, or very early in the morning, before they have reopened, or at night. I would say that the so-called markets have something to do with much of the fighting, but you can't divide business and blood so easily in this country."

"It doesn't look that way from the outside!"

"Of course it doesn't."

Jeebleh murmured to himself: Warlords, market forces!

With subliminal grief on his face, Bile continued, "Some people, as a matter of fact, trace the falling-out of StrongmanSouth and StrongmanNorth to the arrival of billions' worth of Somali banknotes flown in from England, where they had been printed for the former dictator's regime. All hell broke loose when the plane bringing the banknotes in from Nairobi was diverted to an airstrip in the north of the city."

"By StrongmanNorth?" Jeebleh asked.

"The excessive greed of both strongmen produced fragmentation, then a civil war," Bile said. He stopped suddenly and turned to Jeebleh: "Here we are!"

"Where's *here*?"

"The Refuge."

THE GATE SLUMPED ON ITS HINGES, CREAKING FORWARD, ITS BOTTOM EDGE almost touching the ground, its paint flaking off. Jeebleh assumed that it was seldom closed, and imagined children and abused women walking in, the children to be looked after and fed, and the abused women to receive comfort and professional counseling. You didn't need to close such a gate.

As he and Bile passed through, Jeebleh saw a number of bungalows. There was a sign saying "HOYI"—shelter—in prominent capitals, and a smaller one announcing "The Refuge." "In days now long gone," Bile explained, "when schools ran morning, afternoon, and evening sessions, most of these bungalows served as dormitories. Day students of several secondary schools in the neighborhood, whose parents lived in other towns, used to stay here."

They walked past a low-ceilinged cottage where youths in dark overalls were gathered around a broken-down vehicle, being instructed in motor repair. As they walked farther, the din grew louder, and younger too. A bell rang, and twenty or thirty teenagers, most of them boys, came pouring out. Jeebleh and Bile stood aside. A door behind them opened, and more boys and girls, younger than the previous group, came out, running with the uninhibited enthusiasm of youth. The girls were giggly, the boys full of chase. They seemed so much younger than the armed youths at the airport, or the runners at the hotel.

An elderly woman greeted Bile by name, and then acknowledged Jeebleh's presence with a nod. Jeebleh learned that she was in charge of the children, with the help of several younger women. To one side, a man was bending down to tie the shoelaces of a very small girl.

Peace reigned here, Jeebleh thought. Bile had created several overlapping worlds, ideally conceived: the flat he shared with Seamus; The Refuge; the clinic, which Jeebleh had yet to see; and Raasta and Makka's world too, temporarily interrupted as that might be. These worlds were contrasted starkly with what one might experience in the rest of the city. They were oases of comfort in a land of sorrow.

Bile pushed open a door to the anteroom of an office. On the wall were photographs of children, some in school uniform, some not. For a moment, Jeebleh was lost in reverie, forgetting where he was. He stared at images of boys and girls receiving awards from an Italian monsignor. There were captioned photographs of a swimmer receiving a medal, a chess player who had finished second at a competition in Prague, a runner who had been second fastest in a steeplechase competition.

"Did you choose this place?" Jeebleh asked.

"Do you recall what it used to be?"

"I remember we used to call it 'The Dormer.' When we were in our teens, it was a dormitory run by the Roman Catholic Church. It was a home to abandoned children, who were looked after by the fathers. And before that, it belonged to a Sicilian who had named it Villa San Giovanni."

"Well done!" Bile said.

"Now tell me more about it."

As it happened, Bile had walked into the building by chance one day, a few months into the civil war. He was on some errand or other, and for some reason took a detour. Maybe a mysterious force had led him here. He came upon a child in a corner, wrapped in a blanket and smartly dressed in pants and a handsome T-shirt with writing in Gothic script. The presence of the girl in an empty dormitory made no sense, and there was no way of knowing who had left her there. When he returned home with a girl for whom he had no name, Shanta and Faahiye, with whom Bile shared the house then, decided on one for her, because she kept pointing to herself and saying something close to "Marta," or was it "Marcia"? They called her Makka, and sure enough, she responded to it.

They fell silent as a young man entered the office without knocking. He brought them tea on a tray. Bile nodded a thank you and waited until they were alone to speak further. "In another sense, you could say that Raasta brought us all here."

"How's that?"

"Or rather, I should say that Raasta brought her mother here, as a prelude to her being born. And then guess what? Dajaal met Shanta here, again by chance."

"I won't ask what Dajaal was doing here either."

"He was in charge of the force holding the district."

"Go back to Shanta, or how Raasta brought her here."

"It's all fascinating and complicated," Bile said, and paused. "Shanta was very pregnant with Raasta, eight months or so. She had gone to an appointment with an obstetrician, but because of the fierce fighting between the clan militia and the Tyrant's forces, the doctor wasn't there. Shanta had walked a great distance, all the way from Digfar hospital. The fighting between the clan militiamen and the regime was very fierce, bombs were falling everywhere. But at no time, Shanta would tell me later, did she fear for her own life or her baby's."

A handheld radio on Bile's desk came to life, and the static in the room made him silent. They listened as two women talked about provisions for The Refuge, which one of them was supposed to obtain.

When they signed off, Bile continued: "It was probably Shanta's weighty bladder that brought her here. She was in need of a toilet, tired, so she found a bed and fell asleep. Sometime later, after it had gotten dark, Dajaal, who was in command of the group fighting against the Tyrant's forces in the district, woke her up. He went to get her husband, who helped find a midwife. Then Dajaal led me to her, in time to deliver Raasta into the world. So we're all connected to this place!"

DINNER AT THE REFUGE PROVED TO BE AN EYE-OPENER.

Jeebleh had to sit on a mat on the floor. If he needed a reminder that he was physically out of shape, then here it was, drilling pain into his knees, his upper thighs, even his heels. He could not tuck his feet under his body, as the others all managed to do with ease. Even though he ached terribly, he remained in a crouch, and kept changing position. Finally he squatted, balancing himself on the tips of his toes.

"Who are these children, and why them?" he asked.

"In the main, there are periods when there is little or no fighting, and periods when the strife is more intense," Bile replied. "The bulk of the children, those who form the core group, we refer to as 'inmates.' A third of the children you see qualify as 'tourists'—they've fled the fighting in their villages, but they plan to go back when the fighting dies down."

The refectory was noisy. There were younger children, numbering about thirty, and adults supervising their eating. There were teenagers and young men. They sat on the floor, close to where Jeebleh and Bile were sharing a large plate with Dajaal and the driver. There were nine massive plates in all, with seven or eight people to each one.

"We've resorted to the traditional method of eating together daily from the same *mayida*," Bile said, "in the belief that we create a camaraderie and we'll all trust one another. Some might consider hogwash the idea that those who look one another in the eye as they eat together are bound closely to one another. But our experiment bears it out—anyone meaning to do harm to a fellow sharer of the *mayida* will not dare look him, or anyone else, in the eye. Around here we say that many people prefer staying away to coming and sharing the *mayida* when there is bad blood. And when we share the *mayida*, there can be no bad blood."

"A brilliant idea," Jeebleh agreed.

15.

"YOU MUST TELL ME ABOUT RAASTA AND MAKKA," JEEBLEH SAID.

"I'll be very pleased to," Bile replied.

They were now back in the apartment, the light in Bile's eyes suggesting sorrow coming home. For his part, Jeebleh was restless again. They sat on the balcony, a touch of salt in the early-evening breeze.

Jeebleh told Bile that for his own belated benefit, he wanted to know better what had happened on the day the two girls disappeared.

"We've been able to piece together, from talking to two women who work at The Refuge, that Makka was the first to go missing," Bile said. "This is because something unusual occurred earlier that day. A girl around six or seven years old probably, arrived at the gate, dressed in an outfit made up of colorful beads, similar to the kind that bare-breasted Zulu maidens wear. She stood where she was for a good while, but wouldn't come into the compound. Neither of the two women knew who she was, where she came from, who had dropped her at the gate, or picked her up when she eventually left, about twenty minutes later, walking north, vanishing into the mystery that had brought her forth. Makka saw the girl at the same time as the two women did, and soon afterward started acting like she was under some sort of spell, shaking. The two women agree that our Makka was so taken with the girl's beads that she followed her when they were called away to attend to some problem."

"And then what happened?"

"Makka returned, alone," Bile said. "And a short time later, Makka went out again, apparently in search of the beaded girl. The two women remember Makka saying that she had come for Raasta, so they could go 'play beads' with the other girl, or something like that. And she said something about a man and a woman. Many things are not clear."

"And Raasta?"

"Raasta was very agitated to learn that Makka had gone off on her own. And she went in search of her."

"Then?" Jeebleh asked.

"The women saw a fancy car with tinted windows, engine running, parked at a road to the south of ours. By the time we mounted a search in the neighborhood, we couldn't find any sign of the car. A neighbor claims to have seen one of the men. He had shades on, the kind often worn by gangsters in American films."

Jeebleh mused aloud, as though to himself, "I wouldn't have thought that fancy vehicles would be commonly seen in the potholed streets of civil war Mogadiscio."

"There is such a fleet, which once belonged to the now collapsed state," Bile said.

"Is this why everyone assumes that a warlord is behind the disappearance of the two girls?"

Bile picked his words with caution: "To spare her from worrying too much unnecessarily, we haven't told Shanta everything we know. Only the two women and I know about the fancy car."

A long, long silence followed.

"TELL ME MORE," JEEBLEH SAID.

"They're so unalike, it's incredible," Bile said. "But they have become completely dependent on each other, and are beginning to look alike, in their own fashion. You know the story, when a man and his wife have lived together for many years, they begin to sound alike. In fact, Raasta and Makka do sound alike, to a certain degree." Bile paused, perhaps suddenly conscious of his natural use of the present tense, a sign of his belief that the girls were well and unharmed.

Jeebleh remained silent. He did not mention that he had spoken to Caloosha about the girls, because he wished neither to raise Bile's hopes nor to dash them.

"Except for the day of their disappearance, neither girl does anything or goes anywhere without the other knowing about it," Bile continued. "They're like Siamese twins, neither makes a move without the other being there."

"So whoever separated them on the day they went missing knew what they were doing—lure one away and you get the other," Jeebleh guessed. "Could it have been an inside job?"

Bile wasn't ready for speculation. "Where Raasta intimates care, Makka communicates boundless, generous love. No one knows exactly how old Makka is, or how she came to be sleeping in that room at The Dormer where I found her. She's given to kissing, to touching, and to trusting people. There's a smile forever on her lips, and she displays joy at every opportunity, seldom crying, rarely showing any depression, which other children in similar circumstances might. Often I tell myself that she's held together within the framework of a narrative not yet known to us, that she's an untold story. Her every word points to so many unasked questions needing answers. At The Refuge, she is treated with great affection, because of her special qualities. Everyone is kind to her. She smiles crying, and cries earnestly, laughing. Compared with her, I feel a great lack."

This was how he had found her: He heard a bizarre sound coming from what he presumed an integral part of the mystery that is nature. He was in The Dormer all on his own, when he picked up a sound between a gargle, a clearing of the throat preparatory to making a long speech, and a growl, a form of communication more associated with animals not endowed with speech. Once he found the Down's-syndrome girl, a little bundle in the fashionable clothes of a child from a well-to-do family, it had taken Bile several minutes to decide that she was speaking not Somali, but a language that sounded like German. He wished Seamus were there, as he might have

known whether it was German or Flemish or Dutch. Bile could only assume
that she was half Somali, half European, the European half unspecified. The
sounds she had mumbled—deciphered and rearranged in his head—did not
form a phrase, and led him nowhere. She had a nasal form of speech, *n*'s colliding with a handful of *g*'s. It was hopeless to try to understand what she was
saying. It was a lot easier to comprehend Raasta's babbling than to disentan-
gle the jamboree of Makka's words.

Whereas Raasta made progress by great leaps and bounds when it came
to the mastery of language, Makka did not. She was fond of repeating a
stock phrase: *"Aniga, anigoo ah!"* This Somali phrase meaning "I myself
am!" would be considered sophisticated in any language. But was it what
Makka meant to say? Rendering the phrase to Seamus as "Me, myself, I,"
Bile couldn't help wondering whether there was a purpose to the Down's-
syndrome girl. It didn't take long for Raasta to prove to all concerned that
Makka was a genius of sorts. The two girls were friends to peace, to harmony.

Then one day, three years to the day on which she first appeared mysteriously, Makka began to thread and unthread rosaries. She took to doing this
whenever she was awake, busy as someone who had discovered her vocation.
Bile found her as many spools of thread as he could. She was very diligent,
and was blessed with a concentrated look that defined her. It was charming to
watch her, her lower lip distended, a trace of saliva as clear as a raindrop in
the recesses of her open mouth, the wrinkles on her forehead thick as home-
spun cotton. She was in the habit of muttering things to herself, frequently repeating *"Aniga, anigoo ah!"* He thought of the phrase as a unique feature of
Makka's.

She had more words now, thanks to the therapy given to her by foreign
specialists, Irish volunteer teachers who spent a few months at a time at The
Refuge. Makka's words wove themselves into an embroidered pattern—her
ellipses.

A wonder of affection, Makka gave huge kisses—and liberally. Raasta
more than anyone else mined her wealth of emotions from deep down, where
only she could tap, willy-nilly. Hugging Makka to herself, their cheeks touching, Raasta would mumble words, and Makka would repeat after her, altering

the sequence slightly or changing the pronunciation. Then Makka's mouth would remain open, and the words would fail her.

Everyone congregated around them, loving them. The girls helped the others cope with the stormy weather of clan politics. If there was one huge difference between Makka and Raasta, it had to do with memory. Makka was in the moment, and the moment was innocence, pure and simple. She was in no one else's camp, only in her own. She belonged to no clan and to no one but herself. The Refuge provided her with a family, and she provided The Refuge with her absolute loyalty. By contrast, Raasta had been taught who she was, that is to say, what her clan family was, from the instant she opened her lungs with the cry of life.

"What was Faahiye's attitude toward Makka?"

Bile rose in an instant surge of unease. "Just a minute, please," he said, and was gone.

Minutes later, Jeebleh heard a toilet flushing, then footsteps returning.

IT APPEARED THAT BILE HAD REACHED FOR AND RETURNED WITH A NEW VOICE, retrieved from deep within. He was much calmer. "You see," he said, "even though Faahiye may have been present physically, it seemed to those of us in daily contact with him that he was not all there."

"How was that?" Jeebleh asked.

"Some of us felt he was on some sort of suicide trip. He behaved recklessly, going to the areas of the city where deadly fighting was raging. He'd take along a camera, like a tourist on a suicide mission."

"Did he show anyone the photographs he took?"

"He wouldn't even bother to print them!"

"Didn't he train as a lawyer?" Jeebleh asked.

"A lawyer in a lawless land, jobless and unemployable."

"Didn't he commit come of his free time to The Refuge at least? Didn't he help run it?"

"We all wished he had," Bile answered.

Voltaire had said that good, honest work done in God's name banished three of the greatest evils—boredom, vice, and poverty. Thinking about Faahiye's lack of commitment to the jobs at hand made Jeebleh wonder whether he would have been easier to deal with if he had had jobs and worked at them. And would the same have stopped Somalis from going down the inevitable road of self-destruction, self-hate, waste, and famine? Evil and envy gain a solid foothold in the mind of the jobless. His thought led him elsewhere: to sex. Jeebleh imagined that Faahiye was starved of love and sex. He asked Bile as much: "Did sex occupy a prominent place in his mind?"

You might have thought that the earth had been pulled from under Bile. Jeebleh was regretting his question.

"Why do you ask?"

"Yeats said that sex is the subtext of every ruined relationship. Or am I misquoting him?"

"We'll have to ask Seamus about that."

"About Faahiye and sex?"

"No, about Irish poets and sex!"

Jeebleh repeated, "Was sex the subtext in Shanta and Faahiye's embittered relationship?"

"Put that question to them when you see them."

HALF AN HOUR LATER, BILE'S FEATURES HAD ROUGHENED AT THE EDGES, LIKE frozen butter exposed to sudden heat. He said, "I knew very little of what had gone on before I came. But it became obvious that my presence was causing a great upset in the home they had set up for themselves. I admit I was insensitive at first too. Of that I am certain, and I regret it all the time."

"What did you do?"

"We shared a limited space. We were on top of one another, and spent a lot of time together. Shanta and Faahiye quarreled so savagely in the first months of Raasta's life that I moved out and set up my own place, within easy walking distance. By then Faahiye had tried to force himself on Shanta, soon after the traditional forty-day convalescence period. I didn't care to know about it, but I got to hear of it because Shanta told me of her own free will. There were subsequent quarrels, in which he became unbearably offensive, at one time suggesting that Shanta was saving herself for the only man she had ever truly loved, namely me. Then they worked out a modus vivendi agreeable to both. He looked after Raasta in the early hours of the day— Shanta doesn't wake up until noon, she's that kind of person. And she looked after the girl in the afternoons and at night. This way, I managed to have uninterrupted time with Raasta when it was Shanta's turn. It was all very complicated. There were so many borders we couldn't cross, and so many things we couldn't do. It's a great relief that Raasta—and later Makka, when she joined us—didn't collapse into a pair of tearful misfits. I've no idea how, but the two girls knew where the paths to doom and despair lay, and they kept well away from them, thank God."

Bile was in the vortex of a huge sorrow, but he concentrated his mind wholly on the telling of the story. His features took on the darker hue of fabric soaking overnight in water. Now that he was immersed in his sorrow, Bile's expression put Jeebleh in mind of the color of southwestern Nigerian *adire* cloth at its finest.

"Do you think he's taken the girls hostage?"

"I don't know," Bile said.

Jeebleh could see the weight of Bile's gloom lowering him into further despair. His pupils reduced to a darkness extending inward, into infinity.

"With help from Caloosha?"

"I wish I knew," Bile said.

Jeebleh watched another cloud of sadness descending on Bile, much like the one before, an acknowledgment of a huge loss. A few seconds later, he sensed a pale reverie spreading itself over his face.

"The sorrow that's home to us!" Bile cried.

Jeebleh wasn't sure whether Bile was articulating a difficult concept with death in mind, but he was obviously withdrawing into himself, barely aware that Jeebleh was in the room with him.

"I think I am the cause of the hurt of which Faahiye has never been able to speak, given that he is so correct and proper in his demeanor," Bile said. "It's possible, however, that the source of his hurt, which in the end ruined their relationship, was sex, or rather lack of it. Memory is regret! Memory is regret. But what can I say?"

Jeebleh reached out to touch Bile, pat his knee.

"If only he had left when he should have, and taken his wife and daughter with him," Bile said, "things might have been different for all of us. Now sorrow permeates our air, pricks it, and we hurt. Everyone hurts. And there's no hurt like that of an innocent man wrongly accused of a crime he hasn't committed, no hurt like that of a wife spurned, a love not reciprocated, a matrimonial bed abandoned, children turned into battlefields."

Bile held his head between his trembling hands, and Jeebleh was not sure if he heard a faint sobbing. He could hear his friend's breathing, soft like the patter of a baby's footsteps. A big hush, then Bile lifted his head. His cheeks were moist. "It was a real shame!" he said.

"What was?"

"That Shanta accused Faahiye so unfairly."

"Of what? What did she accuse him of?"

"A crying shame!"

"This is why he left?"

But Bile wouldn't go into more detail, he wouldn't answer the question. His head shaking, he would only say, "I believe Faahiye is innocent, a man wrongly accused!"

Jeebleh could think of nothing to respond.

"Let's blame it on the civil war," Bile said remorsefully. "Let's blame it on our sick minds, on the tantrums that belong in our heads. Let's blame it on the endemic violence, the cruelty that's been let loose on the weak. Let's blame it on our damaged sense of self."

"But what did she accuse him of?"

Still Bile wouldn't say, and he left the room.

16.

"HAVE WE GRIEVED ENOUGH?" JEEBLEH ASKED.

"I doubt that we have," Bile replied.

"Do we know how to grieve? And if we don't, why not?"

"I don't know if it is possible to have a good, clean grief when people have no idea how big a loss they have suffered, and when each individual continues denying his or her own part in the collapse."

"Aren't many Somalis mourning?"

"We mistake a personal hurt for a communal hurt," Bile insisted. "I find this misleading, I find it highly unproductive."

Jeebleh recalled Bile's early loss of his own father, allegedly at Caloosha's hands. Seamus had lost his brother, a sister, and his father to sectarian violence in Ireland. Does a child mourn a loss in the same way an adult does? Is there a time limit, a cutoff point after which grieving becomes ineffective?

"How have you coped?" Jeebleh asked.

"I've kept myself infernally busy, and I attend to other people's needs, not mine. I haven't had the time or the strength to grieve or to deal squarely with the ruin that is all around. Instead I wallow in my sorrows often enough, and feel a more profound despair when I think I might have achieved something more substantial if I had intervened politically, and tried to make peace between the warring sides."

"Why haven't you tried to do that?"

"I hadn't realized until seeing you that I jumped in at the deep end on the day I gained my freedom and decided to stay, and when I chose to set up a refuge, look out for Raasta, be close to Shanta, who is forever needy, and not enter what passes for politics hereabouts."

"Is there anybody for you to talk to?"

"It's too late for me to search out interlocutors worth taking seriously and trusting, too late for me to get involved in peacemaking now."

"Why is that?"

"I would be like an ant that got distracted and went out of the line and is now trying to find its way back into the ranks after a storm has disorganized the line."

Bile's worries were posted on his forehead, visible signs of what weighed on his mind. Jeebleh's own restless thinking led him to his preoccupations. Unlike Bile, who had stayed away from "what passes for politics hereabouts," he had taken the plunge into the chaotic energy of the place. Now, as a consequence, he was getting lost in the claims and counterclaims of clan politics.

A cat entered the room as though it had more rights to be there than Bile, the resident of the apartment, or his guest. To judge from the way Bile stared at the creature, they were strangers to each other; Jeebleh sensed an unspoken hostility. The cat looked at Jeebleh, then at Bile, then blinked at them both, and made itself comfortable as only cats can in a place where they do not belong. It took its feline time, stretching, yawning, looking at them again. It looked at Jeebleh and smiled, then at Bile without smiling, and caressed its whiskers, Jeebleh thought, in the brooding manner of a man pretending to be thinking.

"Have you met StrongmanSouth?" Jeebleh asked.

"I've never met him, and I have no desire to shake the hand of a murderer," Bile said. "Nor would I want anyone to misunderstand the purpose of my visit, if I were to visit him, and give it a clannish spin, considering that we belong to the same bloodline, he and I. I've chosen to take my distance from him, not least because I want everyone to know that I do not approve of his murderous policies, precisely because The Refuge is in the territory under his nominal control."

"Have you considered asking him to give a hand in recovering Raasta and her companion? After all, the abduction took place in the territory under his nominal control."

"To what end?"

"You don't think he will help?"

"I am doubtful that he will."

"But do you think he knows of the abduction? Might he even be behind it? Or do you feel that he won't help you in any way, knowing that you are a man of peace and he is not?"

If one's life was made up of a million moments of truth, Jeebleh thought, his sending off the clan elders and his subsequent intervention on behalf of the Alsatian were among his *momenti della verità*, actions that were undeniably significant, leading, as they did, to a sea change in him. It wouldn't do to dwell on these grave moments of truth.

At long last Bile spoke, but only to say, "I don't know."

"Why haven't you been in touch with Caloosha?" Jeebleh asked.

Bile looked quizzically at Jeebleh: Had he too heard a knock on the door? A moment later, their gazes traced the tapping to a sparrow throwing its weight against the windowpane. The cat looked up expectantly. Bile rose, hesitating over whether to let the bird in or not, and then opened the window to let the sparrow decide. The bird flew in, wheeled around the room, turned, and flew off, safe.

"I wish not to have any dealings with either Strongman or Caloosha," was all Bile was prepared to say.

"A boy murders his brutal stepfather in cold blood," Jeebleh said. "Does such a boy, who has suffered years of cruelty at the murdered man's hands, mourn his death? Does the son of the murdered man, a half brother to the killer, mourn the loss of a father he's never known?"

When Bile didn't react, Jeebleh recalled the words of Bile's mother, couched in regret, referring to her own role in raising Caloosha. "It's very difficult," she had said, "to rid yourself of the monster whom you've given birth to yourself, fed, raised, and looked after, and then let loose on the world." She was responding to the clan elders, who were all men, and their tendency to blame women and point to what they called "the lax side of a mother's nature." Caloosha had killed his stepfather, yet the clan blamed his mother for it.

HAGARR, THE MOTHER OF CALOOSHA, BILE, AND SHANTA, MARRIED THREE times. She was a strong-minded woman, and didn't hesitate to do as she wanted. When the opportunity to go to Italy on scholarship to train as a midwife presented itself soon after the *nikaax*, her engagement, she went, in opposition of her future husband's wishes. Later, when he suggested that she give up working, because he could afford to provide for her and their son, Caloosha, she refused to do so. She was one among a handful of Somali women who had finished their secondary education, and could earn their own keep, and she dreaded the thought of relying on a man's handouts. A woman with foresight, she knew that the day wasn't far off when her husband would look for and find a younger, prettier woman, one prepared to do a wealthy man's bidding. And as soon as this happened, Hagarr insisted on a divorce.

She moved out of his house into that of her elder brother, where she and Caloosha, then a three-year-old, were given a room with a separate entrance. It wasn't long before she discovered that sharing space with her sister-in-law was no easy matter. She found accommodation in a rooming house, and hired a series of young maids to look after her son. She didn't care when society accused her of what some called "dereliction of duty as a mother." But she was bothered when her husband threatened her with court action.

Caloosha was a very difficult child to raise. He was impossible to discipline, and he displayed unusual cruelty early on. Already at age three he was adept at throwing knives, the way you throw darts at a dartboard, though he preferred living targets. He lit matches out of mischief, nearly setting the house on fire. Many of the young women Hagarr hired to look after him left within a short time.

She had her job and made a sufficient income, but Caloosha was too great a challenge for her to raise as a single mother. So she contracted a second marriage, as she believed that the boy needed the sobering hand of a male to bring his wild, satanic cruelties under control. Within a month of the wedding, there was considerable change in Caloosha's behavior. He was much more restrained in his dealings with the house help, and was calmer, less prone to violence. Hagarr attributed this to her husband's calming influence. But then she discovered bruises on the boy's body. Once his eyes were swollen shut for days, his nose bled, and his wrists and back were sore. It turned out that her husband was in the habit of tying Caloosha's feet together and hanging him upside down. Hagarr came home from work one day and found her son hanging there. She didn't know what to do, short of threatening her husband to move out. The trouble was, she was close to having their first child, her second. And even though he had been beaten to the point of death, Caloosha seemed to have made peace with his own and his stepfather's violent natures. He never complained. He took the beatings "as a man."

Caloosha was nine and in the second grade at school when he had a particularly unpleasant altercation with his stepfather. A few days later, his stepfather was found dead, a poisoned arrow stuck in his throat. Hagarr was away on night duty. According to the two sisters of the dead man, who'd shared a room with the boy, there were no untoward noises during the night. Only the following morning, when the maid knocked on their door, did they learn of their brother's death. He was buried the same day. There was suspicion that Caloosha had shot the poisoned arrow, but there was no proof. The boy showed no outward signs of guilt.

Hagarr went to her grave believing that her son had killed her second husband. And Bile would insist, at least in public, that he bore his half brother no grudges for seeing to an early grave the man who had fathered him.

JEEBLEH AND BILE SAT WITH THE COFFEE TABLE BETWEEN THEM. JEEBLEH was studying the photographs in an album: Raasta in her mother's arms, in her father's, the pictures showing clearly how engaged she had been since birth. The gaze of the one-week-old followed the movements of the photographer.

Now he wanted to know what Bile's first thoughts were when he joined Shanta and Faahiye.

"I feel embarrassed when I look back," Bile told him. "Regrettably, I haven't shared my shame with a living soul. It grieves me to remember what I did."

A hush, as quiet as early-evening shadows, descended on Bile's face. He tilted his head slightly toward Jeebleh, in the posture of a pet being stroked.

"Why is that?" Jeebleh asked.

"I wanted to touch," Bile said.

"Just to make physical contact?" Jeebleh recollected the urge to make contact when his solitary confinement came to its abrupt end. "I remember that feeling."

"I wanted to be touched," Bile said, "to be held in a human embrace. The desire to touch and be touched was so great that I nearly smothered everyone I met with a hug. I'd have been one of the happiest men on earth, if someone had touched me and I had touched them, innocuously, but lovingly too."

"How did you satisfy the urge?"

"When I look back on those days, I recall being alive, free—but alas, I lived in a house that wasn't my house, with a sister I hardly knew, whose husband I didn't get on with, and I had plenty of money that wasn't mine. The first few days, I thought about my mother, who wasn't a physical person, maybe because, as a midwife, she looked on the human body as a shoemaker looks on leather—not intimately. Shanta was a touch-touch person and, when she was young, would cuddle up to you. Caloosha was so cruel he didn't 'touch' you—you know that yourself—he hurt you. Often I remembered with pleasure the women I had loved, especially the women who had touched me where I liked to be touched, and whom I touched where they liked me to touch. I was in a needy, touch-me-please mood when I met Dajaal, soon after I gained my freedom."

"And he dropped you off at Shanta and Faahiye's?"

"That's right. As it happened, I walked in through the front gate and heard a moan, which had some urgency to it. Dajaal had alerted me to Shanta's condition as soon as I introduced myself to him. I suppose the groan I heard helped make the urge to touch less important, for a while at least. And before long, I was washing my hands and rolling up my sleeves, ready to get down to work.

"I wish I had seriously considered the ethical implications of a brother delivering his younger sister's baby, but there was no time—the lives of the mother and the baby weighed heavily in favor of an intervention, mine. These were abnormal times. There were no hospitals functioning, and I had no way of finding another doctor to help my sister. So I did what I had to, and got down to work right away, conscious of the conditions I was working in, which were far from ideal."

"And where was Faahiye all the while?"

"He was there, all right."

"Doing what?"

"I seem to remember that he was as nervous as an adolescent," Bile said. Raasta was their first baby, the first for both. His anxiety grew, and he kept knocking at the door, coming in and going out, and putting sophomoric questions to me.

"I had no idea he would want to hold his baby as soon as she opened her lungs with the welcome of life. Not many Somali men would want to hold a baby soon after birth. For me, however, everything was unreal, and I took delight in touching, hugging, being touched and hugged, because I didn't remember what I had just done—helped at the delivery of my sister's baby, which by medical standards in our country is unethical. We quarreled over who would hold her longer.

"I hadn't the calmness of mind to comprehend why Faahiye was fussing, or sulking, and why he was walking out of the room. Whenever I didn't hold her, I regretted my error of judgment, regretted that I was hogging my niece's company, and regretted that I didn't take into account the fact that Faahiye was as eager to hold and touch the baby as I was. Only it was too late. We were two men of advanced age, one a father, the other a maternal uncle, and we were ready to fight over a baby, just born! But never in her presence."

"And then?"

"My sister was dead to the world for much of the first day, and when she came to and held the baby, she spoke of how she had fallen under a quiet spell. We sensed calm within ourselves whenever we were close to Raasta, and if we had to fight or argue, we would go out of the room where she was. She mattered to us all, because she guaranteed our safety. She was a child born to peace, she was an alternative to attrition. She was a protected person, so anyone physically close to her would be protected too. That's what we believed."

Jeebleh asked, "What became of the duffel bag?"

"I had clean forgotten about it," Bile said. "Faahiye found it in the house and confronted me, asked where I had gotten the cash. We argued, and he accused me of robbery and murder. I was at peace with myself, and my conscience was at peace with the truth, as I knew it, and I knew I was no murderer or robber. But I had a problem explaining, and felt affronted by Faahiye. I was hurt. We got off to a bad start. That was what it was. And then there was Shanta's sickness."

"What was the matter with her?"

"She had an acute inflammation, which worsened soon after she started breast-feeding. This led to abscesses. Within a day, her breasts were swollen, and because there was increased hardness toward their lower edges, I decided the baby should be bottle-fed. But then Faahiye forbade his daughter to be fed on powdered milk bought with looted money. Shanta told us that as a woman she didn't want to become a victim of what she said were 'men's endless petty quarrels over matters she considered to be of no importance.' To her, what mattered was that the baby had milk, not where the milk came from, or in what form. Faahiye sulked. It was all pretty horrid."

In another long silence, the two friends looked at the cat, now busy pulling at a doll into which it had dug its powerful claws.

"SHANTA'S TROUBLE IS THAT SHE IS SHANTA!"

"What do you mean?" Jeebleh said.

"She describes herself as having her hands tied with a rope of tears. By which she means she cannot help being weepy," Bile responded. "But she can be equally tough, and refuse to compromise. When she's in an obstinate mood, she becomes a tit-for-tat person, and lets the world burn in its ashes."

Bile explained how proud he was of her politics, what he called her "civic consciousness," and how she would engage Caloosha's politics with foolhardy courage. "Since Raasta's disappearance, however, she's started to demonstrate worrying signs of change. While she still despises his intimacy with the warlords, she's moved closer to Caloosha ideologically, not least when it comes to clan politics."

"How does Faahiye react to this?"

"He belongs to the old world! He can be deferential to a fault, at least in public," Bile said. "But he can prove hard to take in private, reducing all Shanta's grievances to a woman's nagging, a naught. All the same, he behaves in an upright, old-world manner, like a man who believes in his own dignity and in the honor of the family. In contrast, she is given to outbursts, and to making a spectacle of herself in public."

"What's been your relationship with him?"

"We've been civil with each other, as in-laws, ever since he accepted my explanation of how I came by the money in the duffel bag."

"That's a relief."

"We got along quite handsomely until he disappeared," Bile said. "He and I never exchanged a harsh word over his and Shanta's difficulties, for I saw how this was an affront to him. I stayed out of it as well as I could. I tried to intervene by speaking to my sister when things got out of hand, or when, in my presence, she behaved in an ill-mannered way."

"How did he behave when she flipped?"

"He was very restrained."

"Even when her behavior became unbearable?"

"There was the occasion when she made uncouth comments, described him as sex-starved, and claimed that he wanted her to 'give' it to him every night. I remember how he looked at her as an adult might look on a spoiled child," Bile said.

Jeebleh said nothing.

"There's nothing sadder than when someone you love takes leave of her senses right in front of you. Nothing as disturbing as when a well-brought-up, sane woman behaves uncontrollably badly in public."

It was time to change the subject. "Who named her Raasta?" Jeebleh asked.

"We named her Rajo, in the belief that the girl represented every Somali's hope. But then people misheard it as 'Racho,' and we didn't want anyone to assume she was an orphan, so I nicknamed her 'Raasta,' on account of her dreadlocks. She was born with beautiful natural curls, which when washed, stayed as firm as jewels."

Jeebleh remembered a detail from several articles he had read about Raasta and The Refuge, which stated that many people lived under the aegis of the dreadlocked girl. He hoped he could meet her before he left.

Bile yawned, mumbling about wanting to rise early, and Jeebleh agreed that they should turn in. But neither moved or said anything for a while. Then Jeebleh asked, "Do you think it will be possible for me to visit Shanta?"

"She'll be happy to see you, I'm sure."

"Maybe I can try to see her tomorrow?"

"I'll arrange the visit," Bile said.

17.

JEEBLEH WOKE WITH A NAGGING ANXIETY ABOUT HIS IMPENDING VISIT with Shanta, worried that he might upset her more in her already weepy state. He wondered if he shouldn't postpone the visit until more was known about the fate of the girls.

He wished more people would speak in a tongue of regrets, as Bile had suggested in his meandering way when they talked earlier, and instead of insisting that they are not to blame, would admit to their part in the collapse, to their culpability in the failure. Maybe then they would benefit from Bile's humility, his honesty and magnanimity, these being assets in themselves, and seldom found in the same person.

There were night shadows and foreboding silences in the bedroom. He thought he had heard noises after midnight, and he wondered whether Bile had sneaked out of the apartment, like a man embarking on a dangerous mission, or a lover honoring a late appointment with a partner. He had exchanged good-night greetings with Bile soon after their conversation, ready to drop into the comforting well of a deep sleep.

The day before, he had called home and given his wife and daughters his doctored version of the truth, notable for its omissions. His wife, who knew him better, queried his decision to move south.

"I couldn't stand staying in that hotel."

"But you've often spoken of the excessive violence in the south of Mogadiscio," his wife said. "Does it make sense for you to move there?"

Jeebleh replied with a formidable sangfroid: "I've moved in with Bile, that's how I see it. What's more important now, anyway, is that I feel safer in his company and in the setup here."

He exchanged a few words with his daughters, to whom he offered more of the same waffle. He interpreted his action as the acceptable behavior of someone being protective toward his family. There was no reason to make them worry unnecessarily.

Jeebleh thought that he may have been woken by a ringing telephone, but he wasn't sure. He looked at the clock—about three in the morning—and decided to get some water from the kitchen. On his way, he noticed the door to Bile's room was wide open, and the bed empty. He thought of attaching the door chain for security, but he wasn't sure if, or when, Bile might return. He stayed awake for quite a while, reading, then fell asleep to the sounds of the displaced families lodging in the improvised spaces below the apartment. Much later he heard a key turning as the door was gently locked from the inside, and chains and bolts being put on. He lay obstinately asleep, like a schoolchild at wake-up time. His unconscious got to work, and he had a dream in which peahens played their part in a young woman's self-arousal. How intriguing!

At eight in the morning or thereabouts, a gentle knock on the apartment door woke him. When he came out of his room, he saw several pieces of luggage in the corridor. Probably Seamus's, he deduced from the fact that the door to Seamus's room was closed. So who could be knocking? When he asked who it was, Bile responded, "The breakfast man is here!"

To let Bile in, Jeebleh removed the chains, of which there were at least three, then slid back the bolts, of which there were two. He wasn't convinced that these impediments would stop a determined man, armed and ready to shoot his way in. All the same, it took him an inordinately long time to get the hang of undoing the chains and bolts, and Bile had to instruct him what to do when he got stuck. Finally, he unlocked a padlock on which he set eyes for the first time, a lock in a class of its own, an Italian-made affair as big as a full-grown gorilla's jaws. When he had pulled the door open and faced Bile, Jeebleh confessed that he had had no idea there was so much hardware on the door. "I doubt there is anyone in the world who's as clumsy with bolts and chains as I am!"

"I know several people who won't even have locks," Bile told him, as he walked in, carrying a professionally packed takeout breakfast. "Since arriving in Mogadiscio, Seamus has developed a fad for bolts, heavy-duty locks, and chains. Being from Belfast, he'll tell you that he knows what guns do to people, and that he's seen it all. Which is why he refuses to keep or own guns."

"How many bolts, how many chains, my God!"

Bile said, "When you share an apartment in a violent city, you accommodate each other's sense of paranoia. We bolt it up, chain and lock it, because it eases Seamus's paranoia. He refers to this"—he touched the Italian padlock, heavier than a gorilla's head—"as the 'humor-me padlock,' and you can see him holding it in his lap and caressing it, as though it were a cat or a baby!"

"The choices one makes!" Jeebleh said.

"Seamus has developed another obsession."

"What can that be?"

"He loves the sound of chains against chains, loves what he refers to as the handsome feel and sexy sight of heavy-duty padlocks. These turn him on. One of his lovers in Milan gave him the contraption as a present. When he got back to Mogadiscio, he brought it out and spoke of it in the most glowing terms. He might have been a herdsman talking of his favorite she-camel, praising her."

"Would you say Seamus is a fetishist?"

"What do you mean?" asked Bile.

"Of chains, locks, and bolts."

"He is."

"What's your take on lock, bolt, and chains?"

"When we're together, he locks up," Bile said, "I open up."

Since there was a logic built into the relationship between these two bachelors, Jeebleh wondered what his job was going to be in a threesome flat share. Bile went toward the kitchen with the breakfast package, avoiding the seven pieces of luggage in the corridor.

"When did he get here?" Jeebleh asked when Bile returned.

"He rang at an ungodly hour," Bile said, "and told me that his flight from Nairobi had landed just before dark at an airstrip in Merka, he had no idea why. He managed to get a lift from the airstrip, which is about a hundred kilometers from where we are, to a guesthouse in the north of the city. But the manager of the guesthouse had no place for him. It is a house for European Union officials visiting on short missions in Somalia. I was at a friend's house, but Seamus managed to get me on my mobile, and I arranged for Dajaal to bring him to the house where I was. It was in the dead of a dangerous hour in Mogadiscio, close to three in the morning. Then I drove him here."

Good breeding kept Jeebleh from asking Bile where he had spent the night, or with whom. In the old days, it was Seamus who always told you everything about his one-night stands, provided you with their first names or aliases, gave you the size of their brassieres, informed you what they liked and didn't, how they kissed, or whether they were sloppy in bed or not. Details of Jeebleh's own infrequent forays came out sooner or later at Seamus's badgering. Bile, however, was unfailingly discreet; he wouldn't tell you a thing.

Jeebleh said, "I bet Seamus won't stir until midday."

"Always dead to the world in the mornings, our Seamus."

After a pause Bile asked, "Would you like an espresso?"

"If it's homemade and by your good hands, I would. A double!"

JEEBLEH TOOK A BITE OF HIS BRIOCHE. THE HONEY RUNNING DOWN HIS chin reminded him how much he used to enjoy these delicacies. It was comforting that life had plotted to bring the three of them together again, all this time after their days in Italy, and he couldn't help praying that they would still live in the country of their friendship.

The espresso was majestic; there was no other word to describe it. Full of vigor, stronger than the kick of a young horse. It was dark, grainy, and concentrated like a Gauloise. It reminded him of their days in Padua, and he was tempted to ask for a cigarette even though he had abandoned the habit two decades earlier. Life was young in those smoke-filled days, days full of promise, all three friends eager to make their marks on the societies they had come from. Dreaming together, the three inseparable friends, and the two women whose presence became de rigueur for Seamus and Jeebleh, smoked their lungs away, and consumed great quantities of espresso.

In those long-ago days, you would see Seamus going off lonely and alone into the darkened moments of memory, as he recalled what had happened to his family in Belfast, blown up in their own apartment, a grenade thrown through an open window from a passing car. He had lived with constant worry about sudden death. He would talk like a man deciding to forget, but not forgive. And he would remind you time and again that two brothers, a sister, and his father had died in the massacre; only he and his mother had survived, because they happened to be out. Mother Protestant, father Catholic, he had been brought up to live as inclusive a life as he could, in which sectarian differences were never privileged. And then the massacre. He was hard-pressed to know what to do. There was something in the way Seamus told the story that made Jeebleh think that he had exacted revenge. And on several occasions he had heard Seamus screaming in his sleep, "The bloody dogs are done!"

Bile now asked Jeebleh, "Did you sleep well?"

"Yes, I did. I dreamt too."

"Do you feel like sharing your dream?"

"I saw a one-eyed, five-headed, seven-armed figure," Jeebleh told him. "Maybe you'll help me interpret it, the way you used to."

"Was the one-eyed figure with multiple heads dancing?"

"Yes."

"Were there voices in the background chanting narrative sequences to the tale being mimed?"

"How have you worked out all this?"

"Just answer my question."

"Yes."

"And was the movement of the figure with the multiple heads extravagant, the gestures now rapid, now deliberately slow, and were the index finger and the thumb held away from the rest of the body, and the arms of the dancer shaped into a wide circle?"

"Yes again."

Silence settled on Jeebleh, as if permanently. He remembered the calmness as he watched the figure dancing, and saw several faces known to him. He was sorry he couldn't put any names to the faces—maybe they were from an earlier life, now forgotten.

"Was the figure garlanded and in costume?"

"Y-e-s!"

"Hindu deities have a way of presenting themselves in movement," Bile said, "some boasting an enormous headgear and the costume to go with it, others arriving while riding a rat. I'm thinking of Ganesh, whose intercession is sought whenever a Hindu embarks on a journey or an enterprise, whose potbellied image, with an elephant trunk and tusks and shiny countenance, is paramount at the entrance to a great number of temples." Bile rubbed his palms together excitedly and asked with a grin, "Was there a peacock?"

"There was a peahen!"

"Not a peacock?"

"Why do you ask?"

"Because you saw Mira in your dream—a peahen!"

"Mira?"

"Miss Mira Meerut," Bile said. "Our—that's to say, Seamus's—Mira from the city of Meerut, India, possibly the most beautiful woman to join our tables in Padua. She was in love with Seamus."

Jeebleh's ears throbbed, the skin tightening, the rhythm unnerving, his heart beating faster and faster. "Mira wasn't from India," he corrected. "She was of Indian origin, all right, but she was from Burma."

Bile agreed that she may have been traveling on a Burmese passport when they met her, but she was from southern India, culturally speaking. Her parents had migrated from Gujarat, in western India.

"She was the one who brought along a couple of exquisite woodcarvings," Jeebleh said. "I remember those."

"That's right," Bile confirmed. "She was besotted with Seamus, who, in turn, was besotted with the carvings. The figure he fell for was caught in the process of movement. Such a vivid rhythm, I recall. We had it on our mantelpiece in the apartment in Padua."

"I remember that there were carvings," Jeebleh said, "but my memory of that particular carving is vague."

"She was a beauty," Bile said. "She wore peacock feathers and what a train of sari colors, of a silk I've never seen anywhere else. I was smitten with her too, but I dared not speak of it. She was breathtakingly beautiful, irresistibly charming, her almond eyes exceptionally large and in constant motion. I can't believe you don't remember her. Miss Mira Meerut moved about with a large following of admirers. She was like a peacock with a harem of peahens. Until she met Seamus."

Mira's father, Bile related, was a diplomat based in Rome—or was he with a UN agency? In addition to her striking beauty, she was also a first-class brain. She was ready for her finals, when her parents made her withdraw from the university because she was pregnant. Bile took this personally, because he was the only person in whom Seamus had confided that he was the baby's father. To intercede on her behalf, and ask that she be allowed at least to take her finals, Bile presented himself at Mira's parents' apartment. An Italian woman opened the door when he rang the bell, and told him she was the new tenant. Bile learned that Mira and her parents had left the country, precise date unknown. He found this difficult to believe, and he walked from room to room in the apartment, hoping that somehow he would find Mira or her parents. The only trace of her he discovered was a drawing of a peacock in green-and-blue blossom, with a cropped tail. Bile took ill, and barely passed his exams that year. "And guess what?" Bile asked.

"What?"

Bile faltered as he spoke. "Mira Meerut was here in Mogadiscio less than two years ago, as a UNICEF consultant. She was the mother of two children, and the happy wife of a man several years her junior, an American. She was stunningly pretty, but not as free-spirited and wide-eyed with wonder as when we met her. She had resigned herself to being the ordinary wife of an ordinary American financier, on whom she doted. And when she and Seamus met, they had a ball remembering the good times, and even enjoyed recalling the bad times, the very depressing moments. But she wasn't at all pleased to learn from Seamus that he had left the woodcarving in storage in New York, and didn't take it along everywhere he went."

"How fortunate that her tour of duty here coincided with Seamus's presence," Jeebleh said. "I bet it was wonderful for you to see a train of saris and to relive the past."

"She was deeply hurt, though."

"And she didn't hide it?"

Bile shook his head no.

"How did you figure out my dream?"

Bile said, "You may not have remembered it for what it was, because there's a photograph of Mira, taken by Seamus, on the wall in Raasta's room. You probably saw it before you fell asleep, and the image of this stunning woman in motion insinuated itself into your dream. She still loves Seamus!"

"It is possible that my deep unconscious also became aware of Seamus's presence in the apartment. Maybe the dream is in part a recognition of his arrival, a welcome event."

And suddenly Seamus was there: in full flesh, grinning.

18.

JEEBLEH'S EYES WERE TOUCHED WITH A SMILE THAT SPREAD SIDEWAYS
to his cheeks and down to his chin. Seamus's eyes, like a falcon's, were a dark
brown, the pupils hardly visible.

Jeebleh held his breath in suspense, waiting to hear which language Seamus would speak. When they met last, in Padua, they used Italian. Would
Seamus, knowing that Jeebleh had now lived in the United States for close to
twenty years, choose English? In those long-gone days in Italy, the world had
been in flux, but now things were very different, and they were meeting in
Mogadiscio; both were keenly aware of this.

"We're all jumpy, aren't we?" Seamus had chosen English.

Jeebleh guessed from his tone of voice that Seamus would not lapse into
some piss-elegant Irish English as he used to. He had lived in England during his teens, then had gone on to Cambridge, where he had taken his first degree. And he had spent time in Italy, France, and Egypt.

"Understandably jumpy," Jeebleh agreed.

Seamus came closer and said, "Never you mind, we'll sort it out." He
opened his arms wide. "But let me give you a good, warm welcome hug to
comfort you!"

Seamus was a well-built, beer-drinking man. He was as tall as he was
wide, and sported a liberally grown beard, the kind a devout Sikh might wear

to a temple on a Guru's remembrance day and be showily proud of. He had beady eyes, bloodshot red, and thin arms that made his wrists appear scraggy. Physically, he had changed greatly since he and Jeebleh had last met. Younger, of course, and handsomer then, he had been much leaner too, clean-shaven and with a waist that might have been the envy of many a model. But Jeebleh would have recognized him anywhere, despite his girth.

Jeebleh let go first, so as to hold his friend at a look-and-see distance, and eventually to hug him yet again, even if briefly and more for effect.

Bile, who had been standing nearby, watching the goings-on, now sneaked out of the apartment. Neither friend paid him mind.

"Mogadiscio has been awful to you!" Seamus said.

Jeebleh noted a characteristic of Seamus's that hadn't changed: he exploded into a room, like a missile arriving on the quiet and detonating with a rush of excitement. His entry today was not as dramatic as it used to be, and he was quieter on the whole, growing only moderately louder the more he spoke. Would he make his usual sharp, insightful comments? Jeebleh, who associated him with an impressive presence, wore a wary expression, similar to that of a dog on whose pee-marked territory a wily cat has begun to trespass.

"My clansmen have been awful."

Seamus went to the kitchen to make coffee, and Jeebleh followed. Seamus had unkempt fingernails, edgily bitten and dirty. His toenails were long, so long they put Jeebleh in mind of a museum postcard of a Neanderthal man in all his excessive wildness, as imagined and drawn by a modern illustrator. Jeebleh guessed that his wife's remarks about unruly toenails would have cut Seamus to the quick, and made him deal with their disorderliness. Maybe he could grow his fingernails and toenails as long as he pleased because he wasn't sharing his life or his bed with a partner.

"Bile's told me how they behaved, your clansmen," Seamus said. "What a repulsive lot! Fancy asking you to pay for the repairs of *their* war machine. Do they think you are a warlord? They don't know you as well as some of us think we do. But what cheek!"

"I told them off."

"Glad you told them to sod off!" Seamus was getting a little excited, and louder. "I know how you feel. I told mine off, whingers the lot of them. I told them to naff off, the moaners. I was a little tyke then, and I haven't lived in Ireland since, because of my family. How I hate whingers. But you want to know what I think? I think you must be careful next time you meet any of them, if there is a next time. They'll stick a knife in your back, easy as taking a toffee from a baby. They're all plunderers, every single one of them. But then, you know that, don't you?"

"I do!" Jeebleh agreed.

"And they bury you fast here," Seamus said.

"Don't worry. I won't let them."

"Good for you!"

"I refuse to die. My family wouldn't want me buried here. My wife is an American, you know, and calls this place 'a jerkwater of a ruin.' I've other responsibilities elsewhere, a loving family to love."

"Glad to hear it."

There was a brief pause.

Jeebleh said, "It's lovely to see you."

"You know what pisses me off?" Seamus said.

"Tell me."

"What pisses me off no end is how easily they dispense with the formality of a postmortem. They cart you off and away with the enthusiasm of a two-pot screamer heading for the pub, murmuring a few verses. I won't stand for any of that. I've drawn up my will, and Bile has a notarized copy of it in the event of anything unexpected. I don't wish to be planted in the earth fast. In fact, the mere thought of it kills me. I've provided Bile with a pile of cash locked in the safe. I want to be flown out of here, with the leisured slowness of an Irishman, and I want a wake and lots of drinking and feasting. That's what I want!"

Then all at once, he wore an expression that Jeebleh didn't know how to interpret. He remembered Seamus's charming cheekiness, his posturing, his clowning.

"How's your mother?" Jeebleh asked.

Seamus looked sad, and exhausted from jet lag. The color rose in his cheeks, and he said, "She's tough as nails, and obstinately holding on. Thanks for asking." His eyes dimmed and after a pause he said, "Sorry about yours. Please accept my belated condolences."

Jeebleh looked steadily at Seamus as he poured coffee from the espresso machine into two cups, then passed one over. "Tell me your latest," he said, "and then let's work our way back to when we last met."

"I've just come from Ireland," Seamus said, obliging, "with a duffel bag of money to top up what Bile and I had between us, so we can keep The Refuge going until we run out of charity money again. As you can see, we're all fine, may God help us, and the fat is not in the fire yet! We're optimistic, despite the disappearance of our dearest, Raasta and Makka."

"I'm not sure Bile's told me how you got here the first time," Jeebleh said. "If he has, I don't remember. Anyway, he and I still have to catch up with each other. It is a bit of a blur, all that I've learned. So why Mogadiscio?"

Seamus was so still that Jeebleh thought he had seen a green-eyed fairy. "My life was gathering dust," he said, "cobwebs forming in the corners, because of my nine-to-five job. The more the dust gathered, the more fits of uglies I had. I traveled a lot, but my travels were always work-related. I would spend a week in New York, two in Bangkok, a couple of days in Melbourne, then a month in New York, and another in Nairobi, always traveling and always working. I was in terrific demand as a simultaneous interpreter, and the pay was top-notch. I couldn't complain about being everyone's favorite, but it was getting to me."

"What's wrong with pegging away at work?"

"I hated becoming a gun for hire," Seamus said. "You'll remember I speak seven languages that are understood in areas of the world held apart by the guttural, the tonal, the diphthong, and other tongue-twisting differences. Well, I was on the road for long stretches of time. I made pots of money, but that wasn't good enough, and I was on the verge of freaking out. I was lonely, and my life felt as though it had no purpose."

Jeebleh said, "What passport do you travel on?"

"British."

"Your loyalty lies with Britain or Ireland?"

A lightning sense of humor flashed in Seamus's eyes, and he grinned. When Jeebleh looked at him, puzzled, Seamus said, "Funny you should ask that."

Jeebleh waited patiently. In Padua, Seamus used to describe himself as "a colonial"! And since he was at a loss to find an equivalent word in Italian, he would often just use the English, and explain it to those who had no idea what he was talking about.

Now he said, "My loyalties do not lie with the Union Jack, for sure. Mine's an all-inclusive Irish loyalty, with a good measure of cosmopolitanism. The idea of owing allegiance to a country is foreign to me."

"You haven't answered, Why Mogadiscio?"

"Because Mogadiscio was *there*, in Africa!"

"What about Mogadiscio? What about Africa?"

"I used to donate a little more than a third of my earnings to charities in Africa, when cobwebs laden with the memories of a spider started to waylay me. Thinking of our friendship and our closeness turned to Africa into a cause. For me, Africa became my cause!"

"You never thought of Ireland that way?"

"No. I ruined Ireland for myself a long time ago, did some things there I couldn't go back and live with."

"And what might that have been?"

Seamus's eyes dodged, and his conversation followed. "Mogadiscio seemed to be the ideal place for me."

"Hiding out with warlords and mercenaries?" Jeebleh countered jokingly.

"And Bile too! But yes, you're right."

"I was on the run most of the time anyhow," Seamus said, after a silence, "spending a week on a curry-and-chow-mein tour, Delhi for a weekend, Hong Kong for a day. This wasn't work, but run, run, and run, a lifestyle with no room for reflection, a life meaninglessly held together by a major absence: love! I'm not speaking of loving a woman or a man, don't misunderstand me, but of a good, plain, old-fashioned, sixties-style personal commitment to love."

"And what have you found coming here? Love?"

"Will you forgive a cliché?"

"Go ahead."

"I've run into my self, coming here."

"Is this good or bad?"

"There's a purpose to my life now: Raasta!"

Then he was back to when he decided to come to Mogadiscio: how he bought the *New York Times* Sunday edition at midnight, in San Francisco; how he read about a UN-funded job in Somalia; how he applied; how he was short-listed; and how he was selected. He packed lightly, convinced that he would hate it. But he didn't. He met Bile—"It was more like running into my self"—and Raasta; he stayed. "Perhaps there's some truth in the wisdom that there is no happiness sweeter than the happiness built on someone else's sorrow. And this city has enough sorrow, with much deeper foundations."

"That's how Mogadiscio has struck you?"

Seamus replied, "Mogadiscio, because of Raasta, is what a straw dripping with water is to a man dying of thirst. I'm aware of the fact that it's a death trap, and because of this my heart goes out to those who're caught up in the fighting, and those who cannot help losing themselves in its politics. I am here to stay, that's what matters."

"And the cobwebs?"

"Vamoose!"

Jeebleh wished he could say that about himself. But then, he hadn't come to sweep clean the corners of his life that had grown dustier from neglect. And while eluding death, he would lay his mother's troubled soul to rest. He knew this was a tall order, but worth trying.

"Tell me about yourself," Seamus said. "Why are you in Mogadiscio?"

"I've come to ennoble my mother's memory."

Seamus knew that there were occasions when it was best not to say anything, not to even bother with condolences, because there are no words with which to express one's sentiments satisfactorily. He had heard a great deal about the mothers of Jeebleh and Bile, but it was difficult for him to imagine them alive, a lot easier to think of them as dead. He had a vague memory of some controversy to do with Jeebleh's letters, but Seamus wasn't sure if Caloosha had been involved, and in what capacity. He seemed to remember it was Shanta who had spilled the beans on this aspect of the controversy.

"How do you plan to achieve that?" Seamus asked.

"I'm working on it."

"Is there anything I can do to help?"

"Thank you."

Seamus now had a disheveled expression as he asked, "Have you seen Caloosha, since coming?"

"I've seen him. Have you?"

"I haven't had the desire to meet him ever," Seamus said. "The things I've heard about him haven't encouraged me to."

"I met him briefly, that's all."

"And Shanta?"

"Not yet, but I plan to."

Jeebleh looked at his right hand, palm up, and stared at where the heart line veered toward his middle finger. He asked, "Have you met Af-Laawe?"

After some reflection, Seamus said, "Af-Laawe, the Marabou, is sure to discover the whereabouts of the dead, in whatever state they're in. I would seek him out if I hadn't any idea in which of the many cemeteries someone was buried. The man's death instinct contrasts well with Bile's life instinct."

"What do you think about him?"

"He gives me the shudders."

As the conversation paused again, Jeebleh remembered their youthful, energetic days, when to pass the time they took turns completing each other's unfinished sentences. When they engaged each other in that kind of banter, fellow students who joined them found it difficult to keep up. Often, even the languages changed—from Italian to English, then perhaps to Arabic. Toward the end of their stay in Padua, Seamus had picked up the basics of Somali.

Jeebleh would have to run a fever of nerves before reintroducing the see-sawing games of their younger days in Italy. Most likely, it wouldn't work here, in troubled Somalia. He asked, "Did you come to Mogadiscio before or after the Marines landed?"

"I arrived in Mogadiscio in 1992," Seamus said. "I was head of an advance team charged with assessing the needs of the United Nations offices. I was to set up the translation units. The UN intervention was estimated to cost more than one hundred million U.S. dollars for that year alone. We put up a guesthouse, which doubled as our office. Because we hadn't the authority to hire any local staff, New York imported Somalis with American passports. And you had old British colonial officers running the show: former BBC staffers, chummy with the former dictator, who served as consultants to the UN. I remember an Englishman who kept yattering at me about clan warfare, and how the combined efforts of the U.S. and the UN would sort out the mess. Sod it, it was utter rubbish. Left to me, I would've committed the lot to a nuttery, the self-serving imbeciles."

"How did you and Bile meet?"

"I shared a table at the guesthouse with an Italian-American woman who was on an advance mission to open the UNICEF office," Seamus said. "She mentioned his name in passing. I looked him up. It wasn't difficult to find him."

"Was he living alone then?"

"He was spending a lot of time at Shanta's, with Raasta, even though he was living in shoddy settings. He had the bare minimum when I first visited him. We talked, and he shared some of his visions with me, visions that took a different form every time we met." As he spoke, Seamus bit at his fingernails, to the flesh, at times making it difficult for Jeebleh to understand what he was saying.

"Did you recognize each other when you met?"

"He didn't recognize me," Seamus said.

"Because of the beard?"

"I hadn't grown one then." He looked into Jeebleh's eyes, as if focusing on some distant horizon, and then sipped his coffee.

"You didn't expect him to recognize you?"

"For one thing, my name would've been the furthest thing from his mind," Seamus said. "Also, the civil war had had a disorienting effect on him—he was concentrating on minimal survival. But he recognized my voice the moment I spoke a full sentence.

"I went to visit him at The Refuge. He was quieting a toddler who was having a convulsive crying fit. The girl fell silent on seeing me come closer, and from the way she stared at me, you might have thought she knew me from somewhere else. She rose to her full height and wobbled away, past me, up to the new playhouse, where Raasta was playing with blocks."

"And then?"

"A thousand memories were condensed into a giant singular memory, which dwarfed all others, and I recited a verse from Dante's *Inferno*, in which enslaved Somalia was a home of grief, a ship with no master that was floundering in a windstorm."

"Then he recognized you?"

"And I stayed to help at The Refuge."

"Just like that?"

"Just like that!"

"What else?" Jeebleh asked.

"I don't know why I thought about olives then—olive fruits, olive trees, and olive wood," Seamus said. "Or why my mind went quietly about its thoughts in the way bees go contentedly about their motion, each droning note resulting from the previous one. I had no idea if the thought about olives came to me because we had been in Italy when we last met. Or if the fine polish of Bile's smooth skin reminded me of olive leaves, dark green on one side, silvery on the other. It could be that I was comparing our friendship to the olive tree. Because when the top branches die, a fresh trunk with a new lease on life emerges. And the tree bears fruit between the ages of five to ten years, and may not reach full maturity until after twenty!"

Thinking about friendship and about olives and their fruits, Jeebleh recalled the times they had been through as friends, and asked himself where he had heard the phrase "the country of our friendship," and decided that Bile had spoken the words; now the image Seamus used to describe his and Bile's friendship was an olive tree. When he turned to his friend to ask, Seamus's eyelids were like moths at rest, leisurely wrapping their wings over their bodies, in contented contemplation of their own mortality.

"And then what?" Jeebleh said.

"Raasta took to me," Seamus said.

"Right away?"

"She consented to sit on my lap the first time I invited her. It was love at first sight, mutual."

"What of Faahiye?"

"I didn't meet him until after my third visit. And when I did, I had the feeling that there was something wrong, and that he and Shanta had ballsed up their marriage. I could see that was affecting Raasta in a negative way. I worked out for myself that Faahiye was the primary source of the discord."

"What was Raasta like?"

"She was very striking."

"Because of the dreadlocks?"

"Actually, you might have assumed she was Bile's daughter if you hadn't known, because of the family resemblance. Also, she was very comfortable around him. They touched a lot, the two of them, they touched all the time." Tears filled Seamus's eyes.

"And when you eventually got to know Faahiye?"

"He made me think of a tree that has never flowered," Seamus said. "You might think he was from another, older world. He took everything personally, and because of this, he hurt easily."

Not knowing what else to say, but wanting to make a remark, Jeebleh said, "I hope the girls are unhurt."

Seamus, looking exhausted, covered his mouth and yawned. "Is there anything I can do for you before I go back to bed?" he asked.

"Could you give me directions to Shanta's?"

Seamus obliged, then returned to his room.

19.

BRIDGES SEPARATE THE TWO SIDES THEY JOIN, JEEBLEH THOUGHT, AS HE took long, eager strides on the way to Shanta's. He kept consulting the mass of squiggles passing for a map that Seamus had drawn as though from bad memory. Now he came to a stop, and looked this way and that, and then at the piece of paper, which he held at trombone distance. He had forgotten to bring along his reading glasses. With no prominent landmarks to guide him, and no street names either, he was unable to determine whether some of the asterisks represented two- or three-story buildings reduced to rubble or crossroads. Was he to turn left here, go a hundred meters or so, then turn right at the next destroyed building? He went on nonetheless, with the confidence of a man who knows where he is headed.

A hungry dog, its emaciated tail between its skinny legs, followed him. It kept a safe distance, its nose close to the ground, but its eyes focused mainly on him. The dog was on full canine alert, Jeebleh noted, ready to take off at the slightest hint of threat. It stopped and waited whenever he paused to take another look at the piece of paper, and didn't move until after he had resumed walking. Jeebleh relived the incident with the Alsatian. He hadn't thought he would get into trouble or risk being shot at if he stepped in to prevent a spoiled brat, the son of some minor warlord, from torturing a dog. He hadn't counted on having to deliver the puppies, but he was glad he had been there.

With the bush dog still following, Jeebleh came upon several sick-looking goats. Then he saw a cow taking famished bites of a plastic bag and swallowing it, and watched as she coughed, like someone with a chest ailment. After this, he saw two elderly men lifting their sarongs until they showed their bare bottoms, preparing to defecate in full view of the road. When he had lived here, this behavior would have earned a reprimand or an immediate fine if someone from the municipality had seen them emptying their bowels.

A little later, he and his canine companion came upon a throng of men gathered around something on the ground. Jeebleh decided this was a curious crowd, and not likely to turn into a mob. But why were some of them bearing clubs and others firearms? Was it for self-protection? He could see the men concentrating on the same spot and pointing. Was it a corpse, the carcass of a dead goat or some other, more unusual animal? Before getting any closer, he made sure that he knew where the hungry dog was, worried that he might be held responsible if it bit someone, or went berserk at the sight of a corpse or a carcass. He stopped within reach of the dog, just in case he was forced to intervene.

What distinguished him from the men in the crowd, apart from the fact that he had neither a club nor a firearm, was that they were all wearing sarongs. He had on trousers.

The men made space for him, and he moved forward with the mindset of a man prepared for peril, all the while wondering whether it was wise to enter what might be a trap set to lure strangers like him into it. And yet he went forward. All at once a man with a prominent gap in his upper teeth blocked his path.

"Are you a doctor?" GapTooth demanded.

"I am not."

Heads turned and stared, and many of those at the back of the crowd craned their necks to see. Were the men more interested in him than in the man who lay unconscious on the dusty ground, his body in a tortured posture, folded into his sarong? GapTooth volunteered the information that the man on the ground had just had an epileptic seizure. "But no one in this neighborhood knows him, or knows where he comes from or why he has had an attack and fallen right where he is lying."

Jeebleh assumed that GapTooth had advised everyone in the crowd to keep a safe distance from the epileptic, a meter at least. But he was not saying anything of the kind to Jeebleh.

There was a rawness about the way the crowd looked at the fallen man, who lay unconscious, his eyes scarily wide open, his legs apart, and his lips traced with dried saliva. A tall, bald man standing to Jeebleh's left wondered aloud if there was a divine purpose to the presence, in their midst, of an epileptic. This set several of the men to talk all at once. BaldMan intervened, hushing them, and said, "If there is a divine message, what is it? That we're out of control? Handicapped? Brain-dead? Stuck in some state where we're neither living nor dead?"

Those present turned themselves into a debating society, with several men reacting viscerally to what BaldMan had said. It seemed he was someone they listened to, even if his pronouncements were meant to be provocative, or downright offensive to many there. The talk shifted from the epileptic as a divine message to Jeebleh's presence among them.

GapTooth, pointing at Jeebleh, said to BaldMan, "But what of this man, here? Do we know who *he* is? Is it a matter of time before he falls sick and drops forehead first into a heap of nervous disorder? Will his eyes begin rolling, his teeth clench, and will his tongue stiffen like a bridle in a horse's mouth? Will his breathing become noisy, will froth run with the blood coming out of his mouth? Will he fall into a convulsive fit, lie unconscious on the ground, and when he opens his eyes, not recognize any of us? Will he remember our conversation? Will he die mysteriously, leaving the problem of where to bury him? I would say that the man lying unconscious on the ground, whom we are shunning, has more things in common with us than this newly arrived stranger here, who is upright, on his feet, and apparently healthy, walking through here in his trousers with his mangy dog. It is this man we should be worried about!"

Heads turned back and forth, eyes focused now on Jeebleh, now on the epileptic. Two possible scenarios came to Jeebleh's mind, in instantaneous reconfiguration. In one, the crowd turned into a mob. In the other, he was taking part in a TV game show in which the contestants pressed buzzers when they were ready to answer.

GapTooth asked, "If you're not a doctor and you're not sarong-wearing, and you do not suffer from epilepsy, then who are you?"

Trusting his instinct, he replied, "I am a guest."

"Of the epileptic?" asked GapTooth.

"No, I am Bile's guest!"

"Bile, the doctor?"

"That's right."

"Have Raasta and Makka been found, then?" GapTooth said.

"Who are they talking about?" someone called out from the fringes of the crowd. "What manner of name is Raasta? It is not Muslim, not even Somali."

"Have you not heard of the Protected One?" someone next to him said.

"I haven't had the pleasure," the man said.

Before Jeebleh could speak, another man stepped forward. "The trouser-wearing stranger in our midst is new to the city, as you can obviously see. But at least he is no enemy and no threat to us, if he is Bile's guest. And I am sure most of you have heard of the Protected One, Bile's niece, and the Simple One, both missing for a while now. Unless you do not listen to the BBC Somali Service?"

Another man admitted to not having heard of Raasta.

"A pity you haven't had the luck to meet either the Protected One or the Simple One," GapTooth said rather theatrically. Jeebleh couldn't tell whether some of them were teasing one another, as friends do. They could've been actors manqué, for all he knew, performing an impromptu play, staged for the benefit of anyone who happened to be passing.

With his hand extended to Jeebleh, GapTooth said, "Please remember me to the kind doctor when you see him next. And I hope, for our sake, that we find Raasta healthy and unharmed."

"What's your name, so I can give it to Bile?"

"Alas, I have no name by which I wish to be known in these terrible times," GapTooth said, "nor do I answer to my old name, because of the associations it has for me nowadays. Possibly, the good doctor would know who I was if I resorted to my former name, but I would rather wait until peace has come to stay."

"I understand," Jeebleh said, even if he didn't.

At the mention of Bile's name, the crowd had begun to relax, and so had Jeebleh. But he reminded himself that it was when you dropped your guard that someone could hurt you. He imagined panic descending on him in the unlikely form of a faint heart, his own. Then he felt ill at ease, and began perspiring, until the sweat soaked through his shirt, and his back became too wet for comfort. He kept his panic under check, even though he was short of breath and nervous. Finally he plucked up enough courage and then knelt to check on the epileptic. A man with a front-row view of the spectacle asked if there was nothing he could do for the poor man.

BaldMan asserted, "If I haven't said it before: We do not bother with people we do not know!"

"But he's a human being just like you and me!" Jeebleh shouted, whirling to his feet. "He needs to be taken to a hospital. Why do you need to know his clan family before you help him? What's wrong with you? You make me sick, all of you! Out of my way, please."

The crowd stepped back fast, clearing a large circle around Jeebleh and the unconscious man, only to close in shortly, gawking. The hungry dog, which no one had bothered to shoo away, stood nearby, waiting and watching. As Jeebleh glared at them, he assumed that many in the crowd thought he had suddenly gone mad, and might harm them. In the quiet that followed, as they gathered around him in the attitude of spectators assembling for the timeless pleasure of it, he knelt down again.

It seemed that the epileptic had started to undress before losing his consciousness and falling. His hands a little unsteady, Jeebleh rearranged the man's sarong as well as the circumstances would permit, and straightened his legs. But he had no idea what to do next. So he took the man's head in his hands, believing that this would help release the pressure of his teeth on his tongue.

The crowd came closer, their expressions changing from barefaced indifference to total concern. When the epileptic stirred in an agitated way, the spectators, thrown into a mix of fear, shock, and relief, fell back, some invoking several of Allah's designations, others remaining silent with the panic overwhelming their hearts. Jeebleh, oblivious of their doings, tugged at the epileptic's limbs one at a time, until the sick man responded with a tremor, like the fury of a madman unchaining himself. The epileptic shook so violently that Jeebleh had difficulty holding him on the ground.

It was in this moment of despondency that Jeebleh heard first the voice of a woman and then a car door being opened and closed. Was he conjuring things, imagining the words "Let go, let go"? When he looked up and found his eyes boring into Bile's, he relaxed his grip. Finally he let go, happy to leave the epileptic in the capably professional hands of Bile, who would know what to do.

Now he sensed Shanta's discreet, caring presence. She was saying to him, in the voice of a parent to a frightened child, "Come with me, then."

Taking a moment to look at her, he was surprised by her unimposing beauty, diminished as it was by her overall expression, which was suggestive of mourning. She was tactful despite the awkwardness of their encounter. It wasn't lost on him that someone always came to his assistance whenever he committed himself to a clumsy act. Now it was Bile and Shanta's turn to help deal with the problem. He felt like a mischievous child who kept getting into trouble. Perhaps the time would come when he would run out of people to offer him a lifeline.

"Tell me everything!" Shanta said. But she didn't even listen. Instead, she led him by the hand, away from where the epileptic had collapsed.

That the hungry dog was gone was a relief to him.

THEY HAD WALKED SCARCELY TWENTY METERS WHEN HIS SENSES AWOKE TO the pervasive smell of excrement and the rotten odor of waste. Shanta's questions helped take his mind off the overwhelming smell. "Tell me about the dog!" she said.

"Which dog?"

She linked her arm to his and kept pace with his slow gait. "Tell me about the dog and the cruel boy in fancy clothes."

He told it to her in a short form.

She said, "Has it occurred to you that you cannot be good in a conscientious way in a city in which people are wicked and murderous through and through?"

He let that pass without comment.

"Now tell me about the elders!"

Again, he gave her an abbreviated version.

She said, "Do you realize what you've done?"

"What have I done?"

She wondered aloud whether he realized that he was rubbing pepper and salt on the communal wound, reminding them of their human failures. She pointed out that the source of his problem was fundamentally this: He always occupied the moral high ground. She added, "Because of this, you had to be humbled."

He was having difficulty breathing, not because the smells were new to him—they weren't—but because they had become even more overpowering. People living in such vile conditions were bound to lose touch with their own humanity, he thought; you couldn't expect an iota of human kindness from a community coexisting daily with so much putrefaction. Maybe this was why people were so cruel to one another, why they showed little or no kindness to one another, and why they were blind to the needs of a bitch in labor or an epileptic in a convulsive seizure.

They came upon crows partaking of a spread of carrion. Three or four of these grotesque birds separated themselves from their colleagues and caught up with Shanta and Jeebleh in their leisurely walk. Bolder than he remembered them, the crows scoured the road ahead, hopping forward, then slowing down, like dogs on an afternoon stroll with their masters. The crows could equally have been bodyguards, assigned to escort dignitaries across a dangerous terrain. Shanta strode ahead as if unaware of the birds' presence, even when they flew into the air, in an attempt to keep pace, and croaked reproachfully overhead. They might have been hungry children urging their parents to take them home and feed them.

Jeebleh and Shanta came to a locked gate. Shanta bent down and worried a stone out of its position in a nearby wall. Her hand came away, palm up, maybe to show she had no key in it. The gate opened. Jeebleh recalled how often the city's residents had to fall back on their own ingenuity. How on earth do you open an automatic gate when electricity is intermittent? People had to find inventive ways of activating electric gates manually, and find them they did. On closer scrutiny, he saw that Shanta had pulled at a string hidden in the wall, to release the gate. There!

She let him go past and pushed the gate shut, then slid the bolt up into the metal frame. As they went on, past what had been the front garden of a two-story house, his sixth sense told him that someone was pointing a gun from the upper floor. He was beginning to feel unsteady in the knees, when he saw a small boy training a toy gun on him. Did the boy belong in the house, and if so, who was he? Was he a squatter, a dangerous species camping in a re-doubt? He followed Shanta into the living room, and remained standing and looking around.

"Tea?" she asked.

"Without sugar, please."

She suggested that he sit in the chair she indicated, and went to prepare tea. He made himself comfortable and took in the contents of the living room. He guessed that a child had occupied the center stage of life in the house, a child whose presence determined the shape of things in it. But the toys were all pushed out of the way into a corner, treated without much regard, aban-doned. They made Jeebleh think of the provisional nature of a child's play left unfinished, after the flagrant defilement of peace.

He couldn't tell from the contents of the house whether its original occu-pants had fled before their lives were cut short. From all indications, though, the place had been home to people of different ages, backgrounds, and pro-fessional interests, at different times. He deduced this from the titles of the books on the shelves, books now in disorder. One of the former occupants might have been an architect, another a nurse. Several others, younger in age, must have been high school students, some at the Egyptian secondary school, some at the Italian *liceo classico*, others at Benaadir, where the medium of instruction was English—in short, a house of polyglots.

"Here we are," Shanta said, "tea and nibbles!"

20.

"LITTLE RAASTA FELT SHE FIGURED OUT FOR HERSELF WHAT MARRIAGE IS like, when she was only four," said Shanta—given name Shan-Karoon, meaning "better than any five girls anywhere"—her voice drenched with emotion.

She faced him with the demure posture of a woman entertaining a potential in-law. Why was she ill at ease? Her clothes weren't a mess. In fact, she was smartly dressed. All the same, there was something about her that disturbed him. But he couldn't say what.

She would have been much younger when he was bundled out of the country. For all he knew, a lot of terrible things about which she spoke to no one, not even Bile, might have happened to her. He was on edge, like a man daring to stand on wet soap. He asked, "How did Raasta manage that?"

"You would know if you'd met her," she said.

"But I haven't!" He gave her a sharp glance, and the wells of her eyes filled with tears. He couldn't tell how she managed to contain them precisely where she liked them, brimming on her lashes. He insisted: "In what way did Raasta work out what marriage is like, at the age of four?"

Like a bird feeding, Shanta moved her lips soundlessly. He sensed then that talking to her would to be an undertaking that needed special skills. She was likely to be evasive when it came to Faahiye, and might be given to improvising or making up stories too. He wouldn't put it past her to make unsubstantiated innuendos, as many spouses might, when, in self-justification, they talked about their partners. She had trained as a lawyer, and joined the law firm set up together with several colleagues, including Faahiye. She had practiced her profession until the country collapsed into total lawlessness.

Now she spoke when he least expected her to, and, instead of answering his question, changed the subject: "Bless the house that our mothers built. Please accept my condolences over the death of our mothers.".

"Would you know how to locate Mother's grave?"

"I'm sure I would," she said.

But he was not one hundred percent certain she had understood that he was referring to *his* mother, not hers, and was sorry that he had not been clearer. He waited for her to speak; he didn't wish to be the one to draw attention to this lapse.

Obliging, she indicated that she had gotten his meaning. "I planted two trees at our mothers' graves," she said. "For the unparalleled sweetness of its fruit, I planted a mango tree of the Hinducini variety, imported from India, at your mother's grave, and a lemon tree at my mother's. I also placed four medium-to-large stones with your mother's name written on them. I haven't been to her grave—or my mother's—for quite some time, but if I put my mind to it, I am quite sure I'll find it, no problem at all. We can ask Dajaal to take us there, if you want me to come. He's useful in that department, and can find anything."

"You wouldn't know how to find her housekeeper?"

"Why do you want to find her?"

"Because I would like to know all I can about the old woman's last days," he said. "It is important that I talk to her. I have a number of questions that only she might be in a position to answer."

"I'm afraid I've no idea where she might be."

It was his turn to commiserate with her over the disappearance of Raasta and her companion. And because she snuffled, he felt shut out by the new circle that she now drew around herself. He was relieved that she knew how to locate his mother's grave if all else failed, and sorry he couldn't share all he had been told about Raasta's possible abductors. He intended to talk to her about his plans for his mother: to construct a noble memory for her in some way, gather a few sheikhs to speak words of blessing in remembrance of her—and of Shanta's mother too. He knew he had to wait until it was appropriate to bring up these matters, trifles in comparison to what Shanta was going through. He hoped there was time yet for his priorities.

She spoke fast, as though she had a dog at her heels, chasing her. "One way of putting it is that I've lived in a dark house, with the blinds drawn, and where the air is sour, and where I am alone, even though I haven't chosen to live by myself. I live in hope, though. I say to myself every hour that one day my daughter will be back, she who worked out for herself what marriage is like, at the age of four, and said so to me."

Jeebleh sucked at his teeth, sensing there was no point asking the same question for the third time. He suspected she wouldn't be goaded into giving away more than she wanted.

Now it was Shanta asking a question: "Why do you think Faahiye had a hand in my daughter's disappearance? I understand from talking to someone that you believe this to be the case."

"I don't remember saying any such thing to anyone."

"You've been to see Caloosha," she said, "and you've talked to Af-Laawe, and you've also spoken at length with Bile. What are your views? What are your conclusions?"

"I haven't come to any yet."

"Has Faahiye kidnapped her? He would need help from one of the Strongmen. Or has he done it on his own? And if so, why?"

He noted this time that she spoke her husband's name like a curse. Then she lapsed into a ruinous state of mind, appearing overwhelmed with the genuine emotion of a love gone sour, or hate gone seedy. Self-consciously, her hand went close to but dared not touch the well of her eyes. He remembered her as a child, remembered how she used to cry at the slightest pretext. By all accounts, hers was a life of high-flown emotions now, of days filled with incessant weeping.

"We're under a curse, as a family," she said.

"What makes you say that?"

"Caloosha had you and Bile, his own brothers, locked up, and is suspected of killing his stepfather. More recently, since our mother's death, several events, one after another, have turned what I, for one, first imagined to be blessings—the birth I had looked forward to all my life, and freedom for a brother who had been in prison and whom I waited to welcome—into curses. Times being abnormal, Bile touches me where he isn't supposed to, and does taboo things that he isn't allowed to. There's talk of murder, and there's talk of robbery. My husband questions, I take sides. We quarrel, my husband and I, and he leaves. My brother is hurt, and spends more time sulking than I've ever known him to do, telling me in so many words that I've brought ruin on our heads. My daughter and her playmate vanish mysteriously. Are they kidnapped? Have they been taken hostage? And if so, who's got them? Does their disappearance have a political angle? When I was young, not given to reflection and not in the know, I used to think there was something remarkable about our family, something unique. Now it seems we're uniquely cursed. And things aren't what they've appeared to be for much of my life."

"Has Faahiye been in touch?" Jeebleh asked.

"The phone rings."

He stared at her, saying nothing, puzzled.

"My phone rings, and when I pick it up, it falls silent," she continued, snuffling. "It rings again, and again no one speaks, no one says anything. So I don't pick it up anymore."

"Why would the kidnappers call and then say nothing?"

"I'm sure it's Faahiye!"

"Why would he be doing that?"

"To torture me!"

Jeebleh waited warily for her to explain further, but she ceased speaking altogether, swept away by a violent torrent of emotion. There was a feverish intensity to her behavior. He offered her his handkerchief, which she accepted and held in her hand, staring at it as if she didn't know what use to put it to. Again snuffling, she said, "Raasta was a wonder child!"

"Why 'was,' why not 'is'?"

"Because when she's returned to us, she'll have changed from the child I knew as my baby, and will have become a total stranger to me. She'll have been tortured. No child can survive this kind of torment. Her days of captivity will haunt her forever. My daughter is living in fear."

"No hard news about her, none whatsoever?"

"No one tells me anything."

"Why haven't you spoken of your worries to Bile?"

"For fear that he might think I am inventing things," she said.

"I feel certain that he won't," Jeebleh said.

"Unless it rings when he is here, he won't believe me, he'll assume that I am a distraught mother inventing things, like the ringing of a phone with no one at the other end. It's possible that someone is keeping an eye on my movements, and on whoever comes here. The phone rings after Bile has come and gone, not when he is here. Am I mad and imagining things? I don't know. Maybe I hear the phones ringing in my head, because I wish someone to get in touch with me. I am alone for much of the time, you see. I've no friends left. Many of them avoid me, because I keep talking about Raasta and Makka. But even in my madness, my daughter wants to come home, to me, away from the deceivers!"

When he heard her say "deceivers," he concluded that she wasn't completely mad, for he knew whom she meant. He felt more bound to her now, felt a deeper kinship, as a fellow sufferer at their hands.

She said, "I am a mother, deprived of the company of her loving daughter. It shouldn't surprise you or anyone else if I follow a bend and go where madness, beckoning to my sense of despair, is the supreme authority."

"You're not mad!" he assured her.

"I only have circumstantial evidence," she said, and the sad memory of what scanty evidence she had made her bend over. She held her head between her knees, sobbing.

They were back in her preteen years, when she used to embark on bouts of intense caterwauling, crying her throat sore until she got what she was after. Now she was a tantrum-throwing kid. She could contain herself one minute in lawyerese, her syntax perfect, her logic impeccable, and in the next minute burst into tears, and look mad and miserable.

He wouldn't lose hope. He would badger her until he got some adequate answers out of her: "Has anyone that you know of seen Raasta?"

"Af-Laawe has seen Faahiye!"

Clever at taking advantage of anyone with needs, Af-Laawe qualified as one of the deceivers. He had the knack of turning up to offer a hand. Who was Af-Laawe, and what was his role in all this?

"Have you mentioned this to Bile?"

"I have."

"And his reaction?"

"He promised he would look into the matter."

"Will he, do you think?"

"I doubt that he ever will!"

She was on firmer ground now. This was clear from her body language and her voice. She sat facing the curtainless window, now open, and the sun reflected in her eye made her appear less sad, but a trifle sterner.

She said, "Because Af-Laawe sees himself as a rival of Bile's, and as the other, that's to say, Bile's darker side, he's difficult to catch out. Af-Laawe will tell you that he's committed to the well-being of the dead, as if the dead cared, and that he buries them at no charge, which isn't true, of course, and that, like Bile, he came upon a windfall of funds with a mysterious origin. The truth is different. We know where Af-Laawe's money came from, that he is a devious fellow, and that Caloosha is his mentor—the overall head of what I'd like to call, for lack of a better term, the cartel. And don't think I'm mad or a raving paranoiac—I'm not, I'll have you know."

She was making a convincing case, but he wanted to know: "What cartel? What're you talking about?"

"The business interests of the cartel are suspect," she said. "Initially established by Af-Laawe as an NGO to help with ferrying and burying the city's unclaimed dead, it's recently branched out into other nefarious activities. The cartel, my reliable source has it, sends all the receipted bills to a Dutch charity based in Utrecht. But that doesn't bother me. What bothers me is what happens *before* the corpses are buried. Terrible things are done to the bodies between the time they are collected in Af-Laawe's van and the time they are taken to the cemetery. A detour is made to a safe house, where surgeons on retainer are on twenty-four-hour call. These surgeons remove the kidneys and hearts of the recently dead. Once these internal organs are tested and found to be in good working order, they are flown to hospitals in the Middle East, where they are sold and transplanted."

Jeebleh sat upright. Outlandish as it all sounded, he remembered being present when the corpse of the ten-year-old at the airport was transferred into Af-Laawe's van, and that the young man killed in his hotel room was put in the same van. He remembered how quickly Af-Laawe had acted to move the bodies, and how he had arranged for Jeebleh to ride in another car from the airport, although he had clearly intended to pick him up. Maybe there was some grisly truth in what Shanta was saying?

"Is Bile aware of all this?"

"It's not in his nature to talk, even if he is."

"Why not?"

"Because he doesn't wish his integrity questioned."

A latticework of shadows fell on her face, and Shanta's features made Jeebleh think of an old canvas in the process of being restored. He saw crevices where there were darker shadows, and imagined scars where the shadows were lighter.

"And you think it's the cartel that has kidnapped the girls?" he asked. "To get them out of the way so there will be no refuge for those fleeing the fighting? Or are Af-Laawe and Caloosha getting at Bile, each for his own reason?"

"Everything is possible."

"But the cartel, assuming it does exist, won't allow the girls to come to harm, will it? Especially if, as you say, Caloosha has something to do with it?"

Shanta was no longer in a mood to answer his questions, and her chest exploded into a mournful lament. She managed to say, despite her emotional state, "The cartel is in the service of evil!"

"Have you spoken to Caloosha about your worries?"

"I have."

"His response?"

"He says he is doing all that he can to have the girls traced. He says they are probably being held in the south of the city, which is not under his—StrongmanNorth's—jurisdiction, but StrongmanSouth's. But you know why I think he too won't help at all? Because the cartel's source of corpses will dry up if Raasta is back in circulation."

"*Che maledizione!*" Jeebleh cursed.

Snuffling more mightily, she trotted off, head down and body trembling, in the direction of a door that he assumed would lead to the toilet, presumably to complete her crying away from his gaze. He heard the boy moving about upstairs and muttering, perhaps entertaining himself with talk. But who was the boy? What was he doing here?

Shanta was away for at least fifteen minutes, and when she returned she sat from across him, not quite recomposed. She crossed and recrossed her legs, reminding him of an agitated mother hen fighting with all her might to save her chicks from the vulture preying on them.

AT JEEBLEH'S SUGGESTION, THEY MOVED OUT TO THE GARDEN, WHERE THEY sat on a bench under a mango tree, its shade as sweet as the fruit itself. Unwatered and ravaged by neglect, the garden was a comfortless witness to the nation's despair, which was there for all to see.

"Whose house is this?" he asked.

She looked away, first at the mango tree, which had begun to bear fruit, and then at a colorful finch hanging over one of the branches, cheerfully young and full of chirp. "Our own house is in an area that in the days when you lived here was known as Hawl-Wadaag but that has recently been named Bermuda. The neighborhood was destroyed in the fighting between StrongmanSouth and a minor warlord allied with StrongmanNorth. This house belongs to friends of mine who've moved to North America."

"Have you lived here for long?"

"We've been very unhappy," she said.

Jeebleh looked about, distressed.

"Perhaps the deteriorated state of the garden and the house explains why we've been unhappy here," she said.

How unlike one another are unhappy families: Tolstoy?

"We've stayed on a collision course, Faahiye and I," she said, "quarreling a great deal and unnecessarily. We've been in the sight of an evil eye, that's seen much ill!"

"Because of what?"

"Because of the curse of which I've spoken."

"But Bile at least had no choice," Jeebleh reasoned.

Yet there was no reasoning with her. She said, her voice shaken, "He touched me in ways that he shouldn't have. And because of this, we've earned ourselves a curse, this way harvesting nature's ill intentions."

"In his place, what would you have done?"

"In my rational mind, I know that it was a matter of life and death, and he had to make a decision, and voted in favor of life, voted for life. I am alive, and Raasta is a wonder child and, thank God, healthy. You ask what the problem is? Well, the problem is that what's been done can't be undone. The problem is that the curse has become part of us, affecting us all."

Her expression reminded him of the oval face of an owl in the dark, seen from the advantaged position of someone in the light. "Was that part of the curse, what happened between Bile and Faahiye the moment they met?"

"They were at each other's throats, because of what happened," she said, "and it fell to me to make peace between them. It's always fallen to women to forge the peace between all these hot-blooded men, always ready to go to war at the slightest provocation. Faahiye and my brothers are no different from the majority of men who've brought Somalia to ruin! Why do men behave the way they do, warring?"

"What do you think?" he asked.

"Maybe because they've got no sense of grief?"

He let this pass without comment, and waited for her tears to subside.

"Tell me who the boy in the house is."

There was smugness in her gaze as she turned in the direction where the boy was playing by himself. "He belongs in The Refuge. He came here to play with Raasta the day she disappeared, and has since refused to go anywhere else until she's back. He has become a kind of insurance policy, mine, that there will be a child in this house!"

It struck Jeebleh that for his entire visit, she didn't seem mad at all. Emotionally charged, yes, but that was more than understandable in a woman whose daughter was missing. In fact, she was confident enough to pleasantly offer him a plate of warmed-up food—yesterday's leftovers—if he had a mind to eat. And she was talking in a straightforward manner and answering his questions, and saying and doing nothing far-fetched or deranged. No one would doubt that she was as sane as he was.

He shifted the conversation: "Whose idea was it, do you know, that dinners at The Refuge should be a communal affair?"

She wasn't sure specifically, but thought it could only have been a woman's idea, even if it had come from Bile, who might have relied on the women around him. Women, after all, often ate in this way and knew the benefits accruing from it.

He nodded, remaining silent.

"For one thing, women waste less food," she said. "For another, eating together from the same plate is more gregarious. Besides, as you well know, we women have always eaten together, after serving our husbands. That women are content with seconds or leftovers suggests that we're prepared to compromise for the sake of peace. Not so men!"

He let the silence run its full course, and then asked if she had any suggestions about how he could reach the woman who had kept house for his mother. Her stare as hard as stone, she looked ahead of her, as though not aware of him at all. Again her lips moved like a bird feeding. Then her lips stopped and formed an O. "I knew where she lived, in Medina, before the collapse. I haven't seen her since then, as I had no reason to. But it shouldn't be difficult to find her if she's alive and in the city."

"Caloosha tells me she's left for Mombasa."

"Isn't that what he says about Faahiye too?"

"That's right."

"Have you asked Dajaal to look for her?"

He responded that he hadn't, and she reiterated that Dajaal could find anyone or anything; he was useful that way.

"Bile tells me that, among other things, you've come here to honor the memory of your mother," she said. "I would like to join you in doing so for our mother too. They raised us together as one family. What did you have in mind?"

His prayers for his mother began right away, in his imagining, with the whistle of a red-and-yellow-breasted robin perched on the branch of the mango tree.

He said, "I would like somehow to mark my mother's passing, perhaps with a day of prayers, a gathering of some sort, most likely at The Refuge. But first I'd like to locate her grave and pay a visit, and then maybe commission the raising of a stone in prayer, in her memory. Nothing extravagant, like a mausoleum, but it would be good if I could in some way reclaim her troubled soul from the purgatory to which Caloosha helped relegate her."

"The idea of using The Refuge to commemorate her life is wonderful," she said. "I like it very much, and hope that Raasta is there to celebrate the marking with us."

She released a long-suppressed snuffle.

He fell silent, ready to ask her pardon and take his leave, as soon as it was decent to do so.

21.

WHEN HE RETURNED TO BILE'S, JEEBLEH INSERTED THE KEY IN THE LOCK but had difficulty opening it. The key would turn loosely, without engaging to move the bolt. Then he heard footsteps approaching cautiously, and guessing it might be Seamus, he announced himself: "It's me, Jeebleh!"

The bolt was released at once, the door opened, and Seamus stood there, broad as his smile.

"Is she off her rocker, as Bile believes?"

Jeebleh didn't answer, and walked past Seamus into the living room, where he sat down. His friend joined him. When he'd brought Seamus up to speed about his visit with Shanta, Jeebleh fell silent, exhausted from the effort of remembering what he had been through.

"What about the boy?" Seamus wanted to know. "Is he still there at Shanta's, refusing to leave until Raasta returns home to play with him?"

Jeebleh didn't reply, because he had other worries on his mind. He wore a sullen expression, his stare unfocused, as if he couldn't see or hear a thing.

Seamus, disturbed, tried to reach out in sympathy: "Are you okay?"

"I am."

"But you've got the shakes!"

On edge, Jeebleh was getting worse by the second, and looking as if he might have a nervous breakdown right in front of Seamus. He held his stomach and, bending double, made as though he might bring up his worries. A portmanteau of jitters, he was short of breath, his eyes startled, as if his guts were being emptied, to be flown out of the country, as parts. He was showing a passive side to his nature, like someone not responsible for what he was doing. Yes, something was happening to the action man, and he wasn't able to fight it off. Jeebleh, known for his tough stances and rational behavior, looked unlike anything Seamus could ever have associated with him. "I don't like what's happening to me," he said.

"What's happening to you?" Seamus asked.

"I'm now part of the story, in that I've taken sides, and made choices that might put my life in danger."

Seamus shook his head in sorrow, as if he knew exactly what Jeebleh meant. "I know too many people who couldn't help getting too involved, couldn't avoid becoming part of this nation's trouble. You need to return to being your usual self—a father to your daughters, a husband to your wife, and a professor to your students. You should leave the country while there's time."

"What are you saying?"

"It's time you left," Seamus said.

"It is, but I won't leave yet."

"What's holding you back?"

"Some unfinished business awaits my attention."

"I hope you know what you're doing!" Seamus told him.

In response, Jeebleh took refuge in a Somali wisdom about a man who bit the stronger of two fighting dogs on the ear in anger, because it was molesting the weaker one, torturing it. He added: "I've already made a name for myself, haven't I, standing up to my clan family?"

"For goodness sake," Seamus pleaded, "they tried to murder you."

"I won't risk my life unnecessarily, I promise!"

Seamus ignored the promise. "It makes me sad to think that you'll not only become part of the civil war story, but get totally lost in it, because the story is much bigger than you, and might prove deadlier than you can imagine. My only advice is that if you won't quit, you watch out and make sure you aren't sucked into the vortex."

"I'll be very careful," Jeebleh said.

Seamus tried to steady his look before speaking. His arms folded across his chest, his manner ponderous, he said, "I've been there too at the crossroads, where arrivals meet departures, and where self-doubt meets with certainties and self-recrimination. *And* I've avoided becoming part of the story!"

Jeebleh now watched Seamus busy himself with some domestic chore or other, acknowledging silently that he could've left without trying to tie the necessary loose ends. Now this was impossible. If he left, he would be walking away from a part of himself—and leaving behind a piece of his history too. He didn't want to do that.

"For years now," Seamus was saying, "people have been coming to Somalia, every one of them intending to do their bit and then leave. The Americans came, as their then president put it, to do God's work! God knows they didn't do that. But then, did they just leave as they had planned? No, they were drawn into the vortices of clan intrigues, and when they left, they left parts of themselves behind. Making a choice and then acting on that decision and leaving: these are out of our hands before we're aware of where we are."

Jeebleh asked, "Why have you stayed?"

"Sometime during my second visit," Seamus said, "I realized that I'd mislaid something of myself here during my first visit, and I had to return for it. Instead of retrieving it and leaving immediately, I've stayed. It's possible that some of us cannot help losing ourselves in the sorrows of other people's stories. I can vouch that you've changed since your visit to Shanta's, I can see that. If you asked what Somalia is to me, having stayed, I would respond that it is the Ireland of my exiled neurosis."

"My story cast in misanthropy!" Jeebleh said.

"You're doing whatever it is you're doing out of empathy, not hate," Seamus suggested. "You feel deep love for justice. I'm moved to hear you tell the story of the man who bit the stronger of the two dogs. After all, there isn't much of a story in 'dog bites man,' because it happens all the time. But when a man bites a dog for reasons to do with justice, it's a big story, worthy of a newspaper headline. So could you explain to me, in the light of all this, why you've returned to your country in its hour of tragedy? I've been told that you've come to visit your mother's grave. But you've done bugger-all about *that*! So what made you come?"

Jeebleh reached inside his mind for the strength he sensed he now lacked, and found himself in a corridor as narrow as tunnels are dark. He tried to locate the arrows that might point to an exit, but there were none. His hands in front of him, he fumbled forward, and finally fell back on a version he had rehearsed to himself several times before. Retelling it for Seamus's benefit, he described his unpleasant brush with death, when a Somali, new to New York and driving a taxi illegally, nearly ran him over. He conjured it all like a film shot on a busy New York street, demonstrating the startled look on the face of the Somali, and revisiting his own days recovering in a hospital. He slowed down to prepare himself for a challenge from Seamus, well aware that his friend could argue that by coming to Mogadiscio, he was not so much thinking about his mortality as seeking out death.

"Have you come to court death, then?" Seamus asked.

"It's no longer clear why I've come," he said.

"Would you be ready to bite the stronger of two dogs on its ear, in anger, as the Somali wisdom has it?"

Jeebleh assured him that he would.

"Are you prepared to kill and to be killed?"

"I could be, depending."

"On what?"

"What's at stake."

Apropos a question not asked, Seamus said, "The violence that's war, combined with the violence that's famine, run in my blood and in the veins of my memory, and so I understand where you're coming from, and where you find yourself."

Agitated, he took his drawing pad and traced a half-human, half-animal figure, a man of advanced age, supporting himself on a walking stick and begging. Then he drew the figure of a woman à la Matisse, strong lines, prominently Fauvist in their pursuit of self-release. Jeebleh knew that Seamus would continue drawing until he provided the woman with a singularly abundant breast. And if he was in the mood, he would draw a baby, whom the woman would suckle. He would grow calm only when the drawing was done, and once the baby wore the capricious expression of a cynic.

Jeebleh put this down to Seamus's childhood terrors: a grenade had been thrown into the window of his family's living room, killing Seamus's father, his sister, and two brothers—everyone but Seamus and his mother; in frequent childhood nightmares, Seamus would wake from his sleep, shouting, "But why me?" He would talk expansively about the incident, but not about the fact that the man alleged to have thrown the grenade had later died violently himself. At being asked pointed questions about this, Seamus would drop into a depressive silence. After regaining his tongue, he might tell you that although he had been in the area when the man died, he hadn't been charged, and that the police had cleared his name within a few days, for lack of evidence.

But Jeebleh risked asking about it. He felt he had to hear about it. "If you didn't have a hand in the man's death, and I'll assume that to be the case," Jeebleh said, "why were you accused of it? How was it that your presence in the area had been noted and you were suspected?"

"Because no one living in a country in which a civil war is raging is deemed to be innocent. Here in Somalia too everyone is potentially guilty, and may be accused unfairly of crimes they've committed only by association. If you are a member of the same clan family as a perpetrator of a crime, then you're guilty, aren't you?"

"Do you still wake up, shouting 'Why me'?"

"Not anymore I don't," Seamus said.

"That's a relief!"

"Living in Mogadiscio, seeing so much devastation and death from the civil war, and working at The Refuge have cured me of that."

Jeebleh had heard the passion in Seamus's voice when he spoke of Raasta. He obviously adored her, as though she were his own child. His affection seemed to border on obsession. That morning Jeebleh had seen Seamus's room in the apartment. There were photographs of the girl everywhere, on the walls, on key rings. Two photographs that he had taken hung on either side of his bed. In addition, he had many drawings of Raasta, stacks and stacks of them. Seamus was apparently in the habit of drawing her when he was nervous, which was a great deal of the time, and he drew rather competently, at times almost like a professional. "She gives a purpose to my continued stay in Mogadiscio, despite the risks," he said now.

"What is she like?"

"A halo of comfort to me," he said. "An elated sense of peace descends on my head when she is around me. In her presence, I am as happy as a yuppie throwing his first housewarming party."

It occurred to Jeebleh that Seamus, the polyglot from Northern Ireland, might have some thoughts related to his pronoun obsession. He tried it on him: "What pronoun do you think is appropriate when you refer to the people of Belfast? Not in terms of being Catholic or Protestant, but just people?"

"I'm afraid you've lost me."

"Do you use 'we' because you see yourself as part of that community, or 'they'—a ploy as good as any to distance yourself and to distinguish yourself from the sectarian insanity of which you're not part?"

After some serious thought, Seamus said, "I don't know if I'm as conscious of the pronouns as you are. Anyway, what pronouns do *you* deploy?"

"Myself, I use 'we' when I mean Somalis in general, and 'they' when I am speaking about clan politics and those who promote it. This came to me when I was refusing to contribute toward the repair of *their* battlewagon, for I didn't want to be part of *their* war effort. I left *their* side of the green line and relocated in the section of the city where the other clan family is concentrated. It's as if I've written myself out of *their* lives."

"Enemies matter to those who create *them*," Seamus responded quickly.

"I'm not with you."

"When you think of them as 'they' and therefore create *them* yourself, then it follows that you become an enemy to *them* the moment you opt out of their inclusive 'we.' As it happens, you are worth a lot more to them dead than alive, assuming of course that they can lay their hands on the wealth you had in your room or on your person."

Jeebleh nodded in agreement. "Another Somali proverb has it that the shoes of a dead man are more useful than he is."

"How cynical can a people get."

"I would say we're a practical nation."

"Deceitful too," Seamus said, and after a pause went on: "I bet Af-Laawe would've helped them to effect their clannish claim on your cash and so on. He'd be attending to your corpse in jig time, before anyone else knew you were a goner."

"Is he as much of a shit as Shanta depicts him to be?" Jeebleh asked. A wayward silence gave him the luxury to recall Af-Laawe's thoughts on pronouns. But when other memories from other dealings that had passed between him and Af-Laawe called on him, Jeebleh felt his body going numb, as though his limbs had been rendered lifeless. Nor could he shake off the shock of hearing Shanta's suspicions about the cartel! Shanta was a mother with a missing daughter, and at times she was clutching at straws, but some of her speculations made sense to him. "Tell me about Af-Laawe."

"The man is in the thick of every wicked deed," Seamus said. "Unconfirmed rumor places him in the role of go-between, something he's apparently good at."

"Where else does rumor place him?"

"I understand he ran an underhand scheme," Seamus said, "in which four-wheel-drive vehicles were spirited away with the help of Somali drivers and some UN foreign employees. Again, he acted as a go-between, linking the UN insiders and the Somali drivers. But he received the biggest cut, because it was his racket. The Somali drivers would vanish into the city's no-go areas, and the Lord knows there were many, and some UN bureaucrat would get his commission in cash. And the vehicles would end up in Kenya or Ethiopia! You'll probably have heard of the four-million-dollar heist, the one that made it into the international press."

"Why do you think he hasn't quit, retired on his millions?"

"He's past the stage when he can just walk away," Seamus speculated. "I presume he gets a kick out of courting danger on a daily basis. Sure as eggs is eggs, he's *his* own story now, and too big a man to lose himself in other people's fibs, or to care about them. My guess is that he'll eventually tempt Caloosha's wrath, and he'll end up dead."

Jeebleh looked disconcerted: "And the AIC?"

"What about him?"

"Did he become part of the story too?"

"Fools are famous for the gaffes they make," Seamus said. "We weren't on first-name terms, the AIC and I, but we got on reasonably well until he lost his way in the complex plot of Somalia's story. He may have meant to do 'good,' but his methods were highly questionable. In the process, he ended up behaving very much like StrongmanSouth, whom he meant to expose."

"He too became *his* own story?"

"And he compounded the problem by misinforming the American militariat and the UN too. I don't wish to be unfair to him, but I think that in the end he mislaid his marbles."

"Would you say he was evil?"

Seamus's worries made him look more careworn, and a little paler. "I would say he was banal."

"No one's going to think of anything else when 'banal' comes this close to 'evil.'"

"He was true to type, and American."

Not knowing what to make of this, Jeebleh let it be. He concentrated his stare on a gecko at the bottom of the wall, within reach of his hand, and a fly washing its head reflectively, as though tempting the gecko.

SEAMUS'S EYES CLOSED VERY, VERY SLOWLY, LIKE THOSE OF A CHILD RESISTING sleep. Then the phone rang, and Jeebleh answered it. Shanta was at the other end. There was a life-or-death urgency to her voice. She wanted Jeebleh at her place right away, but wouldn't tell him why. Assuming the worst, he got in touch with Dajaal, who promised he would take him there at once.

22.

NO SOONER HAD JEEBLEH PUT ON HIS SEAT BELT THAN HE APPROACHED Dajaal about joining his cause. He broached the subject with the timidity of someone who had no wish to spend another day behind bars in a detention cell.

"Supposing that I set my sights on destroying a man who's wrought havoc on my life and done irreparable damage to others close to me," he said, "and supposing I were to ask you to help, would you give me a hand?"

Sounding as if he had given the subject some thought, and had been expecting the request to come for some time, Dajaal answered, "Of course I would."

Jeebleh mulled this over and then said noncommittally, "You realize I haven't a clear idea of what's involved?"

"Nor have I much of an idea what you're talking about, come to think of it," Dajaal said, "but there's time to develop these plans, plot and fine-tune them. In my previous experience as an army man, and as a long associate of Bile—I'm eternally devoted to him—I have undertaken tough jobs. My training has prepared me, and I am always willing to accept risky tasks in the line of duty."

Jeebleh assured him that he hadn't discussed the topic with anyone else, and that it was too soon to come up with a blueprint. In any case, they wouldn't make any moves until they were clear in their heads about the fate of the girls. Till then, Jeebleh said, mum's the word!

Dajaal told Jeebleh that as an army officer he was trained to share secret information on a "no-name, no-packdrill" basis. He, Dajaal, would honor that.

"What about Bile?"

"What about him?" Dajaal asked.

They had arrived at Shanta's gate. "How will he take it?" Jeebleh said.

"He's aware of your plans?"

"I haven't spoken to him at all about my plans."

"When I met him at the clinic this morning," Dajaal explained, "Bile alluded to how a female bee mates with any drone she meets in the course of her honey-making business."

"Have you any idea what he was saying to you?"

"Not really," Dajaal replied. "But he explained it this way: that for his self-fulfillment, a torturer will be content to torture a victim wherever he may come across one."

When Jeebleh said, "Thank you," he did not know whether he was thanking Dajaal for the lift or for the details of what Bile had said, or simply bringing their conversation to an abrupt end because he was feeling uncomfortable.

Jeebleh got out of the car. Dajaal chose not to accompany him, but to wait outside until he was sure that his presence was no longer needed.

JEEBLEH WAS SURPRISED THAT SHANTA DIDN'T EVEN BOTHER TO WELCOME him or thank him for coming promptly. As soon as she saw him, she cursed: "The son of a bitch has called."

He was tempted to say, "Where are your manners?" but decided to make an allowance for Shanta. Of course, he could guess whom she meant, and he waited for her to say more. There was rage in her voice, old rage mixed with new.

"Did he say where he was calling from?"

"He sounded so close that it could've been from the house next door," she said. Then she turned her back on Jeebleh and, again cursing like a drill sergeant—"The son of a bitch"—walked away. He didn't follow her inside immediately.

He averted is gaze, finding no pleasure in seeing her curves through the diaphanous dress she wore, a garment adorned with fluttering birds. He thought of his wife, to whom he had spoken the day before.

Shanta made him even more uncomfortable with her abusive language. "The son of a donkey has rung, but doesn't want to speak to me. Can you believe it?"

He entered the house and shut the door. He reminded himself how he had been reared in a venerable tradition in which you pretended that nothing untoward had taken place if a respectable person misbehaved in your presence.

"Would you like a cup of tea, while we're waiting?" she asked.

He wondered whether it was wise to have tea with her or even to wait, when he didn't know why he was waiting, precisely for whom or for what, or for how long. That she continued to swear irritated him greatly, he had no idea why. He spoke slowly: "Tell me if I'm right. Faahiye, your husband, called between the time I was here last and the time you called me at the apartment, and he said he'd call again, but didn't give a definite time or reason. Did he name the person he wanted to talk to?"

"He wants to speak to you." She nearly flew into a fresh rage. "'I want to speak to Jeebleh.' That's how he put it. 'I want to talk to that man and no one else, and I want you to ring him and get him, and I'll call!'"

"I hope you're not blaming me."

"Have you been talking to him behind our backs?" She looked like a floor cloth, untidy in her moment of sheer rage. "Tell me the truth!"

"No, I haven't."

"So why has he rung you, if you haven't?"

"I wish I knew."

"It doesn't make sense, does it?"

"If Faahiye and I had spoken, as you say," Jeebleh challenged her, "would he not have a better way of reaching me?"

"I suppose you are right." She settled into the sofa, shifting in it. She rubbed her forehead with her hand, as though this might help reduce her pain. The minutes passed slowly. He thought of trying to assure her that he was not offended by her insinuation, but chose not to, certain that it would be of no use.

"He rang me soon after you left," she said.

Jeebleh thought that maybe one of Caloosha's security operatives who was keeping tabs on him had seen him with Shanta, as they walked away from where the epileptic man had collapsed. When the word got through to Caloosha, he might have called Faahiye and asked that he speak to Jeebleh. It was safe to assume that Faahiye would do what he had been told.

"Did he say anything about Raasta?"

"No."

Even though it wasn't in Jeebleh's nature to see the bright side of things, he felt he needed to be optimistic. The words came to him easily, but he was having difficulty in delivering them convincingly, so he repeated them to himself over and over. Faahiye wouldn't be making contact unless he had decided to bring the crisis to an agreeable end; he was free to make such a decision on his own, and not at someone else's suggestion. But Jeebleh couldn't pass his optimism on to Shanta, as he feared that she would become more aggressive.

And she would not give up. "Why, of all the people in the world, has he chosen to talk only to you, if you haven't been in touch with him on your own?"

"I have no idea," Jeebleh said.

"There's got to be a reason," she insisted. "I've never known him to do anything unless he's given it a lot of consideration, and studied it from every possible angle."

Jeebleh said, "Maybe he thinks it'll be easier to talk to me, because I'm the only one who's known him for donkey's years and with whom he hasn't quarreled?"

"I am Raasta's mother."

Jeebleh was on the verge of saying that that was beside the point, but it dawned on him that the opposite was the case: The fact that she was Raasta's mother *was* the point. He speculated aloud: "Maybe he looks on me as a neutral person, or an impartial judge, able to listen to the two sides of the argument judiciously?"

"What two sides? There *are* no two sides! I want my daughter back, and I want her now. He can go where he pleases, something he's already done. I don't care. I want my Raasta back."

"We're assuming, without knowing it for a fact, that he's holding Raasta hostage," he countered.

"Why do you say we're assuming that?"

"Because we are," he said.

"Isn't he?" she asked.

"We haven't established that."

Shanta grew more and more tense, and then, exhausted, slumped back lifelessly. He sat forward and, turning slightly, saw a slim book in Italian written by Shirin Ramzanali Fazel, a Somali of Persian origin. He recalled reading the book in New York, and thinking that it was no mean feat for a housewife to write about her life in Mogadiscio, and then her exile in Italy. He was pleased that Somalis were recording their ideas about themselves and their country, sometimes in their own language, sometimes in foreign tongues. These efforts, meager as they might seem, pointed to the gaps in the world's knowledge about Somalia. Reading the slim volume had been salutary, because unlike many books by authors with clan-sharpened axes to grind, this was not a grievance-driven pamphlet. It was charming, in that you felt that the author was the first to write a book about the civil war from a Somali perspective. He asked Shanta what she thought about the book.

"I hadn't been aware of the depth of her hurt until I read it," she said, "just as I hadn't given much thought, I confess, to the suffering of many Somalis of Tanzanian, Mozambican, or Yemeni descent. The civil war has brought much of that deep hurt to the surface. I hope that one day we'll all get back together as one big Somali family and talk things through."

"Who's to blame for what's happened?"

"I hate the word 'blame,'" she said.

"Is Shirin Fazel Persian? Or is she one of us, Somali?"

"She is a deeply hurt Somali, like you and me," she said. "When you are deeply hurt, you return to the memories you've been raised on, to make sense of what's happening."

"Do you reinvent your life?" Jeebleh asked.

"It is as if you see yourself through new eyes. And then you reason that you're different, because you are after all from a different place, with a different ancestral memory."

"You feel left out when you are hurt?"

"I suppose that is what Shirin Fazel feels. Left out and victimized, because she is of Persian descent."

"Is Faahiye hurt in a similar manner?" Jeebleh asked.

"Because his family was different from ours?"

"Did he speak about it?"

"That would be uncharacteristic of him."

"Because he belongs to the old world, in which you don't speak about what hurt you, is that why? Or is it because he believed that the clan business had nothing to do with his hurt? That it was personal?"

"He belongs to a world," Shanta explained, "in which he expects that those hurting him will realize their mistake of their own accord and, without being told, stop hurting him any further."

"What do people do when they're hurt?" he asked.

"Tell me."

"Some people go public, and they show the world that they're hurt. They accuse those who've hurt them, they become abusive, vindictive. Some become suicidal. Some withdraw with their hurt into the privacy of their destroyed homes, and sulk, and whine. To someone who's hurt, nothing is sacred."

Jeebleh felt oddly comforted by the thought that Shanta, no longer tearful, was attentive. No outbursts of emotion, nor did she behave neurotically when they talked in general terms. He must take care not to spring a question on her, lest she drop into a state of nervous tension.

"Why, why, why, why?" she asked.

He disregarded her question; he should muster the strength and the wit to make her relax until Faahiye called or Bile arrived—Bile would, he thought, show up at Shanta's sooner or later—whichever came first. Then he became aware of her fixed stare.

"He turned our private quarrel into a public spectacle," she accused. "He left, so the world would talk about him. And do you know why he did that? He did that to exact vengeance." She was calm, composed as she spoke, and nothing indicated that she would go weepy on him. "By going public," she went on, "he brought his hurt out into the open, as though he expected to receive a proper redress. Did he think how I might feel, how Bile might feel? Then Raasta and Makka disappeared."

Jeebleh realized that she was staring at him, in fact focusing on a dribble of saliva dangling from his lower lip. Embarrassed at his dribbling like a baby, as he was prone to do whenever he concentrated, he sucked it in with a gust of air. He remembered that he had lent her his handkerchief, so he dried his chin with the back of his hand. He was about to excuse himself, when she started to speak.

"A wife is not likely to display her hurt in public the way a husband does. A woman doesn't go blatantly public until after she has tried other ways of communicating with her spouse. Women keep these things under wraps for much longer than men do. It's only when a woman can no longer deal with it that she speaks of it, first to her friends, then to her spouse. Only when no solution to the problem is in sight does she speak to others. It takes a very long time before outsiders hear of the marriage problem from a wife. By the time a woman makes it public, we can assume that the marriage is doomed."

He couldn't help thinking that this sounded like the crossroads where the Somali people stood. Like Faahiye and Shanta, they were not prepared to talk directly, but only through intermediaries—in the case of Somalia, through foreign adjudicators. Interfamilial disputes had a way of becoming protracted, at times requiring an eternity for the parties in the conflict to sit face to face and talk—alone!

They both looked toward the door, then at each other. Jeebleh wasn't sure if he had heard a car door open and then close. The optimist in him wondered whether that might be Faahiye coming home, with Raasta? He waited for the noise to make sense, but none came. He had almost given up, when the gate outside creaked. It was then that he stood, bracing himself for an unpleasant surprise. But when he opened the door, he saw Bile at the gate, waving to Dajaal as he drove off.

. . .

JEEBLEH, SHANTA, AND BILE SAT AND TALKED, AND BILE WAS INFORMED OF the developments relating to Faahiye. Though their hearts were not in it, they chatted about other things, not to kill the time, but because they were nervous, the three of them, for different reasons.

"All this waiting is getting us nowhere," Bile said, "and we have no idea why we are waiting."

"We're waiting for Faahiye to ring."

"This is ridiculous." Bile addressed Shanta: "While we wait, perhaps you can repeat the precise words Faahiye used, for my benefit."

Shanta obliged. "The mobile rang and I answered it, saying hello. I said hello several times, and then Faahiye spoke. He said that he'd called for 'that man.' I asked to explain whom he meant, and he said to pass his message on to Jeebleh, to whom he wants to talk. I offered to give him the number of Jeebleh's mobile, but he said that that was not what he wanted to do. He wanted Jeebleh to come here and to wait for his call on the landline."

Bile turned to Jeebleh. "How long ago has it been since you got here?" He looked at his sister and waited.

"About an hour and a quarter."

"Does this mean we'll be here forever, waiting?"

Jeebleh suggested they wait as long as they could.

"I don't like devious people," Bile said.

"To hell with it all!" Shanta exploded, and hurried from the room, breathing like someone who needed a good, hearty cry, in private.

JEEBLEH AND BILE TALKED WHILE THEY WAITED FOR SHANTA TO RETURN, AND for the phone to ring.

"What becomes of a nation when there is such a great disharmony that everyone is dysfunctional?" Jeebleh said.

"The young ones will play truant," Bile replied, "the civil servants won't do their jobs properly, the teachers won't teach, the police, the army, the entire civil service, nothing, and I mean no institution, will function as it should."

"In short, you'll have a dysfunctional nation?"

"It's only when there's harmony within the smaller unit that the larger community finds comfort in the idea of the nation. The family unit acts as a counterbalance to the idea of the nation. And in order for the nation to function as one, the smaller unit must resonate with the larger one."

Jeebleh, silent, pondered this.

Bile said, "You asked if sex was the subtext of Shanta and Faahiye's ruined relationship? Or did you ask if sex was the fault line in their marriage? I recall being embarrassed by the question, and have since thought it over. I think that one never casts aspersions on a wife, a husband, or for that matter an intimate, without self-diminishment! This is a lesson we've learned the hard way, from the civil war."

The landline rang, and Jeebleh answered.

IT WAS AFTER NIGHTFALL WHEN JEEBLEH AND BILE LEFT SHANTA'S. THE DARK sky spread above them, the ten-day-old moon a reference point. Jeebleh was relieved that Faahiye had kept his word and called; he had promised to call again, probably the next day, to arrange a face-to-face meeting with him, alone. But he hadn't said anything about Raasta, and he kept repeating, "We'll meet and talk!" Bile had stood close by during the conversation, his imperious demeanor sufficient to remind Jeebleh not to do or say anything that might complicate an already complicated situation.

But something about the call had made Jeebleh's heart stop, though he didn't speak about it afterward. When he had finished talking with Faahiye, Af-Laawe had come on the line. He said that he would meet Jeebleh the following morning at a crossroads south of Bile's apartment. He told Jeebleh that he would bring his mother's housekeeper along, and the three of them would go together to the cemetery where the old woman was buried.

As they walked back to Bile's apartment, Jeebleh trembled like a candle caught in a storm. He had reached at least three certainties: Af-Laawe was more involved in these nefarious activities than he had let on. And if the two of them met, and the girls were released unharmed, Jeebleh would put his own plan into motion, with help from Dajaal. And at possible risk to his own life, he would not divulge the proposed encounter with Af-Laawe to anyone, not even Bile or Seamus. Maybe to Dajaal, but he would have to think about that. As he walked, he sometimes felt he was about to collapse at the knees, or his legs were about to take a tumble; he would then straighten his back, steady his body, and stride forward. Bile would extend a helping hand, asking if he could do something for his friend. Shanta's accusation—that he had secretly been talking to Faahiye—resounded regrettably in Jeebleh's ears. He wished that he had spoken of the rendezvous that Af-Laawe wanted, shared it with Bile there and then, as soon as he had hung up. Now Jeebleh would have to keep the appointment secret, and honor it, at great cost to his own standing if he was discovered. He was damned either way, whether he spoke of it or not.

When Seamus let them into the apartment, he noticed Jeebleh's pallor. "Oh dear, dear, you're a wreck, aren't you?"

And even though he wouldn't hear of either friend's helping him to his room, Jeebleh accepted a bowl of broth and a cup of hot chocolate, in bed, when they were offered.

23.

JEEBLEH WOKE UP FEELING ASHAMED AT HIS INABILITY TO MENTION HIS appointment with Af-Laawe to Bile or Seamus. He got in touch with Dajaal, however, calling him on his mobile to inform him that he had arranged to meet Af-Laawe and go to the cemetery.

Bile had now gone to work, and Jeebleh needed someone to talk to. He woke Seamus, and over a breakfast of Spanish omelette with him, Jeebleh was physically unsteady. He felt as though he had been emptied of life itself, like an egg out of which a weasel has sucked everything.

Seamus had sensed Jeebleh's unease from where he sat across the table. "If I were you," he said, "I would be careful before committing myself to an action that might complicate matters for all concerned."

"I look nervous, do I?"

"You look like a teenager right before his first date," Seamus said. "Anyway, whatever you're up to, please don't embark on a job if you aren't prepared to follow it through. Besides, you must steel yourself for an unexpected challenge if you're up against a no-goodnik of the local variety. I'll offer any assistance you require."

Jeebleh thanked him and pushed away the omelette, which was cold as a morgue. His innards stirred with the adrenaline of a daddy longlegs crawling out of a ditch a meter deep. Saying no more, he went to keep his appointment with Af-Laawe.

FOLLOWING INSTRUCTIONS, JEEBLEH TURNED LEFT WHEN HE WAS OUT OF THE building, then right and right again, looking this way and that to see whether he was being tailed. He waited at the designated corner where he was to be picked up. He was like a child playing at being an adult. He did not like what he had been reduced to, a marked victim. After all, Af-Laawe and his cohorts could do away with him if they so chose.

He had just decided to cancel the appointment, and was pulling out the mobile phone to call it off, when he heard and then saw a black stretch limousine approaching. He had been listening for the bumpy clamor of Af-Laawe's jalopy; this was totally unexpected. Or was it? Had he not been told about a fancy car seen in the neighborhood of The Refuge on the day the girls went missing? His ears beat with the rhythm of a funeral drum.

For a moment he thought he was mistaken, because the black Mercedes cruised past him, raising a storm of dust. But then it turned and came toward him again, as fast as a getaway car leaving the scene of a crime. The driver cut the speed, until the car was as slow as a hearse, and came to a halt. The back window opened, and there was Af-Laawe, sitting showily in the row of seats by himself. All smiles, his index finger bent and beckoning. "Get in!" he said.

Jeebleh took his time, and had a glimpse of two toughs, one at the wheel, the other in the second row of seats.

Af-Laawe cried, "Hold tight!" and the car was off in a rattle of gravel.

Not wanting to show that he was frightened, Jeebleh held tight, as he had been instructed. Af-Laawe was visibly agitated, and Jeebleh wished he knew what had excited him so. He prayed to God they wouldn't have an accident: the hospitals were barely functioning, and what if he needed a transfusion? Was the blood supply safe? If Shanta's so-called cartel was truly in operation, his heart and kidneys might end up somewhere in the Middle East! And this pimpmobile was a clear sign, if he needed one, that Af-Laawe was not to be trusted. Disjointed words fell pell-mell from Af-Laawe's mouth.

"Where are you taking me?" Jeebleh asked.

"To your mother's housekeeper!"

AND BEFORE JEEBLEH KNEW IT, THEY WERE THERE, AND A WOMAN WHOM Af-Laawe introduced as the housekeeper was hugging him and kissing his cheeks, then his right shoulder, then his hands one at a time. Jeebleh was overwhelmed with emotion, although he and the woman had never met. Try as he might, he couldn't remember the name by which he had known her. He was of two minds whether she was genuine or fake, for he couldn't be certain whether the name by which she was now introduced matched the one he had sent monthly *xawaala* remittances to.

To the best of his memory, he had had no hand in hiring her, and he couldn't recall who had. He remembered agreeing to transfer the funds through an agency based in New Jersey to an account in the woman's name at a Mogadiscio bank. He had received a letter from his mother, written with the help of a scribe, informing him of the woman's employment. In addition, he had been given a neighbor's telephone number for her. His mother would not countenance a telephone in the house, for in those days, phones were a nuisance: if you were one of the few subscribers in a neighborhood, your phone would quickly become community property. He felt guilty that he hadn't been there for his mother, yet he had done what he could, and he tried to have her join him in America. But there was a problem, something to do with her not having a passport; the authorities—read Caloosha—would not issue her one.

Jeebleh and the woman now sat on a threadbare couch on the porch of a small house with a very low ceiling. Af-Laawe stood apart, his back to them, intently watching the road while he eavesdropped on their every word. The two muscles standing guard at the door made a dramatic impression on the woman. Whereas Jeebleh spoke to the woman in a low voice, she made a point of talking to him loudly, so everyone could hear. Although he assured her that he wasn't hard of hearing, she continued to talk as if to a deaf person.

This was no routine encounter for Jeebleh: he was meeting someone who claimed to have looked after his mother's daily physical needs, nursing her through advanced age until her death. If she was genuine, he might have looked upon her as a mother to his mother. But he sensed that he was being duped, so he was not in awe of her or of what she might tell him. He had an unpleasant question about letters that had been returned to him unopened. He meant to ask why they had been sent back, not about the monthly remittances. But a drought raised its parched head inside him, and he could come up only with an innocuous question: "What were my mother's last words?"

"She was happy to go, when her time was up."

"What else do you remember?"

"I remember the shine on your mother's cheeks."

"Her last words?"

"She was happy to go, when her time was up," the woman repeated, with more care this time, and added: "But she was very sorry that you, her only beloved son, weren't there to bid her good-bye."

They lived in a world of pretense, the two of them. He talked with caution, well aware that his life depended on it. She spoke to please Af-Laawe; most definitely she feared him too. But Jeebleh had to set a test for her, to see if she was for real.

"Like many Somali children," Jeebleh said, "I never knew my mother's age precisely. Would you by any chance know?"

"She was close to seventy."

"When she died?"

Af-Laawe stepped in. "If we had her papers we would be able to answer your question with more precision."

His mother had had a strong and youthful spirit, and had been more together in mind and body than many others of her advanced age. Jeebleh knew that although she may have appeared younger, she was actually in her early eighties when a housekeeper was hired to look after her.

The woman, contradicting an earlier statement of hers, said, "She wanted so much for you to return before her final departure, and as I said earlier, she was sad that she had to go."

He pictured her in his mind, a hardworking and determined woman, prepared to outlive the Dictator. She wouldn't have been happy to go without seeing her son. In fact, on the few occasions when he had called on the neighbor's line, she would tell him that she would preserve herself until he came home. Now that he remembered the phone calls, it struck him that this woman was not the person to whom he had spoken when he had telephoned: that woman had had a local accent, while the woman in front of him had a more pronounced accent from the north, probably from Galkacyo.

He had seldom written to his mother, and was cautious when he did. Not only did he think there was no good to be gained from raising her expectations, but he did not want to cause her unnecessary distress. She never sounded keen on the idea of having his wife and two daughters visit. "What will I say to them?" she asked once. "I don't speak a foreign language, and you haven't taught them Somali." And when he spoke to her again, asking her to think further about it, she said, "It'll only worry me to no end if they come. Besides, I won't be able to sleep a wink, night or day, expecting a knock on my door, and waiting for someone from the National Security to harass us." She was a woman with an agenda, the preservation of her son and Bile, whom she loved as though he were hers too.

Jeebleh asked the housekeeper to tell him what his mother thought about his unannounced departure from Somalia.

"I don't like to hurt your feelings," she replied.

"How do you mean?"

"Your mother died believing you were a traitor."

He knew the woman wasn't telling the truth, and was sure she had been told to say this. He shifted his gaze away, refusing to look in her direction for a while. When he had her in his sights again, he asked, "How often did Caloosha visit her?"

It was her turn this time to appear drained of blood, her face becoming pallid. "I don't wish to get involved," she said.

"What do you mean, you don't wish to get involved?" He pretended to be enraged. "What has my question got to do with your getting *involved*? Involved in *what*?"

He knew and she knew where he intended to take her with his questions. And he understood why she didn't want to go there with him, to a land of further attrition. Af-Laawe, he noticed, was agitated again. Jeebleh decided to interrogate her further. "Did my mother suffer any lapses of judgment?"

"Why do you ask?"

"Because I doubt that she would think of me as a traitor, unless she had suffered great lapses of judgment."

"I wouldn't know."

"Did she die fully alert?"

He had been kept so ill informed about her state of health that he did not even know about the deterioration until she was just about dead. He had seen this as symptomatic of a country whose people cared little about one another. On the one hand, there was deliberate indifference to her condition on the part of the state apparatus, because she was his mother. On the other hand, there was an incurable apathy everywhere. Someone like Shanta, who had visited the old woman and in all probability looked after her now and then, still hadn't stirred herself sufficiently to show that she cared, by writing to him.

He and his mother had never talked about his departure from Somalia: it would have been unwise to discuss his controversial one-way ticket out of the country on an open telephone line belonging to a neighbor. He had heard of his mother's deteriorating health, and tried to telephone, but could not get through because of the bad connections. Then he received a newspaper clipping, anonymously posted, in which her death was announced. Now he repeated, "What was my mother's mental state when she died?"

"Your mother died on her own terms," she said.

"She was fully aware of what was happening?"

The woman nodded.

He imagined Caloosha calling on his mother, sitting at her bedside day in and day out, and describing her son as a traitor. Could she, in truth, have seen as a traitor someone who belonged outside the precincts of the human community? No. He knew she wouldn't have thought of him as a Judas. Alas, he had no one to support his side of things. His voice as hard and unbending as iron, he asked, "What about my letters to her? Why were they returned, unopened and unread?"

"I've no idea about letters' being returned."

"You weren't aware?"

"I read her the ones I received!"

"What did you do with them?"

"Burned them."

"Why burn them?"

"Those were my instructions."

"Who gave you those instructions?"

"She did!"

If this was true, then it could only mean that his mother had attained the bitter age when nothing hurtful could have touched her anymore. He had failed her, and was blaming others for his foibles: that was the sad truth of it. He had come too late. What in hell did he expect in a country weighed down with the grievances of its people, dwelling in a land burdened by destruction and death? His own letters returned, unread? Now he asked, "Were you alone with her when she died?"

"We weren't alone."

"Who else was there with you?"

"Caloosha!"

She would give no further details, and resorted to shaking her head back and forth, then up and down. She paused for a brief spell, then shook her head now to the right and now to the left, in the gesture of someone ridding herself of a terrible thought.

Jeebleh imagined his mother dying, and then total quiet descending, a butterfly no longer stirring, with its wings folded, still.

He heard Af-Laawe say, "Now to the cemetery!"

ON THEIR WAY THERE, JEEBLEH UNDERSTOOD THAT HIS MOTHER HAD DIED restless. It no longer mattered to him whether the woman now sitting behind him in the Mercedes, next to Af-Laawe, had served as her housekeeper or

not; nor did it matter if she had lied to him. He and his mother hadn't ultimately made peace with each other. His visit to her grave and his wish to
build a headstone were but attempts to effect reconciliation with her spirit,
which had departed in a troubled state.

He assumed that Af-Laawe and Caloosha would feed him half-truths and
apparent facts. Having bothered to bring him all the way to the cemetery,
they would probably show him a tomb marked with a board bearing his
mother's name. Thanks to Shanta, he knew what to look for: a Hinducini
mango tree with seasonal fruits bigger than the head of a grown man, and four
medium-to-large stones with his mother's name on them. He sat between two
men in shades, with guns.

"What about the money?" he asked the woman.

"We used every penny of it," she told him.

He could only contemplate a life of regret, one in total ruins. If the woman
was to be believed, the last words on his mother's lips amounted to a curse. If
he was being fed on half-truths, was it possible that even though the woman
was as false as counterfeit money, the low-ceilinged house to which he had
been taken really belonged to his mother's housekeeper? And was this one
reason why he hadn't been allowed to go past the porch—because they were
worried he might see many of his mother's things, things the genuine housekeeper had appropriated or had been given by his mother? What gave this
woman a certain credibility was that although she was a fake, she wore a
dress his daughters had bought and sent as a gift to their grandmother.

Like it or not, he was visiting a land where demons never took a break.
There was so much distrust that demons didn't need to top things up, make
sure there was enough to go round, give everyone his or her commensurate
share of misery.

AT LONG LAST, THEY REACHED A GATE WITH A BROKEN SIGNBOARD, WITH THE
words "The Sity's General Cemetary" written in the shaky hand of a semi-
literate. The road was choked with low shrubs, leaving only a narrow point of
entry for the car. Traces of the old tarred road were visible, as was a broken-

down shack, which once had served as a guardhouse. From the few times he had come here, Jeebleh remembered a caravan of vehicles waiting at the entrance. In those days, you had to present a death certificate from the municipality to be allowed to bury your dead here. Civil wars, anathema to bureaucracy, do away with the authority that is synonymous with normality. Civil wars simplify some matters and complicate others.

They drove for quite a while before the vehicle came to a stop at the command of the housekeeper, who saw the landmark she was looking for. The first to get out, Af-Laawe went around and gave the housekeeper a hand. Jeebleh got out and walked forward with a clubfooted gait. The huge loss was at last getting to him, weighing him down with more guilt. Had he been by himself, he would have sunk to his knees and stayed there, taking comfort from his humbled position. He heard his name spoken in a low whisper, and the housekeeper's announcement: "There, I can see it!"

He took a good hold of himself and looked around. There was no mango tree with a sweet shade close by. Nor could he see four medium-to-large stones with writing on them to mark the grave, as Shanta had described. He didn't know what Af-Laawe and the housekeeper expected him to do. He went on his knees, not because he wished to humble himself in prayer, but because walking or standing upright was proving difficult. Of course he knew that the moment toward which he had been moving all these years, to be face to face with revelatory death, was further away now than he had imagined. "This is not my mother's grave," he told the housekeeper.

"But it is," she insisted.

"It isn't!" he said.

Af-Laawe came nearer to find out what was happening, and the two musclemen with shades and guns approached as well. Jeebleh prepared for the moment when he would sink deeper into a reverie, and waited.

All the while, the woman pointed at a mound of earth that wasn't his mother's, saying, "There!" Who was she? Why was he still on his knees? From the way the woman indicated the mound, her forefinger extended, she might have been Columbus pointing at a new world beyond the horizon.

"That grave doesn't belong to my mother," he said.

Af-Laawe said, "Does a grave belong to the person in it, or to those claiming it with an authoritative apostrophe, as when someone says, 'My mother's grave'?"

Jeebleh wasn't sure which Af-Laawe was getting wrong, his pronoun or where to place the apostrophe. Nor did he like Af-Laawe's lip. But then what could he do about it, considering that there were two muscles who would kick him to death if he challenged him?

The woman came to him now, and towered above him. With her head inclined, her smile diffuse, she took his hand and led him to a mound that had collapsed on itself. And pointed at it. "Here she is!" She picked up a strip of zinc with his mother's name recently inscribed in the hand of an autistic child. "Your mother's here!" she said.

"My mother doesn't belong in here!" he insisted.

With mouthy rudeness, Af-Laawe said, "She may not belong in the grave herself anymore, given her condition, but her bones do."

One of the musclemen moved into Jeebleh's field of vision, blocking it. He pretended to help Jeebleh to his feet, while his companion prodded Jeebleh sharply with the professional accuracy of a nurse giving an injection.

Jeebleh's stomach turned, and he dropped deeper and deeper into nausea. He could not get up, and was so weak that he felt almost lifeless. By the time he managed to crawl closer to the mound and lay his head on it, the squeamishness had disabled his knees. Finally he fell, forehead first, as though he were dead.

PART 3

". . . Murderers and those who strike in malice,
as well as plunderers and robbers . . .
A man can set violent hands against
himself or his belongings. . . .
Now fraud, that eats away at every conscience,
is practiced by a man against another
who trusts in him, or one who has no trust."

                                    (CANTO XI)

Who, even with untrammeled words and many
attempts at telling, even could recount
in full the blood and wounds that I now saw?
Each tongue that tried would certainly fall short
because the shallowness of both our speech
and intellect cannot contain so much.

                                    (CANTO XXVIII)
                                    DANTE, *Inferno*

24.

HOW DID HE GET *HERE*?

He was in a restaurant, sitting by himself at a table, and before him was a cup of tea—which, he found by dipping in his finger and touching it to his lower lip, was highly sugared. There was a huge gap in his memory. He couldn't recall what had happened between the moment his knees gave way, after the jab from the muscleman-cum-medico, and now.

He studied the curious faces surrounding him and concluded that he didn't know who they were, and hadn't the slightest idea how or why he had been brought to this place, or by whom. His memory had run out, abandoning him at the mound. But in his mind he replayed Af-Laawe's rude remarks, which he hoped Af-Laawe would pay for sooner rather than later. Jeebleh remembered the supposed housekeeper pointing at a grave, her forefinger extended, and saying, "Your mother's here!" Then Af-Laawe's sass . . . and then what? Did the jab come before or after he had had enough of Af-Laawe's lip and the woman's lies?

The mystery was now cast in a framed moment that was difficult to define. He had been on his knees when he felt the jab; he had smelled something noxious, although he couldn't determine its nature. He had seen the shadowy presence of the muscleman in the corner of his vision, then a second muscleman's hand insinuating itself into the lamp of his consciousness, making him go out as quickly as the flames of a fire extinguished with a miasmic liquid. He had heard the voices of the two men in shades, before a needle pricking him on the upper thigh interfered with his thinking. Now he felt his stomach to make sure that he hadn't undergone a surgery in which an organ of his had been removed. He touched where the needle had prodded, and it ached. He hoped he wasn't developing an exaggerated sense of paranoia, in which, like Shanta, he would detect the hand of the cartel everywhere.

What would become of him now, he wondered, as he listened to a miscellany of male voices. Af-Laawe was somewhere near, he was sure. And he was damned if he knew the purpose to all this, or where his new reality began and where it might end. But why did "they" have to resort to these crude methods?

He heard someone calling his name.

TALL, BUCKTOOTHED, THIN AS A CANE, FAAHIYE STOOD BEFORE HIM. DISSOLVing into the shadow he cast, he was as elusive as a mirror reflected in the image of its own shiftiness. Jeebleh stared up at him, and he wouldn't take a seat. Jeebleh focused on the toothpick in the corner of Faahiye's mouth, which his tongue was busying itself with, moving it here and there, back and forth. He had the drawn-in cheeks of a man of advanced age. Jeebleh made sure that he was seeing no visions. He thought it safe to assume that Faahiye, who had come out of hiding, should be the one to say something first.

And that was how it came to be. Faahiye took the toothpick out of his mouth and said, "I'm surprised you recognize me."

"Where am I?" asked Jeebleh.

"I was told you'd be here."

"Who told you that I'd be here?"

"I am not at liberty to disclose that particular detail."

Jeebleh said, "Sit down anyhow," and Faahiye did so. Then, because they hurt, Jeebleh closed his eyes. He took a deep breath, then exhaled, counting to thirty, and praying that he wasn't hallucinating, seeing things and thinking weird thoughts at this most crucial moment of his visit. Faahiye sat close to him, their thighs touching, Jeebleh's itching. How he wished he could scratch the spot! But uncertain what to make of Faahiye, he did not dare.

"We've all been through it!" Faahiye said.

"We've all been jabbed, have we?"

"Jabbed?" Faahiye asked.

"Poisoned!"

"I meant that all of us who've lived in this civil war have become someone other than ourselves for brief periods of time, in which we've entertained moments of doubt, or dropped into a deep well of despair. Have you too become someone other, in spite of yourself?"

Listening to Faahiye was working positively on him, and he was managing to take it easy, despite himself. Faahiye's words had taken him to a comfort zone, where he didn't mind dwelling for as long as they were in the teahouse. Jeebleh would have been the first to admit that it would be unwise to meet up with Af-Laawe, after he had been told about him; Af-Laawe would put him through a grinder, he suspected. But now he was looking at the brighter side of things: at least he had gotten to meet Faahiye, never mind his dissipated condition. Who knows, he might even get to meet Raasta and take her home shortly, back to Shanta and Bile!

"We've all learned to be someone other than ourselves, and have relaxed ourselves into accepting our perverse condition," Faahiye was saying. "This makes living easier, less tedious."

Jeebleh felt as naked as a cat with singed hair. Were Af-Laawe and his cohorts making him jump through hoops of humiliation in order to warn him that worse things were to come unless he stopped being a nuisance? His tongue was now in a tangle, in part because he didn't know whether it was wise to confide in Faahiye. After all, if trusting Af-Laawe had gotten him to where he was now, jabbed and in pain, then where would trusting Faahiye lead him?

"I know I am someone other than myself," Faahiye said. "At times it's pretty hard to figure out who I am, especially when I am by myself. This gets a lot more challenging when I am with others, who are themselves others!"

"What about when you are with Raasta and Makka?"

Jeebleh felt uncomfortable, because Faahiye's expression didn't change at all, as if he didn't even recognize the names of the girls. To interpret his interlocutor's shiftiness, Jeebleh willed himself into becoming as humble and calm as the metallic silver of a mirror. This way he might make sense of the shadowy apparition moving at the deeper end of what was reflected in Faahiye's features.

"You know it and so do I," Faahiye said. "You become someone other than yourself when you spend many years in isolation, or live separated from those who mean a lot to you. You become someone other than yourself when you live together with your jailers, whom heaven wouldn't admit into its courtyard, and whom hell wouldn't deign to receive."

"Why did you opt out?"

"I am sure you've heard the proverb that says that even a coward, alone and untested, thinks of himself as a brave man?"

"I know the proverb, all right," Jeebleh said.

"I left because I thought I'd do better if I struck out on my own, away from the constraints of in-laws and so on. And because I didn't like the false lives we lived."

"False lives? What false lives, whose?"

"It would be unbecoming of me to name names."

Faahiye beckoned to a waiter, who came and recited the menu of meats and pasta dishes. When he had taken Faahiye's order, and it became obvious that Jeebleh didn't want anything, the waiter relayed it at the top of his voice to the kitchen, about ten meters away, through an open hatch. Jeebleh drew comfort from the fact that he was meeting Faahiye in a restaurant filled with absolute strangers. Because no one there was carrying a gun—at least not openly—and no one appeared worried or frightened, Jeebleh remembered Mogadiscio as it used to be, peaceful. Not far from where they sat, several men were busy counting piles of Somali shillings, then handing them over to other men in exchange for U.S. dollars. Jeebleh guessed they were close to the Bakhaaraha market.

Faahiye continued talking. "Memory runs in awe of all that's false, mean, and wicked. Myself, I'd ascribe my failure to adapt to life with Bile to the fact that before his arrival on the scene, Shanta and I had all the time we needed to construct a world out of dreams. I was, I must say, unprepared to live in an intimate way with Bile at the same time as having Raasta. It was all too much, too soon—I found it unhealthy, and contrived. Before his arrival, Shanta and I had dreamt dreams the size of a huge home with all its comforts, dreamt that we would enjoy our child's love and companionship to the fullest extent. I had dreamt that I would relish being a father to Raasta, whom I hoped to rear on a diet of affection.

"We began our lives, Shanta and I, as a twosome, a loving couple, rarely raising our voices in anger at each other. We spent much of our time together, loving, bonded, tied to each other by the mutuality of our needs, the need to survive the war, which was then between the Dictator and the clan-based militias. Neither of us imagined life without the other. There was joy in our sharing of pure love, and we melted into each other. She was my barber, and devoted loving time to giving a smoother shape to my straggly toenails. I paid attention to all of her needs in every detail. We would shower together, soap each other's bodies, and then make love."

The waiter brought Faahiye his order, but wouldn't go until he was paid in cash. Faahiye touched his pockets, then showed his palms, indicating that he had no money. Jeebleh offered to pay, but he had only dollars. "No problem," the waiter assured him, and took the bill to the money changers nearby, who gave him Somali shillings.

Between mouthfuls, Faahiye continued to speak, saying that when Shanta became pregnant, both he and she felt that if she carried the pregnancy to term and gave birth to a healthy baby, then such an issue, given Shanta's age, would be a miraculous one. "If only I could bid yesterday to return, and make it explain why Bile's arrival changed everything, why I didn't take to him, couldn't stand him, and why he didn't take to me and couldn't stand me either. Perhaps it was because we lived on top of one another. Moreover, the civil war was entering a very tense new phase. Or maybe it was because he took over the running of our lives, ruining what prospects there were for Shanta and me to enjoy being parents to Raasta together—I don't know!"

The noise of the teahouse ascended in cigarette smoke toward the low ceiling and then descended as an indecipherable din. The ceiling fans turned and turned, but didn't produce cool air. Straining his neck, his eyes focused on the window farthest from him, Jeebleh saw a jalopy resembling Af-Laawe's.

"Before Bile came, Shanta and I had lived in mutual dependence, to the exclusion of everyone else," Faahiye said. "We both held the view that hell is a blood relation. Myself, I can take my blood relations only in small doses, never in concentrated form. We got together a year after her mother's death, some time before yours passed away. She was a wonderful woman, your mother, God bless her soul, and I was very fond of her."

Jeebleh was more moved to hear this than he might have expected.

"Your mother was the first to hear of our wish to marry, because Shanta treated her like a second mother. Sadly, we had very little time for anyone else, and we seldom visited her. But whenever we did, she was warm and caring. Her housekeeper was a brave woman, able to tell Caloosha off when he got out of line. She loved you, your mother, and had nothing but praise for what you stood for."

Tears coming to his eyes, Jeebleh asked whether Faahiye had any idea how he could reach the housekeeper.

"I know where she is," Faahiye said.

"Where?"

"She and I lived in adjacent rooms in the refugee camp in Mombasa. She was penniless, depressed, and lacking in energy. She came to life only when she was angry and cursed Caloosha, or was full of joy and praised your mother's generosity of spirit—or yours!"

"When did you get back from Mombasa?"

"This morning."

"Tell me more. Please."

"I am not at liberty to do so," Faahiye said.

"And why not?"

"This is too complicated to get into now."

There was a long silence.

"Anyhow," Faahiye said finally, "Bile came when Shanta had lain on her back for almost two days, in labor. We were cursing our misfortunes, to be bringing a baby into a world falling around our ears. The Dictator had fled, and many members of my own clan family had been rounded up and killed en masse. So bad was the rabble-rousing rhetoric that Shanta, between groans, kept suggesting that I leave, that maybe it wasn't safe for me.

"Bile came. I've got to hand it to him, he knew what to do. He turned the baby to a position that would make for a healthy delivery. He delivered Shanta of a baby in a shorter time than it took him to decide whether to put aside the moral and psychological constraints of his medical ethics. Then he touched Raasta."

"*Touched* Raasta?"

"He appropriated her soon after delivering her. I understand now that he touched her out of human tenderness, which he must have missed, given that he had spent many years in solitary confinement. Later, I noticed that she quieted down whenever he picked her up, whereas she was in great distress when I held her. Raasta was jinxed, I thought. Why, she'd make as if suckling at his breast. I went ballistic, and on the attack. I spoke of murder, and of robbery. I had the proof. Bile had arrived with a duffel bag full of money. Where had he gotten it? No one leaves prison with a duffel bag full of money. He gave me some incredible spiel about stumbing on the funds, but I wasn't satisfied, and demanded proof of his innocence, which he couldn't provide."

"Why did you leave without any explanation?"

Faahiye replied, "I was irreconcilably hurt by Shanta's flippant remarks, spoken first in jest and in private, then in anger, in total seriousness, and in public. I had felt since Bile's arrival that she was a changed woman. Occasionally, she behaved as though her brother's presence turned her on sexually. And when I called him a murderer and we exchanged rude words, she took his side, saying how she hated having to deal with two children, one of whom was a grown adult—meaning me—and the second—meaning Raasta—a baby at her breast. I was reduced to an outsider in my own home, made into an ogre in front of my friends, and treated like an embarrassment in the presence of acquaintances. I withdrew in shame. I was of use only when they needed a fourth at the card table. Then they would ask me to join them."

"Did you at any point suspect that Bile had it in for you, because the two of you belonged to different clans?" Jeebleh asked.

"That never crossed my mind."

"Did you talk to Bile?"

"According to him, there was no basis for what he referred to as my self-exclusion. And the fact that he turned things around and made me feel that I was excluding myself didn't help matters at all. I quoted to him a proverb: 'A cow got while on a looting spree doesn't produce a calf that's legally yours.' And I forbade my daughter to be fed on the powdered milk that he had bought. The battle lines were drawn. We were engaged in a war of wills over what was right and what was wrong!"

Jeebleh had heard enough about Raasta, and so he asked: "Where's Raasta?"

"I haven't any idea."

Faahiye struck Jeebleh as straightforward.

"How about Makka?"

"No idea either."

"When did you last see them?"

"I saw them before I left for Mombasa."

"At Bile's or at Shanta's?"

"At one or the other's. I can't be certain."

"Where are you staying now?"

"I am not at liberty to disclose this detail."

"With Caloosha? With Af-Laawe?"

"I am not at liberty to disclose this," Faahiye repeated.

There was another long silence.

Jeebleh wondered if the cartel—and there was clearly a cartel, he told himself, organ-stealers or not—had flown Faahiye in from Mombasa, promising that he would see his daughter and Makka on the condition that he kept certain secrets to himself. He asked, "Will you call me if they will let me meet with Raasta and Makka after you're allowed to see the two girls yourself?"

Faahiye's eyes became evasive. He looked around, as if searching for someone tailing him or eavesdropping on his conversation. And then, with a knowing smile covering much of his face, maybe out of relief that Jeebleh had worked out the mystery for himself, he replied quietly but urgently, "I'll see what I can do!"

Then, without much ado, both got up to leave.

ONCE OUTSIDE THE TEAHOUSE, JEEBLEH USED THE MOBILE TO PHONE DAJAAL and ask that he pick him up. Dajaal questioned him about where he was, and set a spot to meet him.

Before the two men bid each other farewell, Faahiye told Jeebleh a folktale.

"It happened a long, long, long time ago," he said. "A son, reaching the age of twenty-something, marries. Blessed with children and a loving wife, the son takes his blind, now senile father to a tree very far from the family dwelling, gives the old man some water in a gourd and some milk in a pitcher, and leaves the helpless old man there. He promises he'll return for him shortly, only he knows he has no intention of doing so. The old man dies from exposure to the elements. But before dying, the old man curses his son.

"The years come and go, and the son grows to become an old man, his sight weak, his hearing gone, almost an invalid, a burden to his family. One day, his own son takes him for a walk, away from the hamlet to a desolate place. He puts two gourds, heavy with milk and water, close to him, and vows that he'll return for him before nightfall.

"The old man remembers what he, as a young, strong man, had done to his ailing, blind father. So he calls back his son and says, 'My father cursed me for doing to him what you're doing to me now, because I left him, a senile old man, to die alone. I lied to him, he cursed me, and so from then on, misfortunes called on me frequently. I'll pray for my father's pardon, and I'll pray that God blesses your every wish with His approval. May good fortune smile on you and your family, my son!'

"The son takes his father back to the hamlet, and the chains of curses, guilt, and more sorrows are thus broken."

Then Faahiye was gone!

25.

AFTER DAJAAL PICKED HIM UP OUTSIDE THE RESTAURANT, JEEBLEH judiciously related some of what had transpired since he left Bile's apartment. He withheld the part about his visit to the cemetery with Af-Laawe, his musclemen, and the supposed housekeeper. Then he asked Dajaal's interpretation of the folktale.

"I would assume that he is now prepared to return to the fold of the family." Dajaal clutched the machine gun lying in his lap. After a silence, he added, "I doubt that it'll be a let-bygones-be-bygones return, though. He'll lay down his conditions, that's for sure."

"Why do you say that?"

"I have the feeling that he is being blackmailed. But however you look at it, it's definitely a relief that he is ready to break the cycle of curses and to reconcile himself to his new situation."

Jeebleh said, "He's from the old world, all right!"

Dajaal drove without talking, visibly hampered by the gun on his lap, which slipped whenever he took a bend. They were headed back to Bile's, and were less than a kilometer away when Jeebleh asked if Dajaal could do him a favor.

Dajaal slowed the car. "Y-e-s!"

"Could you take me to the cemetery, please?"

"Why?"

"I wish to visit my mother's grave, to pay my belated respects to her, to say a brief prayer in peace there. I'll be in your debt forever if you get me there and back."

"How do we find the grave?"

Jeebleh explained that Shanta had given him directions, and that he knew what to look for.

"We'll have to let Bile know."

"I don't think that's necessary," Jeebleh said.

Dajaal gave this a moment's thought, and then deferred to Jeebleh's decision. Even so, he fidgeted as he drove. The gun kept slipping off his lap, and he kept grabbing it with his left hand just before it dropped to the floor.

"Since I am playing truant today, I might as well hold the gun," Jeebleh offered. "At least that'll make your driving easier."

Dajaal had yet to come up with an answer when Jeebleh took hold of the weapon, turning it this way and that. Admiring it. He surprised even himself when he said, "This is a beauty, isn't it?"

"It's well put together, I agree." Then a rider: "Mind you, go gentle, okay?" Dajaal might have been warning a toddler about the dangers of fire.

This was the first time in his life that Jeebleh had held a firearm. What worried him was his spellbound, facile adoration of the gun. The muscleman had injected him with a potion that had altered his nature and personality, and soon he might no longer challenge a statement like the one spoken by Af-Laawe on the day of his arrival: that guns lack the body of human truths! As he fondled the gun, he realized that he was a changed man, different from the one who had left a loving wife and two daughters back home, promising to be cautious, and to bring back the life, his, of which he was a mere custodian.

They arrived at the broken signboard that marked the entrance to the General Cemetery, and drove around in search of the landmarks Shanta had told Jeebleh about. He was sweating with worry when they passed the section where Af-Laawe had taken him; he remembered what had been done to him, and how rude Af-Laawe had been. But he chose not to speak of any of this to

Dajaal. He was relieved as the uncut wild shrubs impeded their progress, and they had to take a long, roundabout way toward a large mango tree.

Jeebleh apologized for making Dajaal go through all this. "If my mother had not departed the way she did," he said, "with her soul bothered and her peace troubled, I should not have insisted on your bringing me here now."

As soon as he discovered a straight path to the mango tree, Dajaal revved the engine. He parked the car under an acacia, and stayed there, covering Jeebleh with the machine gun—they could not be sure, Af-Laawe or his cronies might be lying in wait. Jeebleh got out of the car without fear and, no longer tired, strode forward with a fresh spring. Now that he had found the spot marked with four medium-to-large stones bearing his mother's name, Waliya, he looked around and saw how close he had been to it on his previous visit. He doubted that the purported housekeeper knew where the grave was; Af-Laawe, however, did. From where he stood, Jeebleh could see that here too the earth had shifted, and several mounds had collapsed on themselves.

He sank to his knees, humbling himself in prayerful memory of a mother whom he felt he had failed. In this crouched posture, he resembled a haunted creature from prehistory deferring to a sky god. His eyes opened wide onto an endless day of prayer, and an eternal night of commiseration.

He was now more at peace with himself than at any time since his arrival in the city of ruin. And when Dajaal came to him, suggesting that it was time to leave, Jeebleh requested that they call at Bile's mother's grave. Again, he crouched in supplication, the boundary marked with a fruitless lemon tree which offered hardly any shadow, and four medium-to-large stones bearing the name: Hagarr.

AT THE APARTMENT, HE TOLD BILE AND SEAMUS MORE THAN HE HAD BEEN prepared to share with Dajaal, about what had been done to him and how he had suffered at Af-Laawe's hand. Then he explained what he had done, and how, soon after calling at the graves of his mother and that of Auntie Hagarr, peace had returned to him.

When Shanta, who was in a party mood, joined them, Jeebleh purged his story of the mention of the jab he had been given by Af-Laawe's muscleman. Nor did he bother to inform her of his thought that the muscleman was a doctor on retainer to the cartel. Yet Jeebleh harbored his own worries. His hand kept returning to the spot where he'd been jabbed, and he wondered whether it would grow larger than a boil before the night was out. Earlier, he had shown it to Bile, who promised that they would go for tests at the city's only lab with a pathology facility, rudimentary as it was. Jeebleh's mind kept returning to the many occasions in their youth when Caloosha had subjected him and Bile to torture; he knew that he had come to a point in his life when he should face his demons, and in some way deal with them. To take his mind off his worries, he emphasized Dajaal's opinion that Faahiye was a victim of blackmail. When she heard that Jeebleh had called at their mothers' graves, Shanta became more boisterous, kissing, ululating, a woman in celebration.

The four stayed up most of the night, talking, engaging in conjecture. No one wanted to break up the improvised gathering, and of course, Shanta had no wish to go back to an empty, desolate home; she preferred instead to sleep on the living room floor. Whereas Shanta, in her nervous optimism, felt that Raasta and Makka's return was imminent, the others were not of that view, especially Bile. All the same, the apartment was charged with Shanta's renewed energy. They tried to imagine their way into Faahiye's mind, speculating over the same ground: Why did he keep telling Jeebleh that he wasn't at liberty to disclose this or that bit of information? How was Raasta bearing up, and what was her mental state? Was Faahiye telling the truth when he said that he had been at the refugee camp in Mombasa? With Shanta's spirits so high, the three men were careful not to say or do anything that might spoil her flowering enthusiasm.

For fear of being thought a party-pooper, Bile acquiesced to Shanta's demand that the generator run for much longer than was customary. All sorts of drinks came out of the cabinet, soft, hard, and in between. Seamus helped himself to several bottles of beer and as many generous tots of whiskey as his tumbler could contain. A wine bottle of excellent Italian vintage, bought in Rome, was uncorked. Coffee was made, and tea brewed. Glasses that hadn't been dusted for years, since no one could think of a good enough reason to celebrate, were passed around. Shanta insisted on a very sweet orange drink.

Bile, though not unnecessarily mistrustful of Faahiye or his motives, was by nature ill disposed toward hatching his eggs before he had a hen to lay them. He couldn't help returning to the same questions: How was Raasta doing in captivity? How was Makka coping? How much help, if any, had the abductors received from Caloosha or Af-Laawe? What purpose was the abduction meant to serve?

The posse of security personnel—discreetly recruited from within the displaced community nearby—was on the alert, busy watching over the entire neighborhood. And because there was electricity for them from the generator for much of the night, there was gaiety among the security detail too, a modest calm informed by self-restraint.

The three men did not abandon their instinct of caution; while one moment Seamus and Jeebleh agreed that there were positive signs pointing to an early reunion with the missing girls, the next moment Bile wondered whether they would be able to meet Faahiye's conditions, whatever these were.

It wasn't so with Shanta, who was overwhelmed with joy, her tongue where her heart should have been. She kept jabbering away, at times making it difficult for the others to get a word in edgewise. Not once did she say anything terrible about Faahiye. What's more, she asked for Jeebleh's forgiveness, because of the results obtained. "I wouldn't have accused you unfairly of talking to Faahiye behind our backs, if I imagined for a moment that you were capable of achieving miracles." Embarrassed, he looked away, remembering being told that she was given to speaking of herself as a mother "damned to tears and sorrow." With an expression of pained wonder, she went over and for the second time kissed him on the brow, almost tumbling on top of him. She regained her balance and caught her breath, and kept saying, "Thank you, thank you, thank you in the name of our mothers!"

Now the past, which Shanta had smuggled in by alluding to their mothers, became the fifth person in the room, assuming a larger presence than anyone had been prepared for. Bile admonished them to desist from introducing the past, as a contraband idea, as this would exclude Seamus. Nor could the three friends and coevals speak of their more recent past, as this would exclude Shanta. Seamus stepped in to steer the conversation away from the present to a past not close to anyone's heart: the role the United States had played in Somalia!

"I've my misgivings about saints and angels," he said, "especially as I fear that people describe the Yankees as 'good angels' come on a humanitarian mission, to perform God's work here. Do you think Yankees ceased being angels, because of the conditions they met here, conditions that wouldn't permit them to perform any work but Satan's? When do angels cease to be angels and resort to being who they are, Yankees? That's a topic worth pursuing, wouldn't you agree with me, my American friend?" And Seamus looked at Jeebleh, teasing.

Jeebleh was comforted by the prospect of affording his mind time to dwell on another subject, and he thought, half remembering a quotation attributed to J. M. Synge, that there was no one like Seamus to soothe and quiet one's nerves on an evening such as this. Meanwhile Seamus's unerring sense of kindness toward everyone made it possible for him to speak a gentle reprimand in the very idiom that made you think he was praising you. The man thought of the world, Jeebleh reflected, in images that surprised even Seamus: unpredictable in an interesting way.

Shanta was excited to high heaven, and so was her voice, as she addressed Seamus, who now assumed the role of a moderator at a panel discussion, but only momentarily. "They ceased to be angels," she said, "which they weren't in any case, and became who they were, Americans, when they used overwhelming force in such an indiscriminate fashion and lots of innocent Somalis died."

Bile agreed, adding that, from the moment they landed and started putting on a circus for the benefit of prime-time TV back home, you felt they couldn't have come to do God's work.

"Why did they come, then?" Seamus said. And when no one spoke, he gave his theory: that everything that could've gone wrong for the Yanks had gone wrong because they saw everything in black and white, had no understanding of and no respect for other cultures, and were short on imagination, as they never put themselves in anyone else's shoes. They were also let down by their intelligence services, arriving everywhere unprepared, untutored in the ways of the world; he brought up the collapse of the Soviet Union and the former Yugoslavia, Iraq's invasion of Kuwait, and the disintegration of several ramshackle states in different parts of the globe. "They came to show the world that they could make peace-on-demand in Somalia, in the same dramatic fashion as they had made war-on-demand in the Gulf. They came to showcase peace here, as a counterpoint to their war effort elsewhere. Iraq and Somalia had one thing in common: both were made-for-TV shows. Christ, they were uppity, but they never lost their focus—the prime-time performance was their focus all along." He turned to Jeebleh, who looked ill at ease. "I am agreeing with you. What's your gripe?"

Jeebleh pondered for a few seconds. "Doesn't the sound of a gunshot make the birds perched side by side on a telephone wire take off in fright, all at the same time?" he asked rhetorically.

"Y-e-s?" Bile seemed interested.

"But a few seconds after taking off in fright," Jeebleh said, "don't many of the birds that haven't been hit come back to sit on the same telephone wire, or another one very much like it?"

"What's your point?"

"The Americans shouldn't have permitted the armed vigilantes to return to their haunts. They should've disarmed them soon after their arrival, when the irregular armies allied to the Strongmen were afraid of America's military might. They sent contradictory messages to the warlords, and then fell back on this zero-casualty idea. I'd say they lost their focus, all right."

"Perhaps the cutthroat conditions the Americans encountered here, which they had no way of dealing with, made them blow hot and cold?" Shanta speculated.

"There was another problem," Bile said. "A problem to do with definitions."

"How do you mean, definitions?" Seamus asked.

Perhaps because the conversation was no longer about Raasta and Makka's return, Shanta became more garrulous than Jeebleh had known her to be since their first encounter, and couldn't control her enthusiasm. She fidgeted, got up, moved about, then returned to her original seat, mumbling something to herself. No one paid her any mind.

Bile spoke. "The U.S. forces failed to define why they really came to Somalia in the first place, soon after the Gulf War. This was never made clear. The 'good' Americans, just back from defeating Bad Guy Saddam, were seen on TV holding a dozen starving babies at a feeding center—a picture of postcard quality. Later, after the trigger-happy U.S. soldiers massacred hundreds of innocent civilians and turned the life of the residents into hell, we asked ourselves how the Americans could reconcile the earlier gestures of mercy with the bombings of the city, in which many women and children were killed. And did you hear what one of the U.S. officials said when they pulled out after the October debacle? 'We fed them, they got strong, and they killed us!' Do you recall who it was said that?"

"Some U.S. major or other," offered Seamus.

"A spokesman of the UN, actually," Bile said.

"He could've been U.S. Army, though."

"What's the difference?" Shanta said.

"A matter of definition!" Bile said.

Seamus took it from there: "Surely StrongmanSouth's armed youths who shot at the Americans, and killed many UN Blue Helmets of other nationalities, were not the emaciated babies with whom the Marines had those heartwrenching pictures taken in front of the cameras? Surely the spokesman of the UN military was mistakenly equating the small group of armed militias who fought against them with the whole of the Somali nation?"

"Don't Somalis take the part and mistake it for the whole too?" Jeebleh knew he was in a distancing mode, apart from "them."

"I agree," Bile said. "We too mistook the small group of senior officers and the military on duty here for the whole of America. You'd have thought from listening to the ranting of a supporter of StrongmanSouth that America had gone to war against the whole of the Somali nation, which of course it hadn't. When one takes the part for the whole, one seldom bothers to distinguish between the uncouth soldiers with whom we've become acquainted and other, well-meaning Americans. I am sure there are millions of Americans who are good people, and millions of Somalis who wouldn't hurt an American fly. When you think of it, the Americans, by their actions, made a hero out of StrongmanSouth, and this prolonged the civil war. After all, it was after their hasty departure that he nominated himself president. I'd say the American-in-Charge met his equal and Faustian counterpart in StrongmanSouth."

"What of the Belgians, the Italians, or the Canadians?" Seamus asked. "They didn't act less uppity or more humanely toward the Somalis, did they?"

Shanta now addressed Jeebleh: "Did you know that in everyday Somali, the term *amerikaan* means 'weird'? Why do you think that is so?"

"I know too that the term *amxaar*, the Somali word for 'Ethiopian,' means 'unkind,' 'brutal,'" Seamus said. "And I can tell you why."

"The coinage of *amerikaan* to mean 'weird,' I should point out, precedes the Somali people's recent encounter with Americans in the shape of the Marines and Rangers who shot the daylights out of them," Jeebleh said. "Maybe it came about as a result of the Hollywood movies we've seen?"

"I think it's in the nature of the strong and the weak to define each other in ways that make sense only to one of them, not necessarily to both," said Seamus. "To the Somali, the Amerikaan is weird, to the American GI, the Somali is an ingrate and a skinny."

"And I would hate it if a GI Joe not worth a quid of chewed tobacco were to make up our minds for us about America!" Jeebleh replied. "Moreover, let's ask ourselves a question: Can we blame them? Is a whole country responsible for a crime committed by one of its citizens? Can all of America be held responsible for the gaffes made by one of its nationals, however high-ranking, or however representative of the power invested in him?"

It was then that Bile reminded them of how the rotors of one U.S. helicopter had blown a baby girl, barely a year old, out of her mother's arms and up into the dust-filled heavens. They all fell silent, affected by the unimaginable horror. Jeebleh wanted to know if Bile had ever met her.

"She was brought to my clinic," he offered.

Jeebleh remembered Dajaal's mentioning that his granddaughter had been blown away in a helicopter's uprush of air.

"Dajaal came along to the clinic with the girl and her mother."

"I've been meaning to see her," Jeebleh said. "Perhaps Dajaal can take me to her."

Shanta was the first to yawn, and the yawning became contagious, everyone agreeing that it was time to turn in. Bile reminded Jeebleh that just to be on the safe side, he would take him to the lab first thing in the morning.

Shanta overheard and worriedly wondered if all was well with Jeebleh.

"Just a checkup," he reassured her. "I'd also like to go to the barber for a haircut," he told Bile.

"I'll ask Dajaal to drive you. And maybe on your way to or from the barber's you can make a detour and visit his granddaughter and her mother."

Shanta said, "Good night, then!"

Instead of saying good night, Seamus left Jeebleh with an admonition: "Let no madness hurt you into bearing a gun!"

Not rising to it, Jeebleh said, "Good night!"

"Night-night!"

"Night-night!"

26.

"WHICH DO YOU PREFER, WALKING OR TAKING THE CAR?" DAJAAL ASKED, when he and Jeebleh, back from the lab, met the following morning.

"Are the two places far apart?" Jeebleh paused, feeling awkward, after taking a step. He put on the sarong he had brought from New York, and borrowed a conical cap and a shawl from Bile, wanting to look like a local when he went to the barber's, and to visit Dajaal's granddaughter and her mother.

Dajaal replied, "At most, it's half an hour's walk from my daughter-in-law's to the barbershop. I've arranged for Qasiir to meet us there."

Jeebleh had had a slight fever during the night and had been awake almost until dawn, tossing and turning, at times deciding to pack his bags and leave, then changing his mind and persuading himself to stay the course. Now his swollen glands were causing him discomfort, and several of his joints were burning from pain. Bile wouldn't commit himself to a diagnosis until he had heard from the lab technician, who had promised to get back to them before the end of the day, tomorrow at the latest. If anything, Bile said, Jeebleh was lucky that he had a constitution as strong as a horse's; Bile felt he was in no danger of imminent collapse.

"Let's walk," Jeebleh said.

"Are you sure?"

"Walking will do me good."

The memory of what he had gone through hit him afresh with agony and anger. He felt an upsurge of masochism within, like a river rising in the Sahara. He told himself to withstand the pain with unprecedented stoicism, but not to forget what had been done to him, so that he might link yesterday's agony and anger to those of yesteryear, and to what had happened to him as a child.

"Let's walk and talk!" he said.

DAJAAL LED THE WAY AND JEEBLEH WALKED ALONGSIDE, CLUTCHING THE candies he had brought for Dajaal's granddaughter. Death was no longer in every shadow cast by every wall. When he first arrived, he feared being ambushed by an unexpected death, and worried that he might die anonymously, killed by someone who did not know him and had no idea why he was administering death to him. Since then, he had wised up, coming around to the view that in the Mogadiscio of these days, death was seldom anonymous: it had a face and a name, and you were more likely to be killed by someone supposedly close to you or related to you. It was becoming rarer for total strangers to kill one another for no reason. Gone were the days of random killings. Lately, murderers were more calculating, factoring in their possible political and financial gains before killing you. Was it Osip Mandelstam who had said that only your own kind would kill you? To elude death of that sort, Jeebleh had fled south, where he was supposed to be an *other*, and where— here was the irony—he felt safer.

Dajaal interrupted his thoughts. "Are you happy in America?"

"America is home to me, but I doubt that I would use the word 'happy' to describe my state of mind there," Jeebleh said tentatively. "I'm comfortable in America. I love my wife and daughters. I love them *in* New York, where we live. I can't help comparing your question with one that I asked myself when I got here: Do I love Somalia? I found it difficult to answer."

"Do you?"

"Of course I love Somalia."

"What about as a Somali in America?"

"When I think about America from the perspective of a Somali, and reflect on what's occurred following the U.S. intervention, then I feel I'm in a bind."

Dajaal took a tighter grip on the ball he kept squeezing to help the blood in his hand circulate. You could see that he too was turning a thought in his head, stirring it, agitating it.

"Something happened that I hadn't reckoned on," Jeebleh said. "I discovered that I was not saddened by the deaths on either side as much as I was saddened by the ruthlessness displayed by the young fighters." He watched the flight of an eagle briefly before turning to Dajaal to ask, "What did you think of the Marines and the Rangers as fighters?"

"I couldn't fault the junior officers."

"What about the commanding officers?"

Dajaal took an even firmer grip on the rubber ball, his knuckles protruding more prominently and appeared a shade paler than their natural color.

"My heart went out to the young Marines and Rangers," Dajaal said, "even though on the night of the third of October, when I confronted them—man to man—I gave each of them as much of a piece of hell as I could. But during the lull in the fighting, I felt as though each of them was alone in his fear, like a child left in the pitch-darkness of a strange room by parents who were enjoying themselves elsewhere. I imagined them wondering what they were doing in Africa, away from their loved ones, and asking themselves why some skinny Somalis in sarongs were taking potshots at them. I imagined them questioning in their own minds the explanations put out by military spokesmen at Pentagon briefings. But you want to know what I thought of the commanding officers. From the majors upward, including the AIC?"

"Tell me."

"I hoped to God they would be court-martialed, and wished them hell and much worse." Dajaal squeezed the ball as though he might eventually succeed in getting blood out of it. "The senior officers were too ignorant to learn, too arrogant. If only they had had enough humility to put themselves in their subordinates' shoes, I kept thinking. Their behavior was loony. But the young Marines and Rangers redeemed themselves with their fighting. They held up

well, fought fiercely, and gave back as good as they got. As fighters, there was
a major flaw in their character, however. They thought less of us, and that was
ultimately the cause of their downfall. You should never think less of your
opponent—we were taught this at military school. If you respect your enemy,
you can be easier on yourself later, especially if you lose the fight, and it is of
high moral value when you win."

"They belittled StrongmanSouth's militia?"

"They belittled all of us, fighters or no fighters," Dajaal corrected him.
"StrongmanSouth didn't fight. I was there, and he didn't fight. That was to
prove the Americans' undoing, the fact that they belittled the fighters."

"You're saying that pride can cause one's ruin?"

"A lot of terrible things were done that night and the following morning by
both groups, ours and theirs," Dajaal said, "all in the service of the raging insanity. We had hardly wised up to what was being done on our side when we
witnessed the worst imaginable horror in the shameful shape of youths dragging a dead American down the city's dusty roads. But then I thought, A mob
is a mob, and there's nothing you can do about it. Mobs run riot, they are good
at that: if they go mad, they do it everywhere, even in America."

"Was there any way someone could've prevented it?"

"It all happened so fast," Dajaal said, "we couldn't have done anything,
even if we had wanted to. We were aware of the mob gathering, chanting the
usual anti-American slogans. Then, before you could say, 'Please, let's not do
that,' the youths, mostly urchins and riffraff, were rampaging, my grandson
Qasiir among them. No one was in control. Many of us were too exhausted
from the nightlong fighting and couldn't be bothered. You must remember,
there were so many deaths on our side, over a thousand by our reckoning.
Many of us went straight from the fighting to the burial grounds. We were all
out on a limb for all of thirteen hours or so, fighting to keep death at bay, and
I doubt if we could've raised our voices against what the youths were doing. I
can assure you that we were shocked. Were you not shocked?"

Jeebleh remembered seeing the scene on TV. He had thought of beasts of
prey roaming the streets of the city and the countryside, beasts inhabiting the

minds of the youths. But when answering Dajaal's question, he moderated his reaction. "I thought of life-in-death, if that makes sense to you."

"The mob had hardly dispersed," Dajaal continued, "and we heard on our short-wave radio that the Americans were leaving, body bags and all. Some of us would've liked to talk things through. I'm sorry that wasn't to be."

"StrongmanSouth wouldn't have wanted to talk?"

"Of course he wouldn't."

"Why not?"

"Because he was a spent force until the AIC gave him a new lease on life by making him 'Wanted' and placing a reward worth thousands of dollars on his head," Dajaal said. "Thanks, but no, thanks, to the AIC!"

Jeebleh remembered the discussion of the previous night, and he asked Dajaal to tell him who, in his opinion, had fought whom. "Americans versus Somalis?"

Dajaal explained that the Somalis, fragmented in their sectarian loyalties, did not see the battle as having been fought between "Somalis" and "Americans." "The fighting was between the clansmen supporting StrongmanSouth, and the AIC," he said. "Truth was one of the first casualties of the war."

"Did you see yourself as a man provoked into deadly action? What finally made you decide to dig up your gun? Were you in a rage?"

"Anger had nothing to do with it," Dajaal replied, "but justice did."

"Were you afraid?"

"I was prone to fear, like the Marines, and alone in my fear too. But I wasn't in a strange country, I knew *why* I was doing what I was doing, and I knew *where* I was, even in the dark! That was the difference between our situation and that of the young Americans."

They came across a zinc wall on which someone had scrawled *"Dal-dalo maidkaada, tagna!"* Jeebleh rendered this to himself as "Take away your corpses and leave our country!" He knew where the line came from. His memory galloping, he recited lines from a poem composed at the turn of the twentieth century by Somalia's greatest poet, Sayyid Mohammed Abdulle Hassan.

"I have no cultivated fields, or silver
Or gold for you to take!
The Country is bush.
If you want wood and stone,
You can get them in plenty,
There are also many termite hills.
. . .

All you can get from me is War.
If you want peace, go away from my Country."

Then a silence, which neither was prepared to break, came between them, like a referee stopping a fight. And into the silence walked a rabble of armed youths, like extras in a film about Mexican bandidos. As though on cue, one youth came forward. He was very short, stocky, and showily dressed as an outlaw—boots, bandanna, and Stetson hat. You could see that he was the kind who would waste you without blinking an eyelid. Jeebleh was expecting to hear a crescendo of gunshots, and death calling, when his worried gaze settled on Dajaal's nonchalant expression. The youth shouted, "Nothing to worry about, Grandpa. We're just having some fun, me and my friends!"

"Come and I'll introduce you to my visiting friend, then," Dajaal told the youth. He turned to Jeebleh and said sotto voce, "He's my grandson, whom everyone calls Qasiir. A rascal, really. He can tell you how he partook of the fighting on the day his sister was hurt. He has been involved in a lot of tomfoolery too."

Qasiir strode as though on a movie set, cameras rolling to catch every one of his antics. The combination of boots and Stetson made him appear taller; he put on a tough expression, thumbs stuck deep into his ammunition belt, teeth biting down on a chewing-stick the size of a cigarillo. Jeebleh imagined a harmonica being played nearby, and Clint Eastwood making a cameo appearance. For all his posturing, he struck Jeebleh as a youth who had come through muck, in which he wallowed; death, which he courted without fear; and humiliation, which he fought hard to subdue in his own way.

His voice firm, on edge, and low, Dajaal told Qasiir that he was fed up to the back teeth with his tomfoolery. "Send your sidekicks away, and follow us to your mother's house, pronto!"

But first Dajaal made a detour to the spot where the helicopter had fallen that October afternoon in 1993. The place looked like any other in a dusty city where furious wars raged. Here, however, there were pieces of metal, once part of a war machine—elegant, noisily powerful, and threatening when up in the air, but unimaginably ugly when fallen and dismantled. A group of rowdy children kicking up a storm of dust abruptly suspended their ball game at Dajaal's bidding, and they gathered close to him and Jeebleh. The children were curious about Jeebleh; they understood he was a visitor to the city. They guessed that he, like a number of other strangers before him, was calling on the disturbed girl and her mother who lived nearby, casualties of a battle that didn't concern them.

Qasiir joined them now, and for Jeebleh's benefit pointed out the battle lines: to the right, where the fighters supporting StrongmanSouth had been, and to the left, where the Americans had been. In a wall improvised from sheets of zinc, they could see evidence of liberal hits from all sides, by bullets of all sizes.

More children joined the group, and a handful of adults came out of their shacks. Dajaal ushered Jeebleh away from the curious onlookers, and led the way to the compound where Qasiir's brain-damaged sister and her mother awaited them. Just as they reached the gate, a cat came out from underneath, flattening against the ground to avoid being cut by protruding nails.

It dawned on Jeebleh that he was acting out of character: there was nothing to gain from a visit to the little girl and her mother. No doubt, they had suffered as casualties of a senseless battle, and had survived huge personal ordeals. But he didn't wish to cut the figure of the war tourist, making a voyeuristic study of a sordid aspect of a sad war that shouldn't have taken place at all. Everything seemed more ominous as they moved into the compound, Dajaal holding back as tradition demanded, stopping outside and announcing *"Hoodi!"* and awaiting his daughter-in-law's welcoming *"Hodeen!"*

before going any further. Qasiir entered the squat building without ceremony. A moment later, music came at them from inside, James Brown screeching, hooting, and grunting to the timbre of his soul.

A HAND PUSHED THROUGH THE CURTAIN AT THE DOORWAY. THEN A WOMAN wrapped in a floral robe, an edge of it held between her teeth, emerged, her gaze deferentially downcast. With one hand clutching her right ear, the other holding a little girl's hand, she came forward. The girl, her gaze diffuse, held the lower edge of the woman's robe. It was clear from the little one's move-ments that all was not well with her. Jeebleh was uncomfortable as he fol-lowed her inside, and he looked away from the pair to Dajaal, who by then had found two chairs for them to sit on. Jeebleh was tempted to turn his back on the whole business, and walk out of the house. But he thought better of it when Dajaal introduced the woman, calling her by name, which Jeebleh failed to catch. It wouldn't do to unnecessarily displease Dajaal, who had been very kind to him all along, and he didn't want to be rude to the poor woman or her unfortunate daughter. He shook the woman's hand when she proffered it. Dajaal called to his granddaughter several times; her delayed re-sponse suggested that she was hard of hearing, or retarded, or both.

"She's deaf from the helicopter noise," Dajaal explained. "And yet she manages to hear ungodly noises, like airplanes, and huge diesel truck en-gines, and heavy-duty motorbikes, and she cries and cries and cries, non-stop. Maybe she senses the earth shaking, I don't know."

The girl stood staring at them, her thumb in her mouth. Jeebleh tried to entice her with the candies, but she wouldn't approach. He tried to engage her in baby talk, but she just stared at him, as though in amazement.

"What's your name?" he asked.

The young thing wouldn't speak. Now he looked up at her mother bring-ing tea, the child almost tripping her. "My daughter hasn't spoken a word all these years," the woman told Jeebleh.

Dajaal tried to bring the girl over to Jeebleh, but she cried so fiercely he left her alone. After a few minutes, when his daughter-in-law had served them tea, Dajaal invited her to come and take the candies out of his own palm. He sat so close to her he could've touched her. The girl's pupils appeared dilated, but her stare was unseeing.

When her grandfather's hand went nearer to give her the candy, she burst again into tears and, taking several steps at once, fell forward. Her mother picked her up, quieted her. The girl, now somewhat relaxed, studied the strange world from the advantageous height of her mother's protective hip.

"She lives in a world of fear," the woman said. "Dust storms disturb her, noises too."

"You say she doesn't speak at all?"

"She can't string two words together."

"And doesn't laugh either," Dajaal said.

"How old is she?"

"Almost five and a half."

Jeebleh didn't know what to say.

"A baby does not suffer alone," the mother said.

Dajaal stayed out of it now, seemingly aloof.

The mother continued, "We all suffer with our babies, share in their suffering, don't we? It's been very difficult to be the mother of a child who's never smiled, and never known laughter or the joy of being young. She cries fitfully, wets her bed and slobbers, her nose is forever moist. We keep trying to make her blow it, but I doubt she'll ever blow it for herself."

Jeebleh looked from the woman to the child and finally to Dajaal, as if he wanted to be helped out of a fix he had got himself into. He rose to his feet hesitantly and stood unsteadily. Then James Brown's honking was no more, and Dajaal was telling Qasiir to tell Jeebleh all that had happened on the day the helicopter's uprush hurt his sister.

Before Qasiir could speak, his mother began: "Children in search of a bit of fun were the first to run to the villa where the two helicopters were hovering menacingly. There were American soldiers in the helicopters, an attack team of about twelve, in big vests worn over fatigues. The earth shook to its foundation, and we were all frightened. We had a routine to follow when helicopters came or when we expected an attack: we would all go together and move north, in small groups to avoid being seen, all of us protected by men with AK-47s. This wasn't the first attack, and as with all the others, we didn't think it would be the last.

"But I couldn't leave, because my daughter wasn't feeling well, and I stayed behind to give her the medicine prescribed for her earache. Besides, the arrival of the helicopters filled my son Qasiir with bravado, and he came into the room we all share, looking for his dirt-brown jeans and his T-shirt with some writing in English. I thought he might help me join the others, but his mobile rang, telling him where to go and what to do. He ran off in haste with several other boys, answering the call of their commander. They knew no fear, my son and his posse."

When she paused, Jeebleh looked at Qasiir, and the youth grinned foolishly. He took up the story where his mother had left it. "I was the leader of the posse, wasn't I? I had on a T-shirt that said 'Frank James is alive and well and living in Mogadiscio,' and I was tougher than all the others. We were useful as spies, my friends and I, and I was the one with the mobile. One of the top men of our militia had given it to me."

Qasiir received instructions via the mobile from a man he had never met, a deputy commander to StrongmanSouth. When he was on the phone, he tried to impress his boys, remaining dramatically silent, nodding in agreement with the invisible commander. Now and then he would proclaim, "Of course I won't share the secrets with anyone else!" Jeebleh imagined the boy switching off the phone and picking up a sliver of wood, placing it in his mouth, and pushing it about with his tongue in imitation of Clint Eastwood in *A Fistful of Dollars.*

In spite of the terrific noise created by the helicopters, Qasiir's posse could hear every word he said, as he told them what to do. He might have been relaying a message received directly from the Almighty, each syllable delivered as though he were honoring it, each vowel drawn out in deference to StrongmanSouth. The boys couldn't tell whether or not he was quoting someone when he said, "Remember that death visits you only once. And so our commander in chief says we must be ready for it, and must welcome it too. How do we achieve the impossible? Discipline." He repeated the word "discipline" several times, until it had the force of an incantation.

They went into a huddle and piled their hands one on top of another, like basketball players at the beginning of a game. They also took a collective oath, reaffirming their fearless commitment to total war against the enemies of StrongmanSouth. They were ready to undertake risky missions now that the assault had begun in earnest.

"And to prove how we were prepared to die for our commander, one of my boys began chanting in rhythm to the rotating helicopter blades," Qasiir said. And to Jeebleh's amusement, he got up and started chanting an imitation of an American gangsta rap. He sang some sort of war cry, *"Dill, dill, gaalka dill, dill, dill, gaalka dill!"* and after a pause, chanted in English, rapping in rhythm and repeating the command "Kill, kill, kill all!" Qasiir's acting was so effective that Jeebleh could hear, in his own mind, the chopper's noise, razor sharp, the blades turning and turning.

The deadly birds continued to hover, Qasiir said, raising an immense cloud of sand. And as the blades rotated faster and faster, the noise grew louder and more frightening, until the swirling currents tore zinc roofing sheets from flimsy dwellings and ripped cardboard from the walls of lean-tos serving as dwellings. A few odd pieces of plywood, no nails to hold them down, were blown away as well.

Qasiir's mother interrupted her son. "None of this mattered to the helicopter pilots or the soldiers in their funny-looking vests! It was siesta time in Mogadiscio, when we all sought shelter from the scorching sun. But on that day it felt like the entire earth was caught up in waves of tremors, each tremor speeding up the pulse of every person or animal in the neighborhood."

Qasiir rose to his feet, acting out more of that day, and Jeebleh was able to imagine the accelerated heartbeats of the ailing, the panting lungs of the infirm, the thrashing of the alarmed, the sand funneling in a mighty whirlwind, people cowering in their shacks, curses spoken, spells cast, homes destroyed, businesses disrupted, lives suddenly ended.

Qasiir's mother described the horrific terror of her baby—then barely a year old—who, torn from her breast, had been caught up in the avalanche of courtyard sand stirred up by the rotors of the helicopters. And when the mother went on her knees, keening in supplication, praying, cursing, cursing and praying, Jeebleh stared, dumbfounded, now unable to imagine the terror.

"I became hysterical," she continued, "and tore at my bare breast, where my daughter had been nursing. I wailed, I wept, I cursed, I prayed, but to no avail. I tore at my clothes, until I disrobed, convinced that my child had been swallowed up in the sand raised by the helicopter's sudden arrival. Then I saw the shape of evil. Rangers pointing at my nakedness and laughing. I stopped wailing, and covered my indecency, and then cursed the mothers who bore these Rangers. I've never glimpsed worse evil than those men cupping their hands at me, their tongues out, pointing at my nakedness."

Qasiir and his team heard her wailing. He shouted to his posse, instructing them not to shoot at the helicopters, fearing that his baby sister might be hurt in the crossfire. Looking back, both Qasiir and his mother speculated that one of the pilots might have become aware of what was going on and, in an effort to help, might have steered away from where the mother knelt, naked, weeping, praying, cursing, wallowing in the sand. "Then"—Qasiir acted it out in a wild charade—"two men appeared from nowhere with RPGs, and they gunned for the chopper. There was a mighty crash: the helicopter was down!"

"And I wouldn't stop wailing," his mother broke in, "until I saw my baby fall to the ground, close to where I was. I crawled on all fours to where my daughter lay, praying that I would find her alive, and unhurt. All the while, my hard, evil stare was focused on the Rangers in the downed chopper. I lifted my baby into my embrace, and half ran, half walked away, aware of the Rangers' eyes trained on my back."

THE STORY WAS OVER, THE MOTHER CLEARLY EXHAUSTED, AND JEEBLEH, NOW prepared to leave, got to his feet. Without thinking, he reached into his shirt pocket and handed over a large sum of money in the local currency—his change from the restaurant—to the mother of the child. The woman looked at her father-in-law, as if to ask, "What am I to do with this?"

"Please let her buy something for the child." Jeebleh's words failed him. He was embarrassed by what he had done so thoughtlessly. He walked out of the compound and, with feelings of guilt weighing him down, waited for Dajaal to join him.

27.

ON THEIR WAY TO THE BARBERSHOP, JEEBLEH, HIS EXPRESSION FORLORN, relied on the strength of his own spirit to overcome the obstacles in his way.

He decided to approach Dajaal right away with specific demands, even at the risk of being turned down. He did not have all the time in the world: soon he would be returning home, back to his family and his teaching: from that distance, a Parthian shot at his present pursuers and his lifetime foe would be impossible. He wanted the job done, and done well—in and then out.

And there was another matter he needed to consult Dajaal about. Jeebleh wanted to hire a mason to build a miniature mausoleum in noble memory of his mother. Nothing extravagant, just a bit of stone neatly put together, in tribute to the woman who had built him into what he had become. His skin bristled as he thought ahead to the moment when, standing before the structure, he could say a prayer or two, in an effort to apologize for his failures. It would take a great deal of love, and more, to help her spirit lie in undisturbed peace.

He looked in Dajaal's direction. The man seemed uncomfortable. "There are two jobs I would like to hire someone to do," Jeebleh said. "Two jobs that are related, to my mind. Would you help me?"

"What are these jobs?"

Worry spread over Jeebleh's face; he looked as wretched as a rusted drainpipe. "How would you go about it if you wished to commission a risky job?"

Dajaal's cagey answer made it obvious to Jeebleh that the man knew where he was headed with his questions. "I wouldn't, for instance, commission my grandson Qasiir to perform a risky job. It would have to be performed on a no-name, no-packdrill basis, with payment on execution."

Jeebleh emerged after a while from his unclear thinking, and sighed with the confidence of a young colt. "Would you have someone in mind for such a job?"

"I would."

Kaahin's name came to Jeebleh's mind. "Like who?"

Dajaal wouldn't commit himself. "I can think of out-of-work former colleagues of mine who'll do the job quietly, efficiently, and cheaply, and who'll spare one all the gory details having to do with the disposal of bodies and evidence linking one to the deed." So Dajaal not only knew what Jeebleh wanted him to do, but had given thought to the details like a professional assassin.

"How much?" Jeebleh maintained his confidence.

"I'll come back to you on that," Dajaal said.

The sun slanted at Jeebleh from the west, and the sand stirred by his feet rose up and caught on his hairy shins: the scratchy edge of his sarong felt drier. He fiddled with the hat, his fingers upsetting its comfortable fit. "Are you carrying a firearm?" he asked.

"I never go anywhere without one nowadays. Without it I feel naked, unsafe. As it happens, I'm carrying two. Now, may I ask, what do you care about firearms?"

"Could you lend me one?"

Dajaal stopped walking and bent down. He pulled out a revolver he had been wearing strapped to his shin, and offered it simply: "Here!"

Jeebleh took it without hesitation. The revolver felt heavier to him than the machine gun he had held on the way to the cemetery. Fear gathered in his throat, choking him. Before walking on, he admired the weapon, then hid it under his sweat-drenched shirt.

It froze his commoner blood to bear the blood-royal elegance of a machine built to kill at the touch of a trigger. The changes wrought in his behavior from the moment Af-Laawe's muscleman had prodded him with that needle were enormous. Even though he had contemplated vengeance on Caloosha, he never thought the day would come when he, a peace-loving man, would resort to using a deadly weapon to settle scores.

"The second job you want done?" Dajaal asked.

"This is a lot more pedestrian." Jeebleh explained the job he had in mind for the mason.

Dajaal asked, "When do you need him to start?"

"I'd say let him start right away."

"Leave both jobs with me, then."

Suddenly they heard a stir nearby. A mob shouting, "Thief, catch him!" was chasing a scraggly youth. Blind with fear, the boy ran smack into Jeebleh and almost knocked him over. The mob stopped a short distance away. The ringleader—a very well fed merchant from the market, sprinkled all over with his wares of flour, rice, and sugar—approached with his arms extended, saying, "Hand over the thief, then."

The thin youth had his mouth full of the food he had apparently stolen, which he was now busy chewing. In his right hand was half of a roll, out of which a piece of meat protruded, like a dead tongue. Eyes as large as his fright, the youth begged in a low voice, "I am hungry, please!"

"How much did the sandwich cost?" Jeebleh asked.

"Hand him over! Hand him over!" the mob chanted.

"I'll pay for what he's eaten, so you can let him go free." Jeebleh looked from the well-fed man to the scraggly youth, and then at the agitated mob, and finally at Dajaal, who stayed out of it, but, as ever, was prepared for any eventuality. Jeebleh addressed the fat merchant: "What's your problem? I am prepared to pay for his sandwich."

"He always steals food, runs off, and never pays!" the trader said. "Hand him over and we'll teach him a lesson. And don't waste our time."

"The boy is hungry, that is why he steals!"

The mob moved in on Jeebleh threateningly. Now cowed, he brought out a dollar's worth of the local currency, and made as though to give it to the trader, who scoffed at the idea of allowing the youth to go free. It was then that Jeebleh lifted his shirt and showed that he had a revolver—and immediately he discerned a change in the mood of the mob, which started to disperse. The trader accepted the money, and the youth scuttled across the road, vanishing into the dust he stirred.

"I'll be damned!" Dajaal said.

DAJAAL LEFT JEEBLEH IN FRONT OF THE BARBERSHOP, AGREEING TO RETURN in an hour or so—he would get in touch with a mason he knew, in the meanwhile—and take him back to Bile's apartment.

Jeebleh walked into the shop with the air of a man who, armed and knowing no fear, was prepared to meet his destiny. The three barbers stopped snipping, and the clients, some waiting on benches against a wall, stared at the stranger entering. He took a seat.

There were seven other customers: one having his hair cut, two having their moustaches and sideburns trimmed, and the rest waiting. Those in the chairs had limp towels wrapped around their throats. On the floor were curls of hair in impossible postures, waiting to be swept away. Even though he couldn't tell who the men in the shop were, he sensed something earthy in their voices. They had been raised probably in the semi-arid hamlets of the central regions, where many of StrongmanSouth's supporters hailed from, and where he recruited a large number of his militiamen.

A cassette of Somali music was playing. Jeebleh enjoyed listening to it. Did the fact that people were eating in restaurants and having their hair cut at the barbers' mean that the most deadly phase of the civil war had ended? The fact that one could pursue these activities without fear suggested a degree of normalcy. Ostensibly, no one in the shop was armed. Certainly, everyone had looked in his direction with ferocious intensity and suspicion when Jeebleh entered, but no one had pointed a gun at him.

One of the barbers beckoned to him with the sweeping gesture of a Mogadiscian welcoming you to his home, indicating a chair vacated by a man whose hair and moustache he had just trimmed to perfection. As Jeebleh took the chair, a scruffy youth came in with a tray holding several metal cups and offered a cup to each of the customers and the barbers. He then began to sweep up the hair on the floor. The men waiting their turn read newspapers and sipped their tea. When the youth was done, he went to Jeebleh's barber for payment, and then was gone, taking the empty tray with him.

Jeebleh just tasted his tea, didn't drink it; not only was it too hot, but it was also sugary. He mused that the youth had brought the tray of tea, and the barber had paid for it; the boy trusted he would get paid, and that he would find the cups when he returned later. These small things represented society's gradual recovery from the terrible trauma of war. Was the worst now over?

"How would you like yours done?" the barber had meanwhile asked.

"I'd like it cut very short." Jeebleh placed the conical hat in front of him where he could see it, so he wouldn't forget.

The barber brought out an electric clipper from under a table, where it had hung on a hook. He adjusted the blade and switched it on, then tested it against his open palm.

"I'd prefer that you use scissors and a comb, please," Jeebleh told him.

The barber started cutting with avuncular charm, and the two of them talked in the soft tones of men confiding in each other. They spoke in general terms, eventually touching on the changes in the clientele of the shop, which, the barber explained, had been the rendezvous for the city's cosmopolitans in the days before the civil war.

Then, out of the blue, the barber asked, "Are you a friend of Bile's?"

"Do you know him?" Jeebleh asked.

"He's one of my customers."

"What about Raasta and Makka?"

"I remember them coming here with him. Have you met them yourself?"

"I've seen photographs of them at Bile's."

"They are so gorgeous, Raasta's dreadlocks," said the barber. "No one other than her mother is allowed to touch them, or tend to them."

"I suppose you'd know Faahiye too?"

The barber went absolutely quiet and shifted uneasily. He took a sip from the teacup closest to him, and stared at the cup in front of Jeebleh, as though suggesting that he should take a sip of his. "Do *you* know Faahiye?" he finally asked.

"I've known his wife for a much longer time."

"I've never met her myself," the barber offered.

"Is it true that Faahiye lives around here?"

"I have no idea."

Nervous, the barber clipped Jeebleh's right ear, and instantly apologized. It was just a small snip, but there was blood. And that worried Jeebleh. An incision with a pair of scissors at a barber's might not be dangerous in many situations, but here, given the AIDS epidemic, you couldn't be sure. Jeebleh's countenance was flustered. He felt the cut with his fingers, to determine how serious it was, how deep. The towel still wrapped around his throat, he half rose and daubed his ear with a bit of cotton dipped in alcohol. Then he leaned forward, staring into the mirror, preoccupied.

He had seen a girl resembling Makka in the deepest recesses of the mirror before him, and was following her movements: then snip! How did he know the girl was Makka, when he had never met her before? Because he had seen her photograph, and felt sure that there couldn't be a facsimile of Makka. Also, the girl's lower lip was drawn down and slightly out, and there was the ubiquitous sliver of saliva, as transparent as the fine knots in a spider's net, lucid and purposeful.

While the barber fussed over the cut, daubing it with more alcohol, Jeebleh looked for Makka's reflection, hoping that she might still be there. The barber held him down, telling him not to move, fearful that he might cut him again. Yes, Makka was there in the mirror, all right; and she was grinning with self-recognition. He watched her watching herself with fascination.

He studied her face. Maybe she was playing a child's game modeled on one that his daughters were fond of playing. One child is blindfolded, and the fun lies in her looking for her playmates, and finding them. If Makka was at play here, could Raasta be far? The thought filled him with excitement. He pushed the barber's hand away and got to his feet, his whole demeanor disorderly. One idea led to another. He decided to go after Makka. He was convinced that she either had a message for him or would take him to Raasta and Faahiye.

He paid the barber as much cash as he could bring out of his wallet, even though the job had been only half done, and badly at that. He dashed out in pursuit of Makka, half his head unevenly trimmed, the other boasting its shock of hair as yet untouched. Someone might have assumed that he was pioneering a new style.

He stood at a crossroads, looking this way and that, and making sure he was prepared in the event of a sudden attack, placed his hand close to the firearm. But he could not decide which way Makka had gone. He continued his search, then he saw her walking ahead of him, into a dusty alleyway. He followed her, aware of his own vulnerability in the city of the gullible.

JEEBLEH FELT AWKWARD AS HE TRIED TO KEEP PACE WITH MAKKA, LOOKING back every now and then, scouring the alleyway ahead. He drew comfort from the firearm; he wouldn't hesitate to use it.

Feeling awkward, and perhaps looking ridiculous, he touched the cut side of his hair, then the uncut side. He had no idea why, but he was sure that even though he might appear ludicrous to grown-ups, he would look fine to Raasta and Makka, who at worst would find his hair funny and might even giggle. Anything that could bring a smile to those children's lips was worth it. The unfinished haircut pointed to his incomplete sense of self: a man who did not know how to use a firearm, and yet was carrying one! He hoped he wouldn't be caught in a web, a trap, as he kept following Makka farther and farther from the barbershop.

It was too late to abandon his pursuit now, too late to return to the barbershop as though nothing had happened and ask the barber to finish the job. He had lost his bearings a few streets back. He prayed that the little girl knew where she was going.

Now he walked faster, and checked to see if someone was on his tail. He saw Faahiye. The two were staring at each other from a distance, almost ready to acknowledge each other's presence by waving. When Jeebleh looked again, Makka was gone. He might as well wait for Faahiye, he thought, and while waiting he touched his hair again—he had forgotten Bile's conical hat at the barbershop.

"What game are we playing here?" Jeebleh asked Faahiye when he arrived.

"I am at a disadvantage."

"How's that?"

"I am at a disadvantage in that I've no option but to play a game whose rules were devised by someone else," Faahiye said. Jeebleh looked at him quizzically, as he went on: "Let's keep talking and stop looking behind us, for we're both being shadowed. One of our tails is at my back, a street away, the other at the corner to the left of the crossroads. Let's not do anything rash."

"Where are you taking me?"

"To Raasta, of course!"

Could he trust himself? For that matter, could he trust Faahiye? Was it a mere coincidence that he'd had a glimpse of Makka when getting his haircut, or had all this been planned by someone? Amazingly, Jeebleh was now prepared to walk into whatever trap there was, to see the girls. And if Faahiye could be believed, and he was really taking him to Raasta, then all the risks would be worth it.

Faahiye's steely expression softened, as he looked closely at Jeebleh's haircut; suddenly he was in stitches, laughing without restraint. "Why, half your hair is cut and the other half isn't," he said. "No wonder you have a lackluster look about you!"

Both were relaxed. Jeebleh smiled, and his grinning gaze wandered away to the clouds, which appeared as lighthearted as he felt now. He anchored his mind to the delightful idea he and Faahiye were on the same side.

When they resumed walking, Faahiye said, "What does one blame—love, because it's gone sour, or hate, because it's gone seedy? Do we keep a record of one another's wrongs, do we go at one another's throats, daggers drawn?"

Jeebleh was weaving himself a shroud of wishes, as he touched his upper thigh, where it still hurt, and then the hidden firearm. He looked to his right, and the world was at peace with itself, the cows behaving as hungry cows do, busy pulling up shrubs at the roots, and enjoying them; he looked to his left, and saw a young herdsman chasing a goat. Close by, two cows were chewing their cud, and they raised their heads, lowed, and showing little interest in him, resumed their chewing. He had been told of cows and goats grazing and digging up a grenade or two, and being blown to death. No such thing happened as he went past, and he took this to be a good omen.

Faahiye crossed a road strewn with uncollected garbage. Following him, Jeebleh thought: All alliances are temporary. He had no idea why he thought this. Maybe because he knew there was no going back now—not until his attempts were crowned with success, or his efforts ended in failure or death. But were they allies now, he and Faahiye? He guessed not: his foolhardy persistence, his call on Caloosha, his insistence that Caloosha help him get in touch with Faahiye and the housekeeper, and his continued search for Raasta had ultimately paid off. Why did he have a childlike trust in Faahiye, whom he hardly knew? Did he feel sorry for the fellow, who could've irritated even an angel into fury?

"May I ask how the girls got here?" Jeebleh said.

"From what Raasta's told me," Faahiye replied, "they were picked up in a fancy car and taken to some house where they were kept in the basement for several weeks."

"Do they have any idea who picked them up?"

"You should ask Raasta yourself when you see her."

"I will."

He listened to the lowing of a cow calling to one of its young. There were cows everywhere, cows communicating their mourning, grieving, lamenting their endangered state, and making sounds that frightened the daylights out of you. A young moon framed by clouds was up in the sky. A curious unease descended on Jeebleh at the sight of a young calf and an older cow fighting over a plastic bag, their horns colliding, both hurting. The tough, translucent material was torn apart, and the older one took a mouthful of it, while the calf stood apart, forlorn and hungry. Several other bags flew into the air, and were blown away to finish flat against a wire fence.

Jeebleh whispered: "Who owns the place?"

Faahiye answered in a mumble, "I have yet to find out myself. Remember, I just got back here."

"Who brought you from the airport, then?"

Faahiye didn't respond. They had come to a gate, at which he tapped hard three times, quick and uninterrupted. The voice of a woman from inside the house told them to wait. Then Makka came out to open the gate, saw Jeebleh, and ran off, back into the house, giggling.

28.

HAVING PRECEDED THEM INTO THE HOUSE, MAKKA HID BEHIND THE DOOR playfully, then came out with the joy of a child welcoming a frolicsome parent. Faahiye took part in the fun with self-abandonment, laughing and loving too. Makka adored him, that much was clear. Instead of asking where Raasta was, Jeebleh watched Makka romp about with Faahiye. When she stopped, exhausted, the sun gathered in her eyes, and her tranquil features were even more of a delight.

She mumbled something in the tawdry tongue of a Marlon Brando doing his Sicilian bit, his cheeks heavy with cotton. Faahiye must have understood her question, for he replied, "His name is Uncle Jeebleh!" She watched him with wary eyes and kept her distance, biting her nails. She didn't come rushing to hug him, as he had expected.

She turned to Faahiye instead, and gave him kisses and hugs, pleased to be holding his hand and fiddling with his fingers. There was such warmth there, gentle, tender, and sweet, even without another word exchanged between them. She waited with childish anxiety for him to return her affections, while he was eager to attend to his guest. When he did kiss her fingers and then her cheeks, her face beamed with the glee of the innocent.

Makka stared at Jeebleh, as if deciding whether he belonged inside or outside the circle of persons to whom she gave kisses and hugs. She hesitated, unsure of what to do, until Faahiye encouraged her: "Go on!" She went to Jeebleh, grinning, her hand outstretched. In her way, she was commiserating with him; or was she apologizing for having taken her time? She pulled herself to her full height and, in an instant, was touching and hugging him, kissing him on both cheeks, before letting him go. She might have been expecting to hear Faahiye's approval for what she had done, and looked sad when neither man moved or spoke.

Jeebleh asked, "Why here?"

Surprising both of them, and maybe even herself, Makka answered. You could see how hard she worked at making herself understood, her forehead furrowed in concentration. Before speaking, she made a sucking noise, reclaiming the saliva hanging from her lower lips by drawing it in noisily. "No here, here!" she said.

Jeebleh didn't ask for an explanation, either from her or from Faahiye. But he remembered the Arab wisdom that from the mouths of the simple you may receive something profound.

"No here, here!" she repeated several times. And again she was on her feet, pointing at herself and repeating, *"Aniga anigoo ah,"* many times. Then she went over to Jeebleh, touched his hair, first the cut side, then the uncut, and giggled excitedly. She mumbled something that Faahiye interpreted for him. "She is saying you are fun and she likes you."

Then the world became a door, and a young girl, age indistinct, walked in. What impression did Raasta make on Jeebleh when he first laid eyes on her? He held two conflicting images in his head at one and the same time. He thought of a potholed feeder road, neglected to the point where it was hardly used, and therefore decidedly quiet and off-peak. Then he thought of a commuter train at rush hour in a big city, packed with workers jostling for standing space in the car into which they had squeezed themselves when the doors opened. It could be that he was already thinking to his return home, now that he had found the girls.

The moment grew in importance; things weren't going to be the same from then on. Raasta was in her own element.

She walked over to her father, whom she embraced, then kissed. And when at long last she came to where Jeebleh was, he didn't rise; instead, he went into a crouch, half kneeling, and waited. He didn't want to be daring; this was not the moment to be brave, take her in his arms, lift her up and plant on her cheeks warm, loving kisses. He let her determine what was to happen. So she embraced him as you embrace someone dear to you, not because you know him but because you've heard his name mentioned often and in an endearing way. She knew how to draw lines, Raasta did. She said to him, in as grown-up a tone of voice as she could muster under all the excitement, "I'm very glad to meet you, Uncle Jeebleh!"

Then because Makka was giggling, her finger pointing at Jeebleh's hair, Raasta put her hand on her lips, both to suggest that Makka stop misbehaving and to stop herself from giggling too. Jeebleh touched the uncut side and said to the girls, "Do you like my haircut?"

They both nodded, giggling.

And then silence.

There was no denying the fact that together and in such a setting, they represented joy itself, their expressions set in happiness, their smiles genuine, and the words they used connecting them lovingly. There was something malleable about their togetherness, as manageable and pliant as dough in the hands of an expert baker. Raasta looked away with amusement every time her gaze fell on Jeebleh's hair. Makka came and touched it again, and then giggled for a long time.

"Who or what did you see on the way here?" Raasta now asked her father.

"We saw a cow chewing a bag, choking!"

The news upset Raasta, who said reproachfully, "Why do you do that sort of thing, talk about a cow dying in misery, when we're doing our best to welcome Uncle Jeebleh?"

"I'm sorry, my sweet!" he apologized.

And he held the two girls to himself, hugging and kissing them. Makka, though not ill at ease, freed herself from his embrace. She took Raasta's face in her hands, a face in the shape of an infant moon, then demonstrated a clock face with her arms, the minute and hour hands in slow forward motion.

Faahiye wore a soft, tender smile as he clowned for Makka, who laughed. Jeebleh stood fascinated, moved to see them all together and happy.

Jeebleh admired the handsome features of the house: high ceilings, exquisite furniture, tiled kitchen floor, fittings still intact, clean and lovely. When he saw the dishes washed, drip-drying in the kitchen, the tea towels clean and hanging where they should, the fresh flowers in the vase on the dining table, he remembered the desolate life that Shanta had been leading, and he was sad. He wondered whether there was another adult sharing the house with the three of them—most probably a woman?

"What would you like us to do now?" Faahiye said.

Makka was repeating something over and over. Eventually Jeebleh figured out the word: "Perform!" He saw that Faahiye and Raasta were both seated and waiting for Makka's performance to start. Smiling all the while, Makka might have been a girl taking pride in her acrobatic skills, showing off what she could do, feats she had seen on television, Jeebleh guessed. When she was done and everyone applauded, Makka was over the moon.

A few minutes later, Jeebleh heard the sounds of a television from upstairs. His memory took him back to his visit to Caloosha's, and the sound of soaps coming from an upstairs room. Understandably, he didn't wish to know more than he ought to, or to get involved in matters that weren't his concern. He looked away, embarrassed, and his evasive gaze settled on a lemon tree in the garden, gorgeously committed to holding what there was of the sun in its leaves.

"I KNOW EVERYTHING ABOUT YOU!" RAASTA SAID.

She was to Makka like a parent to an infant, and she set about organizing a play corner where Makka could keep herself occupied, as a parent wanting to speak to her peers about something important might do. She placed a box of beads close to Makka, who wore a single talismanic bead, blue, around her neck. Makka contentedly started stringing beads together. Faahiye made himself scarce, evidently to tidy up.

"I've heard a lot about you, from Uncle Bile, and you've been with me for a long, long time, from my birth. Now I know your face, and I'm very glad."

Jeebleh didn't know what to say. The questions gathering in his head were growing unruly, tripping over one another, each insisting on being given precedence. The sound of his breathing made him think of a door bolt going home. He fussed at his eye, cleaning it. Finally he said, "I know very little about you!"

"There is time yet," she said. "There is!"

His breathing strained under the tension he felt. The firearm became obtrusive, weighing even more heavily on him. He didn't dare remove it, lest she should see it. Who knows, she might run off, and not want to see him ever again. He didn't want that to happen. Finally he was able to formulate a question: "How have you been?"

"We are good," she said.

"Are you fed well?"

"Better than most."

He asked tentatively, "Are things better now?"

"Things have been better in the last two days."

"Because Daddy is back?"

"They've been kinder, since his return."

"Who are 'they'?"

Jeebleh could sense her instant withdrawal. Her eyes shamefully downcast, she said, "I am not sure."

"Who is the person upstairs?"

"A woman," she said.

"A woman?"

"She cooks for us, looks after us. Washes our clothes, makes up our beds, cleans after us. We found her here. She says little, and does what we tell her to."

"Will you miss her?"

"No," Raasta said. "I miss Uncle Bile, I miss my mother, I miss Uncle Seamus."

She was a formidable girl, able to draw you into her comfort-giving world against your better judgment, if she chose to. He had fallen under her spell right away, because, he reasoned, she was accustomed to being loved, trusted, and obeyed. Looking at her now, and imagining the horrid things that she had been through, not to mention the uncertainties she had lived with as a kidnapping victim, Jeebleh was impressed with her perseverance, her noble bearing for one so young. Her clothes were almost rags, and so were Makka's. Raasta had presumably outgrown hers, and yet she appeared impervious to the state of her clothing, like a duck getting wet in a tropical downpour.

She lapsed into a reflective mood, and withdrew into a private space he was in no position to reach. Jeebleh imagined her to be tough in the self-protective way of a tortoise withdrawing its softer head and legs. Was she thinking through her troubled thoughts? It would be unwise to push her, to try to make her speak. He should give her time, so that the trauma of being held prisoner might melt away. He would let her find peace in her silence, if that was what she was after. He said, "Everything will be all right."

"I am beginning to think so too," she replied, eagerly but absently, as tears appeared in her eyes.

Like all exceptional persons, no matter what their age or disposition, she was as prepared to show her strengths and perseverance as she was willing to demonstrate her weaknesses. And so when it came to weeping, she did so discreetly and undemonstratively, as a mother might in the presence of her child. This grown-up behavior too impressed Jeebleh.

"Shall we go?" she said.

"Where?"

"Home."

Jeebleh didn't know what answer to give. He was not sure whether Faahiye had up-to-the-minute instructions as to what he might or might not do, and did not know what their fates would be if they tried to leave. Nor had he any idea with whom Faahiye dealt, whether communications were by mobile phone, in dribs and drabs, on a need-to-know basis, or in person, direct from the head of the conspiracy. "Let's ask your daddy," he suggested.

"Let's," she said, and was just about to shout and ask whether it was okay to go home, back to her mother, Uncle Bile, and Uncle Seamus, when a ruckus was raised outside.

It was the kind of sound that might have been created by a rutting he-donkey chasing a she-donkey up and down a stone-filled alleyway. It ranked with the hideous racket Jeebleh remembered Italian youths making on their motorcycles through the streets of Padua at siesta time. How were the two girls coping? Raasta, out of sympathy, went to Makka's play corner to hold her in a comforting embrace, to assure her that all would be well, not to worry. When Faahiye asked what on earth was going on, Jeebleh, because he had a firearm, volunteered to find out. He stood beside a window, weapon in hand, ready to put it to use.

Faahiye stayed behind with the girls.

Glancing up the stairs to the second floor, Jeebleh heard that the television had just been switched off. He was tempted to ask who was there, but he chose instead to devote what energy he had to discovering the cause of the ruckus, which showed no signs of letting up.

But he was relieved now to see who was making the noise—Qasiir, armed and Stetsoned, in a car with three of his mates, two of them armed, the other at the wheel. The car was a collectible Ford, a flivver most likely left behind by an American or a European seconded to UNOSOM. Tied to the back, dragging along behind, were several empty tin cans. As soon as Qasiir spotted Jeebleh, who was on the porch, waving, the car stopped, and so did the unearthly noise. "It's only me and my friends," Qasiir said. "This is fun—but maybe not as much as you're having. Look at your haircut—cool! Are you all right? How are the girls?"

Again, Clint Eastwood to the rescue. "What a delightful young man," Jeebleh told Faahiye, who had joined him. He put the firearm away, smiling, and noticed the stale sweat staining the armpits of Faahiye's dark shirt. Jeebleh's face was now daubed with relief.

He waited for Qasiir and his friends to get out of the car before asking how they had traced them to the house. Qasiir and another of the youths were busy untying the cans from the car, when two more vehicles came into view. Jeebleh assumed he and Faahiye were now in trouble; here was the head of the conspiracy come to put an end to the insurgency, they wouldn't be allowed to leave with the girls. Hope drained out of him. But Qasiir called out: "No need to worry. It's only Grandpa, our backup!"

The first car contained Dajaal and a driver. In the second, a battlewagon, were some seven or eight youths with machine guns and rocket launchers. Kaahin was up front, next to the youth at the wheel. Dajaal and Kaahin got out of their respective vehicles and remained where they were, poised to deal with any problem that might come up the road.

Jeebleh's script had called for no fighting, for please-no-guns peace. Accordingly, he went over to Dajaal and gave the revolver back to him, with a whispered "Thank you." Then he lapsed into confusion, as in the script, and paying no attention to the humorous remarks about his fashionable hairstyle, he walked with Raasta and Makka at either side to the warmed vehicle and got in.

They moved in convoy, the car carrying Jeebleh and the girls safely between the battlewagon, now carrying Dajaal, and the Ford. Only when they got to The Refuge did Jeebleh realize that Faahiye had not come.

He wondered why.

But this did not deter him from taking pride in their achievement, the recovery of the girls without a gunfight. Everything would be revealed when Raasta, once she was out of her trauma, relaxed into telling her story.

PART 4

Thus we descended on the right hand side.

(CANTO XVII)

DANTE, *Inferno*

29.

THE STORY OF HOW DAJAAL AND THE OTHERS HAD TRACKED JEEBLEH TO the house where he met the girls was a lot less complicated than the one about how the girls had been taken as captives. After supper, with Makka asleep in The Refuge, Raasta showed herself stronger than anyone had imagined. She was ready to speak of her ordeals. Even though he didn't always follow what was being said, Seamus stuck around to listen, and was satisfied with the summaries he was given—but sorry that, in her trauma, Raasta had forgotten how to string together a sentence in English.

Her story disagreed with the version circulated earlier on one major point: the nature of the car in which they had been driven away. Raasta described it as a black four-door no fancier than Uncle Bile's sedan. In it were four men wearing shades. When pushed into it from behind, she saw Makka lying on the floor in the back, not moving a muscle. The car traveled at frightening speed, a dilapidated battlewagon leading the way. When Raasta resisted, a muscular man held her down to stop her from screaming; he injected her with a hypodermic syringe with a clear solution, which knocked her out.

She came to later in the day, in a dark room draped with heavy curtains. The windows were boarded up, and the only light came from a naked bulb in the corridor. There were people in the house: a dozen men and women, talking all day long, sitting around on the carpeted floor of an adjacent room, chewing *qaat* and watching satellite TV, sometimes in Arabic, sometimes in languages that Raasta couldn't identify. The girls slept on mattresses on a tiled floor, and felt the chill in their bones. The food was not bad, though.

Every now and then, they would be offered special treats: fruits flown in fresh from elsewhere, like apples and large white grapes of the kind not grown locally; cherry tomatoes, because Raasta loved them; lots of sweets, because Makka craved them; ninja toys, because both missed theirs. Only once, however, were they given fresh clothes—and this in the early days of their captivity. The treats coincided with occasional visits from the fat man. He never showed his face to them, but Raasta concluded that he was the head of the visiting entourage; he would waddle past their room, unfailingly surrounded by bodyguards. Would she recognize him if she saw him? She couldn't identify him in a lineup, but she might recognize his voice, which, she said, dripped as if with undigested fat.

What of her father? When did she first set eyes on him, where, and with whom? She hadn't seen her father until he was brought to them. He had seemed devastated, very frail, his eyes bloodshot, as though he had been crying. He had bumps on his forehead, probably from being hit. What did Faahiye say when they met? He wept and wept, sniffing and unable to say much, and he looked helpless. But he was less weepy on the second visit. Raasta had the impression that he had been brought to them blindfolded, because hanging loose around his neck was a mouth mask like the kind Uncle Bile used when attending to very sick patients.

At some point when Shanta was out of the room, probably in the bathroom having a good weep, Jeebleh asked if Raasta could tell them more about the woman upstairs. Raasta was puzzled, she didn't understand the question. So Jeebleh asked if she knew why her father had remained in the house. She assumed that he wasn't allowed to join them, but she couldn't say more.

When her mother came back, Raasta took her by the hand and, bidding everyone good night, led her as a parent might lead a child, saying, "Let's go to bed. No more worries, all will be well. You'll see!" It was Raasta who decided that she and her mother would sleep in Bile's room.

Before saying good night, Seamus told Jeebleh to let him know anything that might be decided on the matter at hand, adding, "Let's brain the lot of them for doing what they've done to our Raasta!"

JEEBLEH NOW TOLD BILE THE STORY OF HOW DAJAAL HAD TAKEN IT UPON himself to give Qasiir the task of tailing him since their visit to his mother's grave, and how Kaahin had organized a battlewagon and crew. He wasn't sure whether Kaahin had changed sides on a permanent basis, but he understood from Dajaal that Kaahin was available to help in getting rid of the riffraff who ran Caloosha and Af-Laawe's cartel.

Not that Jeebleh and Bile agreed or disagreed on what to do about Caloosha and Af-Laawe, yet their conversation pointed to their incompatibility of purpose, neither able to articulate their differences, and both afraid of confronting the uglier aspects of themselves that this reflected. Jeebleh was wound up, living a minute at a time, as he had after the youth was killed in his hotel room. Bile admitted to not knowing how to right a wrong that had brought misery to their lives; killing X or Y wouldn't help in a significant way, or solve the country's problems.

When Jeebleh asked whether he had heard from the lab technician, Bile would say only that Jeebleh should have tests done when he got back to the United States. Pressed further, he became evasive, and got up, ready to bid a hasty good night. Then he said, "Leave it all to me. I know what to do now."

Jeebleh wasn't certain about Bile's meaning: Was he alluding to the lab tests, or to Caloosha, Af-Laawe, and the cartel?

An hour or so later, while Jeebleh was still awake and trying to figure out what was what, or who would do what, Raasta came into the living room. At first, he thought she was sleepwalking, because she rubbed her eyes and mumbled something about wanting to tell him her story. He offered her hot chocolate, then made it for her. She sat in a corner, and after he had brought his double espresso over, she made as if to talk, but she did not. Soon after, Bile, also in sleepwalking stupor, joined them, and Raasta got up and took her hot chocolate with her out of the room without saying anything.

. . .

ALONE, BILE AND JEEBLEH TALKED IN LOW VOICES, NOT WANTING TO DISTURB the others in the apartment.

Bile was surprisingly garrulous—maybe because of the hour, or because he felt he owed Jeebleh an apology for Raasta's unexplained departure. "Until the end of my days," he said. "I will continue to remember the day Raasta was born best!"

"Why is that?"

"I knew right away that she was one of a kind," Bile said, "and I sensed her uniqueness in myself whenever I touched her, and in the others whenever they looked at her. There is something special about the sweetness of memory as I revisit the scene. I think of ants forming a line and having to share a few grains of sugar."

Bile explained that for some time after Raasta's birth, he made a point of gathering as much information as he could from other countries, and learned of other "special" children, born to societies torn apart by internal conflicts. Described in newspapers, magazines, and radio commentaries as "miracles," these children revealed themselves in measured intervals, and in different areas where internecine wars were the order of the day. They were born to unsuspecting parents in Senegal, Kashmir, Tanzania, Somalia, Bosnia, Colombia, Peru, Palestine, and in the mountainous Kwanziris of Uganda, near that country's border with Rwanda and Congo.

Bile looked like a proud parent praising his offspring. Jeebleh listened attentively as Bile described Raasta's uniqueness and pointed out that, unlike the others, his niece had "secular" beginnings, and nothing to do with the religious fervor.

Jeebleh asked his friend to name another "miracle" child.

Bile narrowed his eyes to the size of ants and said, "I can name one such child, sure. A Tanzanian boy, Sherifu, said to have come out of his mother's womb chanting, 'There is no other god but Allah.'"

"Kind of a new messiah?"

"He's been described by some Islamic scholars as an angel, and been welcomed with the pomp and ceremony given to a dignitary in a number of African countries, most notably in Senegal, where crowds have gathered to hear him chant the Koran. Three African heads of state have received him, including Gadhafi in Libya, Kabila in Congo, Idriss Deby in Chad. He's also met the American Nation of Islam leader Louis Farrakhan. He's carried around in a gold-leafed throne by crowds in a frenzy, chanting the names of Allah, and he recites the Koran. Women swoon and collapse, and men fight one another to get nearer to him."

"Now, why do we need a Sherifu or a Raasta?"

"Because people are lost," Bile said, "and they hope to find their way back to Allah or to peace of mind through an intermediary. In fact, Sherifu has been described as a divine instrument, because he could recite the Koran at the tender age of three. Raasta is seen as a symbol of peace because of what she represents for people down here. Moreover, the fact that Sherifu is proficient in a number of languages, even though he has never been to school—he speaks Arabic, French, and a handful of African languages spoken in countries where he has never been—is seen as miraculous."

"What about Raasta?"

"Like Sherifu," said Bile, "Raasta is exceptionally versatile and picks up languages very fast. What's more, she gives shapes to the links between words and their meanings, and then fits them into chains of her own choosing."

"Tell me more," Jeebleh said.

"I recall the day Seamus asked her how she was doing, and she replied that she felt as frightened as a leaf on a tree, drawing itself in, afraid that someone passing by might cut it off. Another day, after one of her parents' quarrels, she compared herself to a tooth rotting at the root, with no gum to hold it."

Bile told of another occasion, when Raasta, not yet three, explained why she had chosen him as her surrogate parent. She did so, she said, because "Uncle and I are bound together with the clear thread of a spider's web, visible only with the rays of sunlight in the background."

Jeebleh asked, "Compared with Sherifu, who could recite verses as a toddler, what could Raasta do at a similar age?"

"Raasta, at two, could speak of the things she knew about when she was a mere fetus, and how she was in touch with things through her own baby-faint heartbeat. She developed fast in the womb of her mother's imagining, she would say, and was fully grown by the time she came into the world."

Jeebleh remembered Bile talking at length about the day Raasta was born, and how his arrival had complicated matters for all concerned. "Would you say Raasta is aware of her own special qualities?" he asked.

"Raasta remembers watching her mother behaving awkwardly, throwing her hands up in despair, remembers hearing her say terrible things about Faahiye, and her parents quarreling fiercely, in private and public. She says that her parents behave as though they have no idea that every birth howls with its own need and is burdened with the histories of its antecedents."

Jeebleh wished he could've seen the young thing, born with a head of raven-black locks. He thought of how full of stir and gorgeous she was, how calming to hold. He imagined her cry like the cawing of an excited crow. "And she asks rhetorical questions, doesn't she?" he said.

"She wants to know if a tree rotten to the core can bear a healthy fruit worth picking."

"People have described her as the Protected One. What does that mean?"

"I don't know whether she herself is protected," Bile said. "I've never actually seen her in imminent danger. But I've never seen her harmed either. I know that people believe that anyone in her proximity is safe from the harms of the civil war."

"Hence a miracle child?"

"She is seen as a symbol of peace, that's right."

30.

JEEBLEH WOKE AFTER A BRIEF SLEEP TO THE SOFT SOUND OF A CHILD'S FEET pattering back and forth in the room. He was a lot groggier than was good for him, and he fought hard not to make much of his state of exhaustion or confusion. Clumsily rubbing his eyes, and then becoming conscious of the unfinished business of his uncut hair, he willed his expression to change instantly to one of delight at the sight of Raasta standing over him.

He scrambled out of bed, and then apologized. Perhaps he would have preferred it if she had not come upon him sleeping, or tired. Already dressed and ready to face the day, she was elegant in her composure, waiting. There was something noble in how she held herself, as though ready for an event of extraordinary nature.

Here was the rub: For one so young, she had a face as ancient as the roots of a baobab, and yet young-looking, a joy to gaze at and adore. He reckoned she was in her public mood, and it was time he prepared himself for what she had to say. He cleared his throat, took a solid grip of himself in good time, and said, "How are things with the world this morning?"

"Dajaal wants to talk to you," she said, and seeing that he looked so bedraggled, she smiled to herself.

At the mention of Dajaal's name, several of the latent worries he had lived with for the last few days came out. Had death, which kept a close watch on his movements, paid a visit to someone, and if so, on whom had death called? "Where is he?" he asked.

Jeebleh caught sight of her as she withdrew into her private world, where she behaved like the child she was. But for these occasional slips, Jeebleh thought Raasta could offer the best tutorials in their art to the most professional of actors. She completely inhabited the role she had been assigned to play. She stood still, like a ballerina awaiting her music. "He said that you should meet him at the clinic," she replied, "and from there he'll take you and the builder to the cemetery."

He could tell from her delivery that there was a second, more serious part of the message, and he waited, relieved that this time she didn't appear to be lapsing into a kid's universe. "Anything you haven't told me yet?"

She turned nimbly away from him. Was she about to explode with the intensity of the part of the message she hadn't yet delivered? His wandering mind took him back to his childhood, and to an Arabian folktale about a man who is about to be murdered: The victim asks his murderer to promise that after his death, he will visit his village, and recite to his orphaned children half a stanza of a poem he has written. The children understand their father's coded message, and the murderer is apprehended.

Raasta looked up, his question perhaps resonating in her head, as taunts do. She said, in words carefully and properly enunciated, "Dajaal said to tell you that what needed to be done has been done."

Even though Jeebleh understood what the words meant, he didn't know precisely what had been done to whom. He was in no doubt, however, that Dajaal had packed a lot into the briefest of messages, which was why the two of them would have to meet and talk before he knew with any certainty what had happened. He was sure of one thing, though: The news wasn't the kind you shared with a child so nervous as to unbuckle her sandals and dig the toes of one foot into the heel of the other. Solicitous, he wondered aloud if Raasta was okay. When she nodded, he said, "You've delivered a very important message, and I thank you very much," in a tone that suggested that he wanted to get on with the rest of the day.

"Would you like me to take you to the clinic, where Uncle Bile and Uncle Seamus are, and where you are also to meet Dajaal?" she said.

"I would," he said, "after a shower. I'll be with you in a few minutes."

Good as his word, he was quick about his shower, and he managed to shave, and trim the uncut side of his hair. When he emerged from the bathroom, she looked up at him and smiled, but said nothing. She led him to the clinic, without speaking, using shortcuts, her hand forever in his.

STILL HOLDING HANDS, JEEBLEH AND RAASTA WALKED IN ON BILE IN HIS consultation cubicle. They might have been lovers out on a promenade. And not having bothered to knock on the door, they gave poor Bile a startle when he saw them. Jeebleh wondered why he appeared so disturbed when seen taking pills similar to those he had taken the previous night. What were the tablets for? Were they for his depressions, or other complaints?

Bile stared at Jeebleh, then at Raasta, but didn't say anything. His hand went to his mouth, covering it, then eventually to his chest, as though checking whether his heart was where he presumed it to be, and functioning. He was clearly at a loss for words. Sighing and still looking dumbfounded, he sat down, his face pallid, his body drained of life.

Raasta looked from Bile to Jeebleh, bewildered. But she too could not express her confusion, again because the words failed her. Her face said that she knew something terrible had happened, but she had no idea what. She seemed to sense too that the disquiet, earlier on Jeebleh's part and now on Bile's, differed from the uneasiness her parents were in the habit of driving each other into when they argued. This was a much more serious matter, and she had better not make inappropriate remarks, or ask infantile questions.

Bile beckoned to her to come closer. He held her at arm's length, as though having a good look at her for the first time in years, then took her into his tight embrace, nearly hurting her. Jeebleh, not one to be left out, joined them in the hug—Raasta weepy, Bile almost ready to speak but still unable, and Jeebleh undecided.

Jeebleh stepped away from them, his thoughts drifting toward culpability, wondering what it was that had upset Bile. He leaned against a wall, listening sadly to Bile's softly murmured words to Raasta, who was sniffling. Jeebleh became aware of the presence of a fourth person in the cubicle, a young girl. On impulse, he spoke to the sick child, whose chest was bare; her ribs protruded, her jaw was prominent, and her eyes were marked with unwashed sleep. "What's your name, young lady?" he said.

Bile shook his head, moving it back and forth as a worshipful Sufi might. Raasta, no longer weeping, wiped her face dry with the back of her hand. She took notice of the sick child and did what she could to make her happy: she held the bony fingers in her hand, and kissed them one at a time. She continued kissing them until she brought a smile to the child's lips, and that was heartening to watch.

Slowly the mood in the cubicle changed, and the space, with its fluorescent tube and humming generator, felt bigger and brighter. To Jeebleh, it was wonderful to see a smile gradually forming on Bile's lips. The distant look in his friend's eyes worried him, but there was no mileage in putting too many questions to Bile all at once, because the dark mood might descend again. It was possible that the years spent in isolation had, with this recent upheaval, begun to impose a mental imbalance on Bile, heavy depression descending on him with the cautious approach of an owl in a lighted compound.

Unable to stand the thought of seeing his friend in such a state, he prepared to leave the cubicle, to go in search of Dajaal or Shanta, hopeful that one of them might know what had caused Bile's discomfiture. He closed the door as gently as one would the door to a room in which a child is sick, and an image etched itself on his mind: three heads dipped together, like three colts drinking side by side from the same ditch.

RAASTA TALKED UNCLE BILE THROUGH HIS DELIRIUM GENTLY. SHE KISSED him on the forehead just as it darkened with the pain trespassing there. She spoke to him as a mother might talk to a child unwilling to eat his meal. She had done so before, helped him through the worst panic attacks, helped him live out his hell in the quiet, and emerge from it, with little or no memory of what he had been through; he was capable of taking refuge in amnesia. His eyes were foggy, his mind in a mist of its own making, his thinking dogged by the formidable double-take of someone suffering the effects of guilt. He kept repeating, "Look at what *they've* made me do!"

AFTER A WHILE, BILE RID HIMSELF OF THE DEMONS, AND HIS HANDS GREW AS steady as a doctor's again. Raasta was ready to ask him about the sick girl, who tried to get up on her feet but couldn't stand upright; her knees wobbled, then buckled. Bile asked Raasta if she could guess the girl's age.

Before she had time to think, Makka joined them. She held one of the sick girl's fingers, which she touched to her own lips, and placed her head on the girl's frail chest in a one-sided cuddle. The sick girl took Raasta's finger—not Makka's—and stared up at her, the pupils of her eyes not dark, almost pale.

Raasta guessed, "Five?"

"Not five," Bile said. He sounded his usual self, congenial, convivial. At least his voice was normal, if not his posture; he leaned to one side, like a house about to collapse.

When Raasta looked at the girl again, she saw her face in a new way, and it was the face of a much older person, with no muscles, wasted. Her loose, wrinkled skin came away with your fingers if you pulled. And her belly was swollen. Raasta couldn't recall the word Uncle had used to describe what was the matter with the girl, a big word, which sounded to her like some Italian ice cream, or a Chinese takeout meal. And what eyes she had—very large, the size of healthy onions grown in fertile land, which made you cry a lot if you cut them. The girl's eyes were the most active part of her body, forever moving, aware, and alert to any changes around her. Except for that of her eyes, every bodily movement exhausted her, it seemed, and made her short of breath.

Raasta, Bile, and Makka stood in silence, in a circle. Raasta saw tears in the corners of Uncle's eyes. This undermined her self-confidence: she thought she had dealt with his unease and talked him through it, released him from his troubles. She was used to her mother's dashing out of rooms, into bathrooms or bedrooms, and crying tearfully. She might have believed Bile was weeping in sympathy with the ailing child, who hadn't a future in the land of collective sorrow, but she knew that wasn't true.

Suddenly the door to the cubicle opened: Seamus was there, not making the disarming entrance he often did, but remaining in the doorway, not moving. Raasta could not tell why he was staring at Uncle Bile, as fiercely as a parent might stare at a child misbehaving in public. Could it be that he was just studying Uncle? He was preparing to say something, but perhaps being polite, waiting for the right moment. His expression overflowed with such sympathy he looked as enticing as a full moon.

Shanta arrived and walked past Seamus into the cubicle, bringing with her a lot more unease than had been there earlier. The silences grew as long as evening shadows, and a hush unlike any other fell on the room. Raasta, desiring to calm the tension, moved to hug her mother.

"Uncle hasn't been well!" Shanta's words were reduced to a whine.

Raasta regarded Bile, who now looked fine to her, and thought to herself: But what on earth is Mother talking about?

She gave her mother a sweeter hug, which took in her sorrows, as one might draw up a skirt that's too long. She talked to her mother, then to Makka, then to the sick girl, in an inclusive way. She beckoned everyone to join in a hug. But when she looked up to invite Uncle Bile and Uncle Seamus, they were not to be found, and she had no idea when or where they had gone. Restlessly, she pulled the sick child closer, as though going down a slide together, down and down until their hearts were in their mouths. Raasta was a little scared going down slides. Shanta rarely gave such all-inclusive hugs to anyone voluntarily.

Raasta now thought of a neater way of closing the brackets her mother had opened when she spoke of Uncle's not having been well. "Uncle Bile looked fine to me," she said. "Tell me, what do you think is the matter with him?"

"It's a long story, my sweet!" said Shanta.

Raasta knew that she wouldn't get to hear the story. But never mind, she thought, because on the whole she had had a wonderful life, compared with other children; she had had fun, and had been looked after by wonderful people, whom she adored. She knew it would be greedy of her to ask for more. After all, there was no joy in making demands that were impossible to meet. It wouldn't do to ask Uncle Jeebleh to stay on in Mogadiscio, when he had a family in New York, and a job to go back to. She had met him face to face only yesterday, but she loved him dearly, because of his courage.

Raasta sensed that she had an attentive audience in her mother, Makka, and the sick girl, all three of them eagerly waiting. But since her return, she had been struggling to find her tongue. It was curious that words were avoiding her lately, as though she had betrayed or abused them; they no longer leapt joyously to her tongue as before, when she could speak effortlessly and make them do as she pleased. She looked around self-consciously and saw Shanta studying her with more care—perhaps wondering if the past ordeal had imposed silence on her.

It took a long time, a lot of patience, and a great many questions before mother and daughter passed words back and forth, and in the end resolved what Raasta meant to say. "I'll never sit on his lap, ever, or hug him or kiss him." And yes: she knew about the terrible things he had done to Uncle Bile and Uncle Jeebleh decades before, knew about the blood on his hands. There was so much blood he would not be able to wash it away, even if he prayed fifty times a day for the rest of his life.

But there was a hitch. Raasta could not bring herself to use the word "hate" to describe what she felt. The word would not come off her tongue, it just would not, even though for the first time in her young life she felt she hated someone—Caloosha, whom she would never call Uncle again, because he had been very wicked. She believed he was holding her daddy prisoner. And she was certain that he had ordered her abduction and that the job had been carried out by some of his friends. Although she had not seen his face, she suspected that she had heard his voice.

"You're too young to hate!" Shanta told her.

"I know from what Uncle Bile has said"—Raasta spoke with unprecedented ease, not because she grew more articulate, but because she was quoting her favorite uncle—"that there are too many people fighting over matters of no great consequence."

For a few moments, the words she ascribed to her uncle gave her as much joy as a new toy might offer another child. Her face beamed as she spoke in a tongue borrowed from her uncle, of how every time militiamen fight and kill, a new twist is given to the old fighting, which then takes on the shape of a new quarrel. And when there is the possibility of peace, a new fight erupts, based on an old complaint, and which some people call justice and others madness. "And," she asked Shanta, "do you know what Uncle Bile said about civil war?"

"Tell me."

"That in a civil war there is continuous fighting, based on grievances that are forever changing."

31.

JEEBLEH'S EYES, WHEN HE SAW THEM IN THE MIRROR WHILE SHAVING THE next day, were proof enough that Caloosha's death did affect everyone in the close-knit family of choice in major ways, whether they admitted it or not. But how had the death of the monster been achieved? Dajaal? Had Kaahin and his associates, or Qasiir and his boys, lent a hand?

He was surprised to read in a report in one of the Mogadiscio rags, by its correspondent in the north of the city, that Caloosha had died in coitus, croaking on top of his young wife. Other tabloids had a field day too, one topping another in their scoops. A paper based in the south of the city, deemed to be more sober in its analysis and less vitriolic in its assessments, identified the wife as a young woman whom Caloosha had abducted a few years earlier, after killing her entire family. According to this article, he had kept her as his sex slave under lock and key in an upstairs apartment. She belonged to the Xamari community, and was her captor's junior by at least forty years. Another paper, claiming a valuable inside source, reported that an unidentified woman had summoned Bile to the villa to help resuscitate his brother. He had gone there immediately, together with two other doctors. But their attempt at resuscitation was too late, and he was declared dead at the villa at about five in the morning. Yet another rag emblazoned its front page with the

sensational headline "Blame It on Viagra!" Perhaps the editor was simply in-
dulging in some cheap underhand joke at the expense of the dead man.

Jeebleh was surprised that no one expressed the least bit of sorrow at the
death of a man whom they knew, and with whom a number of them had had
dealings. At worst, he had expected some of those who'd benefited from their
association with Caloosha to speak well of him. He wondered whether there
would be any mourners at his funeral, or would he be buried alone, no one to
attend but the gravediggers?

ON HEARING THAT CALOOSHA HAD DIED, SHANTA REACTED WITH UNBECOMING
rage. She described him as a spoilsport.

Cursing, filled with the sappiness of her fury, she let the lava of her anger
spill over, but made sure that it didn't assume the solid form of hard evidence. When she began to cool, she complained: "What peeves me is that he
isn't letting me and Raasta enjoy our reunion in undisturbed peace."

There was no evidence that Caloosha had committed suicide or that he
had willed his own death, as far as Jeebleh could tell.

She raged on regardless. "He won't grant us the pleasure of enjoying
Raasta's return, nor have we any idea what or who is keeping Faahiye from
joining us. It's Caloosha's accursed intention to make us all look bad in
everybody's eyes."

"And how does he do that?"

"I'm saying that even in his death, he is a snob," she went on. "Look at it
this way: The fellow is now spoiling the *alla-bari* party for your mother tomorrow afternoon. What will people say if we throw a party a day after his intern-
ment? And have we decided if we're going to his burial, as tradition demands?"

"Are you?" asked Jeebleh.

"Are we?"

Silence took both of them by the throat. To complicate matters further,
some unasked questions lay between them, on the low table in Bile's living
room: not-yet-composed questions now for Shanta, now for Jeebleh, like flies

on the unwashed faces of malnourished children taking breathers after lavish compensatory feedings. One unasked question had to do with what Bile was up to, in the darkened room, with the door closed.

DAJAAL HAD MADE HIMSELF SCARCE AFTER THE VISIT HE HAD ALLEGEDLY PAID to Caloosha in Bile's company. Jeebleh met him only once before he did his disappearing act. And he asked him pointed questions. Dajaal, in his circumspection, related the exchange between the two half brothers. Apparently, Caloosha had glibly told Bile that he would need more than bullets to kill him, that he wasn't "of the killable kind." He boasted that there were very many others like him around and that soon enough another "unkillable" would take his place, and things would remain as they had always been. He ended his declamation by assuring his half brother that the rot in the soul of the nation had set in, and that killing him off would do little to reverse the process.

BILE HAD TAKEN TO BED EARLY, IN THE QUIET WAY IN WHICH A MAN WITH IRON in his soul suddenly lapses into a dark mood. Jeebleh resolved not to disturb him, guessing that he couldn't stay awake for sorrow. His friend was best left alone in his private world of desperation.

But then Jeebleh wasn't sure he and Dajaal had understood each other as conspirators do. That Dajaal had not made detailed references to the alleged visit, and had chosen not to divulge much of what he'd witnessed—save the conversation between the brothers—owed much to his military background, his no-name, no-packdrill training. In the end, this served as his sleight of hand, further strengthening the efficacy of the conspiracy.

Bile was decidedly in a sad state. Yet there was comfort in the fact that he wasn't alone in the darkened room. Raasta, sensing the seriousness of her uncle's despair, had pitched her play space in a corner of the room, and invited Makka to join her.

.   .   .

AND WHERE WAS SEAMUS? HE WAS AT THE CEMETERY, HELPING THE MASON
whom Jeebleh had commissioned to build his mother's sepulcher, to a height
no greater than the span between his thumb and his little finger, as Islamic
tradition demanded. Seamus had gone there with Qasiir and his posse of
armed youths, in a battlewagon lent through Kaahin's good offices. Seamus
had spent much of the morning in the apartment, drawing *his* women, every
one of these looking as if she could have had a walk-on role in Fellini's *8½*,
babies at the women's singularly abundant breasts, the women's features like
the Madonna's. He wasn't due back until after the mason had finished the tomb.
Seamus had to be there, offering any help he could, because the illiterate mason could not work from his sketches, which he found most intimidating.

Jeebleh now remembered the cutting remark Seamus had made in reaction to Shanta's rage over her half brother's death. Caloosha had owed "heavy
debts in blood" to many people, Seamus had said, so it was natural for people
to take vengeance on him now that he was dead. What an apt phrase—heavy
debts in blood! Jeebleh wondered who might exact the heavy debts, and to
what purpose? Would the same person or persons exact repayment of similar
debts from Af-Laawe? What might his own contribution to the campaign be,
his role in the business of overdue payment in blood? Would he serve as a
mere catalyst? Or would he put the collection of debts into motion?

His mobile phone rang, and it was Seamus saying that Jeebleh should
come to the cemetery at once, to approve the design and the construction of
an enclosure with a patch of green, a kind of garden. They wanted him to see
what they had done. To the question of how he would get there, Seamus responded, without the slightest hesitation, that he would send Qasiir and his
friends along in a battlewagon, and they would escort him. Jeebleh couldn't
help noting sadly what their world was coming to: He and Seamus were rubbing shoulders with armed youths and accepting lifts in battlewagons! He
was about to share his worries aloud, when Seamus asked how Bile was doing. Jeebleh replied that their friend was in his darkened room, in bed, lost
to the world, and contemplating the ceiling.

"Alone?"

"Raasta and Makka are with him."

"What bothers me," Jeebleh added after a pause, "is that our friend is soreheaded, and as quiet as a physician retrieving a bullet from a patient's skull. And he's his own patient."

The two agreed that a man in Bile's state of mind couldn't be left alone. Whereupon Seamus suggested that Qasiir take a detour on his way to the apartment and escort Shanta there.

AT THE CEMETERY, SEAMUS, THE MASON, AND TWO ASSISTANTS WERE AT work, mixing sand and cement, and laying a rudimentary foundation for the structure. Qasiir and his posse were enjoying the sweet shade of the mango tree, the battlewagon parked nearby. They spread a mat where they could sit, and chewed their *qaat*. Seamus wore a hat that from a distance resembled a horse's oat bag but on close inspection proved to be a cloth cap, like what a Yoruba farmer might wear working in his fields. He and Jeebleh chatted while the mason and his assistants pegged away, chanting a work song and moving quickly and deliberately.

Jeebleh felt humbled at the thought of being in a position, at last, to mark his mother's memory with a white stone. And it was thanks to Seamus, the pith and the pillar of their friendship. "What was it you needed help with, Seamus?" he asked.

"For starters, I'd like you to perform the office of placing the marble headstone in the ground yourself, with your own hands. Then I'd like to know if you approve of our building a small cupola into the structure."

"A cupola?"

"A cupola supported by fake marble columns."

"Too ostentatious," Jeebleh said.

"Neither would your mother approve, you think?"

"Nor would orthodox Islam!"

Jeebleh was surprised that Seamus was so conversant with erecting a monument over a Muslim grave, and able to suggest an alternative: a domed tomb that wasn't in the least ostentatious. Jeebleh now performed the office of putting in the headstone so that it faced the Sacred Mosque in the Holy City of Mecca.

Seamus appeared to be in a dither, and Jeebleh asked him what was the matter.

Seamus explained, "One, the builder and I couldn't agree as to the exact direction the headstone should face, even though we were agreed that it should face Mecca. Two, I wanted him to accommodate within the structure both a recess for an oil lamp to be lit for seven days, beginning tomorrow, and a cavity in the top of the headstone, in which we might plant flowers. But he wouldn't hear of either, because he has never seen a recess or a cavity built into a headstone except in the tomb of a saint."

"So he says my mother isn't a saint?"

"Not in so many words, but yes."

In an uneasy silence, Jeebleh looked from Seamus to the mason, who was an ordinary kind of guy, and clearly had an unusual way of assigning saint-hood. But Jeebleh had no problem with that. Touched, he turned to Seamus, saying, "You're the real McCoy, aren't you?"

"Not genuine enough, when it came to convincing a builder what is or isn't permitted in Islam, the religion into which he was born, but of which he has little understanding, less than I do. What's more, I rubbed him the wrong way when I told him that although I was born Irish and into the Christian faith, I was agnostic. We communicate only in pidgin Italian, which he could barely use to order a meal at an eatery in Turin."

"I wonder if he knows about Geronimo Verroneo."

"Remind me who he was."

"The Venetian who some say designed the Taj Mahal."

"But your mother is more worthy than the empress in whose memory it was built," Seamus insisted.

Jeebleh, speaking Somali, instructed the mason to create a recess and a cavity in the headstone, as indicated in Seamus's design. Perhaps it was not the language, but the emotion in his voice, or the simple fact that Jeebleh was the son of the deceased, but the man acquiesced and set to work. Moving to further heights of enthrallment, Jeebleh took Seamus in his arms in a kiss-and-tell-all embrace. The mason and his assistants looked at them aghast. Qasiir and his boys first booed, then applauded Jeebleh's action.

Jeebleh released his friend and held him at a distance. "If you're not the most priceless thing that has happened to me," he said, "then I'm done for."

Standing opposite Jeebleh in the brightness of noon, and at that moment looking like a clown without his makeup, Seamus said, "Allow me and my colleagues to get on with the business that's brought us here, please!"

Jeebleh looked away, amused, and his eyes clapped on three cars being driven slowly in procession. One of the vehicles was the kind that dignitaries are chauffeured in, the others were ordinary sedans. He found himself reciting one of his favorite sentences from *Alice's Adventures in Wonderland* and revising it in his head to make it serve his particular purposes. "I might just as well say that 'I see what I hate' is the same thing as 'I hate what I see'!" he told Seamus.

Seamus imagined becoming as many-eyed as a peacock with designs on the object of his elusive desire, when he looked and saw what he too thought he hated—Caloosha. Never mind that he was dead or that this would be the last Seamus would see of him: his funeral cortege.

Now a jalopy came running ahead of the tail of dust following it. Qasiir and his friends stirred themselves into a more restless mood at the sight. With a dark mood clouding his forehead, Qasiir approached Jeebleh, prepared to receive his next instructions. But none was forthcoming.

"From the way the driver's beating that heap," Seamus said, "pushing it beyond its limits, you'd think he was late for his own funeral."

"I wouldn't wish to be early for mine either." Jeebleh found it necessary to elaborate when Seamus looked at him inquiringly. He paraphrased for him the Somali proverb that the mother of a coward seldom mourns her son's early death.

Jeebleh spoke in agitated whispers to Qasiir, suggesting that he and part of his posse drive to the site of Caloosha's grave, and that a second, smaller group, headed by Qasiir's deputy, remain behind. And what was Qasiir to do? He was to stay as low and as still as a dog tag lying where its owner had fallen. Qasiir went off in the battlewagon, excited like a hound scenting the closeness of its prey.

"Is this really what we want?" Seamus said.

"What do you think I'm doing?"

"Do you want a shoot-out?"

QASIIR CAME BACK SHORTLY, WEARING A NEW PAIR OF MIRRORED SHADES through which you couldn't see his eyes but he could see yours. Jeebleh was amused at his own reflection in the shades, and concluded that he had changed a lot in the short time spent in the city of his birth. Not that he bothered to consider the nature of the changes, or if they were to be permanent. He tethered his serious side to the job at hand, requesting that Qasiir kindly remove the shades, then asking where he had gotten them.

Qasiir used a mix of voices—imitation Italian; Arabic, presumably learned from Egyptian films; and Xamari dialect—to answer. A muscular dude, he said, had been wearing the shades; he had acted Hercules-strong and macho. Just to prove the dude wrong, Qasiir had provoked him into a fight, then peeled the shades off his face, threatening to kill him for them if necessary. Jeebleh asked who "the dude" was.

"He had plenty of muscles, but he wasn't strong."

Jeebleh recalled being injected with the liquid solution by a man who met this description. At Jeebleh's prompting, Qasiir explained that it was no use carrying a fancy gun if you were going to chicken out at the last minute, was there? "The dude's gun was for show, and he didn't deserve to keep it, so I took it away from him, to help him, you see. Now I have his fancy gun and his shades too."

Jeebleh felt he was being taken to a territory outside his experience. Not only was Qasiir running rings around him, he, Jeebleh, was becoming more dependent on the young man. Yet he was no more out of kilter than a man walking with his shoelace untied. How much of a change had been wrought on him by living through these experiences? Did it mean—and this was very worrying to him—that Caloosha had won him over to his way of doing things, crudely and cruelly? Jeebleh asked Qasiir how many mourners were at the graveside, and if he could tell him who they were.

"Five or six, maximum."

"Including the guy with the shades?"

"And two military types."

"Who else?"

"Two women."

"One of them his wife?"

"Go see for yourself," Qasiir said.

He knew then he would want to see for himself!

After a pause, Qasiir said, "It was no big deal."

"How do you mean?"

"Cool Caloosha no longer cool!"

"Was Af-Laawe there?"

Qasiir was probably being cheeky, or perhaps knew more than he was prepared to let on, because he said, "They'll be burying him, all right!"

You could've beaten Jeebleh down with a single feather from a vulture, when he noticed several perched in the mango tree, restlessly surveying the extent of the cemetery. "Let's go and see what's what!" he told Qasiir.

Jeebleh took pride of place in the battlewagon, next to the driver, and acted as though he were the commander of a fighting unit. With the heavy gun mounted on the vehicle, they were mobile, fast, and deadly; he feared no one. It took the battlewagon a few minutes to cover the distance between his mother's grave and where Caloosha's was now being dug. It was a sad affair: two miserable-looking military types in dirty fatigues, their bodies unwashed, eyes sore from sleeplessness, their cheeks bulging from the qaat they kept chewing; two women, looking rather like whores paid to mourn; and the muscular man who had injected the solution into his thigh. Jeebleh didn't give in to the temptation of letting Qasiir and his friends turn "the dude" into inedible mince, something they would gladly have done if he had asked them. Nor would he inquire what had become of Af-Laawe, the muscleman's paymaster;

he assumed that they had fallen out with each other, as all thieves do sooner or later. For all he cared, Af-Laawe might have died at the man's hands.

From the way the gravediggers took their time, you would've thought they were performing a thankless task—as if they knew they wouldn't be remunerated for their labor. And where was Caloosha's corpse? Wrapped in a white sheet, it lay close by, still, the freshly dug earth accentuating its sorrowful state. Unburied, his corpse struck Jeebleh as being sequestered in the aloneness of a man whom even hell wouldn't deign to receive.

Good breeding made Jeebleh say a few words for the martyred dead anyway. And before long, he got back into the battlewagon, ready to return to Seamus and the other labors. He planned ahead to the moment when the sepulcher would be finished, and he would call on Shanta, to prepare for the *alla-bari* party. He wanted to arrange the purchase of the cow to be slaughtered at the next day's feast.

ONCE THE TOMB HAD BEEN COMPLETED TO HIS AND SEAMUS'S SATISFACTION, Jeebleh said he wanted to be alone there, to commune with his mother's troubled spirit. He was not a religious man, nor given to saying his prayers or fasting. But he wished to appease her spirit in the best way he could, by consecrating the tomb with a prayer. He knelt down, and saying a brief prayer, imagined two dark angels with blue eyes ceremoniously arriving to interrogate his mother, newly reburied. Sadly, the old woman was unable to provide the right answers to the angels. They were about to order the ground to close in upon her, when she recovered in time to recite the appropriate responses. Whereupon her grave expanded to seventy times seventy paces in length and seventy times seventy in breadth, and the light in the tomb came on. Approving of her, the angels spoke in unison: "Sleep in peace, then, with Allah's blessing!"

Jeebleh joined the others, and the battlewagon took them back to Bile's apartment. He was more pleased with himself and more relaxed than he had felt for a long time. But there was no Shanta in the apartment. Instead, he was pleasantly startled to find Faahiye in the living room. Where were Raasta and Makka? They were in Bile's room, asleep, where Bile was awake, staring at the ceiling.

MEANWHILE, FAAHIYE WAS PERFORMING A RELIGIOUS RITUAL. HE TUCKED HIS sleeves up past his elbows, washed his hands several times, flung the water with his right hand into his mouth, and rinsed his mouth three times. Then he snuffed the water into his nostrils, only to blow it out soon after by closing his nose with the thumb and forefinger of his left hand and snorting. He washed his face three times, then his right hand and arm, and rubbed his wet right hand over the top of his head. He inserted the tips of his forefingers into his ears and turned them around and around, then passed his thumbs upward, behind his ears. He washed his neck with the back of his fingers, and finally, washed his feet up to his ankles, pressing his fingers into the spaces between his toes, one space at a time.

Jeebleh and Seamus watched as Faahiye repeated the ritual of ablution again and again, never failing to recite the appropriate traditions.

"It's as though he has fed his mind on an insane root, which has taken his reason prisoner," Seamus whispered.

"As if a little water will clear him of the deed!"

Jeebleh left, intending to call at Shanta's to make certain that everything was in order for the next day's *alla-bari* feast.

EPILOGUE

"But let us go; Cain with his thorns already
is at the border of both hemispheres. . . .
Last night the moon was at its full."
. . . Meanwhile we journeyed.

(CANTO XX)

DANTE, *Inferno*

THAT NIGHT EVERYONE APPEARED TROUBLED AND ANXIOUS, FOR OBVIOUS and not so obvious reasons.

Jeebleh cast his mind back on everything that had happened, perhaps to sort out what memories to take with him to New York. Could this be why he had stashed away the letter the clan elders had left for him? His intention was to frame it, and put it on his office wall. His hand kept going to his thigh, where the muscleman had injected him. He continued to wonder if his contagion of worry would kill him before he had even had his blood tested at home; he was worried less about the barber's cut, now that it was healing.

He called New York, telling his wife and daughters in an edited fashion what had happened. He touched only briefly on Caloosha's death and his burial, and did not even mention Af-Laawe. He would explain things better once he was back in the safety of home. He concentrated instead on the commemoration of his mother—the construction of the sepulcher, the symbolic reburial, and the upcoming *alla-bari* feast. He told his wife that he was changing his return date, and would let her know about it. Feeling guilty about not offering a complete and true version of things, he laid it on thick when he stressed how much he had missed them all, and how eager he was to return to the bosom of his loving family.

At last Bile came out of his room, where the light was now on. Jeebleh took the slight grimace on his face as a smile, but Bile remained silent. He seemed, however, to be in a cheerier mood than Jeebleh had expected. Perhaps the antidepressants, if that is what they were, had helped him emerge.

As for Faahiye, the poor fellow kept performing a ritual of his own invention, putting his index fingers in his ears and turning them around and around, as if his ears were filled to bursting with wax. Choosing not to raise the devil, because she knew no one would tolerate it, Shanta went to him and spoke solicitously. There was an opaqueness at the center of Faahiye's insanity, as perhaps there was at the heart of Bile's.

Shanta was the one to break the silence, to tell Raasta and Makka that they would be going home early, for they had a busy day ahead of them. As they left, Faahiye leaned against Shanta for support; Makka leaned on Raasta, as though for affirmation. It was a most humbling lesson in compassion.

Where was Seamus? Jeebleh had no idea, nor did anyone else. But this didn't bother him, convinced as he was that Seamus was engaged in an activity worthy of a reliable friend.

WHEN SEAMUS RETURNED LATER THAT NIGHT, SILENT AND EXPLAINING nothing, Jeebleh shuttled between The Refuge—now turned over to several imams chanting the Koran—and the apartment, where his secular friends were camped, barely speaking to each other.

The imams were reciting the entire Holy Scripture, each with his own assigned chapters. At one point, Jeebleh listened to the head imam interpreting a verse for the benefit of his younger colleagues. The imam alluded to a remark ascribed to the prophet Mohammed, about sedition. And perhaps in order to throw more light on the situation in Somalia, the learned scholar paraphrased the Prophet's words: "Cursed with the hearts of the devil in their bodies, some of the 'leaders' will inevitably veer from the virtuous path into iniquity."

Feeling sufficiently instructed, Jeebleh walked out into the starry night to take a closer look at the cow that would be slaughtered the next day. Humbled by the sight, he stood before the heifer as though meaning to communicate with her. Jeebleh thought again about his belated attempt to make peace with his mother in the act of reclaiming her. How he wished he could send her a message and have the sacrificial beast before which he was standing deliver it. In subdued sorrow, unable to give flesh to his idea, he returned to the apartment.

On his way there, it struck him that madness was a country to which many people he knew in Mogadiscio had paid visits. He prayed that neither he nor any one of his friends would suffer permanent damage.

The apartment was quieter than when he had left it. Seamus's door was open, but his room was empty of him. Bile's door was open too, and he was there. Jeebleh wondered where Seamus might have gone, but said nothing to Bile, having no wish to bother him. Then he stretched out on his bed, fully dressed, thinking about what remained to be done. No, he was not ready to abandon himself to sleep.

JEEBLEH WAS UP AND ON HIS FEET SHORTLY, STANDING SHAKILY ON THE wrong side of forty winks, still so exhausted his knees were about to buckle under him. The morning hadn't yet dawned, and he had on the same clothes as yesterday.

He was a changed man. He wasn't quite on cloud nine yet, but he was on his way—aiming at it, hoping for the chance. He had opened a parenthesis with his decision to visit Mogadiscio on a whim, to elude death at the same time that he reclaimed his mother, whom he had neglected into an early grave. Now the parenthesis seemed to be closing, but he felt that it wouldn't have served his purpose for that to happen just yet. After all, he was not prepared to dwell in pronominal confusion, which was where he had been headed. He had to find which pronoun might bring his story to a profitable end.

It was too early to assess the changes that the visit had wrought on his character. Presumably his general personality would be unaltered. No doubt, something in him had given here and there, the way fabric stretches. But the basics remained, gathered at the corners, perhaps sagging or giving at the seams, where the stitching might be faulty. Fancy living in an open parenthesis for as long as Jeebleh had lived in his.

His eyes were no longer drooping with bags of insomnia. Nor was he as harried as he had been the day before, when he went back and forth between the apartment and The Refuge. Granted, it would've been easy for him to kill, just as it would've been easy to die at someone else's hands, in a city where death was treated like an acquaintance. He remembered his exchanges with Seamus on the related topic of burial. How Seamus lamented that in Mogadiscio they buried you quickly; how he found the idea of being buried, no questions asked and no postmortem, so troublesome; how it irked him that no one inquired what someone had died of, and that, at the mention of a name now forever linked to death, people sought refuge in the phrase "the will of Allah," as if this were the alias of the deceased. Seamus would probably want people to have the facts, to know how Caloosha had died, at whose hands, and why. Because he did not wish to play a part in a cover-up, Jeebleh thought it wise to leave before he was tempted to speak of what bothered him.

Soon after his arrival, someone had said to him: "Our people are poor in their hearts. Our people are restless nomads in search of city-based fulfillment." Jeebleh would be well advised to stay out of the people's way, "as soon as the torch of ambition, backed by greed, begins to burn in their eyes." He was damned if he could remember who had said this. It might've been Af-Laawe; it could equally have been Caloosha. That you could receive good wisdom from the mouths of bad men, never mind the names by which they were known or their main purpose in life, surprised him. He wished that he had shot back with a witty remark of his own, that whoever lets his dogs loose should prepare to feed them when they come back hungry. And he would add this for good measure: Take your cynical remarks and sprinkle them on your carbonara like the best Parmesan!

The muezzin called at dawn, and Jeebleh went to the hall where the imams were. He found them ready for a well-earned break. The head imam presented the prayers to Jeebleh, the official "owner of the corpse." He received the blessings, his hands cupped, palms up, in the gesture of a devotee humbling himself before a deity. He handed over basketfuls of money to the head imam, relieved that the scholar had forgotten an earlier condition that he would arrange rides for each of them. When the imams left, Jeebleh returned to the apartment with the express aim of getting some sleep. And even though there was still no sign of Seamus, again he did not ask Bile if he knew where he might have gone. Bile was busy praying, and Jeebleh didn't want to disturb him. Instead, Jeebleh went to sleep.

He woke up again at about eight in the morning.

AND HE WAS IN A MOURNING MOOD. HE WAS ALONE IN THE APARTMENT, AND took his time showering and shaving. He reminded myself of the tradition that a mourner desist as long as possible from changing his clothes. And so he wore the same clothes he had worn the day before, with the slight modification of a fresh pair of underpants.

When he walked to The Refuge, he knew he would have to take the rough with the smooth. As things stood, his own story lay in a tarry of other people's tales, each with its own Dantean complexity. His story was not an exemplar to represent or serve in place of the others: it wouldn't do to separate his from those informing it, or to rely solely on it for moral and political edification. Only when gathering the fragments together would he hold his mother's tale in awkward deference, separating it from the others, giving it its deserved honor.

Jeebleh thought of how the country had been buried under the rubble of political ruin, and how Somalis woke to being betrayed by the religious men and the clan elders who were in cahoots with a cabal of warlords to share the gain they could make out of ordinary people's miseries. The clan elders got their reward in corrupt gifts of cash; the religious elders, turning themselves into cabaret artists, conned the rest of the populace, as they carved an earthly kingdom for themselves. As Bile had put it, money was the engine that ran Somalia's civil war. It stood to reason that money provided the cabals and the cartel with a ladder of lies, which allowed them to ascend out of harm's way. Every other way of assessing the civil war was as futile as pouring wet sand through the interstices of history.

For what it was worth, Jeebleh held a childlike trust that things would work better for more people now that Raasta and Makka were back at The Refuge and Caloosha was out of the way. He trusted that things would improve if Af-Laawe followed in his mentor's footsteps. Now, getting rid of Caloosha was no mean feat! Given the choice, Jeebleh would oppose all forms of violence. But what is one to do when there is no other way to rid society of vermin? Which would he rather be, someone who minds the opinion of others and advocates for peace, or someone who does what he can—despite the risks—to improve the lives of many others? Jeebleh would say, after Thomas Jefferson: "A little rebellion now and then is a good thing." He would go even further and say, again after Mr. Jefferson: "The tree of liberty must be refreshed from time to time with the blood of patriots and tyrants. It is its natural manure." So which would he rather be, someone who kills for justice, or someone helplessly unable to do anything? He would rather he killed than twiddle his thumbs, waiting for others to do the job. To hell with the opinion of others, especially his clansmen, who hadn't the right to sit in judgment on his actions! Jeebleh was all for justice, by any means possible.

NOW HE WAS AT THE GATE OF THE REFUGE. AND A PARTY WAS IN FULL SWING, announced by placards bearing his mother's good name, boldly written in Seamus's upright hand, green on white, and on very fine material, similar to the *subeeci-xariir* cloth in which Somalis wrap the dead when burying them.

A billboard welcomed everyone to The Refuge—"a home to Raasta and Makka, and therefore a place of peace and communal harmony!" Another placard bragged that on entering the grounds of The Refuge, one would "spend a tranquil day among people living in harmonious coexistence with many others with whom they don't share the same clan." Yet another invited the visitor to a place where "even though the residents may not see things eye to eye, they stay together without pulling guns or rank on one another." Tears welled up in Jeebleh's eyes, and his cheeks became wet. How it would have pleased his mother, or Bile and Shanta's, to be here. This, yes, was worth living for!

As he walked farther in, he chatted with the women who worked at The Refuge. They praised Seamus for the signs and for providing the children with their colorful balloons, and commended Bile for being there at all. One woman alluded to his half brother, and said that she hadn't expected Bile to attend a party honoring the mother of a friend right after his own brother had been buried. Others spoke of Faahiye, of seeing him and Shanta holding hands and, trailing them, arms linked, Raasta and Makka. A woman Jeebleh didn't know whispered to him that Caloosha's widow was somewhere on the grounds, and not veiled. Apparently, she was chatting amicably to Raasta or entertaining Makka. Jeebleh was in no hurry to present himself to Caloosha's widow. He made the acquaintance of a few other people, who said how pleased they were that Raasta was back, or how good Faahiye looked, or how nice it was to see a joyful Shanta.

Jeebleh was delighted to see the doors of the dormitories festooned with colorful flags. Where the children were playing in the courtyard, the sky rained a confetti of colors, which clung to his skin. Jeebleh allowed himself to frolic noisily with the children. He helped a young girl blow bubbles, and welcomed a hungry-looking a boy to eat his fill of meat to his heart's content, probably for the first time ever. People mixing, chatting, and looking happy: Jeebleh was pleased to have contributed his small share as the host, and content that his mother had permitted him to use her death as the excuse.

But then, as though darkness had suddenly descended, his progress was impeded. Jeebleh had intended to go to where Bile, Seamus, Shanta, and Raasta were standing. He was prepared to talk to Caloosha's widow. Yet he felt lost, unable or unwilling to decide which road to follow. Until a way was offered to him.

Dajaal was there. And he held Jeebleh by the elbow, as though propping him up. He was entreating Jeebleh to accompany him, he didn't say where. Jeebleh remembered hearing that Dajaal had guided Bile to where Shanta was giving birth. How he wished he had the strength to ask Dajaal whether he had helped Bile do the bloody deed! Instead, Jeebleh took refuge in the variegated meanings of their silence, and silently followed Dajaal. He realized he was being led away from the others. As Jeebleh walked alongside Dajaal and Kaahin, with Qasiir and his posse bringing up the rear, he listened to their conspiratorial voices. One or the other of them spoke of how Af-Laawe had felt the heat and fled the city, how he had been seen in Nairobi buying a plane ticket to France.

Jeebleh knew then that he would leave soon, without his friends' knowing. He would fly to Nairobi to relax for a couple of days, and from there call Bile and Seamus to inform them of the decision to depart—but not why. Then he would book himself on a home-bound flight and, not wanting to tempt fate, get to New York before impulse propelled him in another direction.

Some people hate saying good-bye, some cannot bear to say *arrivederci*. Jeebleh assured himself that he loved his friends enough and that they loved him. He knew that they would visit one another, welcome one another into their homes, and into their stories. He and his friends were forever linked through the chains of the stories they shared.

LATE THAT NIGHT, TUCKED IN BED AND FLANKED BY THE TWO GIRLS, JEEBLEH listened to Raasta tell a folktale.

An ape, finding the throne empty, takes the crown, puts on the robes of the king, and begins to reign. A wildcat convokes the other beasts. These come and heap praises on the new king. Not so the fox, who plots to unseat the impostor. To this end, he gathers luscious fruits, the kind that apes kill or die for, and gives them all to the king. Excited, the ape leaps from his throne, jumping up and down, and to satisfy his insatiable gluttony, surrenders his weighty crown.

Amused, the fox addresses the gathering. He tells the other animals that donning the robes of a king has never made a monarch of a flunky.

And the ape is unseated!

Jeebleh quit Mogadiscio the following morning, without changing his clothes, though he did introduce yet a further modification: he put on clean underpants and clean undershirt.

Bile, Seamus, Raasta, and Shanta learned of his departure only later in the day. He left before the mist in his mind cleared, afraid that he might alienate his friends, to whom he owed his life. He left as soon as he sensed the sun intruding on the horizon of his mind.

AUTHOR'S NOTE

This is a work of fiction, set against the background of actual events that took place in Mogadiscio. The characters and the incidents they are involved in, however, stem from my imagination, and any resemblance to actual persons, living or dead, is purely coincidental.

To write *Links*, I benefited from speaking to a great many Mogadiscians, and from reading hundreds of documents, and numerous periodicals and books. I am grateful to all of those I spoke to, and to the authors whose writings I read. Needless to say, I covered all borrowings with skin of my own manufacture.

The epigraphs at the beginning of the book are from Michel Tournier's *The Ogre* (translated by Barbara Bray; Pantheon, 1984); *The Standard Edition of the Complete Psychological Works of Sigmund Freud* (translated by James Strachey, 1940–1968); and William Blake's *Auguries of Innocence*. The part-title epigraphs are from Allen Mandelbaum's translation of Dante's *Inferno* (Bantam, 1982): for Part 1, from canto III, lines 1–18; canto X, lines 25–42; and canto XXIII, line 144; for Part 2, with slight modification, from canto XIV, lines 16–26, and canto XXIV, lines 88–93; for Part 3, from canto XI, lines 37–54, and canto XXVIII, lines 1–6; for Part 4, from canto XVII, line 31; and for the epilogue, from canto XX, lines 124–130.

The play alluded to in chapter 1 is Carl Zuckmayer's *Der Hauptmann von*

Köpenick. The biblical quotations "Deliver me from blood-guiltiness . . ." and "The sun shall be turned . . ." in chapter 8 are from Psalms 51:14 and Joel 2:31, respectively. The remark "We fed them, they got strong . . ." in chapter 25 is attributed to Major David Stockwell, U.S. Army, UN military spokesman, and is quoted in Keith B. Richburg's *Out of America* (Basic Books, 1997, page 60). The comment attributed to Osip Mandelstam in chapter 26 is from *The Oxford Dictionary of Literary Quotations,* edited by Peter Kemp (Oxford University Press, 1999). The two quotations from Thomas Jefferson in the epilogue are from letters to, respectively, James Madison (January 30, 1787) and W. S. Smith (November 13, 1787).

I found the following invaluable: *Sheekoxariirooyin Somaaliyeed,* a bilingual Somali–English edition of Somali folktales by Axmad Cartan Xaange (Somali Academy of Sciences & Arts / Scandinavian Institute of African Studies, 1988); *The Somali Challenge,* edited by Ahmed I. Samatar (Lynne Rienner, 1994); *Blood Money* by Trisha Stratford (Penguin, New Zealand, 1996); *Dante's Inferno* by Mark Musa (Indiana University Press, 1995); and *Black Hawk Down* by Mark Bowden (Atlantic Monthly Press, 1999).

A number of good friends have been of enormous help, in particular Maxamad Aden Gulaid a.k.a. Caana-geel, Ahmed "Washington" Mohamoud, Lidwien Kapteijns, Tom Keenan, Miki Goral, and David Knowles of Ledig House, where I stayed for three weeks while working on an earlier draft of the novel.

A PENGUIN READERS GUIDE TO

LINKS

Nuruddin Farah

AN INTRODUCTION TO
Links

Links is set in a city that is at once shockingly foreign and hauntingly familiar: Mogadiscio, the capital of Somalia, just weeks after the U.S. troops have pulled out, leaving a decimated, starving city ruled by thuggish clan warlords and patrolled by qaat-chewing gangs who shoot civilians simply to relieve their adolescent boredom. This is the city so disturbingly captured by CNN cameras and in *Black Hawk Down*, but from a startlingly different—and surprising—point-of-view.

Jeebleh is returning to Mogadiscio from New York for the first time in twenty years. Equipped with a clear-minded Americanized perspective and ready to attend to business, this journey is not a nostalgia trip for him—Jeebleh's last residence here was a jail cell. And who could feel nostalgic for a city like this?

Jeebleh is returning to visit his mother's grave and to settle her outstanding accounts—but more urgently, the youngest member of his oldest friend's family has been abducted. Though they have not seen each other in two decades, Jeebleh knows from their childhood that his friend—a virtual brother who remained in Somalia when Jeebleh left—will need Jeebleh to step in. Jeebleh is determined to cut through the swirling, clan-based violence and corruption to rescue the little girl—and, perhaps, a piece of his own identity. Jeebleh's adventure pulls him (and us) into a whirlwind tour of a city where nothing—family or friendship, loyalty or gratitude, betrayal or resentment, tradition or modernity—is simple.

Gripping, provocative, and revelatory, *Links* is the finest work yet from Farah, a novel that will both secure his place in the international literary firmament and stand as a classic of modern world literature.

About Nuruddin Farah

Widely recognized as not just "one of the finest contemporary African writers" (Salman Rushdie) but as "one of the most sophisticated voices in modern fiction" (*The New York Review of Books*), Nuruddin Farah is the author of eight novels. His fiction has been translated into more than a dozen languages and won numerous awards, including the 1998 Neustadt International Prize for Literature, "widely regarded as the most prestigious international literary award after the Nobel" (*The New York Times*).

Born in Somalia, Farah was persona non grata in his native country for over twenty years, able to visit Mogadiscio for the first time in the late 1990s. He currently lives in Cape Town, South Africa.

QUESTIONS FOR DISCUSSION

1. After nearly being run over by a cab in New York City, Jeebleh travels to Mogadiscio to "disorient death" (p. 5). What does he mean by this?

2. Though Jeebleh was born and raised in Mogadiscio, much has changed in the twenty years since he moved to America. Do others view Jeebleh as a Somalian or as an American? How does Jeebleh view himself? What sort of conflicts does Jeebleh's twenty year absence present?

3. Discuss Jeebleh's refusal to give his clan family money for a new battlewagon and his intervention when he sees the child beating the dog. Do you expect this from Jeebleh given his personality and actions up to this point? What do you think causes him to do this?

4. Discuss Jeebleh's relationship with his mother. Specifically, why do you think she never moved to America? How are Jeebleh's actions toward her after her death different from the way he treated her while she was still alive? How are views on the family different between Somalians and Americans?

5. The description given of Hagarr, Bile and Caloosha's mother, on pages 172 and 173 paints the picture of a strong, educated, independent woman. How are other women in the novel depicted? How are their relationships with men depicted?

6. After being injected by the bodyguard in the cemetery, Jeebleh undergoes personal changes. Discuss the nature of his transformation. Would you describe him as more courageous? How does this transformation help him?

7. Dreams and superstitions have a significant impact on the actions taken by Jeebleh and his friends. In particular, there are many superstitious views about Raasta who is viewed as an extraordinary child. What does Raasta offer her family and the people of Mogadiscio that warrants the admiration that she receives?

8. What do you think of Jeebleh's ultimate decision concerning Caloosha? What gives him the strength to make this decision? What do you think the long-term impact will be for the people surrounding Caloosha?

9. Why do you think Jeebleh leaves Mogadiscio without saying good-bye to his friends?

10. What other direction could Jeebleh take at the end of the novel when he decides to book himself "on a homebound flight and, not wanting to tempt fate, get to New York before impulse propelled him in another direction"?

For more information about or to order other Penguin Readers Guides, please e-mail the Penguin Marketing Department at reading@us.penguingroup.com or write to us at:

Penguin Books Marketing Dept.
Readers Guides
375 Hudson Street
New York, NY 10014-3657

Please allow 4–6 weeks for delivery.

To access Penguin Readers Guides online, visit the Penguin Group (USA) Web site at www.penguin.com.

FOR MORE NURUDDIN FARAH, LOOK FOR THE

"Nuruddin Farah, the most important African novelist to emerge in the last twenty-five years, is also one of the most sophisticated voices in modern fiction."
—The New York Review of Books

Links

Before he left for a twenty-year exile in America, Jeebleh's last residence in Mogadiscio had been a jail cell. When he finally returns, it is to a decimated city that U.S. troops have recently abandoned, ruled by clan warlords and patrolled by gangs who shoot civilians to relieve their adolescent boredom. Once back home, Jeebleh finds himself in the midst of swirling violence and corruption as he attempts to rescue a little girl and reunite the family of his oldest friend. Gripping, provocative, and revelatory, *Links* is the finest work yet from Farah, a novel that stands as a classic of modern world literature.   *ISBN 0-14-303484-7*

Secrets

"Hypnotic . . . *Secrets* is a shape shifter—murder mystery, family saga, magical realist thriller." *—Newsday*
Set against the backdrop of Somalia's devastating civil war, *Secrets* is a stunning revelatory novel. The city of Mogadiscio is in crisis when the protagonist, Kalaman, receives an unexpected houseguest, his childhood crush returned from America. Sensual and demanding, Sholoongo announces her intention to have his child, pulling Kalaman back into a past full of doubts and secrets to uncover the startling truth of his own conception.   *ISBN 0-14-028045-6*

Gifts

"Farah weaves together myth, dream, and realism to create literature that is truly world-class." *—Los Angeles Times Book Review*
The second in Farah's trilogy, *Gifts* tells the story of Duniya, a single mother working at the troubled hospital in Mogadiscio. In luxuriant prose, Farah weaves events into a tapestry of dreams, memories, family lore, folktales, and journalistic accounts. Both personal and political, *Gifts* explores the values, challenges, and sufferings of one family—and an entire people.   *ISBN 0-14-029642-5*

Maps

"Startling . . . passionate. Farah's masterpiece." *—Suzanne Ruta, The New York Times Book Review*
A strikingly lyrical novel, *Maps* is the story of Askar, an orphan whose mother died in childbirth and whose father was killed in the bloody war dividing Somalia and Ethiopia before he was born. As a precocious adolescent, he leaves for Mogadiscio in search of a perspective on both his country and himself, and at the hub of violence, Askar throws himself into radical political activity that continually challenges the murky boundaries of his own being, just as "revolution" redefines Somalia's own borders.   *ISBN 0-14-029643-3*